As Imogen had sat up on the wall watching people walking by, she couldn't help thinking this was England at its worst. An ancient monument belittled by gift shops packed full of tat and, hanging outside each one, body boards and flip-flops flapping in the light breeze. Archie had come rushing out wanting to spend fifteen pounds on a varnished shell that had certainly been imported from the Caribbean, and she'd bundled them into the car, though not before Gracie had pointed out a loving message on the car park wall declaring 'Wayne shagged Sharon'.

Meg Sanders and Annie Ashworth are consumer journalists who have written ten successful non-fiction books together. Both have young children and live near Stratford-upon-Avon. *Warnings of Gales* is their second novel. Their first novel, the bestselling *Goodbye, Jimmy Choo*, is also available in Orion paperback.

Warnings of Gales

Annie Sanders

An Orion paperback

First published in Great Britain in 2005
by Orion
This paperback edition published in 2006
by Orion Books Ltd,
Orion House, 5 Upper St Martin's Lane,
London WC2H 9EA

1 3 5 7 9 10 8 6 4 2

A CIP catalogue record for this book is available
from the British Library.

ISBN-13 978-0-7528-8119-5
ISBN-10 0-7528-8119-1

Printed and bound in Great Britain by
Clays Ltd, St Ives plc

The Orion Publishing Group's policy is to use papers that are natural,
renewable and recyclable products and made from wood grown in sustainable
forests. The logging and manufacturing processes are expected to conform
to the environmental regulations of the country of origin.

www.orionbooks.co.uk

To all those brave holidaymakers
who dare to share

Prologue

Penvarick House: Wonderfully secluded, with rural and sea views, this imposing detached property is set in its own enclosed gardens and provides comfortable, spacious accommodation. Sleeps 10–12.

Living room and playroom. Large, well-equipped kitchen with dining area. First floor: two double bedrooms, one with four-poster bed; twin-bedded room; bathroom/WC. Second floor: second twin-bedded room and bunk-bedded room with extra single bed. Shower room/WC.

* Shops 1 mile * TV * DVD *Wm/tumble dryer * M/wave * D/washer * Fridge/freezer * Garden with furniture and children's play area with Wendy house

Padstow is only 4 miles away with its picturesque cobbled streets leading to the old fishing harbour. Many shops and restaurants to be explored, boat trips to Rock or fishing trips. Close to surfing beaches. July/August: Price bracket YY

From: Imogen Fogg
To: Sophie Tate
Sent: 03 January 20.56
Subject: Sand between your toes!

Sophie, darling. Happy New Year! After exhaustive searches I think I've finally found it! It really took some trawling – lots were already booked up, and there's plenty of swirly carpets and Sindy-doll dressing tables amongst those left – but I think this one will suit us all fine. I've pasted in the details about it. Sounds lovely, don't you think? I've been a bit naughty actually, but as it fitted the dates we want and all our criteria – yours and mine – and Caroline's, still leaving her plenty of time for Italy later on (all right for some!), I've gone ahead and booked it. The money's a tad more than we agreed but, fingers crossed, you'll like it. Now all we need is good weather and I can almost smell the fresh sea air from here in deepest Barnes.

Speak soon. Lots of love.

Imo xx

From: Imogen Fogg
To: Sophie Tate; Jo Newman
Sent: 10 July 21.24
Subject: Re: Sand between your toes!

Hi, Soph and Jo, though I haven't met you yet!
First of all, thanks, Jo, for stepping into the breach left by Caroline at the last minute – that was a huge relief! Just

a quick note before we all head west, to say that I'll bring the basics: flour, olive oil, salt and pepper (these places never have the proper stuff) – safer if just one of us does it – and as we'll probably be the first there, I'll do something for supper on the first night. We can sort out who does what after that, can't we? Perhaps, Soph, you could do fruit, and Jo, as I'm not sure what you like, could you bring anything that's particular to you? Don't forget linen and towels, and of course lots of booze! I'll bring a selection of cereal too – my lot are a bit fussy. Sorry we've had to delay the start date for everyone until Sunday. Family weddings hey! Everyone here is very excited about it and it's going to be lots of fun.

Map attached. See you there!

Imogen xx

Chapter 1
Sunday

Sunny to start, with cloud building later,
especially in the South West

'In, in, *in*, all of you. Rory! Where are you? Get in the car now!'

Imogen slipped her hand down the inside of the green overnight bag in the boot, careful not to mess up the folded clothes, and winced as she caught her nail on a rivet in the leather.

'Archie, are you sure you need your rabbit now, darling?' She sucked the blood from her finger, and stuck in her other hand, feeling her way around washbags and soft cotton pyjamas.

'But I'll need him on the journey. He'll be lonely without me.' Archie twisted round in his seat to look over into the boot of the car. Imogen could see his eyes were beginning to fill up with tears.

'Still here?' Guy came up behind her.

'I can't find the sodding rabbit,' she muttered through clenched teeth, then at last her fingers fell on a pair of soft cotton ears and she heard the tell-tale tinkle of the bell lodged in the animal's stomach. 'Thank God for that,' she sighed, and whipped it out from the bottom of the bag like an obstetrician delivering a Caesarean section.

Thrusting the threadbare toy into Archie's grateful hands, she turned to her husband. 'Now *please* don't forget about posting that card to Grandma Min, and Sandra's cleaning this Tuesday but not next, so leave her money out, won't you?'

'Can you just run that past me for the seventy-fourth time?' Guy smiled, planted a kiss on his wife's proffered lips, then patted her bottom and urged her towards the car. 'Come on, get going or you'll miss the best of the day. See you Friday.'

'And water the tomatoes,' she hollered as she waved goodbye and pulled out onto the road, and he rolled his eyes in mock despair.

Perhaps not being able to start the holiday until today because of Cousin Janey's wedding was a blessing, she thought to herself as she swept north over Hammersmith Bridge. With traffic this blissfully light, she'd soon make up the five or so minutes lost locating the rabbit. She did a quick mental mine-sweep: what had they forgotten? She hoped to goodness Rory had put in the sun cream. He'd promised but that was no guarantee. Swimming towels: check. Waterproofs: check. She'd stuffed in a last-minute general-knowledge game in case the journey got tedious, and there was always the new story tape she'd secreted in the glove box – very much a last resort though. Philip Pullman was way beyond Archie.

Though it was still quite early, she could feel the heat of the July sun through the car window on her shoulders as she waited at the traffic lights. Deftly unstrapping her seat belt, she whipped off her sweatshirt and passed it over the seat to her daughter behind.

'Stick that over the back, can you, sweetheart?'

'Muuuurm, you've made me lose my place.'

'Oh Ollie, don't read, darling. It always makes you feel horribly sick and we're not even on the motorway.'

'How long's it going to take?' grunted Rory from the passenger seat, his nose deeply into his Gameboy.

Imogen's heart sank. 'Well,' she hedged, manoeuvring round a bus, 'we're doing awfully well already, and we'll stop for lunch when we get to the end of the motorway, and then we'll be practically there.'

'Can I open my goodie bag now then?' Archie pleaded from the back.

'Hold out a little longer, darling … at least till we cross the M25,' she added under her breath. She'd be stuffed if her carefully prepared novelty was blown by Chiswick Roundabout.

By the time they'd made good headway on the M4, and the signs for Swindon hove into view, Imogen felt elated. Things were going her way. Perhaps the quiz hadn't been *quite* as popular as she'd hoped, and sadly the Pullman tape had had to be abandoned when Archie wouldn't keep quiet, but now Rory was nose down once again in his game, Ollie was quiet and Archie was pointing at interesting drivers they overtook. All three had exhausted the contents of their bags, and the carrier bag she'd remembered to include was now bulging with empty apple-juice cartons and boxes of raisins.

'I feel sick,' Olivia moaned from behind her mother.

'Mum told you not to read,' Rory sneered from the front seat.

'Oh shut up, you,' Olivia snapped back. 'I'm not reading, I'm drawing. You're just—'

'Now, now, you two. Rory, pass her that bottle of water, and Ollie, look out of the window.'

There was a short-lived truce, but by the time they reached the roundabout at the bottom of the M5 and turned into a service station, she had threatened to confiscate Rory's Gameboy for the duration of the holiday and, quite against her principles, had slapped Archie's legs smartly when he wouldn't stop digging his feet into the back of Rory's seat.

'Can we have a burger? They're *bound* to have a burger place.' Rory leant forward excitedly.

'Exactly! Which is why we're having a picnic.' Imogen smiled, and pulled into a space in the heaving car park as near as she could to an area of what might loosely be described as grass. Archie was unstrapped and out of the car in seconds, careering off before Imogen could alert him to the fact that it was, without doubt, a toilet for every holidaymaker's travel-weary dog.

'Arch – watch out for DP!' Then she opened the boot to locate the cool box and mouthed a prayer that he wouldn't fall over in anything.

Ignoring Rory's whine about junk-food deprivation, she waved tuna fish on a brown bap under his nose, inveigled Archie and Olivia into eating hummus-filled pitta bread and some grapes, and took one last look at the map. She'd read it a hundred times already – well, she wanted to have a clear picture in her mind – but the realisation that they still had a long way to go was beginning to bother her. She could feel herself growing twitchy and wanted to be off.

Refuelled, bladders relieved, permission to play in the gaming arcade refused, they were back on the road in under half an hour.

'How much longer?' Olivia's whinge from the back made Imogen's fingers tighten on the steering wheel.

'Oh not long, darling.' She pulled out a CD from the supply she'd stacked neatly into the door pocket. 'You watch, the sky will start to change colour as we get nearer the sea. It's a very particular light. I wonder what the sky's going to be like when we get to Hong Kong.'

'I bet it'll be horrid,' Archie moaned from the back seat.

'Oh no, I'm sure it will be lovely. Lots of sunshine.' Imogen tried to imagine herself sipping Pimm's by a pool in February, but gave up. She slipped the CD into the machine.

'Naaa, Mum. Not that crappy girl band, pleeease!'

'Ollie likes them, and I've asked you before, please do *not* use that word.'

Rory folded his arms heavily. 'Well, they are.'

Imogen gritted her teeth as she looked ahead up the road. Rory hadn't taken the news of the move to Hong Kong well. In fact, ever since his father had mooted the possibility that the bank might want him out in the office there, he'd been sullen and resentful. And who could blame him? He'd be losing friends and everything familiar. Even with his mother's rather over-zealous sales pitch, every time the subject was mentioned he changed it fast. Olivia was no better, though she had showed a spark of interest when Imogen had invented some nonsense about Chinese silk pyjamas. But it was grasping at straws. She'd have to find another tack and launch a sustained PR campaign during the next three weeks' holiday.

Meanwhile, the dual carriageway swept ahead of them, dotted with caravans, cars pulling boats on trailers and estates with roof-rack boxes and boots packed with sleeping bags and kites. Damn, she'd forgotten to pack the kite. She made a mental note to remind Guy to bring it at the weekend. Her mind wandered ahead. Would they have time to get down to the beach this afternoon? It would all depend on what time Sophie and her girls arrived at the house. But good old Sophs, she was pathologically late for everything. Imogen planned to be there to greet them once she'd made the house cosy, and she had a vision of a scrubbed pine table laid with a pot of tea, warm scones and some local bread and jam. In the internet picture the sitting room appeared quite hopeful too. She'd be able to hide those dried flowers in a cupboard somewhere, and the armchairs had to be nicer than they looked.

'Mum.' Her thoughts were brought smartly back to the here and now. 'Where's the sun gone?'

The sky had indeed changed colour, as the bank of cloud that had sat firmly on the horizon for the journey so far suddenly seemed to be dominating most of the sky. But Imogen didn't notice. All she could focus on now was the bank of cars up ahead, a motionless two-laned river of red brake lights as far as the eye could see.

Three-quarters of an hour later, her leg aching from applying the clutch, they had moved barely a mile. Her brain ached more from using up every vestige of inspiration she had to keep the children occupied – how many options are there for I-Spy when your horizon remains unchanged? – and they had eaten most of the packet of chocolate digestives she'd had tucked in her bag for emergencies.

'Now I really feel sick,' Ollie moaned. Imogen pressed the button to open her back window.

'Do you, darling? How many biscuits did you eat?'

'Gooey sticky sickly chocolate,' teased Rory, evilly, leering at his sister. 'Vats of whipped cream, Mars bars dipped in batter …'

'I'm gonna be sick.'

Imogen jammed on the handbrake, and whipped round just in time to catch a handful of warm vomit.

'Rory, baby wipes. By your feet. Now!' Deftly undoing her seat belt with her spare hand, she turned further in her seat, just in time to catch a second helping. Archie started to retch.

'Archie, look out of the window quick! No, Rory, I need a wodge of them, one's no flaming use!' Snatching a handful of wipes, she made as good a job as she could of containing the worst of it – amazed once more at how one can cope with whatever emanates from one's own children – then, grabbing the litter bag, placed it on her daughter's knee. A smell of apple cores wafting out made her feel nauseous too, but it was the best she could do. 'Now if you think you're going to be sick again, do it in there.'

The man in the car behind put his hand on his horn. She muttered fiercely, frantically wiping regurgitated grapes and pitta bread from the front of Olivia's T-shirt.

'Mummy, what *is* a tosser?'

By the time she turned around again in her seat, damage limitation exercised as best she could, there were cars pouring from the left-hand lane into the growing space between her and the car in front, but at least things seemed to be moving.

'Here we go,' she said with a smile, forcing jollity. 'We're getting moving now.'

'It stinks in here. I'm opening the window.' Imogen ignored her elder son, and put her foot down, as if driving up the backside of the car in front would somehow push along the built-up traffic. Quarter of a mile further on, and the reason for the hold-up became apparent. Two drivers were exchanging addresses on the hard shoulder, their bumpers shunted and bent.

'Mum, what's happened? Is anyone dead?'

Really tense now, her mood seemed to dip and rise with every undulation in the road as she willed the cars to keep moving. But the increase in the traffic speed only brought ever closer the dark clouds up ahead and, sure enough, by the time they had got to the turning just after Launceston, she had to put on the windscreen wipers to whisk away the first fat smatterings of rain.

By Davidstow, it was coming down in what her mother would have referred to as 'stair rods'. The only consolation was that Archie and Olivia had fallen asleep, and Rory had given up any pretence of conversation and had headphones glued to his ears, his head nodding to some unheard rhythm on his portable CD player. Free now to think her own thoughts, all she could summon was 'shit'. She could have wept. This was not looking good. This was not how it was meant to be.

A brief phone call to Sophie on her mobile revealed that her friend was a couple of hours behind them and, as if the weather was somehow at her behest, Imogen reassured herself that in two hours anything could happen. The clouds may even have dispersed and an honest July afternoon could yet burst through. Over the thick rounded hedgerows, dotted intermittently with trees bent into tortured shapes by the Atlantic wind, she could just make out the dramatic fall-away of the coastline in the distance, like giant shoulders in a green greatcoat, and was granted instant absolution after the awfulness of the journey. Lord, she'd miss this. Hong Kong Harbour would have to be something else because this view took some beating.

'Rory.' She nudged him out of his rap-induced coma. 'Read the instructions I've written here.' From her bag, she handed him the piece of paper on which she'd noted the route. 'Where does it say we turn? Is it by the pub?'

'If you know, Mum, why did you ask?'

The pretty girl at the letting-agency office was brisk

and efficient with the formalities, and Imogen had time to give Olivia a fresh T-shirt and dash next door into the Late Nite Minimart (she bridled at the irritating spelling) for fresh essentials before following the escort to the house. She knew any hopes of Cornish scones and homemade jams were dashed, however, as soon as she pushed open the minimart door. All it could come up with, unless one wanted cigarettes and Lottery scratch cards, was skimmed milk and a loaf of thin-sliced white.

Suppressing her mild disappointment, she stowed the carrier bag in the boot and latched onto the tail lights of the agency girl's car as she led them through winding and increasingly narrow lanes.

'Nearly there, everyone.' Imogen could feel herself leaning forward in her seat, willing it to be round the next corner as Archie began to wriggle frantically. 'And look, the rain is stopping. I'm sure it is.'

'Can you see the sea yet, Mama? You said it was near the sea.'

'Well, sweetie, the hedges are high, but it can't be far away.'

'I can't wait,' enthused Olivia. 'I'm going to build the biggest sandcastle ever.'

'Mine'll be better,' challenged Rory.

'Here we are, everyone.' Imogen could feel her voice rising with her anticipation. 'We've done it.' Turning into the narrow driveway, she pulled up outside the front door and pulled on the handbrake with a flourish.

There was silence as the four of them peered through

the rain-spattered car windows at the purply-grey granite of Penvarick House. Big sash windows, in UPVC, shone out like startled eyes, reflecting the racing clouds and the grey of the sky. Garish red geraniums in a large tub by the door danced frantically and slapped each other in the fierce wind.

'Is this it? Is this our new holiday house? It's horrid.'

'Now, Archie, I'm sure it will be lovely. Let's jump out and explore.' Undoing her seat belt, she grasped the troublesome rabbit abandoned on Archie's seat and stuffed it into her handbag for safe keeping, then slipped out of her seat to skim her eyes over the view. Across the road in front of the house there was a field that sloped away from them and she could see the roofs of bungalows below. All faced away from them towards what she supposed must be the sea, though there was no evidence of it apart from the vicious wind. She grabbed her handbag and offered up a quick prayer to the god of Holiday Lets that inside it would be all she'd hoped for.

The girl from the agency turned the key in the lock then threw her small frame against the door. 'I remember this one from last time,' she said as she tried again. 'It sticks when it's wet. Ah, here we go.'

The children rushed in ahead of her as she opened the door and bent to pick up a free newspaper from the mat. 'It's been empty this last week, what with the school holidays not yet started. Yours have broken up early.'

'Private school,' said Imogen distractedly, clutching her bag, following her in and standing in the hallway. She gazed around her, trying to ignore the faint musty smell of damp. The children's feet were thundering about in the upstairs rooms and, ignoring the chatter of the girl, she wandered through the open door to her left.

She should have been prepared. She'd seen the pictures on the internet after all and had looked at them again only last night, but somehow her brain must have edited out the worst bits. Realisation dawned. When the copy had said 'comfortable', it didn't, as she had hoped, mean 'tasteful'. Her eyes took in the rose velour suite, thin pink floral curtains, small floral prints and antiqued plates hung too high up on the wall. The fireplace was ablaze with a vase of dried grasses.

Imogen mentally rolled up her sleeves. Time to lick things into shape.

Jo stifled a yawn, had a look through the very long case notes on the screen in front of her, and gave her last patient, a large schizophrenic, the usual pep-talk about taking his meds. Urging him to make an appointment with his own GP, she sent him on his way, still muttering. At least it made a change from junkies and demands for the morning-after pill – that last couple had still been doing up their flies when they'd come in. This red-eye shift from midnight to six was deservedly the best paid – and boy, had she earned her money tonight. She completed her notes, then stood up and packed her case. As she stretched, she could hear her stomach rumbling. There was nothing for it – there would have to be a stop-off at the cab shelter on the way home for one of those fab bacon sarnies and a mug of tea the colour of boat varnish, before home and a couple of hours' kip.

After handing over to the next doctor on duty, she shouldered her way through the heavy glass doors and into the chilly brilliance of the East London Sunday morning. By tonight she'd be miles away, with Finn, wallowing in the cosy and undemanding shallows of a shared seaside holiday – something she hadn't indulged in since she was a child. She smiled wryly as she dumped her stuff on the passenger seat of the car and kicked out the take-out coffee cups from under the pedals. She hoped this one would be an improvement.

Cornwall – hmm. She'd been hoping for Cuba or Costa Rica – something with a bit of cred, like last year when they'd gone to Thailand. But Finn had been miserable a lot of the time, tired and listless in the heat from the moment they'd got there. Maybe this holiday she'd get a chance to rest. Driving home through the awakening streets, she thought longingly of sleep. Being a junior doctor had been bad enough, but the narcotic effect of these on-call shifts was pure hell. Maybe it was age, she thought grimly, taking a quick look in the rear-view mirror at the fine lines around her eyes, but she needed her rest like never before.

Half an hour later, she let herself into the shared hallway, with its perpetual smell of cooked mince, and dragged herself upstairs to the flat. She'd left the heating on all night with laundry draped everywhere in the hope that it would be dry enough to pack and, as a result, the

16

place felt like the rain forest. The stripped floors, pale walls and potted palms contributed to the tropical impression and, had it not been for the strong smell of Ariel, she wouldn't have been too surprised to have come across a gecko rolling his eyes at her. She turned off the boiler, threw open the long windows overlooking the street, and welcomed in the fresh air. Maybe that would help. Must get that sodding dryer fixed.

Pulling down a backpack and a couple of weekend grips from the top of her wardrobe, she dumped them onto the bed, spluttering as the dust flew up. Damn Maria! She'd suspected her cleaner had been slacking for a while. Hoovering round things was her speciality. The Croatian girl's prepositions were undeniably shaky, but Jo was fairly confident she had mimed 'on top of', 'under' and 'behind' clearly enough when she'd hired her. Suddenly, dispirited at the challenges life presented, she sat down and rubbed her face. She'd just pack her potions and lotions before her nap. That would cheer her up.

She surveyed the immaculately organised shelves in her bedroom, and flexed her fingers in pleasurable anticipation. Within thirty minutes she had made her considered selection, starting with the top shelf (shampoo, conditioners, glossing spray, serum), and working carefully down to the bottom one (foot balm, cuticle conditioner, toe separators, orange sticks, files, base coats, varnish, hardening spray), only packing the bare essentials and, of course, her last jar of Paysage Enchanté Healing Balm. What a sod that they'd stopped making it! Despite her frugality, she was dismayed to see that in no time she'd already filled one of the grips with a selection of overstuffed make-up bags (free with two or more purchases). She glanced at the clock. Shit! She'd have to pick up Finn in just under two hours. Not even bothering to close the curtains, she placed the packed bag carefully by the door, shoved the others onto the floor, flopped back on top of the covers and was asleep within seconds.

'Jo, wake up!' Small bony fingers shook her by the arm. 'Come on, lazy! We waited and waited for you to come. Thelma has to go to work now. Come on – we're going on holiday.'

'Wha … wha …? Oh Finn, stop bouncing. Let me wake up at my own speed.'

Finn obliged, jumped off the bed and bounced around on the floor instead. 'Shoes off, mate,' she groaned and rubbed her eyes with the heel of her hand. 'Don't want the old bag downstairs complaining again. And can you get your stuff sorted? Some of it's still drying, the rest's in the ironing pile.'

She heard him snort. The irony! They both knew it was the ironing pile that never got ironed. Thelma's heavy footsteps sounded in the living room and Jo pulled herself up, ready to apologise. But as usual, Thelma's broad, black, smiling face bore no resentment, only mild concern.

'Sleeping again! Why're you working those long nights, man? Them other doctors don't do that.'

'Well, they don't have you to pay, Thelma. You're

worth your not inconsiderable weight in gold, but you're a luxury item all right.'

Thelma's face creased with wheezy laughter as Jo handed over a crumpled handful of notes. 'You have a lovely holiday, now. Where is it you're goin'?'

'Cornwall. North coast, somewhere near Padstow. You remember Sophie – blond and fluffy, two little girls? – well, she's booked a house for us all.' She yawned and pulled a face in response to Thelma's pitying glance at Finn. 'Yeah, I know. But there's another woman too. I've never met her, but she's got a boy a bit older than Finn and a couple of others. That's the main incentive, really. I wouldn't have taken him out of school early otherwise, but it's the ideal opportunity to keep the Finnster occupied and out of my hair so I can get on with some serious vegging.'

Thelma pursed her lips and sucked on her dazzling false teeth. 'A women's commune? God help you, darlin'. Worse than having men around.'

'Oh go on, you old misery. It'll be fine.'

Finn reappeared with two cups of tea on a tray, his tongue sticking out in concentration. 'Thanks, Finn – you're a honey.' The women sipped the steaming brew in silence for a while as Thelma surveyed the chaos in the living room. 'You planning to get there this week?'

Jo look around in resignation, and shrugged. 'Got to get it dry first, then we'll have to stop at the supermarket for provisions. We've received our instructions.'

From along the corridor came sounds of scuffling and muttering. '… bloody batteries! Know I've got some here somewhere. Where the hell are they?' Finn appeared, scowling, now changed into shorts and a loose T-shirt. 'I can't find batteries for my Gameboy, and my sandals are too small.'

Jo heaved a heavy sigh. Thelma shook her head. 'Well, looks like you got everything under control here, so I'll go to work. I'd rather be coming on holiday with you though and my precious boy. I never went to Cornwall.'

Jo shrugged. 'I imagine it will be lovely. Just think, Finn, the house is right on the beach apparently. Won't that be terrific? You can go straight out there in the morning.'

'Yeah, whatever. But what about the batteries? You know I'll only drive you crazy in the car if I don't have any. We bought some the other day, didn't we? I bet you've gone and put them in your radio.'

Thelma blew a kiss and let herself out. Jo turned back to Finn, whose green eyes were sparkling mischievously.

'OK you win, crafty thing. You can take them back then. Your need is greater than mine. I suppose they have things like batteries in Cornwall or perhaps it's all wind-powered.'

Finn skipped along the corridor to his bedroom and the muffled grunting and cursing continued to the accompaniment of some early Hendrix on his CD player. Damn it, the kid had taste. Jo set about shaking and folding the driest clothes, and moving the wetter ones closer to the windows.

By midday, she was starting to wonder if it was

possible to dry clothes in the microwave. 'How about we go out and get some lunch?' she suggested. 'There's sod all in the fridge.'

But Finn was anxious to be off. 'Can't we eat on the way? Oh, come on, Jo,' he complained. 'Let's get going. I don't want us to be last as usual. I thought you were going to get the drier fixed.'

Jo bristled. 'And just when have I had time? I've got two full-time jobs, if you haven't noticed. Looking after you and tending the sick, most of whom are bloody lead swingers anyway.' There was a short silence. 'I'm sorry, mate,' she said at last without looking at him. Finn came over and slipped in behind her on the sofa then started to rub her neck. 'I'm sorry too, Mummy. D'you want another nap before we go? It's a long drive.'

She tilted her head back against his curly dark hair, and sighed. 'Oh Finn, don't tempt me, babe. I'm just so bloody knackered. I'll be fine. Tell you what, I'll have a large latte with two extra shots. That'll keep me awake, even if I have to stop to wee at every service station between here and Land's End.'

After a lunch of Brie and cranberry on brown for Jo, with the vital quadruple-shot latte, and toasted panino with a deluxe hot chocolate (mounded with marshmallows, whipped cream and chocolate curls) for Finn, they returned to the flat in high spirits, giggling and shoving each other along the pavement, to find their jeans just about dry enough to wear.

'Hooray!' called Jo, as she struggled with the zip. 'This is a good omen. I've got a great feeling about this holiday.

Let's get the stuff in the car. Did you pack your toothbrush and everything?'

Finn bounded into the room, baseball mitt in hand. 'Yup. Are you taking your Gap jacket?'

'Nah, too thick. I think I'll take that one I got for the Dominican Republic.'

'I'm taking mine.' Finn jumped up and down until he had unhooked the jacket, then stuffed it into the bag he'd brought from his bedroom. 'Are you nearly ready?' he asked, looking pointedly at the chunky watch on his thin wrist.

'Yeah, almost done here. I'll just wash my hair quickly and put on some slap.'

Finn sighed in resignation, leant against the wall then slid down it to sit on the floor and fished a comic out of his bag. He was halfway through the second one by the time Jo emerged, feeling human again. 'Come on, let's hit the road. It's the start of our big adventure. Have you got the map?'

Finn hunted through the pile of luggage on the floor and emerged triumphant. 'Here it is! Have you got directions? Unplugged everything? Got the keys? Your phone? Recharger?'

'Yes, yes.' Jo ushered him out of the door. 'Stop fussing, Dad! Everything's under control.'

Finn said nothing, but rolled his eyes as they shut the door behind them.

The traffic was solid long before they even reached Exeter. As Jo had predicted, thanks to the latte she'd had to stop several times, but it was a chance for Finn to have a run round. As usual, he was irresistibly attracted to the games machines. 'Not only are they a waste of money,' Jo called embarrassingly loudly as he wandered inside, 'they rot your brain, you know,' and she went to track down another coffee.

Twenty minutes later, she dragged her reluctant son away from House of the Dead, and they went into the shop to stock up on sweets, drinks and the Sunday papers. The journey dragged on.

'Finn, if you ask me one more time I'm going to set fire to your hair! We are *not* nearly there. We are not even nearly nearly there. You've got the map. When we reach Bodmin, then you can ask me again. That Gameboy was meant to keep you quiet in the car. Don't tell me you got me to buy it under false pretences.'

Silence. Finn turned and looked out of the window for a while.

Suddenly she felt a thrill of expectation. 'Oooh, Bodmin Moorrr,' she exclaimed in a cod Cornish accent. 'Doesn't that fill you with fear an' tremblin', me 'andsome? This area's dead famous for smugglers and mysterious goings on. Bottomless tin mines and contraband brandy. And that dishy bloke Ross Poldark. Oh look, Finn – Jamaica Rrrinn! God, I loved that book – and *Rebecca*. You must read those, Finn. I bet I can get a copy somewhere near where we're staying.'

'Hey, Mum, look at those clouds.' He craned his neck to look up at the sky above. 'That one looks like a stegosaurus chasing a chicken. You reckon it's going to rain?'

Jo glanced over at the stegosaurus, which seemed to have invited some friends over. She shook her head and pulled a face. 'Dunno. What do you think?'

Finn turned to survey his mother's profile. She pressed her lips together and frowned slightly in concentration. He reached over and rubbed her arm gently. 'I think you should have brought your Gap jacket.'

Chapter 2

Monday

*Starting bright, but wind
picking up in the afternoon*

Picking up her cup of coffee from the worktop, Imogen unlocked the back door. The early-morning sun had livened up the rather weed-covered and uneven terrace at the back of the house, and she stepped outside. The plastic garden chairs could have done with a wipe down, especially after last night's rain, but she dried a space for her bottom with the sleeve of her fleece before perching gingerly on the edge.

The garden – huge compared to their postage stamp in Barnes – ran uphill to a thick hedge and a field beyond. It would be fun for the children to explore, with its gnarly apple trees and big bushes to hide in. It had no borders to speak of, though, just a few clumps of shrubs here and there. She could feel her suppressed Gertrude Jekyllism beginning to unfurl. How she wished she could set about it with a spade and a lorry-load of plants.

Less promising was the Wendy house. It was certainly not the timber Hansel and Gretel construction you find in the back of upmarket magazines, which Imogen had imagined from the property's details. Rather, it was a garish plastic version, green with lichen from a winter left outside. She'd have to get the cleaning fluid onto that before she could let the children loose in it.

Later though. For the moment she'd enjoy the sunshine, and she took a slug of piping-hot coffee. Strange, wasn't it, how the water tasted so different from place to place? Perhaps she should have packed the water filter after all. Then, closing her eyes, she let the sun warm her face. Oh bliss.

Well, nearly bliss. She opened them again. The silence had woken her too early. For a moment she hadn't been able to work out where she was, or why she couldn't sense Guy's body beside her, with his familiar deep breaths. Of course the moment she'd opened half an eye to take in the drapes on the four-poster bed and the light pouring in through a chink in the thin, unfamiliar curtains, she'd known where she was and had lain for a moment taking in the room. Her clock had said six thirty-two, and it had felt good to simply steal the moment in the knowledge that with luck it would be a little while before she was joined, inevitably, by Archie.

What a relief it had been to be wrapped in her own sheets – naturally she had had to leave the duvet for Guy, though she would dearly love to have brought that with her too. There was something so unpleasant about sleeping in someone else's bedding – it's what made hotels so distasteful – and the challenge of squashing four pillows into the car had been worth the effort. A stranger's pillows? Too disgusting to contemplate.

The bedroom was pleasingly big – the same size as the sitting room below it – and she felt it was only fair that, with its four-poster and view of the sea in the distance, it should be allocated to her and Guy. She had organised the holiday after all, and it was sweet of Sophie to be so insistent last night that she lay claim to it. What sort of people had woken in this room before? she'd wondered, stretching her feet to the cold patch at the bottom of the bed. Had they also been slightly disappointed by the cheap furniture and attempts at good taste? It had been very satisfying to whip around the house last night gathering up the ghastly ornaments and vases of dried flowers to secrete them in the cupboard downstairs for the duration of the holiday. For the next three weeks she could make the house her domain. Well hers, Sophie's and this other woman's of course.

As she sat outside here now, half an hour later, with still not a peep from Archie – oh the wonderful, soporific effects of sea air – she reflected once more what a shame it was that Caroline hadn't been able to come. But it was rather typical of her to drop out at the last minute. What was Guy's description of her? A 'flake'.

But hell – Cornwall was OK and lots of people Imogen had met came here for the summer. She suspected, though, that they knew which houses to rent and had their names down for them year after year; a bit like they had for their sons' and daughters' public schools. Those same sons and daughters who spent the summer hanging out at that famous pub in Rock hoping to rub shoulders with some minor royal. Those sort of people would have snaffled the houses close to the sea ages ago. How on earth she was going to persuade Archie to walk half a mile to the beach from here she didn't know.

As if on cue she heard his feet pattering across the kitchen. 'Mama?'

'Out here, darling,' and she went to the back door, heaved him up in her arms and sat down with him again on her knee. His face was slightly swollen with sleep and he snuggled his rabbit with one hand, the thumb of his other stuffed in his mouth. His blond hair was spiky and dishevelled and, as she held him to her and wrapped her fleece around him, she drank in his smell and the wafts of his sweet morning breath.

'How did you sleep in your lovely new bed?'

''K,' he mumbled and pushed himself harder against her body. 'Your bed was empty.'

'I know, darling. I was so excited about being by the seaside I decided to get up. The day is too lovely to waste a second of it. How's about you and I go and find some breakfast and bring it back as a surprise for the others?'

''K.'

Ten minutes later, and with the knowledge that there was still an hour to go on the breadmaker (it had made so much sense to bring it with her), they crept out of the back door again. Imogen hadn't wanted to risk the sticky front door, for fear it would waken the others and foil her 'hunter-gatherer' plan to have a fabulous breakfast awaiting them when they got up. She'd left a note so they'd know where she'd gone.

Keen not to fire the car engine, she executed the bump start one of her brothers had taught her when they were teenagers, and pulled out of the gate. Archie began to wake up properly and looked around with interest at the hedgerows and fields around him.

'We're going to the beach later, aren't we, Mama?'

'I expect so.' Imogen was distracted as she worked out where to turn left.

'Will that friend of Sophie's want to come? Have they arrived yet?'

'Yes, darling, they came very late last night. You were fast asleep.'

'His name sounds like win, doesn't it?'

'Nearly. It's Finn, darling. F-I-N-N.'

'Like a fish?'

Imogen smiled. How good children are at bursting balloons of pretension. When Sophie had first told her about the friend she'd found to fill the gap left by Caroline's family, she'd been a little surprised by the name. 'Finn' sounded a wee bit contrived and 'right on' – the sort of name you'd expect in one of those highland dramas on the BBC. Obviously she hadn't had a chance to meet Jo properly. All Imogen knew was that she was a single mother and a GP. Beyond that, Sophie had only provided the scantiest details. Typical of Soph to leave out some rather critical ones!

Imogen had no yardstick to make any judgements by though. When Jo and Finn had turned up last night, they had tumbled into the house, dumping holdalls bulging clothes onto the hall floor and, after a quick cup of tea, had disappeared up to their room. They were probably tired and the last, tricky part of the journey had taken place in the dark. It was just a shame they'd filled up on crisps and chocolate bought at the service station and that they hadn't wanted any of Imogen's casserole. If she'd known, she wouldn't have bothered saving some for the latecomers.

On wider roads now, she accelerated slightly. Perhaps the bakery she'd read about in the 'Fine Foods of Cornwall' leaflet would have something tantalising for breakfast. She wasn't that familiar with Jo's part of East London (occasional forays up to Sophie's for family Sunday lunch being as far as she'd got), but she suspected that her sort 'Sunday Brunched' on something South American that hadn't quite found its way to SW13.

Archie broke into her thoughts. 'Will Fish Finn want to play on the beach too?'

'Oh, I'm absolutely sure he will. Like you he doesn't get to see the sea much.' She briefly wondered how much she should explain about Finn to Archie. Much as she loved her son, he had even less tact than most six-year-olds, and she wasn't quite sure whether the Finn-thing was an issue. 'Er, Arch darling. I don't want you to be surprised, but Finn's not quite the same colour as we are. He's a bit darker.'

'What? Like our dinner lady at school?'

'Well, not quite as dark as that. Just a bit dark.'

'Is his mum dark and fat like our dinner lady?'

'No, darling, she's not. She's very slim really and has light skin like us, and she's got wavy brown hair.' She glanced over at her son, who was clearly thinking this over. 'Perhaps we shouldn't really mention it though. He might feel a bit different and not want it pointed out. OK?'

She wasn't convinced she had his agreement on this, but there was no time to pursue it as they'd pulled up outside the bakery – not quite as quaint and old-fashioned as the leaflet had suggested. The yellow-striped canopy over the window was grubby and torn in places, and a large window sticker was advertising a fizzy drink. The smell inside though was authentic and divine; the aroma of fresh bread mingled with the buttery smell of warm pastry. Ten minutes later and they emerged with two carrier bags full of shiny Cornish pasties for lunch, floury brown baps in case Jo and Finn were vegetarian (maybe that explained the casserole business), a couple of bottles of Cornish apple juice (was Cornwall famous for its apples? she wondered fleetingly), a selection of almond, apricot and plain croissants, and an irresistibly crusty loaf of bread in case the one she had made wasn't enough. The lady behind the counter had smiled at Archie and asked him if he was on holiday. Now this was more like it.

The house was a very different place when they walked in the back door again. The kitchen smelt of bread and she could hear the sound of the TV from the front room.

'What ho, Dr Livingstone. You're an early bird.' Sophie was hunched over a mug of tea at the table in her familiar early-morning slump, her blond curls flattened from sleep, a hooded sweatshirt pulled on over tartan pyjamas. 'You always were better in the mornings than me. Been out foraging? Fabulous idea to bring a proper coffee maker by the way – what a treat. Trouble is I couldn't make it work. Fancy some tea?'

'Oh, I'd adore one.' Imogen dumped the carrier bags on the side and started to unpack them. 'Well, I thought I'd bring the essentials, and I do hate instant, don't you? Arch and I have just found a great little bakery and we got a bit carried away. Too much of this and my bum will be even bigger. Archie?' she called out to the little boy as he headed towards the kitchen door and the source of the TV noise. 'Can you tell whoever's in there to come for breakfast?' Provisions packed away, she started putting bowls, plates and cereal on the table. 'How did you sleep?'

'Deeply and comfortably, thank you,' Sophie stretched languidly, without making any move to pour a cup for Imogen, 'though I kept dreaming about endless motorways. It's rather a cosy little bed actually. How was your palatial boudoir?'

'Passable. All our lot up?'

''Fraid so.' Sophie sighed apologetically. 'Rory is rather surprised I think that breakfast TV has achieved the outreaches of Cornwall. Finn's with them too – I think they're comparing Gameboy games.'

Deciding not to refer to his colour, Imogen settled for, 'Thank the Lord for the lingua franca of the twenty-first-century child,' and went through to rally the troops. On seeing her mother, Ollie got up from her game with Sophie's two girls and put her arms round her.

'Thought you'd run away,' she mumbled into Imogen's stomach.

'Didn't you see my note?'

'Yeah.' Rory didn't even look up from his game. 'I told her where you were. She's just being stupid.'

'Am not, you git.'

'Enough!' Turning off the telly to a chorus of protests, she gently lifted the Gameboy out of her son's grasp. 'Thanks, sweetheart, for involving Finn,' she whispered so only he could hear, then she urged him up and into breakfast. 'Olivia, the G-word is banned as you very well know. Come on, everyone. Cereal time. No one can build empires and sandcastles on an empty stomach.'

Scrimmaging and arguing about who would sit next to whom, they finally found their places and lunged for the cereals. All except Finn, who, still standing by the table, bare-chested and in baggy pyjama bottoms, picked up a bowl, filled it to the brim with cornflakes, took up a spoon and turned to leave the room. There was a sudden silence as the other children watched his progress.

'Er, Finn,' Imogen said quietly, 'where are you off to?'

'Watch TV of course.'

'No, sweetie. We don't eat breakfast in front of the TV. House rule.'

He looked up at Imogen as if he'd never seen her before. His gaze was not defiant as she'd expected. Instead his extraordinarily clear green eyes were wide and innocent. 'I always do.'

Aware that strictly this wasn't her house to make the rules in, she also knew this was a defining moment. It's now or never, Imogen dear, she thought to herself, and glanced over at Sophie who merely shrugged and raised her eyebrows.

'Come and sit here next to Rory and we can all decide what we're going to do today.' Finn faltered for a moment as if considering this, tapping his foot lightly on the floor. Then, precariously negotiating bowl and spoon, he came slowly back to the table and placed them down in the space next to the older boy.

Imogen could feel her shoulders drop with relief. 'Now, who fancies a picnic? Archie, we cut butter from the end of the pat. It's vulgar to scrape it from the top. I've bought some yummy pasties – the big local delicacy – for lunch. Looks a bit like a calzone. We could pack a bag and some balls and go down to the beach – I'm sure you guys would love a game of footie.' She smiled at Finn, admiring for a moment his soft brown skin next to her son's fair colouring.

There was a general yelp of agreement. 'Right, eat up, everyone, then you can get dressed and explore the garden while we pack a picnic.'

Both women squeezed in beside the children and joined in the meal, and everyone chatted about the day, until there was a moment's silence and Imogen noticed Archie staring quizzically at Finn. Oh-oh, diversionary tactics needed, but too late.

'Fi-inn, my mum says we're not to say that you're darker than us, but you're not really that dark, are you? You're just brown, really. Sort of like a sausage.'

'Blimey, Arch – tell it like it is, why don't you!' Sophie threw back her head and roared with laughter.

From the bathroom above their heads Imogen could make out the creak of floorboards. Jo must be up. Great, now they could all decide what they were going to do. Sophie pushed back her chair. 'Imo, are you under control if I go and grab a shower? I'll use the shower room. It'll only be a quickie.'

'Sure. I'll have one after you.' Imogen started to cut into the warm bread she'd taken out of the breadmaker. 'I can't guarantee they'll be any of this left when you come down though – can't resist it when it's fresh and warm.' She tore off a bit of crust and put it in her mouth. 'It's my downfall.'

'I can see that from here,' laughed Sophie, squinting appraisingly at Imogen's backside and shuffled off upstairs in her slippers.

Ten minutes later and Imogen sat and took in the carnage, marvelling at how children could succeed in getting jam on everything. Still, they were fed and having fun. Heaving herself up, she cleared the debris, wiped up the sticky mess and left one place laid out neatly for Jo with bowl, plate and spoon, and surrounded it temptingly with boxes of cereal, butter and jam. There.

Refreshing the coffee maker, she heard footsteps behind her and turned, expecting it to be Jo. 'Crikey, that must be the swiftest shower in history. Hope you did behind your ears!' Sophie's hair was damp, and she looked delicate in pink cotton trousers and pale blue fleece.

'Too right it was swift. It was bloody freezing. Jo's having a bath. I think she must have helped herself to all the hot water.'

*

Jo increased her pace to catch up with her friend. 'What a feast! This picnic wouldn't be out of place at Glyndebourne.'

Sophie glanced across with a little smile. 'And what would you know about Glyndebourne?'

'You're right. I'm more Glastonbury. Does she always prepare this much food? Cos if she does I'll be fat as a house in no time.'

Sophie eyed her in disbelief. 'Fat? You? That'll be the day. I've seen you make short work of my bread-and-butter pudding, but I think you must have hidden it down your socks! Well, I did warn you. You'd better fasten your seat belt but not too tight, cos Imogen's the best cook I know. She always knocked out the best fairy cakes in domestic science and she can do things with pasta that are almost illegal. And her pancakes! Mmm … Oh Gracie! Stay absolutely still, darling. Don't flap at it. It'll go away if you ignore it …' And she was off, bumping along the lane in her flowery flip-flops, completely laden down with neatly packed cool bags, to where her daughter was squealing hysterically at a tiny insect.

On her own again, Jo was reminded for the first time in years of the impromptu picnics her mother used to assemble with distaste on the windy beach at Cromer. Bridge rolls and fish paste, followed by Garibaldi biscuits, all eaten with care to avoid smudging her Yardley lipstick, as Jo shivered in her thin dress, white socks and Start-rite sandals. Her mother's motto had always been 'We'll find something when we get there', or at least that had been her excuse for doing nothing in advance and buying woefully inadequate provisions at the last minute.

It was typical of her mother's whole attitude to her domestic role, which she wore like an itchy shirt. Their kitchen was always too clean to cook in, and anyway her nails were too precious to risk. Her skill at producing meals that involved minimum preparation was nothing less than remarkable. Jo remembered cold tongue and tinned potatoes; pickled beetroot and hard-boiled eggs; iceberg lettuce with a couple of tomatoes placed on top. These were the staples. No faffing about with the likes of raspberry vinegar dressing (apparently Olivia's favourite), and certainly nothing like the homemade sticky ginger cake packed so lovingly earlier by Imogen.

Jo had never dreamt there would be a feast waiting for them when they arrived last night or she wouldn't have stuffed her face with junk. By the time they'd found the house, she had been so knackered she could have slept in the car. The welcoming committee had been too much for her, so she'd used Finn as the excuse for going straight upstairs to the gloomy little room they'd been allocated – the penalty, she supposed, for arriving last. She'd consoled herself with Sophie's emailed assurance that the beach was close enough that they wouldn't be spending much time in the house anyway, but this little route march showed that to be an exaggeration to say the least.

From her position at the rear of the expedition, Jo had a perfect view of the others, straggling in single file along the right-hand side of the lane. Well, single apart from Finn and Rory, glued together over the Gameboys they'd covertly brought with them, in contravention of Imogen's dictat. They kept peeping round furtively to look at Jo, obviously imagining she didn't realise what they were doing. She winked, and watched in satisfaction as Rory gaped in astonishment at Finn, who returned a conspiratorial grin.

Leading the expedition was Imogen. Sophie had mentioned that her old school friend was famed for her efficiency, and here was the proof. Imogen had assembled this gargantuan picnic with practised and unconscious skill, whilst simultaneously directing her children, as if by some mysterious sixth sense, to gather sandals, balls, sunblock and towels from around the house. Striding on ahead now, with her fair hair sensibly tucked behind her ears, Imogen looked every inch the no-nonsense hockey captain she had probably been at school. Broad in the beam and long-legged, she was big-boned and handsome, exuding an out-doorish wholesomeness, her well-scrubbed face glowing in the fresh air.

Walking behind his mother was little blond Archie, closely followed by Olivia with Amelia and Grace, Sophie's girls, who were white-blond like their mother and never seemed to walk if they could skip, but would never skip if there was someone there to hang off. Then there was a bit of a gap to where Sophie was now ambling along, stopping occasionally to look at plants in the hedgerow. Following her equally slowly, were Rory and Finn, both of whom had stripped off their jackets and jumpers. Another reason for Sophie's slow progress: as well as the second instalment of the picnic, she was carrying those too.

Jo watched Finn and Rory together. They had bonded pretty quickly and Finn was clearly relishing the older boy's attention. Rory seemed a nice enough kid, tall, fair and well-made like his mother. Perhaps the dad was a mountainous blond thoroughbred too, like his wife, though Olivia's glossy chestnut hair and more pointed features suggested some rogue genetic strain. The little girl in question had now given up calling back along the row to her brother. Rory was making a point of putting her down in front of his new friend, and Finn had watched the interaction between the siblings with ill-disguised fascination.

Jo herself had been allocated the drinks bag, and a peek inside had revealed a cornucopia of different squashes (organic, natch) and a stack of brightly coloured plastic beakers. She was also carrying the bag with all the towels neatly re-rolled into sausages by Imogen before they left, 'because it makes them so much easier to pack'.

How much further to this bloody beach? Imogen seemed to be fretting too, because she was constantly turning round to jolly on the troops. 'Probably just around this bend now. You'll see, it can't be far.' Eventually, Jo spotted her jumping up and down and waving. The wind carried her words to the end of the line. 'It's here. It's here. It looks perfect.'

And so it was. A broad crescent of clean sand, a generous allocation of rock pools at the far end, and sheltered by dunes. It was the perfect Famous Five setting. Jo was overwhelmed by a sudden earlier memory of

Brittany, and the scratchy grass against her bare legs as she'd clambered the dunes in shorts and plastic sandals while her parents read books sitting side by side on a towel.

The kids were so hungry, they wolfed down everything put in front of them. By the time they finished lunch, the wind had picked up and it was getting a bit chilly. Jo pulled on her jumper, lay back on the sand and closed her eyes behind her shades. Those pasties had been delicious. The first one had barely touched the sides, but she'd taken time to savour the second. 'Imogen,' she had sighed, licking her fingers, 'those were sublime. You can certainly spot a good pasty. Those yummy little slivers of turnip! And the pastry!' Jo had been surprised by the pleasure on Imogen's face. After all, she hadn't even had one herself, only finished off Archie's. But now, at least, Jo understood the reason for the salads and carefully wrapped hard-boiled eggs. Throughout lunch, Imogen had kept glancing at Jo in her bikini and had made some comment about watching her weight.

Now, replete, Jo listened idly to Imogen and Sophie swapping diet lore, and pretended to be asleep to avoid being asked her professional opinion. Dietary advice from slim people isn't generally well accepted.

Jo jolted awake. Brrr, it was chilly now. Without opening her eyes, she reached out for the rest of her clothes and pulled them on. Sitting up, she realised she was alone with the picnic debris and all the other clobber, but way down the beach she spotted the others engaged in what looked like an energetic game of French cricket.

Imogen was bowling, Olivia was batting and the others were spread out for fielding. Jo gazed at Finn, hopping from foot to foot in his excitement, as Sophie dived for the ball. She could see he was laughing out loud, doubled up and clutching his sides the way he sometimes did. She was too far away to hear him but she knew his face would be screwed up with mirth. So like his father.

She shook herself and wondered whether to run down and join them, but then thought better of it. She had to guard the picnic after all. Instead, she sat cross-legged and waved, but Finn didn't notice. She watched for a few moments more, then looked round the beach again. There were other groups, mostly families – not close enough to be a nuisance, but a little too far off to study discreetly from behind her dark glasses. What a shame she hadn't brought a book. Jo started to tidy away the remains of the picnic.

She suspected it was the grey clouds gathering overhead that stopped the game, rather than any lack of enthusiasm. The children came jogging back and she sat up eagerly to hear Finn's take on the proceedings but, engrossed in conversation with Rory, he didn't come over to her. Imogen and Sophie followed behind, wading through the soft dry sand, slightly out of breath, but rosy-cheeked and tousled from their efforts. They looked like a couple of fifteen-year-olds, and she could hear them laughing about something.

'Had a good sleep, lazy bones?' asked Sophie. 'Hope you haven't caught the sun.'

Imogen looked down dismayed at her fair skin. 'I burn terribly easily, and it is the same for the kids. It's factor thirty for us from March onwards. The Far East will be a nightmare.' She sighed to Jo. 'I suppose Sophie told you we were headed en masse for Hong Kong. My husband, Guy, has been posted there.'

Jo watched as Imogen rummaged in the picnic bags, redistributing what Jo had already packed. 'Mm, you told me, didn't you, Soph? Sounds exciting. Lucky you, it's a great place.'

'Oh, you must tell me all about it.' Imogen lowered her voice and leant towards Jo. 'About the sunblock thing – I wasn't quite sure what to do about Finn,' she said confidentially. 'Does he burn at all? I offered him some cream when I was slapping it on the others, but he said you never put any on him. Can that be right?'

Jo felt her hackles rise almost imperceptibly. Was it her imagination or was she being got at? 'Oh it's fine. Lucky little sod doesn't seem to need it. One of the advantages of having a touch of the tarbrush, I suppose.' She could hear Imogen's intake of breath, and wondered why she'd spoken like that. As if to make amends, she indicated the now even neater pile of bags. 'I packed away the picnic, if that's OK. Thought you might want to make a hasty getaway. It's turned so cold. I'm freezing.'

Imogen picked up the children's trainers and clapped them together to bang the sand off. 'Yes, what a pity. Well, perhaps we should have got away from the house earlier. But thanks for tidying up.' Then she turned and cupped her hands around her mouth to call the children who had scattered again far and wide. 'Come on, team, time to get going!'

Jo glanced round quickly, but no one was staring. The children came zooming in from all directions, like sparrows around sprinkled breadcrumbs. 'That's right, well done, everyone,' Imogen gushed.

'Blimey, instant obedience.' Jo laughed in admiration. 'That was impressive. You've got a fine pair of lungs on you.'

Imogen laughed uncertainly. 'Never mind ante-natal classes. What every mother needs is a couple of months' training at Sandhurst.' She turned back to the children. 'I know, why don't we all go home and have a game of Mousetrap?'

Rory groaned, but Olivia and Archie jumped up and down.

'What's Mousetrap?' asked Finn.

'Aha,' exclaimed Imogen conspiratorially. 'You're in for a treat. It's our favourite board game at the moment. And Rory loves it, no matter what he says.'

About halfway back, Finn stopped and waited for Jo to catch him up. 'Wotcha, mate. Come to keep me company? I never knew you were so good at cricket. Did you—'

'These sandals are rubbing,' he complained. 'They're too small. I told you they were. I need some new ones.'

'Oh – all right. I'm sure we'll be able to get some when we go to town. How did you like your—'

'Can you carry them for me? I'll just have to wear bare feet. Here you are.' And he ran off, torn between caution and speed, to catch up with the other children. Stopping for a moment, Jo eased off one of her own kitten-heel

43

mules and grimaced at the blisters forming rapidly on her pedicured toes. Right! A trip to the shoe shop would have to be the top priority.

By the time Jo limped through the front door, the children were huddled round the big kitchen table. The shoes had all been left in the hallway, a prissy habit Jo normally deplored, but she gratefully slipped off hers alongside. Sophie, who was reading the game's instructions, picked up a brightly coloured piece of plastic.

'So this must be the bucket?'

'Yes,' Rory took it from her hands, 'and it fits on the rickety staircase like this.'

Sophie grinned at Jo. 'Cor, you took your time. Stop at the pub on the way? Hope you don't mind, we started without you.'

'Be my guest. Board games bore me rigid. Besides, it'll give me a chance to read the papers at last. I'll be in the sitting room.'

Imogen carefully placed a laden tray on the table. 'Wash hands, please. Then help yourselves to hot choc. There's a little bowl of marshmallows you can pop on top if you like.' The children rose as one and thundered to the downstairs loo.

'Ooh, hot choc! You do know how to live, Imo! Are grown-ups allowed?' Sophie hovered hopefully over the tray. 'Don't suppose you've got any whipped cream amongst your emergency supplies?'

'As a matter of fact, I have,' Imogen admitted with an embarrassed laugh. 'Help yourself, but I won't have any.

44

Might as well apply it directly onto my hips. Would you like some, Jo?'

Jo hesitated for a moment, split between the desire for something sweet and warm and delicious, and a knee-jerk irritation at the cosiness of this tableau. Greed won. 'Yes, actually, I'd love some.' She took the can from Sophie and squirted a generous swirl on top of the steaming mug, then couldn't resist sprinkling marshmallows over the top. She made for the door again and the blissful promise of an hour alone with yesterday's *Observer*, but was beaten back by the stream of children, their barely dry hands reaching for the tray.

Finn turned to her as she left the room, his eyes shining. 'Look, Mum, just like they have in Starbucks! I never knew you could make it at home.'

Jo laughed shortly. 'Thanks a bunch, Finn. Show me up for my domestic shortcomings, why don't you!'

'I could show you how to make it, Finn, if you like. It's easy peasy.' And Imogen turned away to empty the sandy picnic bags. Oh bollocks, thought Jo, and left the room.

An hour later and another burst of laughter from the kitchen. Jo tossed aside the papers and stretched. She'd made herself read them from cover to cover, apart from the sport and the motoring of course, and had even had a shufti at Sophie's *Mail on Sunday*. She stood up and wondered what to do next. Her nails could do with some attention, and a shower and some of that new body cream wouldn't go amiss either. But another gale of laughter, with Finn's triumphant, 'I caught your mouse! I caught it!' decided her, and she went to join the others.

The scent of onions sautéing in butter filled the room, and Imogen, in an apron, looking calm and contained, was moving efficiently round the cooker.

Sophie looked up as Jo came in. 'Great – reinforcements! Passions are running high. Things could get nasty.' She turned to Finn and Olivia, grappling over the plastic hand. 'Come on, you two. Ding! Ding! End of round one.'

Finn was tight-lipped, his face set in a familiar steely determination. 'Shove up, old mate,' Jo murmured, ruffling his hair. 'Can I join in?'

Sophie smiled up at her. 'It's much more fun than the papers, I promise. Your Finn shows a natural aptitude, too. Now we can see if it's genetic.'

'It's only because he kept cheating,' grumped Olivia. 'Cheat! Cheat!' she goaded.

Finn flushed. 'I did not, you bloody bitch!' And angry tears gushed from his eyes.

A horrified silence descended. Rory looked aghast. 'Mum, Finn said—'

Imogen swept in. 'Yes, thank you, Rory. No need to repeat it,' she said tightly. 'Now, let's sort out a few little rules, shall we?' She leant forwards gently across the table towards Finn. 'Let's all agree not to call each other names, especially not in front of the little ones, hey Finn?'

Finn was in Jo's arms now, rubbing his face furiously against her shoulder as she patted him awkwardly on the back. Jo's mind was racing. What line should she be taking here? This was uncharted territory.

'Do you mean rules, like we all make up at home?' Archie asked.

'That's it, sweetie,' continued Imogen. 'But first of all, Finn must say sorry to Olivia.'

'She started it. I'm not,' burst out a still-furious Finn.

Jo gently put her mouth to his soft ear and whispered, 'Come on, mate, I know. Olivia was being a right cow, but it's no biggie. Say you're sorry just to shut her up. Go on.'

Finn pushed out his bottom lip. 'S'ry.'

'And Olivia must say sorry to Finn,' Imogen carried on, raising her voice very slightly. The child reluctantly mumbled her apologies, but they both continued to glower at each other. 'Now, we've all agreed on the first rule? No bad language, no name-calling. That's very important, isn't it? And, Sophie,' she lowered her voice, and turned to her friend, 'could you keep an eye? Perhaps some of them *are* getting a bit approximate about moving their mice.'

The children returned to their game, and Imogen to her cooking. Jo got up as if to leave but Finn's pleading expression made her hover for a moment. Poor kid. He'd been made to look the bad guy, so slowly and deliberately she crossed her eyes and, when she uncrossed them, he was smiling again wanly.

The game continued in relative amity for a while, and Jo sat back, keeping a close eye on Olivia, whilst at the same time intrigued by the goings-on over in the kitchen area. Imogen had luscious-looking vegetables, freshly chopped, laid out on the wooden board in little piles, like a contestant on *Masterchef*. Her movements were economical to the point of being graceful, as she glided between cooker, fridge and worktop. At last she started to undo her apron.

'Right, you lot, clear away. Supper's ready.' Jo frowned and glanced at her watch. Only half past five. What was going on?

'Are we all eating?' Jo looked at the table in puzzlement.

'Don't worry, there's plenty for everyone. I've thrown together a little green salad too.' Imogen placed a large glass bowl of neatly arranged baby leaves and a separate bowl of garlicky-smelling dressing. 'That's one of the best things about the hols, don't you think, Soph? Not having to make supper for the old man. I must admit, though, I've been known to eat with the kids and then again later with Guy. Children's food is always so yummy, isn't it? I defy anyone to resist that last sausage. Er, Finn, er, everybody – let's not start until everyone's served, shall we? It's more polite.'

Finn stopped, looked up and, without taking his eyes off Imogen, neatly spat out his mouthful of risotto. Archie was quick off the mark. 'Yuk, that's disgusting. Spitting's dirty, isn't it, Mama?'

Imogen silenced him with a glare, then offered Parmesan, black pepper, salt, salad and squash to everyone in turn.

'Brilliant! Time for a drinky.' Sophie jumped up with glee. 'I reckon the sun's well and truly over the armpit, don't you, girls? Imo may have brought the entire contents of her larder, but I've emptied our drinks cabinet. Hugh will be distraught when he discovers I've cleaned him out of Sancerre.'

Appalled at the prospect of eating at this hour – God, it was practically high tea – Jo tentatively picked up her fork, then realised to her surprise she was famished. And the risotto was very good – creamy, yet with a slight bite to the rice, just like in restaurants – and with an earthy taste of … mushrooms! She glanced quickly at Finn, who had clearly reached the same conclusion and was picking through his plateful with forensic thoroughness. Imogen spotted it at once.

'Oh dear, Finn, if only I'd known.' She sounded quite put out. 'I could have done you some without. Next time, I'll be sure to remember. Can I get you anything else? Erm, let me see.'

'S'all right,' muttered Finn, embarrassed by the renewed attention. 'Can I have just some more of that bread?'

'What's the magic word?' chorused Archie and Olivia, to Finn's obvious puzzlement.

'Yes, of course, sweetie.' Sophie quickly passed the bread basket.

Finn glanced sideways at her from under his implausibly curly lashes and muttered his thanks, then applied himself studiously to the bread, pushing the risotto aside. Imogen scanned the table anxiously. 'You can't just have bread, Finn. How about some nice cheese?' She bounded out of her chair and went to rummage in the fridge.

Finn blushed. 'Thanks.'

'Oh Imogen, don't fret.' Jo suddenly felt embarrassed by the performance that had ensued. 'The risotto would have been fine – if he wasn't such a picky little git.'

An audible gasp ran through the other children, and Imogen blinked fast. 'Oh,' she exclaimed quickly and slightly too loudly. 'Oh, I … the weather. What's the time?' She whipped round and started fiddling with the radio. From the swirl of static, words began to take shape.

'Malins Hebrides …' intoned the announcer. 'Southerly five to six, veering south-westerly in west later. Rain at times. Moderate or good.'

Imogen listened attentively, bending towards the disembodied voice, frowning slightly and biting her lip. The others finished their meal in silence, with the odd snorted giggle from the girls.

After supper, Imogen left Jo and Sophie to clear up and shepherded her kids off to the bath. 'I've started to write down a roster,' she called as she left the room. 'I'll show it to you both once the kids are in bed.'

The other children evaporated, leaving Sophie and Jo in the grateful silence. 'Well, that was awkward,' Jo murmured. 'Do you think she was really offended? She looked like she'd swallowed a wasp. Great bloody start.'

Sophie took the bowl from Jo's hands and examined it. 'What? About Finn and the mushrooms? Oh I don't think *that* upset her too much. Do you reckon this can go in the dishwasher? Better not risk it.' She looked up at Jo. 'No, the thing you need to know about Imo is that she has to look after everyone properly. She's the original mother hen – always has been – and she'd be mortified to think anyone had left her table unsatisfied.' She started to rinse out the bowl in hot water. 'I remember once she had us to dinner and did this fantastic paella, but there must have been a dodgy mussel cos Hugh heaved in the flowerbed on the way out.' She lowered her voice. 'I had to say he was drunk cos she was so upset. Just go with the flow, Jo. Anyway, I'm so glad you've both met at last. I just know you're going to get on!'

Jo wished she could have had Sophie's confidence and crammed cutlery into the plastic dishwasher basket. 'Shall I put the kettle on?'

'Let's have a celebratory G and T when they're all abed, shall we? Ooh, I can't wait. I'll start rounding the girls up now, in fact.'

'So early?' Jo snorted as she quickly wiped over the plasticised table cloth, another contribution from Imogen's kitchen. 'Finn'll be up for hours yet.'

'Oh will he now?' She was almost sure she heard Sophie giggle quietly, as she slipped from the room.

Chapter 3
Tuesday

Heavy rain clouds gathering
over the South West

Damn. Imogen could hear the rain against the bedroom window even before she opened her eyes. Childhood holidays on the Welsh coast had made her an expert in assessing rain types, and by the pitter-pattering she could tell this was the sort that was set in for the day.

She swung her legs out of bed, careful not to disturb Archie curled up beside her, and pulled back the curtains. A heavy, gunmetal-grey cloud sat over them all the way to the horizon with no break; no chink of hope as far as the eye could see. She'd known it was going to happen of course. The chap had warned as much on the weather forecast yesterday evening. They would definitely have to action plan B.

Slipping a fleece over her pyjamas, Imogen crept out of the room and down the stairs. Despite the sturdy UPVC windows, the kitchen felt chilly in the early morning, and she wondered if she should turn on the heating. But somehow firing the boiler in July smacked of defeat. They'd just have to make do with extra layers.

One thing you could say for Hong Kong – it would be warmer!

Switching the kettle on for tea, she started to unload the dishwasher as quietly as she could. In the silence of the early morning, slipping knives into the cutlery tray soundlessly was almost impossible and took ages. How much easier it would have been had Jo and Sophie separated the cutlery out like she always did. But, by the time she had finished, the breakfast table looked welcoming with cereals lined up in military formation, jam, local honey (a find at the tiny post office between here and the beach) and an unfeasibly yellow pat of creamy Cornish butter. What was it with these Cornish cows?

She paused for a moment and listened. All remained quiet. Then, satisfied that everything was ready – how she'd love to have a kitchen this size – she made herself a cup of tea and curled up on the window seat. It really was a lovely view, despite being obscured by rivulets of rain trailing their way down the window. She realised now that she had played it up slightly to Guy when he'd called last night, but he'd been so uninvolved, as always, with the holiday plans that she, perhaps unconsciously, wanted to make it out to be a complete triumph.

What was it with husbands and holidays? There seemed to be an exponential link between how organised a woman was and how hopeless a man became. But in truth she wouldn't be happy with anyone else organising it. She knew her standards and expectations for a holiday were way above Guy's and so did he – he'd dined out for years on the squalor of his bachelor skiing trips – so they were both happy for Imogen to sort everything.

She wasn't quite sure this house was up to her exacting standards though. It had that inescapable seaside feel to it, but not in the nice Long Island beach house way. Screws on the outside door handles were rusting in the salty air and everything smelt, if not quite damp then definitely coastal. Draining her tea, she climbed down off the seat and put her cup in the empty dishwasher, suppressing her vague feeling that it wasn't quite the success she'd hoped. Probably just the weather. Time to grab the bathroom before the hordes woke up.

Half an hour later, the silent idyll had been shattered. Rory, who could never tolerate anyone being asleep once he was awake, had roused Finn, and in the process had disturbed the girls. The entire troupe had clattered downstairs, followed shortly afterwards by a very grumpy Archie. By the time Imogen was back, washed and dressed in jeans, socks and a loose tartan shirt of Guy's, they were all ensconced in front of the TV.

'Rors?' With a curl of her finger, Imogen summoned her son, who reluctantly followed her out of the sitting room. 'Darling, Finn seems to go to bed later than you—'

'I know, Mum. It's so unfair. I'm way older than him.' His mouth turned down in a pout that reminded Imogen of his father.

'That's as maybe, but it's not what we do. And if he's tired he won't enjoy anything. Do try not to wake him up again, Rory. He needs to sleep.'

'Humph.' Her son turned on his heel and lumbered back to join the others.

Perhaps waffles would cheer everyone up. She dug into the back of the cupboard she'd commandeered for the gadgets she'd brought from home, pulled out the trusty waffle iron then started to make up the batter. Of course if she'd had buttermilk it would be better. Would Finn like waffles? Maybe it would compensate for last night's mushroom fiasco.

There was movement upstairs. It must be Sophie, who she knew was awake as she'd heard her happily humming through the bedroom door. Sophie had always had such a sunny disposition, ever since they'd met in their first few days at boarding-school. The oldest of three, but the last to go away to school, Imogen had been desperate to be like her brothers, who'd romped through a rather Billy Bunter prep school from the tender age of seven. When she'd arrived that first day, she'd been enthralled by the bustle, the piles of trunks with names painted on them, the scramble around the noticeboard to find which dorm you'd been allocated. Her parents had been brusque and businesslike about the drop-off, with a pat on the head and a perfunctory 'You'll love it, darling', and Imogen had tried to be as brave as possible, despite her rising panic. The reality of the tail lights of their car disappearing down the school drive had brought on a wave of terror and a heaving sob painfully suppressed.

She stopped whisking for a moment. Weird. She hadn't thought about that for years. Perhaps the communal atmosphere had brought it on. For so long she and Sophie had reminisced about 'the good times' – school plays, first fags, sunbathing topless on the roof outside the dorm when they were fifteen – and she'd somehow buried the memory of those desperate, blindingly lonely first days.

She started to whisk briskly again. It would have been better, of course, if she'd been the sort of child who cried uncontrollably with homesickness. Those girls were nurtured and held against Matron's ample bosom, until her starched apron was damp from their tears. But Imogen had felt that wasn't the right way to handle things at all. She'd become all businesslike, setting up her teddy and the pictures of her pony in the photocube on her bedside table. She'd got *involved* in things, made herself so busy she wouldn't have to think. Being one of the bigger girls – well, plump frankly – everyone had assumed she had broad shoulders too. It was rather a surprise, then, when Sophie, with her blond curls and pixie little face, had sidled up to her in the lunch queue and introduced herself.

'Bloody hell. You're at it again. What masterpiece are you whipping up now, Nigella?' Imogen started at Sophie's arrival through the kitchen door.

'Oh just waffles. I was thinking about those ghastly breakfasts at school. Do you remember the toast?'

Sophie held up a spoon and the pack of coffee – 'Shall I?' – then started to fill the machine with Colombian medium roast. 'Unforgettable. It was soggy as hell, but they had to toast two-hundred-and-fifty-odd slices. They probably started making it at four a.m. And I entirely blame my inability to shift my spare tyre on school fried eggs. Cooked in so much oil they practically wore arm bands.'

Imogen snorted. 'You might have had the odd bicycle inner tube, but spare tyre? Never. My downfall was treacle sponge. Nectar. I used to persuade that miserable Susan Davies to let me have her second helping.'

'How the hell does this buggery thing work?' grumbled Sophie, grappling to find the flap in the machine for the coffee. 'You have to be a genius to understand these things. Hugh always does ours. He makes a great barista!'

'But I thought he was an architect! Leave it to me, you amateur,' laughed Imogen and taking the bag from Sophie, expertly lifted the flap to pour it in.

'It's no good,' shrieked Sophie, dipping down to get mugs out of the cupboard, 'I'm just a has-bean.' They both snorted with laughter and were still guffawing when Jo appeared around the door.

'Jo!' Sophie wiped tears from her eyes. 'I think Imo has this plan to fatten us all up. She's whipping up waffles.'

Jo, looking gorgeous in white T-shirt and combat trousers, her face glowing from yesterday's sun, winced. 'It's a conspiracy! I shall have to go back to that bloody gym again.'

Imogen turned away, fussing unnecessarily over plates for the waffles. All at once she felt hefty and obvious; embarrassed by the trouble she'd gone to over breakfast. Would Jo think it silly? Imogen had visions of her at home, with her curly hair caught up loosely on top of her head, her low-slung trousers, and her flat, brown stomach, eating Special K with skimmed milk whilst leaning against the units like they do in adverts.

'But what the hell?' Jo continued, dropping into a chair at the table. 'Bring them on! It's years since I had waffles, and I bet you make brilliant ones.' Finn and Rory came into the room. 'Finn my man – come sit by me. Do you remember that brunch we had in Manhattan last year? You are about to see it surpassed. Don't suppose there's any bacon too?'

Twenty minutes later there wasn't a waffle left, and the kitchen smelt strongly of fried maple-cure streaky. Imogen knew she shouldn't have succumbed to two rashers, but it was so delicious with the sweetness of the maple syrup. Well, they were by the sea and that always gave you an appetite.

'I think we need a list,' she said to no one in particular as everyone wiped up the last vestiges of crispy rind and waffles from their plates. Between them all they had demolished the two packets Imogen had brought with her, and they'd have to be replaced.

'Scribble down what we need,' said Jo, leaning back in her chair with her coffee mug cupped in her hands. 'I'll do supper tonight, shall I? Finn, Rory, you can come with me and help me choose. Anything anyone can't eat?'

'Mushrooms,' said Finn, and looked sheepishly at Imogen. She smiled and mouthed 'sorry' back to him.

'Cooked tomatoes, yuk yuk,' said Amelia and all the girls pretended to gag in mutual disgust.

'My lot are pretty easy.' Imogen wasn't sure how to couch this, but felt she needed to get things in the open straightaway. 'Rory claims he can't abide chicken but honestly …' She rolled her eyes in despair at the woes of parenting, hoping it would discourage Jo from choosing some intensively reared bird off the supermarket shelf. 'Archie's skin does flare up a bit with cheese, to be honest, and Ollie, you're not to mad about leaf vegetables, are you?' She noticed Jo briefly raise her eyebrows, then she pushed back her chair.

'Righto – that should make it a challenge. Well, I'll go and clean my teeth, then I'll go with the boys and find a supermarket. There can't be one too far away.'

Suddenly, Imogen could feel her plans for the day falling to pieces. 'Er, there's one in Wadebridge,' she said, standing up herself and pushing back her chair, 'but I was thinking … I picked up a few leaflets of things to do locally.' She paused to drop cutlery into the dishwasher, ostentatiously categorising it as she did so. Then, picking up a folder she'd put together, she came back to the table. Jo was suspended between table and door. 'There's a few ideas here I thought might be good for a rainy day and I think we're in for a bad one today.'

An hour and a half later, Imogen was peering through the windscreen at the unfamiliar road ahead. The wipers were batting to and fro as hard as they could, though lorries coming the other way were defiantly throwing great sheets of water up at them as soon as the screen was clear. The farm park was further than she had thought.

'It's not far now,' she muttered to the girls in the back, before they could ask her again.

'I think it's the next turning.' Sophie, map spread out

on her knee, was peering myopically at the signs through her side window. 'You'd have to be Ranulph Fiennes to understand the map on this ruddy leaflet, but I think I saw one of those brown tourist signs just back there … Yup, it's this one.' Imogen slammed on the brakes and steered hard left, the van behind sounding its horn angrily. Sophie looked sheepish.

'Sorry, Imo. That came up a bit quicker than I thought. Perhaps I should have done the driving and you could have done the map bit. You know I'm crap at it.'

But not quite as crap as you are at driving, thought Imogen crossly, but smiled. 'Don't worry. You weren't to know. I hope Jo spots it. Is she any good at following instructions?'

Sophie snorted. 'Well, she is a doctor, Imo, so she can't be that stupid, and Rory and Finn can help find it, can't they?'

'Find it! Rory can't locate his school shoes when they are close enough to bite his bum.'

The uneven surface of the car park was a mass of muddy puddles and, as she'd feared, was full up already. They eventually squeezed in between an old Renault – back seat covered with wetsuits, buckets and spades – and a substantial and brand-new four by four. The sticker announced it came from a garage in Chiswick and Imogen felt vaguely reassured.

The children were damp and cold from standing waiting, and Archie and Grace were beginning to whine by the time Jo's car turned into the car park. 'Thank God,' Imogen muttered under her breath. 'Wait here, you lot. I'll go and get them.' Pulling up the hood of her cagoule, she ran head down towards Jo's car, pointing frantically at an empty space she'd spotted. She ripped open the back door. Heads bent together, Rory and Finn were ensconced in their Gameboys once again.

'Come on, Rors, enough of that. You've been on it for hours.' She thrust out a dripping arm to take the machine. 'You lot *have* been a long time. Did you get held up?'

'Well, a bit,' said Rory, leg up on the seat to tie the laces on his trainers. 'But Jo stopped at a newsagent to get the paper and got us some sweets.' He held up the wrapper of a cola chewy bar.

The farm park bore no relation whatsoever to the images on the leaflet. The demeanour of the cashier, seated in a garden shed that served as a ticket office, set the tone for the 'rural experience' they were about to become a part of. Dressed in a green sweatshirt bearing the 'leisure farm' logo, and popping her gum, she was barely able to contain her *ennui*. After relieving them of £25 – a complicated calculation that involved half of them being a Family Group and a forage in purses to find cash to pay separately for the rest of them – she mumbled something about 'Pat a Pet being available in the lambing barn at two' and 'Milking outside at four, weather permitting'.

'Christ, she must have skipped Charisma Class at finishing school,' muttered Sophie into Imogen's ear.

'Mum, everything stinks.' Olivia curled up her nose with disgust. Indeed there was an overwhelming fragrance of urine, and Imogen wasn't convinced it was all of animal derivation.

'Can we do the gift shop now?' Archie pulled at her wet sleeve. 'I want sweets like what Rory got.'

'Like Rory *had*, and no you can't.'

By the time they were seated around a sticky table an hour later, Imogen had to admit the whole thing was an unmitigated disaster. It had taken threats with menaces to get the children away from the personalised pencils, wildflower book marks and rubber dinosaurs in the gift shop – though perhaps the word 'gift' was giving the array of tat too delicate a description – and to move them on into the park area. They'd agreed to separate into groups with the suggestion they meet for lunch in the Krazee Play Barn an hour later.

Imogen had managed to stick it out for just twenty-five minutes, with rain dripping off the end of her nose, watching Archie pedal round and round a small tarmac track on a broken plastic dumper truck. She'd even peered into a pig sty (anyone who said pigs were clean was clearly deluded), and ooohed and aaahed over hens with feathery legs and a goat called Obediah, but by twelve thirty her tolerance had evaporated, and she lured Archie into the play barn with promises of hot chocolate, only to find Jo and Sophie there already, coats on the backs of their chairs gently steaming, and the other children lost somewhere in the mêlée of plastic balls and yellow plastic tunnels that was the Krazee Barn. The smell of stale chip fat pervaded the whole room and the noise of shrieking children was deafening.

Sophie pulled a chair out for her. 'You are tougher than us, Lord Nelson,' she said with a smile. 'We took one peek at the shire horse – who looked about a hundred and fifty and ready for the knackers – and bolted for dry land. Gracie wanted to find the hamsters but I told her they were hibernating.' She looked bewildered at Jo. 'Do hamsters hibernate?'

Jo's face broke into a broad grin. 'I'm not sure. I don't have many of them as patients, but I don't think they would in July.'

Sophie picked up her purse and stood up. 'Let me get you a cup of something that is the colour of coffee, but bears no resemblance to it taste-wise. Or perhaps you'd rather have a bottle of cream soda. Jo and I were just saying we haven't seen that on sale since nineteen seventy.'

'I'll take the coffee option thanks.' Imogen pulled off Archie's shoes – 'No, darling, socks stay firmly on if you're going in there. Think verrucas' – and shook off her own wet coat. Sophie bustled off to the counter and Imogen ran her fingers through her damp hair, not quite sure what to say.

'I'm so sorry. The leaflet sounded OK and with the rain and everything—'

'Imogen,' Jo put a hand on her arm, 'it's not your fault. It's *fine* – this is a whole new experience for me. Look, the kids are having a great time in there, and no one ever died from drinking weak coffee.'

Sophie put down a plastic beaker in front of Imogen. 'Now here's the menu. It looks like the only thing that comes without chips is the soup, but you can always have them as a side order!'

Imogen cringed and ran her eyes down the seductive

63

list of scampi, sticky chicken wings and cheeseburgers. She could have murdered a plate of fat chips, slathered in salt and vinegar. She remembered the waffles. 'I'll just have soup and a roll,' she sighed. 'And Archie can have the jacket potato and cheese.' She closed the menu and placed it back on the table. The message beeper sounded on her mobile phone. It was Guy: 'Damn 4got it was Tuesday. Left no money 4 cleaner. Srry.'

Heads down and shoulders hunched against the rain, they made a break for the cars. The car park was now heaving, with new punters arriving by the minute, splashing in through flooded potholes and squinting through steamed-up windows, on the look-out for parking spaces as close to the entrance as possible.

Imogen lifted the rear door of her Volvo to provide some shelter. 'Right.' She peeled off waterproofs and shook them briskly away from the children, then sat each of the girls in the boot and pulled off their wellies, securing each pair with a peg she fished from a pocket. She glanced up at Jo. 'Are you sure you're OK about getting to the supermarket? It's the second exit off the roundabout. You could probably get everything in Padstow, if you prefer, when you get Finn's sandals. There's a supermarket there too.' She glanced down at the boy's sopping baseball boots and shook her head. 'Honestly, you'd think at this time of year you could rely on dry weather! I must listen to the long-range forecast when we get back.'

Jo bundled the boys into the car, waved a casual goodbye and left the others to carry on cataloguing waterproofs. 'Now let's see, it was left here, wasn't it?' She peered through the streaming windscreen. 'Finn, take a look at the map, will you? Here you are.'

Finn caught the bedraggled map and smoothed the pages while Rory looked on in admiration. 'Where are we heading?' he asked.

'What did your mum say again? It's off a roundabout. Find a roundabout and we'll head for that.'

They bumbled on for some time, laughing, stopping, reversing. Jo was all for asking for directions, but Finn was confident they could manage. 'God, Finn!' Jo snorted. 'You're such a bloke. What is it with men? What do you do when you're lost, Rory?'

Rory hesitated, glancing at Finn before he replied. 'Weeell, my mum never, ever gets lost because she spends ages memorising the maps and instructions. My dad gets lost because he never reads the maps but he never admits it. He just pretends the way he's going is right.'

'Well, I never read the maps, but I never pretend either. We are hopelessly lost, aren't we?' When they finally arrived at the superstore, Jo sent Finn and Rory out to locate a trolley with four functioning wheels, while she went to the loo. 'Meet you by the melons, OK?'

Rory looked momentarily alarmed at being turned loose this way, but swiftly recovered. 'Er, cool, yeah. See you in a minute then.'

Finn ambled off, pushing the trolley, letting go of it and catching it up, Rory close by his side. Jo smiled to herself as she turned away. Nice kid. He just needed a bit more space to do his thing.

'Gotcha,' Jo whispered, sneaking up behind them a few minutes later. Finn tutted long-sufferingly, but Rory jumped. 'So, you started without me, eh?'

Rory began to apologise. 'Go on, I'm teasing you.' She nudged him conspiratorially. 'Pringles are my fave too. Get another pack, will you?' Now where did I put your mum's list?' She felt in her pockets ineffectually. Damn, she must have left it on the kitchen table. 'Never mind. We'll have to improvise. What do you fancy?'

Gradually the pile grew – sticky ribs, chips, frozen sweetcorn, lime jelly marmalade, prawn crackers, smoked mackerel, Toblerone, crumpets, pumpernickel, and, of course, custard tarts – a special request from Sophie.

They were just about to brave the check-out when Jo slapped her forehead. 'Sandals! Finn, we nearly forgot.'

Rory was astounded. 'You can buy shoes in the supermarket? Do they measure you?'

'Naaah. He's a size, erm, three, aren't you, Finn?'

Jo handed him a couple of pairs to try on, then drifted over to the women's section and started flicking through the racks of underwear with practised ease. Finn slung his chosen sandals into the trolley. 'Oh, Jo, not more knickers!' he groaned. 'You're always buying knickers.' Rory gaped and backed away a couple of steps.

'Yes, but look,' she retorted, brandishing a pack. 'Low-rise thongs. You don't get those just anywhere. And I do hate it when it shows above your trousers – so … tarty, isn't it? Only six quid for four. And in white or black. I'll take a pack of each.'

Rory was scarlet and glancing around anxiously, but

Finn's bored expression seemed to reassure him. 'Just humour her,' he whispered. 'She's got this thing about underwear. Mine too. She throws it all out and buys new practically every two weeks.'

'Oh, Finn, that's just not true.' Jo swept off majestically towards the check-out. 'But I can't stand dingy knicks, and once you've washed them a few times, they're never quite as nice. Come on, boys.'

Back in the car, Jo turned and grinned. 'Gimme the map. I'll do it like Imogen this time, and work out where I'm going *before* I start.'

'Hoo-bloody-ray,' Finn retorted with heavy sarcasm as he passed the map forward.

But Rory protested quietly. 'I think it's more fun your way, Jo.'

The journey back went much more smoothly. Jo slipped one of Finn's CDs into the player and the boys sang along all the way, giving her some welcome head space. The morning had been quite a revelation for her. That barn place had been extraordinary – a bit crowded, a bit smelly but sooo easy. You could just let the kids off the leash and kick back. If the coffee had been even halfway decent, it would have been just about ideal, sitting round the table, chatting about – well, nothing really. Presumably that was what women did when they took their kids out to these places, just relaxed and talked about anything that came up – Pilates, pelvic floors, property prices. It was all very cosy and, well, nice.

Working all bloody day, it was something she'd missed out on completely and, on the rare occasions she made it to the school gate, had felt uncomfortable with the other mothers' effortless ease as they swapped children, news and biscuits. She was aware that some of them treated her differently once they realised she was a doctor – as though she was some superior being they had to impress if possible, or avoid if not. And then there was the single thing. Excruciating dinner parties when you were sat next to some angry divorcee who got steadily more pissed as he slagged off his ex-wife for having taken him 'to the cleaners' in the settlement.

But it hadn't really been like that with Imogen and Sophie. For once, it was three women away from all talk of men, with no supper to plan or shirts to iron. In fact, as they talked, Imogen had revealed a quick wit and Jo was at a loss to understand why she so seldom seemed to let it show. Perhaps she'd chill out and let that military precision drop as the holiday progressed.

Back at the house, there was Drying with a capital D going down. All the chairs in the kitchen were festooned with jackets, Sophie was directing the jet from an electric fan heater at them, while Imogen pored over a printed leaflet, squinting periodically at the controls of what looked like the boiler. The girls, changed into dry leggings and T-shirts, were improvising a frenetic ballet in the sitting room.

'Hellooo,' called Jo. 'The wanderers return! We have food, drink, sandals, Pringles, custard tarts – for my lady's pleasure.'

'And lots of new knickers,' chipped in Finn, and he and Rory dissolved into snorts.

Sophie grinned up from her steamy task. 'Then you deserve a cup of tea, brave pioneer. Welcome to the house of drip. Stick your jumpers and trousers in the dryer, chuck your jackets in this pile of soaking garments, and take the weight off your sling-backs.'

Imogen emerged, having crawled out backwards from the boiler controls, red and a bit sweaty, then smiled broadly at Rory. 'Hello, old boy.' Her tone was warm and welcoming. 'You're back earlier than I expected. Did you get everything? Only I found the list on the table.'

Rory looked down. 'Mum, there's dust in your hair,' he hissed. 'We've been to the supermarket. Got everything there.' He turned away and slouched from the room. Imogen shrugged and gave a tight little smile. 'Charming! Case of the Kevins, I fear. He probably just needs something to eat. Need a hand in with the shopping?'

Jo rootled through the bags where they sagged on the floor and extracted a packet of biscuits, scattering shopping as she did so. 'Here we are. Come on, Imogen. I reckon you deserve a reward for services to central heating.'

Almost imperceptibly, Imogen whisked away the frozen food then hesitated by the bags, which were now disgorging their contents over the floor. Only when Sophie waved her cup of tea temptingly to and fro did she join the others.

'Well, I listened to the weather forecast and, although it doesn't seem likely to improve today, they're promising clear skies tomorrow.' Imogen sighed deeply, a worried frown puckering her brow. 'I do hope they're right.

Anyway, I packed some DVDs just in case of emergencies. If they go stir crazy, I'll unleash *The Lion King*.'

'Ooh goody,' Sophie purred, reaching for another custard tart. 'I love that song, you know the Elton John one. Hugh loves it too …' After a few warbling notes, she trailed off, a misty look in her eyes. 'I miss having him around. Do you know it's the first time we've ever holidayed apart?'

'What?' Jo was astounded.

Sophie shrugged. 'Oh it's OK. We've got the girls billeted with his mum and dad while we go away for a weekend in September … then of course there's skiing in March.'

'Crikey.' Jo noticed that Imogen's face was as incredulous, but was pretty certain it wasn't for the same reasons. 'I hate it when Guy's away – which seems to be more and more often at the moment. But I have to say, we never holiday without the kids. What would be the point?'

Sophie sighed dramatically. 'Cor, I'm glad to get away from the little blighters sometimes.' This was territory Jo didn't understand. 'I hope he's eating properly.'

Jo suppressed a smile and glanced at Imogen to gauge her reaction. With a start, she met Imogen's look and for a moment was nonplussed. Imogen was doing the very same to her. Jo attempted a little conspiratorial grin and, after a moment, Imogen returned it, then glanced away, looking almost shamefaced. A mere nine out of ten for loyalty, Imogen, thought Jo. But you look a lot better when your halo slips a bit.

When the skirmishes and dog fights between the kids

gradually escalated to the point of pitched battle, Imogen rose from her seat, with a steely glint in her eye. 'Right, time for a televisual diversion,' and she left the room, armed with a DVD.

Sophie smiled. 'Oops, this will be interesting. Hope Finn doesn't do his usual *Guardian* film critic act. Bit sophisticated when it comes to cinema as I recall. When he showed the girls *Jurassic Park* that day at your house, I couldn't get them to bed on time for weeks. Didn't it give him nightmares?'

'Nah – he sleeps like a log. He's like me, he'd sleep anywhere.'

Sophie glanced sideways at Jo as they started to unpack the bags. 'Kids do need loads of sleep, don't they? More than you'd imagine. Even if they don't realise it themselves.'

'Mmm, maybe.'

Sophie persisted. 'I mean, does he go to bed earlier on school nights?'

But Jo was too busy staring hard at the collection of purchases she had laid out on the work surface. 'Have I left a bag in the car? This made much more sense in the supermarket. What on earth am I going to make for supper?'

Sophie peeped over her shoulder. 'Beats me. Hate to break it to you, but my girls don't eat barbecue ribs. Deep-fried Toblerone perhaps?'

'Well, chips then. Everyone likes chips, don't they?' Jo started slowly picking up packets and rearranging them on the counter.

Sophie hesitated and surveyed the odd assortment of food. 'Want any help getting it ready?'

Jo smiled ruefully. 'Frankly, yes. But it's my turn, so I'll muddle through. Couldn't bear the indignity of not being able to do it on my own.'

'I'll leave you to it. Tell you what, I'll pour us all a glass of wine. Good luck! *Hakuna matata!*' And Sophie, leaving some for Jo, slipped out of the kitchen to join the others, two glasses of Chablis in hand.

Forty minutes later, things were not looking good. The chips weren't the oven kind after all, and had stuck together in clumps on the baking tray, burnt on the outside and atrophied beyond recognition. The ribs were fine but, sticking her finger in the sauce, Jo realised they were really quite spicy. For lack of any other options, she had made corn fritters, lots and lots, from a recipe she'd found in the book that came with the cooker. She would hold the fried eggs until the last minute and take orders, but she had laid the table, setting out bowls of Pringles and grapes and bottles of Coke and Sprite. It looked rather fetching. She opened the door and called everyone through.

'Cor, can I have Coke?' Archie was the first, followed by the others, all excitedly laying claim to the fizzy drink of their choice.

Jo laughed. This was easy. 'Course you can, guys. Help yourselves. And pass round the grapes, would you? Plenty for everyone.'

The first spill happened as Olivia reached across Amelia to get the grapes. The second was into Finn's lap. The third seeped into the bowl of Pringles. After that, Jo lost track. The remaining crisp Pringles were gone in seconds. Only Finn liked the ribs, although Rory forced one down. 'Better get used to them,' Jo said tightly. 'That's what you'll get in Hong Kong.' The chips were universally scorned.

'Jo-o,' Finn hissed. 'They're crap. They look like dried-up twigs.'

The children burst into gales of hyped-up laughter. 'They look like a bird's nest all smashed up,' added Amelia.

'They smell like hedgehog poo,' chimed in Archie, not to be outdone, despite Imogen's glare.

Jo wasn't quite ready to admit defeat. She gritted her teeth. 'Well, hedgehog poo is full of vitamins, Archie. Everyone knows that. Who'd like a fried egg? No one? Really? Well, me and your mummies will just have to eat that ice cream by ourselves then.'

Imogen had been busy mopping up the spills, but now sidled up to Jo. 'Erm, I've got some tagliatelle, perhaps I could whip up a little carbonara. Did you get some bacon? Well, not to worry. I think there's some ham left over in the fridge. If you don't mind, that is …'

Imogen looked so hesitant, so solicitous, Jo couldn't bear it. It would have been much easier if she had called her a dopey cow – undoubtedly what she was thinking. Jo took a deep breath and surrendered. 'Yes, yes please, Imogen. Whatever you think. Just … just make all this go away. Beam me up, Scottie.'

Chapter 4
Wednesday

Cloudy start but rain holding off.
Brighter later

'Can we go to the beach today?'

Archie curled into Imogen's body, and touched her lips with his fingers, defying her to stay sleeping. Without opening her eyes, she pushed her face towards his and rubbed his skin with the end of her nose.

'You tell me,' she mumbled. 'Go and give me a weather report.' He tumbled out of bed and padded over to the window, pulling back the curtain and letting the early-morning light flood in.

'It's quite bright. Some sun but fluffy white clouds, and Rory has left his skateboard outside.' Tutting, Imogen heaved herself upright and, sitting on the side of the bed, stretched her arms above her head. 'Yesterday's rain won't have done it any good. Right, Archie, my lovely, let's get going on the day. Things to do. Empires to build,' adding under her breath as she pulled off her pyjamas, 'and food to buy so we don't have a repeat of last night.'

Jo's culinary cock-up had annoyed her intensely, and

after she'd gone to the trouble of making a list too. How on earth could a mother, and a doctor to boot, be so stupid as to imagine children would eat that kind of stuff? Didn't she read the papers, and go to other people's houses or did she exercise motherhood from inside some kind of vacuum? As she slipped on her knickers and shook the creases out of yesterday's jeans, Imogen quickly suppressed the feeling of superiority she had from the certain knowledge that her kids ate twenty times better than Finn obviously did, and began to think through her plan.

'Right, everyone,' she addressed the table as the children munched through cereal twenty minutes later. Still no sign of Jo, though Sophie had emerged briefly and had returned to bed with a cup of tea. 'Let's make things easier for everyone. Each of you say what your favourite meals are, then we can plan menus for the holiday, and everyone will get their favourite. Youngest first. Gracie?'

Gracie, her blonde curls and pixyish face so like her mother's, had a mouthful of cereal, but put her head to one side in contemplation until she finished it.

'Sausages!' Archie butted in.

'Wait your turn, Arch,' Imogen admonished. 'What do you think, Gracie?'

'Spaghetti. I like spaghetti,' Gracie whispered, and looked nervously around the table as though expecting derision from the older boys.

'Lovely idea, sweetheart. I'll put that as one. What next?'

Ten agonisingly slow minutes of indecision later, Imogen had finally gleaned a list of options. Rory hadn't helped with useful suggestions like steak and lobster thermidor, there was a definite propensity for chips, and she wasn't sure how the rest of them would cope with Finn's request for bhajis, doner kebab and deep-fried seaweed, thankfully not all at the same time. His suggestions, however, gave her a pretty shrewd idea of where his food came from.

'OK, I shall draw up a menu plan, then everyone will know what's coming and there'll be no *complaints*, Olivia my love,' she said pointedly but teasingly to her daughter. There didn't seem to be a meal invented that Olivia couldn't find something to complain about, but she only pursued her about it gently. Her tastes were pretty catholic after all. How many other children did she know who could cope with tapenade?

As they ploughed their way through warm, fresh bread, Imogen rummaged in her holiday events file, chucking out the leaflet about the farm park with disgust. How could she have been taken in by the flashy sales pitch? The whole place had been nothing short of disgusting, but rather than risk another of Sophie's teasing 'Oh button it, Imo, it was bearable and the chips were good', she'd had to rant on about it to Guy when he called last night. He hadn't been that interested to be honest, but then who could blame him? He was practically allergic to those sorts of 'family leisure' places, referring to them as the 'bubonic plague of the modern world', and she'd always tried to protect him from the horror. Anyway he'd been far too engrossed in telling her that things were 'hotting up at work vis à vis Hong Kong'.

It had been weeks since that Sunday lunch with friends when Guy had idly floated the possibility that he might be posted to the Hong Kong office. Since he was an expert in those markets he'd been back and forth for years, and it was only a matter of time before they sent him there to do a stretch. She'd mentioned it in bed that night, but he'd sounded vague. Things had then gone quiet for a while until – great timing – the end of last week when confirmation had come through. What with the holiday, she'd had no time to plan anything: schools, places to live, the house in Barnes. It was exciting, but there was so much to do and she felt uncomfortable with the uncertainty until she knew more details. She made a mental note to work harder on extracting information out of Guy. But there was no time for that now.

She extracted the brochure she was looking for in her file. 'Right,' she beamed, addressing the table of children and playing her ace. 'Who'd like to learn to *surf*?'

Rory's whoop of glee would be enough to wake even Jo. Finn followed suit, though Imogen suspected that was so as not to be thought uncool, but by the time Rory had explained what surfing involved and had bandied about some 'seriously cool' surf-wear brand names, Finn too was bouncing up and down in his seat with anticipation.

'Can't a woman lie in bed and do nothing in peace?' Sophie appeared at the door in her dressing gown, smiling at the buzz of excitement. Once Olivia and

Amelia had filled her in on the details of the stunning new skill they were about to learn, she was as enthusiastic as they were, but that didn't surprise Imogen one bit. If she'd suggested they should learn crown green bowls or Jacobean embroidery, Sophie would have been up for it. 'That'll be something to add to the old CV!' Of Jo's reaction, Imogen wasn't quite so confident. But if she didn't want Finn to do it, Imogen would simply have to foot the cancellation fee.

'Now, everyone, before we so much as put on swimming trunks, we've got to get this place shipshape. Jobs for everyone.' Imogen raised her voice over the groans. 'Take your own plate and glass over to the dishwasher and everyone must at least make an attempt to make their beds and put jimjams under pillows. This is my holiday too, you know. Now scoot!'

As they ran out of the door to go upstairs, they almost collided with Jo. Her hair was wet from the shower and she looked fresh and pretty. Imogen took in her hooded jogging top, strappy vest and baggy parachute-silk trousers, and felt a large stab of envy.

'Hell, you are impressive!' Sophie was switching on the coffee machine again. Imogen wasn't sure who she was talking to for a moment, but realised Sophie hadn't yet seen Jo at the door. 'Dangling the carrot of surfing in front of them was a stroke of genius. You'll have them hoovering next!'

'Surfing?' Jo sat down at the table. 'That sounds ambitious.'

Imogen looked under her eyelashes to gauge Jo's

reaction, but she was idly chewing on a fresh crust left on the breadboard.

'I booked it ages ago, when our um ... other friend was coming to the house with us. It's for classes next week, but I've got to confirm the numbers with the surf school this morning because it's their "taster session" this afternoon.' Feeling a pang of guilt, she mentally crossed her fingers. 'It's not expensive.' She mentioned the price. 'Quite good value really when you think about it. Er ... do you suppose Finn would like to give it a whirl?'

Sophie put a steaming cup of coffee in front of Jo, who looked down into it in silence for a moment. 'Well, he's pretty uncoordinated, but I spend a fortune on swimming lessons for him. Won't hurt, I suppose.'

'Great!' bubbled Imogen but, as she took her coffee outside, muttered, 'Don't fall over yourself with enthusiasm, will you?' She looked at her watch. After yesterday's debacle at the barn, she couldn't help thinking that the children could do with something a little more highbrow this morning. Something National Trustish that would involve both fresh air and culture.

'Soph,' she called, 'could you bring out that folder?' Sophie emerged from the kitchen where she'd been chatting with Jo and handed Imogen the file. 'What's that ruin place up the coast? That might be fun for the kids to run off a bit of energy this morning.' Jo followed Sophie out, and sat down on one of the other plastic chairs.

'Tintagel,' Jo said, hugging her coffee in the early-morning coolness. 'Believed to be King Arthur's castle but no one knows for sure.' Finding the right leaflet and encouraged by Jo's interest, Imogen outlined her plan.

'Thought we could have a peek at it, then be back in time for lunch. We have to be at Tregant Bay for the surfing by two, but there's plenty of time if we get going.' Hunched over, Jo pulled her sweat top round her, hugging her arms, and looked over at the boys playing up on the lawn.

'Nah,' she said, taking a slug of coffee. 'Sounds a bit too cultured for me. Finn and I will knock about somewhere and meet you back here before the surfing.'

'Meet you back here, indeed,' seethed Imogen to herself four hours later, as she crammed children, wetsuits, beach shoes, towels and a bag of drinks and biscuits into the back of her car. Where the bloody hell was the wretched woman? She knew for a fact that she hadn't told Jo where the surfing was. Split between a wicked desire to just depart and the fact that she'd have to pay for Finn if he didn't turn up, she looked again at her watch. Fifteen minutes to go. Bugger.

But then the whole morning had been a bugger. The Tintagel thing had been impressive certainly, though she'd expected a bit more in the way of a castle, and it had been such a fight getting around the other tourists on the way down that path to the entrance, and a sheer nightmare to drag the children, whining, back up to the car park. Rory had been in a grump because Finn wasn't with them, and Archie had kept stopping dead in his tracks and refusing to carry on at all, until Imogen had been obliged to carry him on her back. By the time she'd got to the top, her face was red and she could feel sweat running down her back. She should have worn shorts of course, but when she'd tried them before they'd left they'd felt even tighter around her thighs than last year and, thinking of Jo and her neat little waist, she'd plumped for her faithful pedal pushers instead. Now she felt lumbering and uncomfortable.

There was no let-up from the children once they'd got back up to the car park either. They had all nagged for an ice cream at Granny Applecheek's Olde Fudge Emporium (or some such nonsense), and she'd said no, with the excuse that lunch wasn't far away. Instead she'd placated them with the agreement that they could have a quick shufti around the shops with Sophie as escort, and she would wait outside. As she'd sat up on the wall watching people walking by, she couldn't help thinking this was England at its worst. An ancient monument belittled by gift shops packed full of tat and, hanging outside each one, body boards and flip-flops flapping in the light breeze. Archie had come rushing out wanting to spend fifteen pounds on a varnished shell that had certainly been imported from the Caribbean, and she'd bundled them into the car, though not before Gracie had pointed out a loving message on the car park wall declaring 'Wayne shagged Sharon'.

Now, back at the house, she slammed the car boot shut and went back up to the front door to grab her purse and keys. Damn the woman. She could find her own way. As she tugged the front door shut she heard Jo's car pull into the drive.

'Hi,' Imogen called, smiling tightly and raising her hand in greeting. 'You're just in time.'

'No peace for the wicked. And there was me hoping for a pee and a cup of coffee before we set off again.' Jo sighed and swung the car out of the drive after Imogen who clearly had a bug up her arse for some reason. 'You did pack your swimming gear, didn't you?'

Finn nodded calmly. 'Yeah, it's all in there. You're sure I can borrow a wetsuit, aren't you, Mum? It looks bloody freezing in that water. I'm not going in otherwise. Wonder if they've got cool ones.'

'I thought all wetsuits were cool by definition,' said Jo, keeping her eyes on Imogen's tail gate. 'They look sexy as hell on – provided you're the right shape, of course. Hope they've got one small enough for you, though, you scrawny rat.'

Finn giggled and squirmed as she stretched across to tickle his ribs. 'Gerroff. Whatever you say back to me, you're a hairy chimpanzee. Anyway, Imogen thinks you're scrawny too. I heard her saying so to Sophie.'

Jo raised an eyebrow, her interest piqued. 'Oh, did she now? What else did you hear her say? Go on. Spill the beans.'

Finn frowned. 'It was this morning, before you got up. She got us all to say what we wanted to eat, and she made a list so we'll all take it in turns to have our favourite. Sophie said she didn't need to go to all the bother, cos it should be a holiday for her too. And Imogen said to Sophie that she had to do it, because if she didn't sort it out we'd all starve, and she said now she understood why you were so skinny.'

Jo could feel her face prickling. For God's sake. Last night hadn't been that bad. Clearly Imogen had been expecting textbook Delia, she was obviously *Good Housekeeping* personified. Jo couldn't believe it when she'd looked out of the kitchen window this morning and seen her scrubbing out the Wendy house. She'd be polishing the grass next.

Jo sighed, her hands relaxing on the wheel. Imogen was one uptight woman, even her driving was prissy, with neat indications and plenty of mirror. Thank God for Sophie – tolerant to the point of inertia. For the first time, she wondered about Mr Imogen. Perhaps he was the weedy type, the type who liked being pussy-whipped. Imogen probably made lists for him too – Jo smiled wickedly at the thought – all the suitable erogenous zones to be stimulated in order, and woe betide him if he did anything wrong.

Jo knew she probably ought to feel miffed about the food thing, but frankly she couldn't be arsed. It wasn't as if it mattered to her. God, no! It wasn't a competition or anything. At least Imogen's lists meant that every day's shopping was now a no-brainer. Finn was humming quietly to himself, feet up on the dashboard, tapping his hands on his thighs in accompaniment to the soundtrack in his head. It wasn't really fair to quiz him again, but it was too good an opportunity to pass up. 'So what did Sophie say back?'

'Mmm?' Finn was miles away.

'When Imogen said that thing about me being skinny? What did Sophie say?'

'Um, she said Imogen should lighten up. She was laughing though, and she told Imogen to be careful.'

'Careful? What about?'

'Oh I dunno.' Finn exclaimed in exasperation. 'I wasn't listening properly, it was just boring stuff. I only went in to get some more of that bread. They didn't even see me. It's really yummy – can we get one of those machines? We could have bread like that every day then. Are we nearly there? Is it going to be cold? I hope I don't fall in. Is it all right to wear goggles?'

Shaking her head slightly in her effort to keep up with Finn's stream of consciousness, she frowned a little as she caught on to the slight anxiety in his voice. She glanced at her son. 'You know, you don't have to do it if you don't want to. I mean, don't feel you have to, just because Imogen arranged it.'

She could almost feel his resolution stiffening as she offered him a way out. 'No, I … I do want to. I wasn't sure at first when Imogen suggested it, but Rory's never done it either and neither have the others. I might be good at it. I might be the best. I might, Mum. That'd be way cool.' He turned round and smiled gappily at her. 'And no one else at school has even tried it. Did you bring the camera? I could show them all. Are we nearly there?'

They peeled off the main road and followed a dwindling lane with a sprawl of bungalows on either side. By the time they had pulled in next to Imogen in a steeply sloping field that doubled as a car park and checked (and rechecked) the handbrake, Finn was pale, almost speechless, with a combination of excitement and terror. He leapt from the car to join Rory for a frantic whispered conversation. Imogen was diligently gathering up bags and doling them out to any child who strayed too close, while Sophie stood on the edge of the dune, surveying the horizon with one hand shielding her eyes, the other on her hip, her curly hair and light cotton shirt fluttering in the sea breeze like pennants.

'Only five minutes before the taster lesson.' Imogen glanced at Jo. 'So we'd better get over to the surf shop. That's where we're supposed to be meeting our instructor.'

'Oh good. Plenty of time,' Jo said breezily. She pulled Finn's swim bag out of the boot. 'I'll just take him to the loos to get changed and we'll join you in a minute or two. Is that it, over there?'

'Yes, right next to the shop. I've been dealing with someone called Matt, but I think he said Dan would be taking the session. I shouldn't imagine there'll be more than one group going out. Erm ...' Imogen paused. 'Probably best not to keep them waiting.'

Jo quickly turned away to conceal her smile. 'Don't worry, Imogen,' she said sweetly, 'we'll be a quick as we can. C'mon, Finn.'

She strode off towards the whitewashed toilet block on the edge of the beach and sniffed gingerly as she got closer. Not too rank, although by the end of the day it would certainly be unspeakable. Best to go now before the floor was awash and the bowls full of unflushed paper.

Jo ushered Finn into the Ladies, despite his reluctance. There was no way she'd have him hopping round changing into his trunks in the Gents, in full view of any old perv who chanced by. He emerged from the cubicle a few minutes later, looking pleased with his new baggy trunks, ordered in haste over the internet. With a design of snarling sharks on a lurid turquoise background, she wondered if they were really the most tasteful choice for a surfing lesson.

Sophie's voice floated in through the sunlit doorway. 'Jo? Are you in there? Imogen's sent me to retrieve you. There's a lanky yoof ready to plunge our tiny offspring into the icy waves and perilous undertow. I think I might need some heavy-duty tranquillisers. Do you have any about your person? Oh hello, Finn, you look cool. Here, give us your clothes. I'll put them with the rest. They're all getting together at the surf shop. Dan'll measure you up for a wetsuit and some boots.'

Finn scampered away, goosepimples forming on his skinny arms, and Jo emerged into the sunshine where Sophie stood waiting for her. 'Oooh, how can you look so calm? Imo and I are both gibbering wrecks.'

Jo laughed, and slung an arm round Sophie's shoulders. 'Just put it down to my well-known serenity,' she retorted. 'They'll be fine, you'll see.'

Sophie elbowed her in the ribs and, scuffling and giggling, they made their way round to the surf shop. Sure enough, the children, plus three others, were lined up near the door in wetsuits, listening intently to the lanky youth in a wetsuit, unzipped and dangling round his waist. He had collar-length sun-bleached hair in a centre parting, but no amount of posing could disguise his under-developed teenage body. He was busy trying to remember their names.

'Right, lil' dude?' he said to the delighted Finn, now zipped up tight from neck to ankle in neoprene, and looking like a child's drawing of a child, all huge grin and stick-like limbs. 'You're Finn, am I right? OK, Fish Finn-ger? Got it now. No worries. I'm visualising you, like, to help me remember your names? Matt told me how? Way cool.'

Jo shuddered, and leant over to whisper to Sophie, 'Why is it every statement is phrased as if it were a question, going up at the end? It drives me mad. What is it with kids? They all seem to do it these days.'

Sophie shrugged, fascinated by the spectacle of the introductory session. 'It's probably cos they spend hours watching Australian soaps after school when they should be doing their homework.'

'It's highly contagious,' Jo murmured, out of the side of her mouth. 'And if Finn starts, I'm gonna brain him. Oh, here comes Imogen. Stand by your beds.'

'Oh dear God,' whispered Imogen as she came to stand beside them. 'I can't stand that awful Australian inflection, making everything sound like a question. The kids are bound to pick it up. It's going to drive me mad.'

Jo and Sophie burst out laughing but, seeing Imogen's puzzled, slightly hurt, expression, Sophie hurried to explain. The three of them laughing together was clearly putting Dan off his stride, so Sophie and Jo went to scout

out the café and shop, while Imogen elected to remain on duty, snapping away with her camera.

The shop was timber-built, had a thin layer of sand underfoot, and smelt of salt. It was packed with racks of enormous surfboards, complicated-looking harnesses, windsurfing rigs and lots of metal bits and pieces whose function Jo could only guess at. On the walls were dramatic, action-packed posters of hunky surfers riding exotic waves in far more exotic locations. Realising she was way out of her milieu, Jo half-heartedly sorted through the racks of bikinis and sweatshirts, until Sophie leant in at the door. 'They do lovely hot choc and latte in here. Can I tempt you? And will you share a Kit-Kat? Imo's gone all strong on me, and I can't have one all to myself.'

Jo nodded enthusiastically and joined her. She and Finn had not eaten properly in Padstow earlier, just snacked from the big deli on the quayside, and she was peckish. She glanced out of the window, framed with stickers promoting clothes and equipment. Was there time to take a snack to Finn? No, they were already down by the water's edge, lying down on their boards and practising. They resembled giant beached turtles.

Sophie stuffed the last finger of chocolate wafer into her mouth. Jo had talked her into getting one each. 'Should we take Imo a drink, d'ya think?' she mumbled.

Jo considered. 'Yes, I suppose we should. She's unlikely to relinquish her post, so we'd better. Tea?' She fitted the plastic lid on the polystyrene cup with difficulty, and carried it out, rounding the corner to where they had left her, but Imogen was no longer gazing after the children. She was facing Jo, talking animatedly to a man whom Jo could only see from behind – but this wasn't another slouching teenage surf dude. This bloke was much older, with dark hair shot with grey, curling and a little unruly. Tall, but not as tall as Dan, he looked very lean, very relaxed, in jeans so stonewashed as to be almost white. Barefoot, he was standing straight on to Imogen, nodding slightly while she spoke, his weight evenly balanced on both feet, arms by his sides. He was wearing a very faded red-check shirt with a conspicuous rip down one side, which was flapping in the wind. She could make out tanned skin, ribs and smooth muscle gliding underneath as he stretched his hand out to take a shell Archie had offered him. Something the little boy said suddenly made him laugh, and he let his head fall back slightly. Jo could see creases at the corner of his eye, a flash of white teeth.

Oh hello, what was this? Jo felt a sudden tingle of interest. Go on, turn around. Let's have a look at you. The man's hand came up to rub the back of his neck as he talked. He didn't look gay, so he was probably married. It was usually one or the other. By his age – and he was no spring chicken – there was always some kind of complication. Jo swallowed, her mouth suddenly dry, then she quickly fumbled in her bag until she found her sunglasses, and jammed them on so that she could continue studying him covertly. It wasn't until Sophie came up beside her that she remembered the tea.

They both went over to join Imogen. Sophie got stuck in straightaway. 'Who's your friend, Imo?'

He turned around unhurriedly and smiled at the two women. 'Hello there. I'm Matt Rowlands.' He turned back to Imogen then stepped back a pace to include her. 'Are these your friends, er, Mrs Tate and Mrs Newman?'

There was a moment of awkwardness until Sophie took the initiative. 'I'm Sophie Tate, this is Jo Newman and Imogen you've met already.' Jo raised her left hand to brush imaginary sand from her cheek, displaying her ringless finger, but she couldn't tell if he'd noticed. Men, she'd found, sometimes consigned you to a 'hands off' category if they assumed you were married. Best to keep her options open. But frustratingly, he had other things to attend to, so after a few pointless exchanges, he left and they settled down on the sand to watch the children.

'Well, you got stuck in quickly there, Imo. What would Guy say?' Sophie teased.

Imogen snorted, genuinely amused. 'Not very much, as you well know. Guy is incapable of imagining that anyone would ever fancy me. He finds the idea quite comical, which is very flattering!' Jo stared in astonishment at this extraordinary revelation, observing how Imogen briskly smoothed out the creases of her sweatshirt, her thick blond hair falling over her face. But curiously there didn't seem to be a trace of self-pity in her matter-of-fact remark, so bald and self-deprecating. She seemed utterly comfortable with this state of affairs, in fact, and Jo remembered Sophie's description of their marriage as being 'rock solid'. She shook her head, incredulous.

'No, Matt's really very nice, isn't he?' Imogen went on.

'And very good-looking, I admit. He's running this place for the summer I gather – does it every year – for a friend of his, a sort of local wheeler-dealer who has one or two touristy businesses in Padstow. He does teach too, but he was telling me he came off his board yesterday and pulled a muscle in his back so he's having a day off.'

'Blimey,' Sophie marvelled. 'What is this? The Spanish Inquisition? Did you also find out his inside leg measurement?' Imogen waggled her eyebrows suggestively. 'Hey, Jo,' Sophie went on, 'why don't you offer him a free consultation? I'm sure he'd be only too delighted to let you see to all his aches and pains.'

Jo pulled her sunglasses down her nose and looked over them at Sophie. 'You're obsessed, woman! We're not all on the pull, you know.' But once her shades were back in place she resumed her covert scrutiny. After all, she wasn't in danger of missing any action involving the kids, because Imogen kept up a running commentary.

'Oh well done, Amelia! Ouch, Finn came off with a thud then. Oh dear, is he crying?'

Jo turned quickly to see Finn wade out of the water and throw his board down in disgust. Dan was still some way out with the other children so she hurried down to see how he was. She was just about to reach him when Matt loped past with long strides. Squatting down beside the little boy, his hands loosely clasped, he listened intently to what Finn had to say.

Jo was flustered. 'He'll be fine. I'm sure it's nothing. You don't need to – oh—'

A wave broke over her ankles, drenching the hem of

her trousers and knocking her off balance. Instinctively she reached for Matt's shoulder to balance herself, then snatched her hand away in embarrassment. Matt gave her a brief smile then refocused on Finn, who was snuffling a little. Jo stroked his curly head and drew him against her, feeling the cold water seep through her clothes. She was almost certain Matt was staring at her now, but couldn't bring herself to look.

'Surfing's very tiring,' he said quietly. 'And he's not got much padding. Maybe he's got a bit chilled. My office has a heater. Would you like to bring him up there until he feels a bit better? What do you say, old mate?'

The little boy raised his tear-stained face. 'But I don't want to miss my lesson.'

Matt nodded approvingly and led them up towards the surf shop. 'Now that is what I call determination. You'll make a great surfer with attitude like that. Tell you what, when you've warmed up, I'll take you out on your own. Just you and me. How 'bout that?'

Jo could feel herself starting to jabber. 'That's very kind of you, but you don't have to. I'm sure he'll be—'

Matt silenced her with an emphatic shake of his head. 'No problem. I'd like to take him out. I'll probably be teaching you next week anyway, Finn. It'll give us a chance to get to know each other.' He glanced at Jo. 'If that's all right with you?'

'But your back – is it all right?'

'How did you know about that?' he enquired, looking at her with quizzical amusement, as he unlocked the door to his office.

'Mum's a doctor,' Finn piped up proudly. 'P'raps she can make it better.'

Matt leant down to turn on an electric fan heater, and she tried not to stare as his ripped shirt fell open. She smoothed her hair back from her face as he stood up and turned to smile into her eyes. 'P'raps she just can.'

Chapter 5
Thursday

*Persistent rain, driven by strong warm winds
from the South West*

This wasn't like London rain, the sort that turns everything grey and puddly, but which you could dodge with a light mac, a brolly and a quick dash to the car. This wasn't even like the rain they'd had on Tuesday. That had been a downpour for sure, but a reliable one that soaked you. No, this rain was petulant and wild. The sort that goes down your ears. Serious, coastal rain that lashes against the windows, driven hard by the wind behind it.

As she folded up pants and played Pelmanism with the socks that she had pulled out of the dryer and laid out on the kitchen table, Imogen tried to squint out of the window and through the mist. Frankly it didn't look good. Guy and Hugh would never be able to play the golf she'd booked at the weekend if it stayed like this. Smoothing out Archie's little boxer shorts and matching up Finn's unusual Simpsons socks – the humour of which was lost on her – she had a sudden recollection of Pembrokeshire holidays with her parents when she and her brothers were children. She'd always remembered the weather as being good, and had memories of them becoming brown as berries as they played all day, every day in the coves, inventing Enid Blyton-inspired mysteries about a local man called Jones the Fish who lived alone in a cottage outside the village. All very Dylan Thomas.

But now as she looked out of the window and listened to the splatter of the rain against the glass, she recalled endless afternoons stuck inside the rather damp rented house, arguing over a game of Cluedo, the box for which was missing the lead piping and Colonel Mustard. He'd had to be substituted with a homemade card so it was always quite obvious who had him in their hand. Anger would inevitably swell between her and her brothers when someone cheated, and her parents, 'putting their feet up', as her mother called it, in the armchairs and reading the papers, would get more and more irate. Imogen, always a bad loser, would throw down her cards in a huff and resort to playing horses on the arm of the sofa until her father would leap up, apoplectic with anger and unsympathetic to the fall-out of sheer boredom. She smiled to herself now. Nothing like parenthood to bring your own childhood back into sharp focus.

Laying the folded washing, and a suspiciously single blue sock of Rory's, at the bottom of the stairs, she paused for a moment to listen to the silence above. Then, picking up the empty laundry basket from the table, she went back to the washing machine to pull out the white load that Sophie had put in before going up to bed.

She could see the missing navy sock up against the

glass before she even opened the washing-machine door. 'Shit.' She muttered the word quietly but with venom. Why the hell hadn't Sophie checked the drum was empty before putting in the next load? Resignedly Imogen pulled out the damp clothes, recognising Rory's favourite and coolest T-shirt amongst the tangled, damp, grey-tinged mess. He'd be devastated. There too were her knickers, Jo's thongs, the lace a grungy grey, and – some consolation – Sophie's pale pink hooded top, now the colour of Germolene.

The chances of finding any laundry-rescue product under the sink were slim, she knew, but a poke around, however, did reveal a bottle of bleach and Imogen bit her bottom lip thoughtfully as she read the label. Reloading the grey mess into the machine, and adding a splash of bleach in with the soap tablet, she switched it on again to Quick Wash.

After last night's supper the dishwasher too needed unloading, so, putting the kettle on for a second cup of tea, she set to it. Weary and hungry from the surfing, the children had demolished the shepherd's pie, Rory's choice, made from the mince in the mound of Sophie's shopping. Her suggestion that *she* make the supper had been entirely tactical. Shepherd's pie was such a personal thing, and she didn't want to risk her fussy daughter turning up her nose at Sophie's version because it 'tastes smelly' as she put it. As it turned out, Finn was the one who ate next to nothing. The day's surfing had rendered him too tired even to eat.

And that was another thing. Imogen had rather

relished the prospect of polishing off the remainder of the pie with Sophie and Jo over a bottle of wine. She'd anticipated trying to engineer the conversation around to how Finn came about and the whereabouts of his dad. She wasn't sure she knew any other single mothers. Divorcees, yes, there were plenty of those at the children's school, but not anyone who'd gone the whole thing alone. And with a black man!

But as she'd begun laying the table for supper and putting on French beans to cook, Jo had appeared at the door, accompanied by Finn, still in jeans and T-shirt.

It wasn't that he had butted in during the evening. In fact, he'd sat yawning at the table as they ate, playing on his Gameboy and ploughing his way through a bag of Bombay Mix, only occasionally looking up. But to Imogen's mind his presence had constrained the subject matter around the table to say the least – and he jolly well should have been in bed. It might have been the wine that Sophie doled out so enthusiastically, but Jo had got more lively than Imogen had seen her to date, making them all laugh with anecdotes about her patients. It was painful to have confirmed what she'd always suspected though: doctors appear sympathetic, but behind your back they put down practically everyone as a 'complete time-waster'.

Medicine was a subject about which Imogen was in awe, and she'd been keen to pick Jo's brains about her complicated labours. But Jo had looked strangely agitated as soon as the word Pethidine was mentioned and she'd stopped Imogen's overtures stone dead with a brisk, 'God, aren't other people's labour stories a complete yawn? You'd think no one had ever done it before.' Imogen had blushed a bit, feeling contrite and knocked back. Perhaps Jo didn't want such things discussed in front of Finn (though Imogen wouldn't have gone into any gory details), but this notion was quickly dashed when Jo started on one of those things-people-put-up-their-bums stories that medics so love to re-tell.

'Christ, I nearly weed myself laughing,' she'd said, shrieking at the memory, 'and then the bloke said, "Honest, Doc, I just sat down and there must have been a hairbrush on the seat!"' Of course they'd all guffawed, and Imogen had felt slightly ashamed to be encouraging Jo in front of Finn, but Finn had simply looked up, tutted, and said, 'Not that ruddy story again.'

Sipping her tea now in the morning-filled kitchen, Imogen realised that, thanks to the wine, they'd all got a bit hysterical and silly as the evening wore on. There had been much teasing about Sophie's prolific sex life with Jo screeching at one point, 'Just how often are you two at it, you old slapper? I thought that stopped when you married.' But throughout Finn had seemed unfazed. Rory would have been agog, but this self-contained little boy, with his loose corkscrew curls and olive skin, just shook his head occasionally, yawned and carried on playing his game.

Imogen couldn't make up her mind about the way Jo treated Finn. He seemed very independent. Perhaps she babied her own kids too much. With his teenage language and passionate desire for gadgets and games –

oh, the nagging – she knew Rory was desperate to be grown up. Parenting him was not unlike holding back a strong and determined pony who, if you loosened the reins, would take off across the field. Even Olivia was already turning up her nose at the classic catalogue clothes Imogen so admired, preferring to prance about seductively in the sparkly Rock Chick T-shirts her godmother had sent for Christmas. Perhaps Imogen should ease up on them a bit.

Oh what would Guy make of that? she thought as she tipped the dregs from her mug down the sink. He wouldn't be too chuffed, as they'd both agreed from the start that no way were they going to raise their brood with wishy-washy parenting. If anything, Guy was a disciplinarian like his father, and was beginning to sound more like him all the time. She smiled as she finished laying the table for breakfast. Lord knows what he'd make of Finn and Jo when he arrived tomorrow. She'd sketched out the barest details about the new housemates on the phone, but for some reason had been evasive. She wanted to wait and see.

'What's this about some cheese place?' Rory lolloped through her bedroom door half an hour later as she was briskly towel-drying her hair after her shower. Topless, his pyjamas were hanging round his hips revealing his soft rounded body, but she could already make out the sturdiness of adolescence beginning to emerge and the planes of his face were defining themselves. He was going to be as good-looking as his father, but he was changing so fast.

'Some what?' Imogen grabbed her comb and, turning back to the mirror, began to de-tangle the knots.

'Archie's just come in and woken me up.' He slumped down on her bed. 'And he said something about going to the Edam Project.'

Imogen snorted. 'Eden, sweetie. Like Adam and Eve, you know. It's a big environmental sort of place with huge greenhouses.' Badly put, she admonished herself, and predictably Rory slumped back on the bed and groaned.

'Noooo. Please no, Mum.' He threw his arm over his eyes dramatically as if the light was too bright. 'It'll be dire and full of old people.'

The response to the outing from the other children over breakfast ran along similar lines, but being faced with a near mutiny only stiffened Imogen's resolve. The alternative was a day kicking their heels and being disruptive, and she wasn't having the opinions of six children sway her when they had nothing better to suggest. Well, five children actually, because Finn was still upstairs and not involved in the heated debate. When he did appear at the door ten minutes later, his face was puffy with sleep and he yawned expansively.

'You want to go and see the Eden Project, don't you, Finn?' Imogen tried to sound as bright as she could.

But Finn merely grunted. 'Never heard of it.'

'It's a boring pl—' Imogen threw her son a withering look.

'Rory, you don't even know. Stop trying to influence him.' Finn sidled into a chair and started to help himself

100

to cereal. Imogen shuddered as, with elbows on the table, he shovelled in the contents of his bowl dry, reading the back of the cereal packet and studiously ignoring the Eden leaflet she put down on the table beside him.

Sophie, though, was a welcome reinforcement to Imogen's camp. 'Ooh I've read all about it in the Sunday supplements – it sounds brilliant. Hugh will be cheesed off he missed it. We'll have to take lots of pictures.' Even Jo, when she eventually appeared, was moderately enthusiastic, though she referred to it as 'just rainforest-lite'.

'The real thing's a bit far for a day trip.' Imogen tried to check the tartness in her voice.

Rory was placated by a bribe of chocolate, but his pre-Minstrel tension returned when his mother discouraged him from travelling in Sophie's tiny car with Finn and Jo. In his sulk, he threw his anorak into the back of her car, clipping Archie on the cheek with the end of the zip. Archie then proceeded to scream and, by the time Imogen had leant in to the back and pacified him, her cotton trousers and T-shirt were soaked. As she drove, the wetness cooled against the small of her back and she felt chilly.

The rain continued to lash against the windscreen and the wipers 'foomp foomped' as they tried to keep up with the demand on them. Despite the wet, the atmosphere felt warm and clammy, and the coolness of the fan clearing the steamed-up glass gave her goosebumps on her arms. She shivered.

'Why do we have to go everywhere in the car?'

whinged Olivia, sitting beside her in the front. Rory, relegated to the back because it wasn't his turn, was slumped with his arms crossed, gazing despondently out of the window. 'Will they have a gift shop?' Olivia continued, her face brightening as the prospect occurred to her. 'And, if so, can I have my pocket money in advance?'

The mood lightened further when Imogen produced a packet of biscuits. Her own mother may have waded in unprompted on most elements of childrearing – many of her techniques being woefully out of date – but she'd been right on the button on this: children need for only three things in life: food, the loo and sleep.

Sleep. Mmm, she mused, thinking of the bags under Finn's eyes, and an idea started to form in her head. 'Rors,' she called into the back of the car to her son, 'I've had an idea about you and Finn. Remind me to tell you later, will you?'

Within half an hour they were waiting at the spot in the Visitor Centre where they had agreed to meet the others. She was glad she'd rung ahead to enquire about the best place. From here they could see the biomes, which seemed to have popped out of the ground like mushrooms covered in bubble wrap. It made one want to stick out one's finger and pop them.

What she hadn't bargained for was the sheer volume of people: bus loads of elderly folk; families with small children clinging to their legs; ecowarrior-types in shorts, anoraks, nifty little backpacks and ugly shoes, all milling around aimlessly. The atmosphere felt steamy, as people dried off in the warmth of the centre. Of Sophie and the others, however, there was still no sign.

'This holiday so far,' she muttered to herself, straining to catch a glimpse of the top of Sophie's head, 'has been spent waiting for everybody else to bloody well arrive.' Her friend's tardiness had always been a point of friction – at least for Imogen – but Sophie never seemed to notice. Suppose you wouldn't, Imogen thought now, gritting her teeth, if you don't wear a bloody watch. But whenever Imogen had made any tart reference to time-keeping in the past, Sophie had simply breathed an airy apology. Damn her, she hadn't even been very contrite about this morning's washing cock-up, or in the least bit grateful for Imogen's success in returning the load to something resembling white.

Imogen's one consolation was that at least over the weekend, when the men arrived, they'd be able to split into families and do their own thing. That did leave Jo and Finn she supposed, looking round to check Rory hadn't moved from his post admiring the renewable house display, but they must be used to being a little unit of two, and Jo could eat with Sophie and Hugh on Saturday night when she and Guy went to the seafood restaurant. She felt a frisson of excitement at the prospect. She'd had to book it in March, for heaven's sake, but she'd heard so much about the place.

Amelia's little form appeared around a group of people standing in front of Imogen, Olivia and the constrained Archie.

'Hi, Ollie,' she said with a smile, her eyes sparkling.

'You're late,' Olivia replied to Imogen's horror. 'We were getting bored.'

Amelia looked behind her to the approaching group. 'It was Finn.' She lowered her voice. 'He threw a complete wobbly in the car and wouldn't get out. It was so funny.' She giggled conspiratorially. 'He and Jo were shouting at each other. Mum had to bribe him out with a Curly Wurly.' Imogen looked at Sophie questioningly as she hurried towards them, but her broadly smiling face gave nothing away. Jo, on the other hand, looked tight-lipped and was trying to cover up the fact that she was practically dragging Finn behind her.

'Sorry about that, troops.' Sophie sounded breathless. 'Bit of a *skirmish* but not to worry.' She glanced around her, rubbing her hands together. 'This all looks exciting. What's the plan, Captain?' By this time Jo and Finn had joined them. Finn, extricating himself from his mother's grasp, was looking at the ground and kicking his foot disconsolately on the floor tiles.

There was a brief silence amongst the group. Jo seemed unable to speak and Sophie was looking at Imogen expectantly. Imogen could feel her irritation rising. Wasn't anyone else capable of making a decision around here? She beckoned Rory over to join them. 'Right, here are everyone's tickets. You can pay me back later. Let's split up into two groups, shall we?' Jo, who had been taking in the surroundings, looked back at Imogen as if she hadn't heard her.

'Sorry, Imogen, you were saying?'

Sod you. Imogen smiled sweetly, and repeated what

she'd just said. Jo seemed happy to go along with Sophie's group so, after suggesting that they communicate by mobile and meet at the self-service restaurant at one thirty, they wandered in the direction of the path down to the biomes.

'Soph?' called Jo, from the back of the group. 'Could you just hang on a moment while I take a quick look at this?'

'What? Found something interesting?' Sophie ambled over, the girls trailing behind her.

Jo checked furtively on Olivia's whereabouts and hissed, 'No, but either we branch out on our own or I'm going to stick her one good and proper. Hasn't she heard of democracy? Bloody hell, Pinochet could've learnt a thing or two about oppression from her.'

'Chill, Jo,' Sophie soothed. 'I know she can be a bit much at times but she means well. Do you think you're maybe a tiny bit stressed cos of Finn's tanty?'

Jo shuddered. 'Tiny bit stressed doesn't even start to come close. The little sod! What's his problem? He's been a major pain in the arse since first thing this morning. At least Imogen's taken him off to a safe distance. Just hope he gives her as hard a time as he gave me. They bloody deserve each other.'

Sophie distractedly did up Gracie's shoelaces, but peeped up at Jo over her shoulder. 'But you don't really mean that, do you? I always hate it if the girls are bratty with other people. Don't mind it so much behind closed doors, but I freak out completely if they act up at their gal pals' houses.' She straightened up and twiddled her daughters' bunches. 'Anyway, are we allowed to proceed now that Colonel Imo and the testosterone troops have a decent lead?'

Jo shrugged as they ushered the girls through the rear doors and out into the rain, now easing up slightly. 'Well, at least she didn't actually witness today's humiliation.' Jo could have gone on: how so far this holiday was doing bog-all for her confidence, how Imogen had done nothing but show her up since they'd arrived. Can't cook, can't buy sensible shoes, can't control one and only child, can't even make hot bloody chocolate.

Sophie called after the girls as, with Olivia in the lead, they started to trot on ahead. 'Not too fast, girlies. Don't bump into anyone.' Down the crowded zig-zag paths they went, towards the base of the workings, verdant and manicured, resplendent with hanging banners and strange sculptures. She turned back to Jo with a look of fond consternation. 'You need to ease up on yourself. This isn't like you at all. You're normally so together. Imo's very kind really and just super-organised. Let her get on with it.' Sophie thrust her arm through Jo's and urged her into a jog. 'C'mon, let's see how many pensioners we can knock over on the way down. And you've got to spend as much time with my girls as you can today, so you can see how utterly vile *they* can be. I guarantee there'll be blood on the coir compost before lunch.'

After half an hour, shuffling in single file along the paths snaking up and down the huge humid dome, following other marvelling visitors in dripping waterproofs, all Jo wanted was to get out into the fresh air again. Besides, her hair was beginning to frizz. But as the only way out was through, they plodded on like Sherpas. Back outside at last, Sophie looked at the time on her phone and looked horrified, then winked at Jo. 'Ages to go until lunch. Now you decide, girls. Would you like to go into the next biome and have a look at lots and lots more plants or shall we have a little break and see if we can find some ice cream? Now that's my method of child handling,' she whispered to Jo. 'Give them two alternatives but make sure the one you want them to choose is the only one that's even a little bit appealing. You know the kind of thing: would you like to do your homework now or would you prefer a nice big spoonful of cod-liver oil? Shall we get on with writing the thank-you letters or shall I feed you to a tiger? Dunno what I'm going to do when they get wise to it.'

Jo laughed in spite of herself and waited outside while Sophie took the three girls into the Ladies. What an amazing place this was. She wondered what Finn was making of it and Imogen's no-doubt exhaustive guided tour. Imparting knowledge was clearly terribly important to her, and she never missed an opportunity to do it. So far, Jo had heard her on the history of tin mining, the best way to poach an egg, and the mating habits of basking sharks. And that was only four days' worth. What was it going to be like after three weeks? Suddenly Jo began to wonder if this holiday was such a good idea after all.

Lunch was another challenge. By the time they managed their rendezvous, the restaurant was heaving and the children ravenous. Rather than stay at the tables they'd bagged and listen to their whining, Jo volunteered to get the food from the achingly worthy menu, and grabbed three trays. Even so, carrying lunch for nine people was a struggle. Couldn't they see she needed some help? But they were all deep in conversation, so Jo selected, paid for and balanced everyone's lunch, taking two trips, plus another for the drinks. Bloody hell, she'd have to do a cashpoint and soon.

As she dumped the random selection on the table, Finn's eyes were gleaming. 'Mum, Rory says I can sleep in his room tonight. Can I, Mum? Can I?'

She raised her eyebrows and regarded him coolly. 'I'm not sure you're in a very good position to be asking favours from me, Master Newman. Not after this morning's little performance.'

His face clouded over and, glancing around self-consciously, he hissed, 'Jo, don't go on about it. Just drop it, can't you? I'm sorry – all right?'

She gestured with her head and Finn moved away from the table and the others' earshot. 'Well you don't really sound it. I'm just not interested in that kind of shit. It's so …' Jo trailed off. She'd been about to say 'childish' but looking down at his now-scowling face she realised how absurd that sounded. 'Look, is there something bothering you? You're far too old to behave like that, aren't you? Do you think Rory would want to share with you if he'd seen your performance this morning?'

That was below the belt and they both knew it. Finn was now looking mulish and she could see if she kept on at him, another outburst would be imminent. But should she give in? What would Imogen do? Imogen, who had got up too from the table and was coming towards them. Jo smoothed her hair and tried to look relaxed.

'Jo, I hope you don't mind about the bed thing. They've been cooking it up on the way round. I'm perfectly happy about it but just with one proviso, Finn. Rory needs lots and lots of sleep at the moment. In fact, he's an absolute beast if he doesn't get at least nine hours, so if you do share, would you mind awfully going to bed at the same time as him?'

Finn and Rory were exchanging gleeful glances, but Jo was still unsure. 'What about Archie? Is there room for all of them?'

Imogen laughed self-consciously. 'Most nights he ends up with me anyway, although that might not be ideal when Guy's here. Archie can start off in there and pootle through to me when he wakes up. You probably think it's awful. But he is my baby, and I actually do love cuddling up with him.'

Jo kept her face carefully blank. She knew exactly what Imogen meant, and was damned if she was going to admit to it. But maybe she'd sleep better tonight without Finn in her bed and his bony knees poking into her back. Maybe.

Lunch consumed, due homage had to be paid to the god of retail in the gift shop, though all three women agreed a firm 'no purchase' policy. Sophie gazed around at the array of merchandise and giggled at the irony of it all. 'Bloody hell, mouse mats out of car tyres? I hope they're Michelin – got better grip!'

Jo had to laugh, as she picked up some glossy tome. 'And how many forests' worth of paper does it take to produce a book about sustainability?' Then at last they were out in the drizzle again, arguing half-heartedly about where they had left the cars.

By evening, all the children were getting fractious and their insults and bickering becoming ever more frequent. Finally, Imogen stood up. 'Right everybody. I've had enough of bad temper. Listen carefully. Anyone wearing socks, go and clean your teeth now!'

On and on it went, and all the children complied with her game, even groaning with disappointment when they weren't picked, until they were all ready for bed in record time and – more amazingly – good-tempered and giggling again. Jo looked on in fascination. You had to hand it to her. Imogen certainly had a knack, and the ability to dredge up that crucial extra resource of energy that seemed to make all the difference. When Jo went in to wish the boys goodnight, she was relieved to see Imogen was there with Rory giving him a cuddle. That meant Finn might accept one too. She'd been dreading a rejection since the idea of room-sharing was first mooted. In the dark, he nuzzled his lips against her eyelids, as he had done since he was a baby, and she waited, astonished, as his body relaxed and his breathing slowed. He was asleep already.

By the time Jo went downstairs again, blinking in the

bright light, Sophie was waiting for her with a large glass of chilled white wine. Imogen was still checking on Archie. 'Cor, you know how to treat a girl,' Jo said with a smile and sank gratefully onto the sofa beside her. She felt tired, but the evening stretched ahead, quiet and calm. She had bought a new book and wanted to get started on it, Imogen had left out one of her yellow card folders ready for when she came downstairs, and Sophie was fiddling about with a camera. They would chat, get on with their own stuff, someone would pour some more wine, Imogen would be sure to listen to the weather forecast. Jo would have a bath, there might be some phone calls to make or receive. But just at that moment, everything was quiet, and Jo felt that maybe, just maybe, this holiday wasn't quite such a nightmare after all.

Chapter 6
Friday

Warm and sunny

Rosemary. Imogen's eyes scanned the array of fresh packaged herbs on the supermarket display. She knew she wouldn't find any in those 'culinary pots', and she had already scoured the garden at the house for a bush of it (and, by looking over the fence, the one belonging to the bungalow next door), but she had held out high hopes that there would be a couple of cuttings here in a sealed plastic bag. There was mint so that was good. She needed some of that for the *vignole*. Coriander (worth putting some in her trolley just in case for a salad). But no ruddy rosemary.

Oh bum. She'd already been in to the butcher recommended in 'Fine Foods of Cornwall' and earmarked a beautiful leg of lamb to be butterflied and collected on her way back (didn't want it sitting in a hot car), and tomorrow night was fish and more fish at *the* restaurant (her mouth watered at the thought of it). So lamb it had to be, but you can't have marinated grilled lamb without rosemary.

There was only one thing for it. She pulled out her

mobile and, resting her bag on the handle of the trolley, rather inexpertly composed a message to Guy about where to find fresh rosemary in Petrelli's (the sublime local deli), which she hoped he would understand. She sighed as she put the phone back in her bag. It was no good. The rosemary had to go in the marinade long before he was due to arrive so, as much as it pained her, she diverted to the dried herb aisle and put a jar of it in the trolley. That would just have to do in the meantime.

She went back to her list, aware that time was now marching on. Inevitably it had taken quite a time to find things in a foreign supermarket, whereas at home she mapped out her shopping list by areas of the shop so she wouldn't waste time. Squinting down the aisles as she went to locate the prosciutto for the *vignole*, she thought about Jo's comment this morning as she'd peered over Imogen's shoulder at her shopping list.

'Christ, are you writing a novel?'

Imogen had found herself blushing – as she seemed to do most unattractively whenever Jo made some personal comment. But then she'd always felt very uncomfortable with that sort of thing from anyone. Guy's mother was the expert, and even after thirteen years of marriage, Imogen could not get used to those comments about her weight every time they met, and when she started on how soft Imogen was on the children, it was all she could do not to sock her one. Jo's remarks today had made her cringe. Yet again she felt fussy and foolish.

'No, no. Just trying to get everything down in case I've forgotten anything.'

Jo had continued peering over her shoulder, reading aloud some of the things on the list and, short of putting her arm around the paper as one might do in an exam, Imogen had had to put up with the humiliation.

'Broad beans in pods,' Jo had read with mounting incredulity in her voice. 'Baby artichokes. *Double* cream. *Two dozen* eggs. Crikey, Imogen, this reads like Mrs Beeton. Either that or you're trying to give us all a thrombosis.' Imogen could feel herself shrink. It was like that moment in the upper fourth when Daisy Pearson had snatched up her five-year diary and read out to the whole dorm, in a silly squeaky put-on voice, how Imogen wanted to 'be a cook when I grow up and then have lots of blond babies and a lovely husband who loves me, and a pony'. Imogen had tried to laugh along with everyone else, but that night she had locked herself in the end cubicle in the bathroom and, clutching her diary and feeling humiliated and violated, she had cried and cried, until her bottom was numb from sitting on the lid of the loo and her slipperless feet were blue with cold.

'Well, the eggs are for the yummy lemon tart I do. Guy loves it. It is a bit heavy on the eggs I know, but it's a treat and perhaps we can do a Pavlova with the egg whites for Sunday lunch. I could get some berries …' Why the hell was she explaining?

Sophie's arrival in the kitchen, arms full of sheets, had given her a heaven-sent excuse to stop gabbling. 'Oh Imogen,' Sophie had gushed, seeing what she was doing, 'another one of your brilliant lists. What are you preparing for us?' Sophie had picked up the cook book on the side and flicked through it. 'Is it a secret?' She'd looked up at Jo. 'You ain't see nothing yet. What Imogen has treated us to so far is merely the tip of the baked Alaska. You wait till she really gets going. Much more of this and I'll be eighteen stone!' There had been a split second of silence, and Imogen was sure she could feel them both thinking that was why Imogen was overweight. Sophie had rushed on: 'Now do either of you want to put anything in this wash before I turn it on?'

Quick as a flash, Jo and Imogen had burst out a heartfelt 'no', and when they'd both caught each other's eye and exchanged a smile, it had been a rather nice moment that was completely lost on Sophie.

But with Sophie's culinary compliments now ringing in her ears, Imogen was beginning to feel pressure to perform. She found the cooked meats aisle and some pre-packed and rather tired-looking Parma ham. Holding a couple of packets in her hand, she deliberated, then put them back on the shelf. Digging around in her bag, she pulled out her phone and texted Guy again, asking him to add prosciutto to his Petrelli's list, then she wheeled her trolley back down the aisle.

But then, what if …? She thought again about his meeting. Turning on her heel, she wheeled back up the aisle and put two packs of the Parma ham in her trolley. Just in case.

Cheese: she'd get a locally made variety at the place next to the butcher. Lunch tomorrow: the men were playing golf, and supper – oh joy! – the others could sort themselves out. She and Guy would be up to their elbows in melted butter, ripping the claws off lobsters!

She loaded the car, left the supermarket car park at record speed, and headed back towards the house, via the butcher's. The seats were roasting, almost too hot to sit on, and she opened the window to let the cool air blow onto her face and through her hair. She glanced at her still pale skin in the rear-view mirror. The odd freckle but really not much colour to show for a week by the sea, but today was looking hopeful. She thought about the packet of condoms she'd thrown into the trolley at the last minute. Guy had always left that side of things for her to sort out and she was fairly certain that he'd be looking for some action this weekend.

What was it about strange beds and being on holiday that made people feel compelled to bonk? It had the opposite effect on her, and besides this heat made her feel big, uncomfortable and sweaty, and disinclined to touch skin to skin with anyone. She indicated to turn left and cringed. The thought that anyone might hear them at it though was the biggest passion killer of all.

The day looked beautiful, and she could see larks diving over the headland as she drove along. The hedges and walls were a dusky pink with valerian, and the deep blue sky and sparkling sea blended into a haze on the horizon. For the first time in the week perhaps, she felt her body beginning to unwind. This was what holidays should be about. Perfect skies with flirty little clouds, and the prospect of a nice evening ahead with the men arriving and lots of laughs. She'd prepare drinks on the terrace. Maybe light the candles. She'd wear her palazzo trousers that felt so comfy round the waist. They'd all be relaxed and at ease, delighted she'd found such a great house.

Suddenly she spotted a sign. Ah ha! She screeched on her brakes and, like Michael Schumacher, lurched into the garden centre to the left.

'Bye! See you later! Gimme a call if there's anything I can get. Bye!'

Jo slammed the front door behind them and breathed a sigh of relief. 'Come on, Finn. Let's get out of here before they think of something for us to do. Phew! What a relief.'

The great arrival was upon them! Hughie and the oft-quoted Guy were due that very evening – time to be announced once Guy had worked out how early he could deprive the London banking scene of his doubtless pivotal presence. And now Imogen had come back from her shopping epic, things were hotting up. Quite why she'd bought that huge shrub, in its ornate terracotta pot, was not clear. She'd muttered something about lamb and marinades, but Jo wouldn't put it past her to be planning a garden makeover project for the occasion.

Jo and Finn flung themselves into the car and gravel spurted from the wheels as they swung out into the lane. 'Where to, Finnster? You're the boss. Anywhere but there will do me.'

Finn made a great show of thinking, miming scratching his head and screwing up his face with concentration, making Jo laugh in spite of herself. Boy, the atmosphere had been supercharged. Even last night, Sophie and Imogen had spoken of little else and, with Finn tucked up so early, Jo had found that the evening had passed slowly despite the promising start. Sophie and Imogen had indulged in a little affectionate husband-bashing, accompanied by lots of tutting and eye-rolling about their short-comings. At times the anecdotes had got positively competitive, until Imogen had pulled herself up short and had gamely tried to include Jo in the conversation. Several glasses of wine inside her, Jo had tried to look cynically amused, rather than expose the gut-wrenching envy she really felt.

At breakfast the other children had talked about nothing but daddies, and Jo hoped she'd managed to deflect Archie's 'Who's your Daddy then?' comment to Finn without him hearing. So, as much for Finn's feelings as for her own, she'd realised that the only safe place to be was somewhere else.

She prompted Finn again now. 'We're fast approaching the T-junction, where all great decisions have to be made. Wanna go to Padstow and do that boat trip? Wanna go and eat worms? Come on, Finn, the world's your lobster.'

'Weeell, what I'd really like is to go back to that beach and do some more surfing.'

Jo glanced at him quickly, but he seemed oblivious to her interest. 'What, Tregant Bay, do you mean?' she asked innocently.

'Yeah, that was it. If I have a go today, I can be better than all the others next week.' He sat back with a satisfied expression on his face. 'Yeah, that'd be brilliant.'

'Sneaky old thing. You want everyone to think you're just naturally gifted!'

He nodded fast. 'Yeah, I hate looking like a dweeb. It was really embarrassing last time. Olivia keeps teasing me about it. But I've been thinking. If I can get Matt to show me some more today and maybe I could get my own board and stuff, then I'd look really cool.'

He fished his mirrored sunglasses out of the travel pouch he wore clipped round his waist, shoved them on and started one of his improvisations, complete with tuneless whistle and knee percussion. Jo shrugged. 'Well, I did say it was up to you, so … er, Tregant it is.' She took a right towards the coast. 'But don't hold out too much hope of getting a lesson in today. You have to book these things up weeks in advance, as our dear Imogen is fond of reminding us.'

Finn gave his mother a searching look over the top of his shades. 'She bugs you, doesn't she?'

'Well, yes. To be honest, she does. But don't say anything to the others, will you?'

'Course not,' he snorted. 'She gets on Rory's nerves too. He thinks she's uncool. But I reckon everyone thinks their own mum is uncool. Well, you're quite cool,' he added hastily. 'But you're not like most mums. I like her. She smells of cake and she's kind but she doesn't want you to notice. When we were playing French cricket the other day, the others were making fun of me cos I didn't know how to play, but she explained it specially and she pretended it was in case the others knew different rules.

119

And she kept telling me when to run and when to stop.'

Jo nodded and judged it best to stay quiet on the subject. How could she explain, least of all to a child, without sounding chippy or possibly slightly paranoid, just what it was about Imogen that grated on her nerves so much: how all that admirable competence felt like a reproach and all that care felt so stifling? How the constant checking and double-checking made her feel like screaming very loudly. How even the cheerful effort not to appeared martyred made Jo want to slap her. No – best not to start down that road. That would definitely be uncool.

And cool was what she was going to have to be if that surf bloke was on duty today. He certainly wasn't a classic hunk, but there was something quite appealing about him. Jo peeped at herself in the rear-view mirror. If she'd known she was going to see him, she'd have done her platinum grooming routine rather than her standard version. Still she didn't look too bad, with her hair roughly pinned up to show the back of her neck. And in the short denim skirt and beaded sandals again now that blister had healed up, she'd be able to do lots of leg crossing and uncrossing, dangling the sandals from her toes. Shame she hadn't brought her bikini with her. Maybe she'd buy one from his shop.

At the bay, which seemed much closer this time than last, Finn was all for rushing off to find Matt straightaway. 'Er no. Let's have a little paddle first, eh?' she suggested.

Finn's surprise was almost insulting. 'What, you? Go

paddling? Yeah! Great – you never normally do stuff like that. C'mon, I'll show you where the rock pools are. Matt said you can sometimes find jellyfish in them.'

Pulling her by the hand, Finn lunged towards the waves and Jo, careful not to look back up towards the surf shop, picked her way over the damp sand, wondering when the best moment would be to casually scoop off her sandals and continue barefoot.

The water was icy and she cursed the goosepimples on her legs, but at least the fake tan looked nice and even. Worth every penny. She concentrated hard on what Finn was telling her, with some effort at first, but soon she was as immersed as he was in crouching over the crystal clear hollows in the rock, curling up her toes to avoid contact with the barnacles, and hunting for the tiny, elusive crabs. When another pair of feet appeared alongside, she jumped.

'You want to watch yourself with bare feet in this sand. There are weaver fish and they can give you a nasty sting. You might want to put your sandals back on.'

Jo straightened up quickly. Bingo! He had been watching their progress after all. He was taller than she remembered. But as she prepared her best 'We've-met-before-but-I-don't-remember-your-name' smile, she realised he'd been addressing Finn, not her. Finn had pulled off his top and tied it round his middle and, through the deliciously silky skin of his little brown back, she could see the precious knobbles of his spine as he bent over the rocks, his hands planted on his knees. His long corkscrew curls had flopped forwards but, hearing the familiar voice, he'd straightened up with a huge grin. 'Matt! Cool. Could I do a bit of surfing today? Jo says you'll be too busy, but I could just come along and listen if you've got other people. Look, I've been practising.'

He adopted the stance, weight low, arms outstretched, and swayed to and fro as if compensating for the swell beneath him. Matt and Jo simultaneously burst out laughing in appreciation of his performance, and Jo caught Finn's sidelong glance. So that was what he was up to – a little amateur matchmaking. It would put a damper on her light flirtation plans. She'd better nip it in the bud. God! That last time, when Finn had hatched plans for her and his deputy headmaster, had been excruciating! Matt was very nearly as unsuitable, although, unlike Mr Dempsey, he did have all his own hair. Jo shuddered.

Time to be brisk. 'Come along, Finn. You can't just barge in on Matt's classes y'know. You'll get your chance on Monday. Maybe we'll get a shrimp net and see if you can get any of those crabs.'

'Mu-um!'

Jo felt Matt glance at her, as if assessing her mood before he spoke. 'Actually, Finn, no one's surfing at the moment. Take a look. The conditions really aren't right today, hardly any waves at all. So that puts me out of a job, for this morning at least. But if you like, I've got crab lines back in the shop and some very tasty bacon. We could go crabbing further round the headland. There's a place I know that's just five minutes' walk. If you've no other plans, that is.'

Matt's glance was so knowing, yet somehow so appealing. Jo hesitated, trying to ignore Finn's restless jigging. She could practically feel him willing her to say yes. She glanced at her watch. She swapped her sandals from one hand to the other and managed to drop them both.

'Come on, Mum, you said you wanted to escape from the house.' He looked up at Matt. 'The other kids all have dads and they're coming down tonight and the mums are going ape shit.' Matt raised his eyebrows in amusement.

Jo winced. Good old Finn. 'Oh, all right then,' she conceded slowly.

'Yessss!' Finn punched the air, and Matt laughed, his eyes crinkling up so much they all but disappeared, reduced to two silvery-grey gleams in his brown face.

They walked back up the beach towards the shop, Jo unusually lost for words, but Finn, thankfully, made up for it with a barrage of questions for Matt. She listened carefully to his answers, sizing him up all the while.

Jo was in an exceptionally good mood that night, but getting the children in bed early was still a relief. Their excitement had gradually given way to rampant hysteria and tears, and they couldn't even be pacified with TV as they'd been barred from the sitting room, which was now gleaming. Imogen was engrossed over the stove, so Sophie and Jo took over bedtime duties.

'Christ, I'm not used to this,' said Sophie, pulling pyjamas over Grace's head. 'This is Hugh's department. I've usually got my feet up with a drink by this time of night.'

'You don't know you're born, Mrs,' tutted Jo, concentrating hard on Archie's molars in an effort to avoid any overtures about her afternoon with 'The Surf-God' as Sophie insisted on calling him. She even volunteered for three-tier story duty, starting with the youngest children. Feeling Archie's warm pyjama-clad body snuggled up tight to hers, and with him absentmindedly rubbing her T-shirt between his finger and thumb, brought flooding back the memory of Finn at that age.

By the time the men eventually arrived, the children were all fast asleep. Imogen and Sophie had made time to disappear upstairs to freshen up and change. Anticipation rather than blusher, Jo reckoned, had lent them both a glow, and the sudden stab of envy she felt made her turn away. At last, the long-awaited sound of taxi wheels on the drive had Sophie and Imogen haring for the door. Jo hung back.

The short, stocky figure of Hugh was the first out of the car, smiley as ever, pausing only to stretch and ease his stiff legs before he grabbed Sophie in a bear hug that had her squealing. 'Hello, girls,' he beamed at the others. 'No need to ask if you've been having fun. You're all looking fabulous – really caught the sun. Imogen, you look as dishy as ever and Jo, you look lovely and relaxed.'

He put his arm around his wife, and they walked into the house together. The still unseen Guy was rummaging round in the boot of the taxi. Imogen rushed forward to help him. 'Thanks, darling,' came a deep drawl and from the back of the vehicle he emerged – and so not the Guy

Jo had imagined that she was momentarily taken aback. In her head she'd had an Aryan man-mountain: jolly and large and corduroyed. An older version of Rory. The man standing in front of her now was certainly tall, but he was dark, rangy and lupine. His business shirt was open at the neck and she could see abundant dark chest hair flecked with grey. The whole impression was sharp and tricky. Now Olivia, with her dark features and bolshy temperament, made perfect sense.

From under a mono-brow, deep-set clever eyes assessed her rapidly, as he continued talking to Imogen. 'I'm absolutely knackered. Yeah, if you could just take that one, oh and the flowers are for you, of course. Yeah, missed you too. Come on, sweetie, let's get inside. I could use a drink.'

He made to enter in front of them, then stopped. 'So, you must be Jo. Delighted to meet you. I'm a bit laden down at the moment, but I'll say hello properly inside – after you.'

'*Darling,*' Imogen peered inside a carrier she was holding, an edge to her voice, 'you *have* brought the prosciutto and the other stuff, haven't you?'

Guy tutted. 'Oh buggeration, I meant to call you.'

Imogen wailed, 'Oh Guy, I wouldn't have asked you if I didn't really, really need it. It won't be the same at all.'

As Jo went back into the house, she could hear him apologising defensively. 'I'm sorry, sweetheart. I've been up to my ears in crap all week, and I've had such a day of it. Nothing but meetings. I completely forgot. Had enough of a job getting away on time as it was …'

In the kitchen, Sophie had Hugh were animatedly exchanging gossip and endearments over the table and large glasses of wine. They'd started in too on the toasted and spiced almonds Imogen had prepared earlier. Between a snog and a hard place. Jo couldn't decide which couple she'd feel less uncomfortable with, and hovered near the splendidly laid table. Imogen brushed past her, looking red and flustered, to go and make the last-minute adjustments that Guy's omission had made necessary. She had the look of a concert pianist asked to perform on a stylophone.

Guy stowed his bags in the hallway and strolled into the kitchen, glancing around the room proprietorially. 'That smells good.' The flowers in his hand – an expensive-looking hand-tied bunch that Jo was prepared to bet he'd sent a minion out to buy that very lunchtime – looked faintly ridiculous and out of place. He started opening cupboards in that half-arsed way people do when they hope someone else will take over and do it for them. 'Any vases?' he asked no one in particular.

Jo took pity on him. 'Cupboard at the end, by the window. I saw a big glass one in there. You might need two – that's a stonking bouquet.'

Guy paused, and shot her a mocking glance. 'Stonking? What kind of a word is that?'

'Oh, an obscure North London argot known only to a select few. Probably hasn't reached sunny Barnes yet.' Jo accepted a glass of well-chilled Pinot Grigio from Hugh and turned away. Within five minutes, Imogen ushered them all to the table, now bathed in candlelight, where they sat in tense anticipation as she carried out the first course, apologising rather pointedly for the packet Parma ham she'd had to use.

Guy groaned. 'My fault, everybody.' He smiled unapologetically. 'It'll still be delicious, but if it's not up to River Café standards, my lovely wife will have me by the goolies. So nobody complain, right?'

'Ooh, yum,' exclaimed Hugh as he helped himself to a slice of bruschetta and a large dollop of what looked like cat-sick. 'You remembered! This is my very fave dish, Jo. Imo always makes it for me. Can't remember what it's called – *La Dolce Vita*, or something.'

Imogen laughed with pleasure. '*Vignole*.'

Jo sniffed the green-grey sludge cautiously. Mmmm – minty, earthy and fresh-smelling – and took a healthy helping. With garlicky, crisp bruschetta, it felt as though angels were dancing a tango on her taste buds – and Jo wasn't slow to say as much. Imogen blinked rapidly and smiled down into her dish. 'Oh, thanks,' she said. 'Just a pity it looks like something a cat might have coughed up.'

She'd taken less than anyone else, but there was still a bit of jockeying for seconds. In the end, Hugh, Jo and Guy split the remainder three ways, while Sophie cleared away. In the pause before Imogen brought in the lamb and while she chatted with Hugh, falling easily into their usual teasing banter, Jo could feel Guy's assessment of her as if willing her to turn to him and talk. He was evidently the sort of man used to being the centre of his universe, but Jo wasn't about to go into orbit round him.

He returned to the limelight again by producing a venerable-looking bottle of wine. 'Here, try this,' he urged, as though letting them in on a big secret. 'I predict you'll find it raaaather special. Chum of mine at work has an interest in a vineyard in Bordeaux. Flinty, isn't it, but lovely nose.'

They obediently sipped, and Sophie pulled a face. 'A bit dry for me, Guy. I only like wine that tastes of gumdrops and Ribena.'

Guy rolled his eyes. 'You see, this is the trouble. All these facile New World wines that people glug down – no one has any appreciation of fine wine any more.'

Imogen plonked down a steaming bowl of mashed potatoes, redolent with olive oil and with curls of Parmesan and coarsely ground black pepper sprinkled on top. 'This is actually an Italian meal, Guy,' she sighed. 'I've got a perfectly respectable bottle of Barolo breathing on the side. I do wish you'd let me know before you decide to treat us to one of your finds.'

Hugh jumped up to fetch it. 'The more the merrier, Imo darling. You know wine never goes to waste when we're around.' He squinted at the bottle and sniffed at the neck. 'Perhaps Guy can have the Bordeaux – shame to deprive you, since you're such a connoisseur and all.'

Jo shot a quick look at both men. Had Hugh meant it as a wind-up? If so, Guy didn't seem to have noticed. She felt a little spark of mischief catch light and leant forward to gaze at Guy over the bowls of steaming veg.

'So what do you do, Guy? Are you a *merchant* banker?'

He looked momentarily perplexed, as if wondering

whether any friend of Sophie's would be so coarse as to use rhyming slang. No, surely not. He smiled. 'No, an *investment* banker. At the coal-face, you know.'

Guy leant across and filled Jo's glass with the Barolo, keeping the Bordeaux for himself. 'Thanks,' she said wryly. 'So what area of the world do you deal with?'

A slow lopsided smile spread across his face. 'Ah, a woman who knows something about bankers. How refreshing. Usually I get asked if I'm manager of the local branch of Lloyds. No, Far East, actually. That's where it's all going to be happening in the next five years, Jo, and that's why we're off to Hong Kong as you've probably heard.' He leant back in his chair, resting his arm nonchalantly on the back. 'Not Japan. No fear. Plenty of people have got their fingers burnt there. There are gains to be made of course – no question about it – but it's a cyclical thing with the Nikkei. No, I'm talking about China. I won't bore you with figures, but believe you me, that's the economy to be backing at the moment. I'd pile in there if I were you.'

Should she? It was tempting. But would it lead to a boring-as-hell, self-justifying recitation along the same lines. Oh, why not? She leant towards him, resting her forearms on the table and lowered her voice. 'What puts me off, Guy, is the human rights record. I'm a long-term supporter of Amnesty and the reports we receive from China are quite horrendous. I'm sure making money is terrific fun and very rewarding but, well, I just couldn't enjoy it if I knew it had been made off the back of someone else's misery. China may be the smart place to make a fast buck, but it's a system I'm not prepared to buy into.'

He took a slug of wine and tutted. 'Oh Christ, one of those bleeding-heart liberals, am I right? Well, we've got a whole department that deals with your lot. We do have a stewardship fund. Does pretty well. It'd be right up your street – no tobacco, no arms, no pollution. They've even won awards. But they don't make the big killings. That's for sure.'

Jo smiled tightly. 'Exactly my point. Here, Imogen, let me help you with that.'

Imogen's embarrassed look made Jo feel rather guilty. She had baited Guy needlessly, but something about his arrogance, that air of entitlement, had rubbed her up the wrong way. And he was so different from what she'd expected – a bluff Hooray Henry City type, friendly and affable, like a Labrador. Instead here was a wolfhound: sharp and challenging. Obviously he and Imogen had found their level, but it wasn't the type of relationship for her – although come to that neither was Sophie and Hugh's. Maybe she was just too hard to please. Maybe that was the problem.

Jo resigned herself to the role of observer for the rest of the meal, although she couldn't prevent herself exclaiming over the deliciousness of every single mouthful. 'Imogen,' she said reverently, after eating her second piece of lemon tart, 'this is worth an embolism! Delicious.'

Before Imogen could respond, Guy leant over and slung his arm proprietorially over his wife's shoulders.

'I'm a lucky, lucky man, aren't I? She knows how to look after me, don't you?' And he planted a kiss on her mouth.

'Hear, hear!' laughed Hugh, and pulled Sophie close. 'Cheers, everybody. It's great to be here.'

Chapter 7

Saturday

Fine and breezy to start,
with rain possible later

Imogen could feel something was different before she'd even opened her eyes, and then realised that for the first time all week she didn't have any bony knees in her back, or Archie's soft breathing on her cheek as he lay beside her. Instead she could feel the weight of Guy's body on the other side of the bed and hear his rhythmic deep breaths. She rolled gently onto her back, slowly so as not to wake him, opened her eyes to see the sunlight already playing on the ceiling and began to analyse the feeling of anticipation she had about the day ahead.

It was going to be a goody. The men were here to share the burden of entertaining the children – Rory could have his longed-for game of cricket on the beach later with Guy, who would be satisfied because by then he'd have had a round of golf in the sunshine. The children would have a picnic on the beach and maybe a swim. Then there was the prospect of glowing skin by teatime, a leisurely bath for her with a glass of wine at about six thirty and the ferry over to Padstow for dinner at eight.

She felt herself smile. Yes. All in all there were the makings of a good weekend.

Yesterday evening had gone to plan too. OK there hadn't been time for drinks outside as she'd envisaged, but at least the men's lateness had ensured the children had been out of the way, and dinner had been the triumph she had hoped. She was still pretty pissed off about the prosciutto-issue, but the packaged stuff seemed to work quite well, or at least nobody said anything about it, and she'd watched with glee as Jo had seconds of everything.

She looked over at Guy beside her. He was lying flat on his back, mouth fallen slightly open, with dark stubble now very pronounced around his chin. Which of the boys would inherit that? she wondered. It was hard to imagine it would be either of them, they were both so fair, like her family, and their skin was so smooth and soft now. What a shame that men grew hairy. She smiled to herself again; perhaps it would be Olivia who had to cope with a moustache.

There were pronounced shadows under Guy's eyes. He must have had a busy week, but that was nothing new, and he hadn't been specific. All he'd mentioned was that there'd been 'some bugger of an issue' to sort out and he'd left it at that and, when they'd gone upstairs, he'd merely made some comment about Jo being a bit of a 'tight arse'. Then he'd got into bed, complained about it being smaller and more uncomfortable than the one at home, and had fallen asleep without attempting to make love to her. For that she felt mildly relieved.

The conversation at dinner last night had been a bit tricky at times, she had to admit. At dinner parties at home Guy would usually hold forth and then, as the evening wore on and the Merlot took hold, he would get into some deep political discussion with someone else – inevitably a man. When they'd first met (at a dinner party, natch) she'd been intrigued and rather seduced by the way he became so embroiled in intense and intelligent conversation, and she would listen avidly even when the subject held no interest for her whatsoever. These days she would just raise her eyes to the ceiling and turn back to whatever she had been discussing with one of the other women.

But last night for once Guy had met his political match, and in a woman. Jo had taken his predictable comment about her being a 'North London liberal' with ill-concealed contempt. 'I'm glad to see you are such a broad-minded thinker,' she'd commented tautly at one point, and that had set the tone for exchanges for the rest of the night: tight and barbed, but disguised behind benign smiles. The subject Imogen had dreaded most eventually broke the surface, but Jo swiftly put Guy straight. The NHS was badly funded, she agreed, but she gave short shrift to the topic of private medicine: 'Do you honestly believe any of the people in my waiting room could afford to contribute to the cost of having a verruca removed, let alone pay for a hip replacement? Get out of your ivory tower, Guy, and find out how real people live.' It had all been delivered affably enough, but her meaning was unmistakable: she and Guy may live in London, but they had clearly never travelled on the Clapham Omnibus.

Imogen had jumped up at this point, desperate to defuse the atmosphere, and eulogised about the Cornish cheese she'd bought. Hugh had stretched and said how lovely it was to be here, Sophie had done her usual tension-pricking trick of feigning ignorance on any subject political, and they'd all moved on to talk about plans for tomorrow.

Now, as she lay here in the sun-filled bedroom, she couldn't wait to get up and make the day as perfect as possible. Guy stirred and rolled over onto his side, his arm flung over her body. He pulled her close to him, and started to kiss her ear, his hand moving down to her pyjama bottoms. 'Any chance of a quickie?'

She could feel her body responding despite the lamentable foreplay, but she needed a pee and she was sure her breath smelt. She knew his did. Then salvation, as she heard the thunder of feet down the stairs from the floor above, their bedroom door was flung open, and Archie stood there like John Wayne arriving at the Last Chance Saloon.

Guy groaned in her ear. 'Here comes the Mini Pill. The best contraceptive known to man.'

'Daddy!' And both he and Imogen dived under the duvet to protect themselves as four stone of raw boyhood landed on top of them.

Several hours later and she was sitting on the picnic rug on the beach finishing off Archie's discarded Scotch egg. Rory lay with his head on her knee, chewing on an apple core. Putting his hand up to protect his eyes, he asked sleepily, 'What time did you say Dad would be back? I want to play cricket with him.' It was now well after lunchtime but Guy had never been able to see the romance of picnics – he said he took issue with the crunch of sand you get in each mouthful of a cheese-and-tomato sandwich – so they'd agreed that he and Hugh would have a 'bite to eat' in the clubhouse after their round. But she really had thought they'd be back by now. She squinted in the direction of the car park.

'Didn't they say two thirty?' she called over to Sophie, who was making a picture out of shells with Gracie.

Sophie looked up, her curls all wind-blown and her face freckly and pretty. 'Oh, they've probably got absorbed in a pint and some boring discussion about fives and threes or bogeys or whatever it is in that blasted game.' She went back to arranging mussel shells on the roof of her beach house picture. 'I never have understood the attraction of hitting a small ball a couple of hundred yards in the vain hope you'll get it into an equally tiny hole. Bloody pointless if you ask me.'

'But, Soph,' Imogen giggled, 'I was only thinking we should take it up. I've always rather fancied myself in tartan trousers and a yellow V-neck.'

'Oh me too,' mumbled Jo sleepily from where she was lying a few yards away. 'And what about those dinky peaked things, like a baseball hat only without the hat bit, to hold your hair back while you tee-up?'

'You see, Jo,' Imogen teased, 'I knew there was some county in you somewhere. You've a closet desire to live in

Royal Berkshire, haven't you?' Jo snorted. Imogen ran her hands through Rory's hair. 'Why don't you go and play with Finn? Look, he's over there looking for sand worms. He might like some company.'

'That's babyish.' Imogen looked up quickly hoping Jo hadn't heard, but her face was impassive. 'Anyway I want to wait for Dad.' Imogen watched Finn in the distance down by the waterline, in T-shirt and shorts, crouching over something interesting he'd found in the sand. For all his precocity, he seemed rather small and vulnerable against the giant backdrop of the sea and the sky.

Who's the wog? It still made her jolt, Guy's comment this morning as he'd looked out of the bedroom window on the boys playing in the garden below. She felt a bit guilty now that she hadn't filled him in on Finn and Jo, and she knew he wasn't racist really (although he had refused to live in Wandsworth), but she was glad Jo hadn't overheard. Needing to prime Archie was one thing, but honestly! He'd made some further comment about interracial relationships, and she'd taken him to task. 'Besides, I don't know anything about it. It hasn't been mentioned and it's none of our business. And he's a lovely boy, so don't you dare mess things up.'

'Want something else to eat, Arch?' She put an arm out for her youngest son, who came plodding over and flopped down beside her, sand stuck to his knees and fingers. He nestled into her tightly. 'Your lips are a bit blue, honey. Need another fleece on?'

'Not hungry. Can I have a drink?'

Imogen reached over to the picnic bag. '*Please*. I've got

one of your favourite bickies here too, with the caramel hiding under the chocolate.' She held one up expectantly but he shook his head. She paused for a moment looking at it. Oh sod it, it was too fiddly to put one biscuit back into a packet, and she popped it into her mouth.

'Oi you, Mrs!' Sophie looked up in mock reproach. 'I hope you're not going to spoil yourself for monkfish in some scrummy creamy sauce this evening.'

Imogen smiled guiltily and pushed a crumb in from the side of her mouth. 'Oh, I've no doubt I'll find room for a soupçon somewhere. Nothing comes between me and a mussel. Talking of which, hold in your stomachs, girls. Isn't that the hunk of surfing gorgeousness over there talking to Finn?' She couldn't resist shooting a sideways glance at Jo who, rather too slowly, rubbed her eyes and pushed herself up onto her elbows to squint down the beach.

'Looks like it.' Jo lay back down again. 'So long as it's not some old perv trying to pick him up. What's all this about this evening then, Imogen?'

'Didn't Imo tell you?' Sophie gushed enthusiastically. 'She and Guy are having dinner at the Seafood Restaurant in Padstow. She booked it aeons ago, clever old thing. I'm dead envious. We're never that organised, Hughie and me. God, Imo, do you remember all that fuss with our passports before our honeymoon?' She turned to Jo, still wincing at the memory. 'Hugh's brother had to do a mercy dash to Gatwick with them or we'd have missed our flight. Oh I've just thought – what are we going to do tonight without the chief chef? Looks like we'll have to forage for ourselves, Jo – just you, me and Hughie. Won't that be fun!'

Imogen had never seen anyone move from horizontal to vertical quite so quickly in her life. But within what felt like seconds Jo had sat bolt upright and then, like a gazelle, was striding off down the beach towards her son, who was now chatting animatedly to Matt.

Sophie looked after her, bemused. 'Was it something I said?'

Imogen was saved from having to respond by the appearance of two unmistakable figures emerging over the top of the dunes: Guy tall and loping in navy polo shirt, and Hugh, the shirt he'd borrowed from Guy to satisfy golf club rules straining across his broader figure. Imogen waved to get their attention. 'Rory, look, darling, Dad's back.' Rory was off, racing across the beach towards them, spraying sand up behind him. Imogen could see him saying something to Guy, then watched as Guy ruffled his son's hair and Rory's stance slumped. He lolled back towards her behind his father, kicking sand, until all three reached the rugs where they were waiting. Guy threw himself down beside Imogen, planting a kiss on her cheek, whilst Hugh rummaged through the picnic basket for scraps.

'Who won then?' laughed Sophie, slapping her husband's hand affectionately.

'Ballesteros here as usual.' Hugh ducked out of her way as he stuffed a mini pork pie into his mouth and mumbled, spraying crumbs of pastry, 'He showed no mercy to a poor Islington architect. These ruddy bankers

– I reckon they spend half the week on the golf course.'

Guy rolled onto his stomach. 'You're just a bad loser. Where's the good doctor, by the way?' Imogen shaded her eyes and scanned the view.

'She's down the beach with Finn, I think. Rory,' she looked up at her son who was sitting some distance away now, sulking and burying his feet with sand, 'run down and see if Finn wants to play cricket.'

Rory raised his head up and pouted. 'But Dad promised he'd—' Imogen shot him one of her I'll-talk-him-round looks and jerked her head down towards the sea. Rory got up and slouched off.

'Come on, darling.' She turned to her husband as soon as Rory was out of earshot. 'He's been nagging about it for the last hour at least. You did promise you'd play.' Guy groaned and slowly pushed himself to his feet.

'Christ, when can a man relax around here? Come on, Huge. Move that arse. You're wicketkeeping.'

Imogen watched for a while as the boys, Amelia, Olivia and even Gracie gathered around Guy. Sophie too had strolled over and put her arm around her husband. Imogen was relieved to see Finn had come running up the beach with Rory and that he was being involved again at last. Matt too was heading towards the group, egged on by Finn (who'd run back briefly to collect his catcher's mitt), and was ambling up the beach with Jo beside him, her hair working itself loose from the hair tie in the gathering breeze, the curls falling attractively around her face. She must be cold because she had her arms firmly folded against her chest as she walked.

As usual Guy had appointed himself umpire and captain, and within moments he was directing players to various fielding positions. It never ceased to amaze her how people just fell in with his wishes. She'd watched his natural dominance at tennis matches at the club where they played. Even the children seemed to jump to it when their father metaphorically clicked his fingers. He conducted life with a conviction that was hard to resist. She watched as he bowled then lunged dramatically as the ball was returned powerfully by Hugh, intercepting it from being fielded by Matt, who was standing some way behind. Further back still stood Jo, arms still held tightly around her body as if in self-defence.

Imogen moved herself gingerly from her sitting position, her arms going numb now that the clouds had chased away the sunshine, and from holding on to the nestling Archie. 'Come on, you, let's go and join in. You can play deep in the outfield with me and we'll build a sandcastle when no one's looking.' She looked down at her son, his head resting against her, and pushed his fringe gently off his forehead.

'Arch, you're all clammy, sweetheart. Whatever's wrong?'

Jo was holding up the *Observer* Review to her face, trying not to listen to the animated voices coming through the closed kitchen door.

'Don't be absurd. I'm not leaving him like this.' Imogen's tone was high-pitched, and had Jo not known better she'd have thought she was admonishing Rory.

Guy's words were less clear, but out of the deep timbre she could make out enough to guess the rest. He was clearly trying to state his case, a wheedling tone creeping in, and Jo could make out 'looking forward' and 'only a tummy upset'. Would Imogen crack?

Jo started as the kitchen door opened suddenly and Imogen's voice was clearer as she came into the hall. '… just not prepared to leave him. I couldn't enjoy it, and besides it's not fair on Sophie and Jo to have the responsibility of a sick child.'

Guy's tetchy response followed Imogen up the stairs. 'But you've even got a sodding doctor in the house. He couldn't be in better hands.' Through the crack in the door, Jo could see his look of despondency, as he jammed his hands into his pockets like an overgrown boy and heard him mutter, 'Well, that's buggered that then.'

Imogen's feet hurried across the landing above to the darkened room where little Archie had been puking his guts up since mid-afternoon. This time it was Guy's turn to start as he spotted Jo. He made a half-hearted attempt to smile and Jo had to acknowledge that she'd overheard.

'It's the old umbilical cord. You can't come between a mother and a sick child,' she said, with an awkward shrug.

'Tell me about it.' He shook his head slowly.

'Throwing up's the best thing for him. He'll be fine now he's parted company with whatever was bothering him.'

'She'll come round, I'm sure she will,' and he turned back into the kitchen.

This had been building all afternoon. From the moment they'd got home from the beach, Archie shivering in Imogen's arms, Jo had attempted to stay out of it as best she could. Once she had checked Archie over for temperature, rashes and rebound, and reassured Imogen that he didn't have typhoid, meningitis or appendicitis, and it was probably caused by the sea water, she'd retired behind the papers.

Perhaps it was time to admit that she wasn't actually going to be there to babysit that evening anyway. The prospect of playing gooseberry to Sophie and Hugh had freaked her out so badly that she'd leapt at the first solution that presented itself – Matt. What must he have thought when she bolted up to him by the waterline just after lunch, quickly gesturing at Finn to lose himself for a minute or two? Matt had looked at her with cautious amusement in his eyes, obviously realising something was going on – so much for her inscrutable cool!

'Matt, I … I wouldn't ask you this if it wasn't an emergency, but is there any chance you might be free tonight?'

He'd paused for a moment. 'And hello to you too. An emergency, eh? Thought you were the doctor. Tell me more.'

'Yes, hello. Sorry. Well, it's more of a social emergency actually. Imogen and Guy, that's her husband over there who's just here for the weekend, are going out to that seafood restaurant tonight and that just leaves Sophie, her husband and … er, me. And – well – let's just put it this way, three's a crowd and I don't want to cramp their style.'

She had been encouraged when he started to laugh and had continued, 'Could you, d'you think? I'll pay you a million pounds. If we could just go out for a couple of drinks – my treat …'

She had watched, mortified, as he'd slowly crossed his arms and seemed to be considering, then horrified herself even more when she'd blurted, 'It's just anything to get me away from the bloody Mills & Boon going on back up at the house. It's not like I want to go out with you or anything—'

This time he had burst out laughing. 'How flattering! Any port in a storm, hey? Well, this is a first for me.'

God, what a cock-up! Jo had felt her face burning, and the awful possibility had crossed her mind for the first time that she'd got it terribly wrong. He might be attached. Kids even. 'I didn't mean it like that. Of course I'd love to go out with you. I mean … not like that, but for the evening I mean … It won't take long.'

He had smiled slowly. 'Oh I *see*. Just a quickie then. I'll do my best. And I'm so glad you'd love to go out with me, even if it's *not like that*, whatever *that* is.'

Massively relieved but keen to escape the agony and his slow, teasing smile, she'd speedily fixed a time and place to meet, and felt immeasurable gratitude to her son when he rushed over again to drag Matt to play cricket. But Archie's projectile puke into the sand shortly afterwards had, mercifully, put an end to the match that Guy had been persuaded to start.

And now, Jo folded up the paper and consulted her watch, it was time for her to get ready to go out. With her shower stuff and the basics of her make-up tucked under her arm, she peeped out to make sure the coast was clear on the landing, then padded along to the bathroom which she was relieved to see was free. She sniffed cautiously – well, you can never be sure with men around – then pushing razors and shaving gel out of the way on the crowded shelf, laid out her bottles. She could feel a strange fluttering in her stomach, and hoped she wasn't coming down with whatever Archie had.

The reflection that stared warily back at her in the mirror didn't look too wrecked and the shadows under her eyes were definitely beginning to shift. OK, so it wasn't a date *as such* but there was still work to be done and, by the time she stepped into the shower, she'd de-fuzzed and exfoliated with zeal. Back in her room, and wrapped in a towel, she cracked open the achingly expensive moisturising cream, breathing in its delicious lemony fragrance. Bit too nice to waste on a surf bum, even one with nice grey twinkly eyes. Now, what to wear?

By the time she got downstairs, happy at last with her choice of clothes, the children – minus the puking Archie – were finishing their bowls of spag bol (Gracie's choice) with noisy enthusiasm. Even before she entered the kitchen, she could hear Finn's husky voice singing tunelessly that unbearable song Sophie had, unaccountably, taught him in the car.

'I've got a song that'll get on yer nerves, get on yer nerves, get on yer nerves. I've got a song that'll get on yer nerves, and I'm gonna sing it all day!'

'Was that you, Jo?' gasped Olivia, eyes wide, as Jo

slipped into the seat between her and Finn. 'My tummy never rumbles that loudly. You must be very hungry.'

Jo eyed Finn's bowl hopefully. 'Do you want all that?'

He placed a protecting arm round it and glared at her. 'Yes I do, gutsy. You're always doing that. Get yer own bowl. Imo's made loads. You can have yours later, when they've gone out.'

Jo hesitated. 'Actually, I'd better have a word with Sophie about that.' And assuming Guy had talked Imogen round and she'd gone up to change, she reluctantly left the pasta behind her and went out into the back garden to find Sophie. But only Hugh and Guy were seated at the recently scrubbed and Imogened plastic table, each nursing a glass of Scotch and casually dipping into the remains of the almonds from the night before.

'Relax, why don't you?' she laughed, cuffing Hugh on the head playfully. 'Where's that dish of a wife of yours? I wanted to tell her, well both of you, that I would be out tonight as well, and to ask her if she's OK about keeping an eye on Finn. Will that be all right because I need to get going?'

She turned to walk back into the house, but Guy called after her. 'Haven't you heard?' His voice was resentful. 'There's been a change of plan.' She turned back to look at him as he refilled his tumbler. 'Imogen's put her foot down about leaving Arch, so Hugh and Soph are gamely taking our reservation. Sophie's upstairs getting ready now and Imogen's administering cool flannels.'

Jo could feel a wave of disappointment. Would this

screw everything up? 'I'm so sorry. What a shame. I know you were both looking forward to it …'

Guy shrugged. 'Well, that's Imogen. Look, there's no reason why this should wreck everyone's evening. Leave the boy with us. It'll be fine.'

'Well, if you are sure …' And she checked her watch again, went to break the news to Finn, and rushed out of the door.

The surf shop was in darkness, the car park empty. For a moment Jo wondered if he'd forgotten, but as she walked over the firm sand towards the door, she noticed a desk lamp on in Matt's office. He was on the phone, and she watched him through the lighted window, smiling and nodding as he spoke. He was wearing a plain white shirt, the ends of his hair looked wet and he rubbed at it absently with a pale blue towel. When she pushed the door open, he quickly ended the conversation, and looked at her appraisingly.

'So, here we are,' he said quietly. She smiled uncertainly. He indicated a director's chair on the other side of the desk and she sat down. He moved out of the pool of light. 'I wasn't absolutely sure you'd show. Y'know, maybe it was a false alarm, bogus emergency call.'

'Things at home have changed a bit, but it's still nice to come out.'

'Mmm.' He smiled enigmatically. 'Well, I'm honoured. I mean, what could a woman like you possibly want with a *surf bum* like me?'

He re-emerged from the shadows wearing a light linen

jacket and patting his pockets. Jo felt herself flush. God, he must have heard her refer to him in exactly those terms to Hugh as they'd packed the picnic away. She hadn't realised Matt had still been with them after the cricket and had merely wanted to deflect Hugh's gentle teasing. She'd meant it, at the time – what *would* she want with a surf bum, really, under normal circumstances? But the idea that Matt had heard her made her feel hot and awkward. Should she say something? No – better not. But Jo could feel her shoulders stiffening as he placed his hand gently on her back now to usher her out into the car park.

The evening air was soft and cool, and the reflection of the setting sun over the sea cast a glowing light across the beach. She turned to him awkwardly. 'I do appreciate you baling me out – really. I know you're busy. I didn't want to impose so …'

He smiled and shrugged. 'Don't. I'm teasing you. If you hadn't asked me, I might even have asked you. And you can forget about the million-pound bribe. A mere ten thousand would have done, but this is my neck of the woods and tonight's on me.'

Jo exhaled slowly and made towards the car but he had another idea. 'Let's walk back along the headland a bit before we go anywhere else. It's one of my favourite views when the sun is going down. C'mon, are your shoes OK? Hmm, not really. Wanna pair of flip-flops from the shop? I'll get you some. One of the perks of being a surf bum.'

This time she caught his teasing grin and, laughing at herself, elbowed him in the ribs as they walked back up to the shop. He rummaged through a box of new stock, rejecting unopened packets until he sat back on his heels with a satisfied smile. 'I noticed these earlier. They look about your size – five, right?'

They were turquoise with an intricately plaited toe loop. She tried them on.

'Jack must have had a rush of blood to the head,' Matt mused. 'He normally only orders the basics. This place could do so much better, I'm always telling him.'

Jo stopped admiring the delicate sandals and looked up. 'This isn't your own business, then?'

He laughed and shook his head. 'No, not really my scene at all. I'm only here in the summer when the surf's up and there's enough tourists to make it worthwhile.'

This was getting worse. He wasn't even a surf bum with his own business. A seasonal fixture, moving on when the weather got cold. Great work, Jo. You've done it yet again – picked a completely unsuitable bloke with no prospects and no stability. How did she do it? She moved away a little and watched him carefully locking the doors. She shrugged her disappointment away and smiled. Still, this was only a holiday thing.

'The sandals are great. Thank you, Jack, whoever you are.'

They didn't get into town for well over an hour. Once they had walked a short way along the headland path and reached the protected sandy cove, they'd sat on the sand, bathed in marmalade-coloured rays of the setting sun, huge as it sank ever closer to the horizon, burning a dazzling path across the sea all the way to them. It had been surprisingly easy and effortless with him, talking and laughing at first, then lapsing into comfortable silence.

It was she who drove them to Padstow and he directed her to a private parking space behind one of the elusive Jack's shops. As darkness fell the streets were busy with a mix of holidaymakers and young locals; the former strolling around and peering into lighted shop windows or making their way purposefully to restaurants, the latter lurching in and out of pubs and calling loudly to each other across the crowded harbour. As Jo and Matt walked side by side, their hands bumped together occasionally, but he made no effort to take hers. Everywhere they went, people hailed him. 'All right, Matt? Good to see you. Stop by, won't you?'

'Does everyone know you?' she asked, enjoying the curious glances.

'Pretty much,' he laughed nonchalantly. 'I grew up round here, and it feels like I never really left, even though I've worked abroad, moved around, I always come back. There's nowhere like it.'

They stopped by the harbour and she shivered slightly as the night air cooled. He glanced sideways. 'Want my jacket? We'll go and get a drink then get something to eat, if you like?'

'No, no. I've already eaten,' she lied quickly. Eating would be too much of a commitment and he was probably just being polite. 'Let's just have a quick drink.'

Jo took in the slight frown of disappointment. 'Oh, if you're sure?' She could have kicked herself, and besides she was starving, but it would sound stupid to change her mind now. So, turning their back on the water, they made their way slowly back towards the pub, passing as they did so the large windows of the seafood restaurant. Matt slowed to a halt. 'Hey, aren't they your friends? Look, at that table over there. Oh, but hang on …' He trailed off and turned to look at Jo accusingly. 'Aren't those the two you're supposed to be escaping from?'

'Yeah, but … Oh, it's complicated. It was supposed to be Imogen and Guy here tonight, but then Archie was sick and … Oh wipe that self-satisfied smile off your face!'

'Jo,' he said with mock solicitude, 'if you'd wanted to go out with me so desperately, you didn't need to make up an excuse. All you had to do was ask … Ow!'

Chapter 8
Sunday

Overcast to start, but cloud
lifting by early afternoon

Imogen slammed the bacon back under the grill and grabbed the bread knife, trying as hard as she could to slice the bread thinly. Bloody homemade loaves. They were always so thick they got stuck in the toaster.

The children were comatose in front of the TV, and Guy was having a shower. This morning he was trying the one on the top landing, having declared yesterday's effort over the bath to be 'as useless as a piss'. The other one wasn't an awful lot better, but she might be able to divert a diatribe of criticism with bacon and eggs and thin, crispy toast.

Fishing out the small orange-juice glasses from the cupboard, she put them on the table. There weren't enough of them, but she knew she'd have plenty of time to wash the ones the children had used before Sophie and Hugh made their way downstairs. She'd heard them come in last night, only shortly after Jo had crept her way up the stairs, and she didn't reckon they'd be surfacing for a while.

Guy, of course, had been asleep by that time, and Imogen had lain wide-eyed beside him. He was always asleep within seconds after they had sex. Funny how it had the opposite effect on her. He went at sex with the same intensity and determination he showed in his business dealings, effective to be sure but not very strong on subtlety. She knew she should attempt to be more imaginative; try out all those positions she'd read about or he'd hinted at, and she had occasionally attempted the odd novelty. But most of the time she couldn't be bothered, and anyway, they were both satisfied with the way things were – regular and brisk if not very tender – and he would slump off her, satiated, and within seconds would be breathing softly and evenly.

She'd slipped out of bed to re-open the door so she could hear Archie if he needed her and she'd looked at Guy's face in the dimly lit room. It was so familiar to her now that she wasn't sure she could have described him to someone else who'd never met him, yet she probably knew his face better than she knew her own. Years ago, when they'd first met, she would drink in every inch of it; run her hands over it adoringly, something he'd found strange but had tolerated. She'd been heady too with the urgency of his physical need for her, carried along with his passion.

But there had been no variety in the urgency over the years, few moments of platonic tenderness in or out of bed, and any signs of physical closeness were inevitably precursors to sex. Inevitably too she knew that she'd transferred her need to give and receive affection to the children, touching them and enveloping herself in them, and revelling in the uncomplicated tenderness they showed. And, she sighed now, God knows it can be hard to be a whore in the bedroom when you'd just unloaded the dishwasher and picked up his discarded boxers off the floor.

Did Sophie feel like that about Hugh? Imogen turned the bacon over now, and pulled the eggs from the fridge. She couldn't do or they wouldn't be all over each other all the time. And boy they'd been up for it last night, she thought irritably, because for ages after they had shut their bedroom door across the landing she'd could hear the creaking of the bed and the bang of the headboard against the wall accompanied by Sophie's suppressed giggles.

She poured oil into the frying pan, an alarming non non-stick version and far inferior to her own at home. The toaster popped up, the bread barely tanned, and she slammed it down more violently than was entirely necessary.

'How could anyone resist a smell like that?' Guy strolled in, turning down the collar of his polo shirt, his thick dark hair slicked back off his forehead. He kissed her perfunctorily on the side of her head by her ear – the top inaccessible as she was nearly his height anyway – and opened the fridge door to survey the contents. 'Any tomatoes?'

'I didn't bother cos the kids won't eat them. I can do you some once the pan is finished with so they don't trace the taint.' She pulled out the grill pan and transferred the now crispy bacon onto a plate before putting it in the oven below to keep warm.

'I'll miss this every weekend.'

Imogen turned to face him, oven glove still on her hand. 'Oh I'm sure we can rustle up cooked breakfast in Hong Kong.'

He munched on a raw mushroom he'd pulled from the bag in the fridge. 'I was going to talk to you more about it last night at the restaurant, or I was until Archie started parking his custard.' How she hated that expression. 'And there didn't seem to be a moment by the time they'd all gone to bed. But pinning down HR about the relocation details has been a nightmare – they are really dragging their heels so it looks like you'll have to do some investigating with your inimitable organisational skills. Malcolm's just come back from a two-year stretch and says his wife loved it. Great country clubs, plenty of tennis and barbecues. It will be fun, and I'm up for a hefty relocation wedge for going so we'll be very comfortable indeed.'

Behind her the toast popped out loudly and made her jump. It was burnt to a cinder. Damn. And damn that she had to do all the sorting.

'Well, it won't be that easy organising it from here, Guy.' She knew she sounded tetchy. 'What the hell are these HR people paid for anyway?'

There was no time to talk any more as the children herded into the room, lured from the box by the smell of bacon. She carefully fried eggs, trying not to break them with the woefully inadequate plastic fish slice. She even rustled up scrambled for Archie who, not surprisingly, was ravenous but couldn't face anything fried. All the while her head juggled questions and thoughts. What with the end of term and coming here, she really hadn't knuckled down yet to sorting out this move. She'd got as far as warning the schools that the children were leaving, of course, and she'd shown Arch on a map where they were going – he'd heard of it because Daddy had been going there on business trips for ages. Now a million thoughts surged through her head: would they make friends? The food – was it edible? What was healthcare like? And where would they live? Would they rent out their house in Barnes? She tried not to imagine someone else making themselves at home in her kitchen. Putting their feet up on her sofa. Having sex in her bed.

'Mum, what are we doing today? And can I have ketchup?' Olivia pulled the crusts off her toast.

'No to the second question. This isn't a transport café. To the first, I'm not sure. I've got a big chicken in the fridge. We could have that, I suppose, and maybe go to the beach.'

'Hold that chicken.' Smiling broadly and weighed down with a huge pile of newspapers, Hugh came in through the back door. 'Fabulous morning. Thought I'd get the papers.' He thumped them down on the kitchen counter. 'Didn't know what everyone wanted, so I brought most of them. No, Imo, you are definitely not cooking lunch today. Sophs and I nicked your fab dinner last night, so why don't we all go out?'

Guy picked up *The Sunday Times* and pulled out the

Sport section. 'How was it, old man?' His eyes scanned the lead story. 'Up to its reputation?'

'Delicious.' Hugh picked up a piece of spare bacon in his fingers. 'What that man can do with seafood! It must be a real privilege to be a lobster round these parts knowing there's a good chance you'll end up on one of his plates. Soph had this seafood platter – and I went for the monkfish. Indescribable.'

I bet there were bloody oysters too, Imogen thought tartly as she fished out jam and honey for toast. She could hardly bear to listen to him waxing lyrical about what should have been *her* dinner, especially when Sophie joined in, appearing at the door looking vulnerable and fluffy in a pink T-shirt with sparkly motif and white shorts, and gushed intolerably about every aspect of the restaurant from the aperitifs to the loos. 'Imo, you've just got to go. I'm sure it would be worth a call. They might have a cancellation.'

'You guys want to go out for lunch?' Imogen changed the subject by addressing the table at large. 'There's that nice-looking place down by the ferry. We're going to have to book though,' she said to the other adults. 'All the best places are always chocka at this time of year.' Hugh announced he'd make that his mission for the morning, and Imogen sliced more bread for toast, as Jo came into the room.

She took in the table surrounded by nine people, and Imogen hovering by the cooker, and came over to take a cup from the cupboard to help herself to coffee, detouring on the way to plant a kiss on Finn's cheek.

'This is all very civilised.' A hint of sarcasm in her tone. 'Everyone sleep well?' There were grunts of assent from the assembled group, the men now deep into the papers, and the children shovelling in toast at top speed.

'Did you have fun with Matt?' Imogen asked Jo quietly, not sure how much Jo wanted her date broadcast.

Jo looked at her sharply, the empty cup still in her hands and an expression of surprise on her face. She evidently hadn't expected the enquiry, though there was no one else she could have gone out with last night. 'Yes thanks, it was … very nice. He seems to know everyone around these parts. Sorry you missed your dinner.'

'I'll have a crab sandwich sometime to make up for it.' Imogen smiled, noticing that Jo offered no thanks for the babysitting service she and Guy had provided. 'It's probably overrated anyway.'

'Quite. One whelk's much like any other I expect.' Jo put her cup under the coffee dispenser on the machine, and lowered her voice. 'Though those two enjoyed themselves by the sound of it.' She caught Imogen's eye, and smirked, sticking her fingers down her throat in mock gagging, and Imogen couldn't help but smirk back.

'Mum, we're going out for lunch. Hugh's taking us.' Finn called over from his place beside Rory.

'Oi, Finn mate, do you think I'm made of money?' Hugh laughed.

Imogen left them all to it, and escaped upstairs. The last thing she could face at the moment was a drawn-out conversation about who would pay for what when her head was full. She hadn't even had time to ask Guy if they'd firmed up the dates for the move. What about jabs? Walking into the bathroom, she absentmindedly picked up the wet towels off the floor and rinsed out the toothpaste tidemarks from the basin.

She fished out Archie's rabbit from where it had fallen down the side of the bed and straightened the bottom sheet. She had visions of him walking down a street of high-rise buildings. Perhaps she'd seen something on TV. It all seemed so strange, but quite exciting.

'Imo?' Sophie's voice carried up the stairs. 'D'ya want another coffee? I'm taking some outside. Stop playing Mrs Tiggywinkle and come and read the papers with us.'

'Won't be a moment.' And as she came down from the top floor, she could see through the door of Sophie and Hugh's room the crumpled sheets in disarray on the bed. QED, she thought as she tightened the bottom sheet on Guy's and her bed, and smoothed down the white bedspread with her hand. QE bloody D.

Ten minutes later and she was out on the terrace, where Guy, Hugh, Sophie and Jo each had their heads buried in the Sundays. Waving away Hugh's offer of a seat, she perched with her cup of Sophie's unbearably strong coffee on the low wall at the bottom of the slope up the garden and watched the children cavorting around the trees.

Guy's guffaw interrupted her thoughts. 'Bloody hell, have you seen this?' And he proceeded to read out to no one in particular some gaff made by the PM at an international conference. Only Hugh looked up from his paper, and made some suitable noises of disbelief, before putting his head down once again.

'Wish the footie season would start again soon. These cricket reports bore me stiff, and the West Indies have stuffed us yet again,' he muttered. Sophie was deep in concentration and nibbling her thumb.

'Hey, darling.' She nudged her husband, pushing a page from the Property section under his nose. 'Look what we could get in Kent for the price of our place. You'd have to be rich as creosote to get anything this size in London. This one is sweet and you could commute.' Hugh sighed and rolled his eyes.

'You are determined to get us out into the country, aren't you? I'll end up like Reggie Perrin. Hey, Guy, didn't realise Global were bidding for UKP.'

'They'll be outbid by the Yanks. Cor, take a butcher's at this tart. Wasn't she reading the weather not so long ago? How's that for a meteoric rise—'

Imogen could stand it no more and, picking up her cup, wandered around the house and out of sight of the group, and surreptitiously poured the coffee down the drain. If there was one thing that drove her nuts it was people who shared the content of what they had just read with everyone else – it was almost as criminal as relaying the plot of a film to someone who hadn't seen it – and Hugh's continued inertia about calling the restaurant to book a table for lunch was beginning to drive her madder. She knew that if she was wise she'd take the initiative herself, but she was damned if she was going to this time.

Two hours later she wished to God she had. Hugh and Sophie, with the glib confidence of the terminally laid-back, had chivvied them all into three hot cars, and they had pulled into the restaurant car park like a presidential cavalcade. She had watched though the window in silence as Hugh had jumped out of his car to enquire 'if they can squeeze us in', only to watch him return a few moments later and give them all the thumbs down.

'I bloody knew it,' she muttered under her breath.

'I'm starving,' Rory whined, and Guy wound down the window as Hugh came over and leant in.

'Sorry, chums, no go. Imo was right. Where shall we try now?'

Three suggestions and three thumbs down later, and Rory's hunger, not to mention Guy's temper, were at boiling point. Once again Hugh came over to the car looking sheepish.

'Sorry, chaps, looks like I've messed up royally.'

'Why don't we go home and I'll make some sandwiches, then we can cook the chicken later?'

Hugh held his hand up to stop her. 'No, Imo, I promised lunch out and lunch out it will be. One last shot – what about that joint on the Wadebridge road? Follow me!'

They did and at two thirty they pulled into the relatively full but not overflowing car park of Hugh's 'joint'. Imogen's heart sank. It was one of those places she referred to as a Brewer's Droop – an anonymous chain of pubs done up in a theme to give each one a 'unique character' based around a barn of some kind. This had always struck Imogen as odd, because barns had little to do with eating. Barns were for pigs and cows.

She could smell stale chip fat the moment she opened the car door, the stench heightened by the heat of the day. She wrinkled her nose and looked at Guy. 'Oh come on, old girl. It won't be that bad, and the kids will think they've gone to heaven.'

'Quite.' She tightened the grip on her bag and followed the group in.

The restaurant looked quite busy, most of the tables full of families, Granny and Grandpa included, having a Sunday-lunch treat. The positive news, after Hugh's charm offensive on the gingham-clad waitress, was that they could squeeze them on to two tables. Everyone dived on the laminated and lavishly illustrated menus. Past caring about her son's nutritional intake now and vowing to make up for it with a broccoli-fest tomorrow, she conceded when Rory ordered a double bacon burger with fries. The other children followed his depraved lead, and Finn gave her a little wink when he ordered a baked potato *and* fries. He really is an engaging little tyke, thought Imogen, winking back at him, and it gave her some satisfaction to know that his happy mood was in no small measure thanks to two early nights orchestrated by her. She'd even managed to have him asleep by eight thirty last night, simply by tampering with his watch while he was in the bath.

Naturally, the food when it arrived – at alarming speed considering the enormous choice on the menu and the size of the order – matched exactly its picture on the menu, down to the placing of the last tasteful parsley garnish. The men had gone for the Sunday carvery, of course, with beef that was the colour of cooked mushrooms, and Imogen was fairly confident her soup had never made acquaintance with a carrot let alone any coriander.

Within minutes, though, the food had hit the spot. Everyone chatted companionably for a while, but the excitement grew as enormous ice creams were ordered to follow. By the time they arrived, each a work of art in chocolate or strawberry sauce with fan-shaped wafers, Rory and Archie were bubbling over, teasing each other across the table.

'Rory, quieten down,' admonished Imogen, giving him a stern look.

For a while he did, and she went back to her sorbet, until out of the corner of her eye she saw him load up a blob of ice cream on the handle of his fork and was too late to stop him slamming his fist down on the prong end.

'Rory, you ignorant little pillock!' Guy's voice boomed across the table, 'Why don't you grow up?' Everything around them seemed to go silent, as the blob of ice cream hit Grace full in the face.

Every eye in the restaurant focused on their table. Jo had an overwhelming urge to laugh and had to suck her cheeks in to stop herself. She wasn't sure that a comment about Rory's accuracy would go down too well.

Then, shattering the stunned silence, came Gracie's piercing scream. Within a split second Imogen was up on her feet, dabbing the little girl's face with her napkin, and

163

attempting to soothe her wails whilst simultaneously glowering at her husband. Gracie's mother, however, was convulsed with laughter and Hugh was looking around in bewilderment.

'Sophie, I'm so sorry. Rory, apologise at once. There there, Gracie. Coffee anyone?' Imogen wittered with forced brightness, her T-shirt trailing in a pool of melted ice cream as she leant over the table.

Poor woman. Jo's sympathy was all the stronger because of the intense relief that, for once, it wasn't Finn who'd disgraced himself. 'Do they do espresso?' Jo looked round hopefully, but the cups on the neighbouring tables revealed the coffee here was the thin variety, served from those horrible little individual filters that fit into the top of a cup, and leave you wondering what to do with the dripping paraphernalia afterwards.

Imogen appeared to take responsibility for this disaster too. 'Sorry, Jo. I reckon we'll be lucky if we get the fag end of a percolator. Why don't we go home for some?'

She looked like she couldn't wait to leave – and Jo could see why. This place had to be the antithesis of all that Imogen held holy with regard to Sunday lunch, and her over-educated taste buds were simply incapable of enjoying crap food.

Guy, still seething, gestured imperiously at one of the teenage waitresses a few times, with no appreciable result, then, with a great display of irritation, he stood up and said quite loudly, 'Well, let's be on our way.'

The bill quickly materialised, and the pantomime started. Hugh was first out with the wallet, but Guy laid a proprietorial hand on the plastic bill folder that had been placed squarely in the middle of the table. Jo hoisted her bag up off the floor. Guy was raising his voice. 'Come on, Hughie. I insist. After all, there are more of us than there are of you – and we eat more too. And you did pay that last time in Richmond.'

'No, no. I won't hear of it. It was my idea. And we did snaffle that delicious dinner of yours last night. My treat – really.'

Guy leant in and tried to retrieve the bill. 'Absolutely not. That meal last night must have cost a bloody fortune.'

Hugh glanced round. People at neighbouring tables were staring again. He shrugged in resignation. 'Fifty-fifty then. Come on, Guy. That's fair enough.'

The others were picking up their jackets and bags. Imogen was organising a loo visit. It was now or never. Jo stood up. 'How about three ways?' she cut in, rather louder than she meant. There was a moment's silence. Both men looked as if their world order had been shaken to the core. Jo was used to this. 'Thirds,' she repeated. 'I'd like to pay our way.'

Guy shook his head emphatically. 'No question, is there, Hugh? Put your purse away.'

Jo could see Hugh glancing nervously at her. He'd witnessed her in tussles like this before and must have known she wouldn't be deflected. 'Fair play, old man. If Jo wants to contribute, let's work it out. Show us the bill, ta.'

Hugh made a show of totting up the numbers, to

Guy's continued tuts, and came up with a figure. From the corner of her eye, Jo could see Imogen dart back into the dining room, take in the situation, hover a bit, then dart out again.

'Fine. Thanks for sorting that out, Hugh. Here we are – that should cover it, I think,' and Jo deposited a bundle of notes and coins neatly on the table and walked out.

In the car park, all was as she had expected, with Sophie sitting on a bench sunning herself and Imogen organising an impromptu game of Seaweed and Sharks. 'That's right, Finn. You're seaweed now, so stay put and wave your arms around. Oh here comes a fish – get ready to catch her.'

Jo watched bemused from behind her sunglasses as Finn gurgled with laughter, doubled over and clutching his sides, completely missing a placated Gracie, who was trotting sedately past, loitering close enough for him to grab. He'd been much better-tempered the last two days. Maybe the sea air was agreeing with him, or he'd got used to being with the other kids all the time. He didn't seem to find it as much of a strain as Jo had expected. Well, that was good, really. Overall.

Imogen sidled up to her as the men emerged and the children scattered to the cars. 'Er, sorry about that. He can be horribly boorish when it comes to money. It's a bit of a male statement.'

Jo looked at her for a moment. 'S'all right,' she muttered, then grinned. 'I enjoy a tussle now and again. Keeps me on form for partners' meetings at work.'

Imogen smiled uncertainly. 'Well, good for you for

fighting your corner,' she said quickly and went back to the car. Guy relinquished the keys, having had the best part of a bottle of Cab Sauv, and Jo could see Imogen adjusting the seat and mirror while he turned in his seat to admonish the kids about something or other. She shook her head and smiled ruefully. Maybe the nuclear family didn't have so much going for it after all. She squeezed Finn's knee. 'Just you and me again, mate. Nice and quiet, huh?'

Finn stared out of the window at the departing cars. 'Mmm, I s'pose,' he muttered, non-committally.

Jo dawdled on the way back to the homestead. She was in no hurry to rejoin the fray, and the tension that had been brewing up between Imogen and Guy made her feel uncomfortable. 'It's a lovely day, F-man. D'ya wanna go to the beach, get another ice cream? One that doesn't come with hundred and thousands and a row?'

Finn considered. 'I'd really like to play football with Hugh and Rory again.'

'What about Guy? Then you could have two teams.'

'I don't want him on my team. He shouts. I don't think he likes me.'

Jo winced. Guy had made some effort yesterday to conceal his surprise at Finn's colour, but not enough, and Jo was quite aware that, had it not been for Imogen's civilising influence, he might have said something. As it was, he'd fished for a bit for information into Jo's past – asked her if she'd spent time in Africa or the West Indies, as if one didn't come across black men in London, for goodness' sake. Well, perhaps one didn't in Guy's little enclave. Jo hadn't risen to the bait. God knows, she was used to balder interrogation than that.

'Well,' she replied carefully now, 'you'll always come up against people you don't get on with. It's just something you have to get used to. For what it's worth, I don't think he likes me very much either. The poor man clearly has appalling taste! Mind you, I don't like him. I reckon he's a bit of a berk. I mean – that thing with Rory and the ice cream ...'

Finn nodded thoughtfully. 'Rory was all excited that he was coming, but I bet he'll be glad that he's going tonight. Doesn't Guy love him?' He paused. 'I s'pose he must do, cos he lives with them.'

Jo could feel the familiar surge of anger at Finn's dad as she slowed the car at a junction. They'd been through this many times before, almost from the moment Finn could talk, but as he got older the questions were becoming more searching. Despite the hurt, she thought he'd come to terms with the absence of a father, but he was increasingly in danger of believing all fathers were perfect. Guy must have come as a surprise. What he needed, she knew, was to work out for himself what a dad may or may not be.

'Well,' she explained slowly, 'there are all kinds of ways people can be with each other, y'know. Families can row a lot and still love each other. People can be apart and still love each other. I mean, we argue quite a lot, don't we? But you know I love you and I'll always be there for you. Maybe it's like that with Rory and his dad.'

She glanced at him. He was gnawing on his lip, clearly

thinking it through. Jo shifted in her seat. Suddenly she felt tired. 'Sometimes adults say stupid things they don't mean, just like kids do stupid things like flick ice cream.'

Finn looked at her with a cheeky grin. 'Yeah, but it was good! Can I really have another one now? A ninety-nine?'

Jo nodded vigorously, relieved. 'Yep, definitely.'

'Could we go and get one from Matt's shop?' Finn was sitting bolt upright again, grinning at her.

Oh heck. Too soon. Jo lied shamelessly: 'He told me he was going to be out today, something about buying more stock, so I expect it'll all be closed up.'

Thankfully the idea of closing a beach shop and café on a sunny Sunday afternoon in July clearly didn't strike Finn as utterly absurd, but he didn't hide his disappointment. 'Aw, shit.'

'Er, Finn – what did we agree about the language, mate? You've got to get out of the habit when there are little kids around. You know Imogen'll wig out if she hears little Archibald coming out with that kind of stuff.'

They cackled unkindly about Archie's name, doing imitations of Imogen and Guy saying it, over and over, until they'd bought and devoured an ice cream and Jo headed the car for home again. Best of a bad job. There was no way she could drop in on Matt, no matter how nonchalantly. No matter how much she may feel like it.

The last thing she wanted was to look needy. Cool – yes. Detached – fine. In control – perfect. But the feelings that had stirred up in her last night would have to be ruthlessly clamped down before she could risk seeing him again. It was extraordinary what a whiff of pheromones could do to a rational woman – especially considering he hadn't even laid a finger on her. To tell the truth, she'd felt a bit disappointed when she'd dropped him back at the surf hut after their prolonged drink. He'd merely pecked her on the cheek and got out of the car, jangling his keys. He hadn't even invited her in for coffee. This was a whole new experience for her. She was accustomed to being the one doing the fending off and now she felt like a randy teenage boy. It had been a fun evening, though. He'd gently prodded her for information about herself and had seemed really interested when she spoke about med school and her problems at the practice. It made a change from the usual self-absorbed blokes she saw who talked incessantly about their latest gig or property prices in Hackney.

When Jo and Finn arrived back at the house, things were superficially fine. The kids were in the garden, and she followed the noise around the side. Hugh was chasing them, making hideous monster noises, while Sophie lay on the grass with her T-shirt pulled up to expose her tummy to the sun. Finn joined in the game straightaway. Jo sat down on the grass next to Sophie. 'I could murder a coffee. Do you think there's any left in the pot?'

Sophie glanced round furtively. 'Probably, but there could be risks involved in getting some. Imo and Guy are ensconced in the kitchen. I think they're having a little discussion following the thing with the ice cream.'

Jo pulled a face. 'Ooer. Well, I'll go on a recce. He was a bit vile, wasn't he? Do I dare go in?'

Sophie laughed. 'It's not Guy you need to worry about, it's Imo. She'll be tearing him off a strip.'

Jo raised her eyebrows disbelievingly, and ambled in through the back door, then froze. Sophie had been right. She could feel the tension in the muffled voices from the hallway even though she couldn't hear what they were saying. Could she back out before they realised she was there? Or would that be even more obvious than just barging in? Imogen raised her voice: 'It's just not on, Guy. All he did was flick some ice cream. He was bored, for goodness' sake.'

'Well, he should learn some bloody manners. If I'd behaved like that, I'd have been given the slipper.'

Imogen sounded almost sarcastic. 'How constructive!'

'At least it's a bit of bloody discipline, which is missing around here.' Jo wasn't surprised by his next comment. 'You're too soft on them.'

'Oh not this again.' Imogen sighed. 'Can't you see it's attention-seeking? He was so looking forward to you coming down, and now ...' Jo had heard enough and started to back away, but her sleeve caught on the open cupboard door and slammed it shut. She was rewarded with Guy's sharp, 'Is that you, Rory?'

'Er, no. It's me. Just on the look-out for a coffee.'

Imogen's face was red, as she bustled in and poured a mug for Jo, muttering vague apologies. Guy pretended to busy himself at the table, lips thinner than ever and a mutinous glare on his face but, seemingly glad of the diversion, he grunted something about packing his bag, and slunk out of the room. Jo also made a strategic withdrawal. The marital battlefield was unknown territory.

The men eventually left to go back to London – two very different leave-takings. Sophie and Hugh hugged warmly, Imogen and Guy were formally polite, like a couple from a thirties movie. The children were lavish in their affections, although Rory hung back and wouldn't look at Guy as he waved from the taxi. Jo and Finn stood to one side, out of it all, and Finn quietly slipped his hand into hers as the taxi drove out of sight. The sense of relief all round was palpable.

Later, much later that night, Jo reached over and emptied the bottle of wine into Imogen's glass. 'All the more for us, then. And I suppose Sophie does need an early night.'

Imogen bit her lip and giggled. 'Thanks, that's plenty. Yes, I'm not sure they slept much.'

'I'm not sure any of us did,' Jo snorted. 'And I, for one, was in no doubt as to what I was missing.' Jo paused, not sure if she knew Imogen well enough to say this: 'There are few things worse than hearing other people having fantastic sex.'

They lapsed into companionable silence for a while. Imogen swirled the wine in her glass, staring into it as though fascinated. 'Look, I'm sorry you were exposed to that, er, disagreement Guy and I were having earlier. It's not like him. He's got a lot on his mind at the moment.'

Jo watched her carefully, then dropped her eyes. 'Yes, well, I'm sure all couples have their moments. Rory's a great kid and he was only doing what any red-blooded boy of his age would do. In fact, I reckon he only beat Finn to it by a whisker.'

Imogen put her glass down decisively and shook her head in annoyance. 'It's so undermining to speak to a child like that. I know Rory can be a pain at times but what ten-year-old isn't? There's always a better way to handle these things than shouting. And now I've had to spend the evening bolstering Rory's confidence. It's too bloody bad of him!'

Jo sipped at her wine and looked at Imogen in surprise. 'That's fighting talk,' she commented with real admiration. 'Of course, I've never had to deal with that sort of thing. It's always been down to me – although that's pretty terrifying too.'

'But how *do* you cope?' Imogen asked. 'Guy's far from perfect, in fact sometimes he drives me mad, but he can be adorable too. And I don't know how I'd manage without him. Someone there to share the responsibility or just to listen.'

Jo was looking down. Her nails needed doing again. 'It's knackering, of course, but I do have him all to myself to enjoy. We rub along, and he's a great little mate most of the time, when he's not being a little bastard, that is.'

There was a horrified silence from Imogen, who looked as though she'd been kicked. Then, as Jo snorted at her appalling bloomer, Imogen tentatively smiled, then threw her head back and guffawed along with her.

Chapter 9

Monday

Bright and breezy

'But what if I'm hopeless? What if I fall off and look silly? Everyone will laugh.' Olivia, bottom lip pushed out, was not helping one bit in the fiddly process of being encased in a wetsuit.

'You'll be just fine. Matt will make sure you're OK.' Imogen resorted to lifting her daughter off the ground, holding on to the collar of the suit and shaking her enthusiastically in the hope that the force of gravity would enable her body to slip far enough down into the rubbery interior so she could squeeze her arms in. 'Now when I put you down, bend your knees like a policeman so the suit fits around your crotch.' She felt positively out of breath. There had to be an easier way to do this!

'What's a crotch?'

'The bit round your dangly bits.' Rory strolled round the car, his wetsuit hanging loosely at his waist in studied coolness.

'But I haven't got any dangly bits!'

'Rory, stop being crude and get your suit zipped up. Now, Ol, breathe in one more time while I get this zip up.' At last she was in, and Olivia, walking like a penguin with her crotch round her knees, waddled over to join the other children.

'Do you need a hand, Rory?' Imogen called to his departing back. 'Or I suppose you can manage,' she finished lamely, grabbing the beach basket and spades from the back of her car and slamming the door shut with an air of finality.

The beach was already quite full, and the squeals of laughter from other children carried across the sand. Many people had stripped off already, the sun quite powerful despite it being only early. Dotted all over the place were bright stripy windbreaks, umbrellas in fierce yellows and oranges, and children in swimming costumes and sun hats, digging in the sand with determination. It looked like a building site for dwarves.

'Yoo hoo!' Beyond the surf hut, she spotted Sophie frantically waving a red spade to catch her attention and indicate where she and Jo had set up camp. Gracie, like Archie too young to join in the surf lesson, sat in her pink hooded top and flowery bikini bottoms, disconsolately making circles in the sand with her fingers. Imogen and Archie waded laboriously towards her through the soft sand, like astronauts on a moonwalk and, by the time they reached them and she'd dropped the bag and spades, Imogen felt hot and sticky in her T-shirt and pedal pushers.

'What ho. Looks like they're all being briefed by that surfing Adonis over there.' Sophie shielded her eyes as she looked down the beach. 'He really is a bit yummy, Jo. I'll have him if you're not interested.' Jo looked up briefly from her book, but Imogen couldn't read her eyes from behind the sunglasses. Sophie caught Imogen's glance and winked.

'What are we going to do, Mum?'

Archie was gazing longingly across the sand to his brother, who was now battling to pull up the zip of his wetsuit. Suppressing the instinct to run down and help him, Imogen watched him struggle until Matt came to his assistance, then the little group – Rory, Olivia, Amelia and Finn, his face gazing up at Matt in rapt attention, and four other children of about the same age – all lay down on their stomachs on surfboards at the water's edge and waved theirs arms and legs about frantically.

'Great! Time for some serious sunbathing,' sighed Sophie and turned to her bag to fish out some sun cream. Imogen noticed that her flat stomach barely crinkled as she bent down, and her small breasts fell forward to fill the cups of her halter-necked bikini. She squeezed cream into her hand, and began to smooth it slowly over her freckled arms, concentrating hard. Sophie had always been slim, moving gracefully from skinny-legged waif to pocket Venus as she grew up. Imogen's gaze slide over to Jo who, laying down her book and bundling up her sweatshirt, lowered her head on to it like a pillow and let her arms fall to her sides. Her turquoise bathing costume lay smoothly over her stomach, and her legs, already beginning to tan, looked slim and shiny all the way down to her neat little painted toes.

Aware that she was standing there staring, Imogen

turned her head away quickly and glanced down at herself. She had known it would be warm – the forecast had said so – but she hadn't imagined it would be hot enough for them to strip off, and now she felt horribly overdressed. Her T-shirt pulled over her bust, and she could see the outline of her bra and the soft mounds of her boobs where they were being squeezed out the sides of the cups. The waistband of her pedal pushers was digging in, and from beneath the cut-off trousers her legs looked pale and speckled from a cursory swipe with the disposable razor last night. She felt sick, just as she had that day shopping in Bath with sixth-form girlfriends when she'd split the trousers she'd been trying on in the changing room.

She couldn't lie here feeling doughy and plump next to these two women. She grabbed the buckets and spades. 'Archie, my boy, come with me. We are going to create an Olympic medal-winning sandcastle that will be the toast of the Cornish coast. People from Newquay and beyond will be buying tickets to admire it. It might even outshine the Edam Project.' She plonked a sun hat on her bemused son's head. 'You too, Gracie. Look sharp.'

Two hours later and the three of them sat back, congratulating each other on their feat of civil engineering. The magnificent edifice stood three feet high, complete with drawbridge, arrow slits and flying buttresses. Gracie had decorated it with shells, and Archie had carefully made little crenellations along the top of each wall. Imogen was beginning to clear up when, out of the corner of her eye, she spotted Rory careering up the beach towards them, like a lightning flash in his fluorescent surf-school vest. She only just managed to put herself between the castle and eight stone of her son, before he could perform a triple jump onto the keep.

His weight knocked her backwards. 'Rory!' she shrieked. 'Don't you dare! Wreck it, and I'll kill you.'

'What is it?' he panted, falling to his knees, perilously close to the bridge and moat, and dripping like a dog. 'Cor, Arch, it's cool.' Archie looked fit to burst from such brotherly praise, until Rory began to poke his finger into the windows.

'Fingers out!' Imogen said firmly. 'Now give us a hand with this lot up the beach and tell me all about the lesson.'

The general agreement from the returned party was that surfing was the best thing ever. Even Olivia had shaken off her early-morning nerves, and was re-enacting moves they'd been taught. 'I almost managed to stand up,' she gushed enthusiastically, at which Rory caught Finn's eye and they both snorted in derision. Imogen doled out juice and a bag of Twiglets each, so as not to spoil their lunch. Jo, however, handed Finn a king-sized Mars bar.

The dark little boy sat down in the sand, breaking the bar in half, his hands covered in a mixture of sand and chocolate, and held it up so that stringy pieces of toffee dangled into his mouth. Rory simmered with envy.

'That surfing was wicked!' Finn grinned exposing

chocolate-coated teeth. 'Mum, I've just got to have the right gear. Can I have a surfboard for my birthday? Can I?' He turned to Rory. 'It's my birthday on Wednesday. What'ya going to get me?'

Imogen handed him a wet wipe from the packet in her basket. 'Is it? How exciting?' She was surprised the impending event hadn't been mentioned before. Birthdays were a constant topic of conversation in their household and Archie usually had his party sorted about eight months in advance. 'We ought to have a party to celebrate!'

'Cool! Yeah, Mum, can we?' Finn turned to Jo who was eating Quavers, her sunglasses still on her nose. 'That'd be brilliant!'

'We'll see,' she mumbled, though to Imogen it was obvious that no such idea had crossed her mind. How curious, when planning children's parties was such fun.

'Well you've come to the right place, Finn my lad,' laughed Sophie, fishing out sun cream from her bag, and applying some to Amelia's nose. 'Imogen does brilliant parties. They are famous throughout London!'

'Oh give over, Soph. You do gush.'

'Well it's true,' Sophie persisted. 'Mine are always a hired disco and catered by Sainsbury's. You did dressing-up for Ollie last year, didn't you? Jo, you should have seen it. We all had to dress up too! Bloody nightmare!'

'Personally parties terrify me,' Jo sounded nonchalant. 'I'd rather have a hundred adults round than ten little brats.'

All at once feeling stupid for being hailed an expert

at something so trivial, Imogen grasped at this as common ground. 'Oh you are so right. Kids are so judgemental, aren't they? When do they learn some tact, for goodness' sake? Imagine if adults talked like them at dinner parties: "This fish is disgusting, can I get down?"' Sophie laughed and even Jo's mouth turned up in a wry smile. 'There's one chap who does the rounds near us. Uncle George. Every wretched children's party you go to he's there, with the same old routine, same crass jokes, a sinister puppet and a box of Haribo sweets. Money for old rope I call it.'

'Yeah, but for lazy sods like me, it means we don't have to make an effort,' said Sophie. 'Us mere mortals can't keep up with the themed dos and arty parties you throw, Imo. Even your fortieth was brilliant,' and she gushed on to a clearly uninterested Jo about Imogen's birthday bash the year before.

'I agree with Imogen,' Jo interrupted. 'These party people are so popular. You have to book them so far in advance, it's like putting your children down for Eton. There was a chap like that when I was a kid – what a creep he was. Made me stand in the corridor at my own party, the bugger.' They all laughed, even Archie tittered at what he suspected was a rude word. Imogen let it pass, just relieved that for once she and Jo seemed to be on the same track.

'Ouch! Aaaaaah!' Olivia's scream burst into her thoughts. Some way away from the group, she was now hopping over towards her mother and stumbling, tears pouring down her face and blood all over her foot.

'Sweetheart, whatever has happened?' Imogen jumped to her feet, grabbing a handful of tissues from her bag. 'Have you trodden on something?'

Sobbing, Olivia let herself be lifted into Imogen's arms who sat her down on her knee, blood dripping onto her trousers, and with a tissue investigated the wound. 'I think it's clean, but it must have been some glass. Poor baby. It must hurt terribly. It's very deep and it's bleeding horribly.' She held the tissues hard against the cut, but it continued to seep through, and with the other hand she reached over for more supplies. Olivia winced each time, her tears now heaving, breathless sobs.

'Oooh that looks horrid.' Sophie peered over. 'Fancy leaving broken glass on a beach. Some people are so witless. I'll go and find it.'

Imogen looked at Jo, who was folding up the Quaver packet and tying it neatly into a knot. 'Jo, I hate to ask when you're off duty and all, but would you mind having a look? Might it need a stitch?'

Jo dropped the Quaver knot into her bag, and got to her feet, brushing the sand off her bottom. She came over to Imogen's rug and bent over Olivia's foot. 'Ooh you poor girl. Looks clean enough.' She touched the skin around it gently. 'No glass left I don't think. Imogen, have you got some mineral water to get the sand off with? Bit of antiseptic and a plaster, and it'll be fine. I take it she's up to date with her tetanus jabs? Keep up the pressure like this,' and she handed Imogen some more tissues. 'I'll go and see if Matt's got a first-aid kit, shall I?' She stood up as if to walk away.

'No, no,' Imogen delved in her bag and pulled out a little green box. 'I've got everything here. Where did you say I should press again?'

Jo stopped, and Imogen was surprised by the look of irritation on her face. 'Here, like this.' She bent down to demonstrate. 'Well, if you have everything you need, I'll leave you to it. Finn, how's about you and me have a swim?'

What was it about that woman? Imogen thought, cuddling Olivia to her and watching Jo and Finn's retreating backs. She really thought they were getting somewhere, and suddenly Jo had cooled the atmosphere. What a strange relationship she had with that child. So imbalanced and precocious somehow. It was as if Finn had fast-tracked childhood, and he was left with none of the best bits to savour. She looked over at Rory, who'd wandered back down to the castle with Archie. Then an idea came into her head.

Once the children had changed, they all went outside into the garden to re-enact their triumphs of the morning's surfing, laughing and chattering loudly, and all the more so because all of them – even determinedly nonchalant Rory – had been full of trepidation about the lesson. Matt's gentle coaxing had taken care of that, though.

Jo and Sophie busied themselves creating lunch, following Imogen's instructions, given with painstaking detail before she'd disappeared outside to make some calls. Olivia was hobbling around gallantly, with a large plaster on her foot, but joined in with the surfing drill Rory was directing on the grass like a sergeant-major. 'Paddle, paddle, paddle. Wave coming. Press-up position. Jump yer legs through. One knee. And up! Slide and trim.'

Chopping carrots, Sophie shook her head in wry amusement and glanced back at Jo, who was grating cheese. 'Look at them on the storm-tossed lawn. They're so funny. Ooh! Archie and Grace are joining in. Hang on a sec.' She wiped her hands on her shorts and darted out of the room, coming back moments later with the little camera she took everywhere.

'How many have you taken so far?' asked Jo, brushing the last flakes of cheese off the cutting board into a glass bowl, before turning her attention to the tomatoes. 'I keep forgetting to take my camera out with us. Mind you, it's a revolting great thing. Really macho-looking, with a huge lens that slides in and out in a horribly suggestive way. I've no idea how to use it. Come on, Soph, you're the expert. Show me how. You keep promising but you never get round to it.'

Sophie was snapping away through the open back door. 'Oh, I'll show you tonight, if you like. Once you understand the basics, it's not that hard. Mind you, it's an awful lot easier when you've got exquisitely beautiful subjects, like our little sprogs. You should have seen some of the gargoyles that used to come to the studio. Ugly chairmen and their uglier children and horse-faced wives.'

'Oh don't shatter my illusions! I always imagined you

as the Mario Testino of the Essex Road, all double espresso and "make love to the camera for me, lovey". No wonder you gave it all up.'

Sophie turned and gave a secret smile. 'Actually,' she began slowly, 'I've got some hot news. I'm joining the ranks of the working mummies again. My old boss Nigel has asked me if I want to go back. I'll have to go all digital, of course. It's going to cost a bomb, and I haven't dared broach that one with Hughie yet … but now the girls are in school I'm itching to get back to it actually …'

Jo was surprised. 'And I had you down as a Starbucker, whiling your days away with a skinny double de-caff latte and a bunch of other yummy-mummies until pick-up time.'

Sophie laughed knowingly. 'Well, shame on you, Doctor, for making snap diagnoses. That's a habit you want to get out of, y'know. No, I do love my girls, but it's so much easier now they're not ankle biters any more. Glad I've got all that arse-wiping over with.'

From the depths of the fridge, Jo's voice floated out. 'I delegated that one to Thelma,' she said abstractedly. 'Did she say to heat up the refried beans or the guacamole? I wasn't really listening.'

'Not listening! Shame on you. Oh, that was a nice one. Got them all looking up at the same time. They haven't realised I'm taking them yet. Isn't it funny the way kids instantly start gurning when you point a camera at them? Refried beans, idiot. Guacamole's always cold.' Suddenly Sophie sounded doubtful. 'Isn't it? I don't really want to go and ask her. She's on the phone to Guy yet again.'

Jo emerged from the fridge. 'I think that's everything,' she said, stripping clingfilm from the pots Imogen had stowed there earlier. 'Wonder if Finn'll eat this. He's never had tacos. Don't want another mushroom moment. I can't take the pressure.' She looked over at Sophie with a conspiratorial grin, but was met instead with an appraising look.

'Jo, you were really off with poor Imo after Olivia's foot thing, you know. Just hared off and left her sitting there. Do you not like her?'

Jo sighed deeply. This was going to be a tricky one. Of course, Imogen having the first-aid kit to hand was entirely laudable, but at the same time so intensely irritating and so typical! And worse still it had deprived Jo of a perfect excuse to seek out Matt – though she felt mildly ashamed for even wanting an excuse. 'Look, it was like I said. Olivia clearly didn't need a stitch, and knowing Imogen, her jabs are bound to be up to date. What was the point of fussing?'

'Maybe,' said Sophie, rolling up the clingfilm that Jo had discarded and throwing it in the bin. 'But don't you think you should have stuck around?'

Sophie had never challenged her like this before. She was normally such a sweet little thing, but Jo could tell she was going to have to defend herself.

She sighed in exasperation. 'Look, you don't know what it's like being a GP. As soon as anyone finds out, they start banging on about their piles and bunions. I spend all day at work looking down ears and up fannies. I came on

185

holiday to get away from all that. It wasn't serious, all right? If it had been, of course I would have suggested A&E, but it just wasn't. Jeez, what do you think I am?'

Sophie looked hard at her for a moment, then shrugged and looked out of the window. 'I just think it's a weird way to act with a friend. It was almost as if you couldn't wait to get away.'

Jo sat in a chair and let her head flop backwards. Friend! Was that really what she thought? That they could all wash up here together in Cornwall, with all their differences and needs, and they would instantly bond into a cosy little matriarchal unit? God, Sophie could be strange sometimes, almost child-like in her naivety. Never mind rose-tinted spectacles, Sophie seemed to have been born with rose-tinted corneas. It must be lovely to be like that – so easily pleased. Her serotonin levels must be off the scale.

She tried another tack. 'Doesn't Hughie get fed up with people asking him about their houses at dinner parties? Whether they should convert the loft, or extend at the back? Doesn't that piss him off?'

'Well, yes. A bit. But, Jo, houses aren't the same as children. When your child is in pain, if feels like the world is coming to an end. You must know that.'

Jo felt a tightness in her stomach and her hands went cold. She knew only too well. She took a deep breath and looked away. It would take a lifetime and more to get the image out of her head of Finn's tiny body, wired and monitored, inside the prem incubator. Time to end this conversation. She shrugged and tried to look penitent.

'I'm sorry. I suppose I'm just a bit tired and, erm, well I've got a lot of sorting out to do for Finn's birthday. I'll check Olivia out later, honest.'

'Of course!' Sophie breathed conspiratorially. 'What have you got planned? Are you going out shopping this afternoon? What fun! I love shopping for the girls' pressies. Are you going to do party bags too?'

God! Party bags. What new torment was this? Jo wasn't even planning on doing a party here, let alone bags. She'd already negotiated with Finn a cinema party and a toy shop blow-out when they got home. 'Oh I don't want to make too much fuss. I mean, the number of parties I've been to where mothers have gone to all the trouble to make plates of hummus on wholemeal, when years of experience have shown that all kids eat at birthday teas is Hula Hoops, chocolate fingers and grapes!'

Sophie considered this for a moment, thoughtfully shredding a lettuce. 'We all know it's daft, but perhaps it's just a part of showing the kids how much we care.'

'No, it's a way of showing *other people* how much you care.' Jo warmed to her subject. 'Then they feel they have to do it too, and so it goes on. No one wants to be the mother who doesn't make the pointless sandwiches. Women don't need society to oppress them. We do it ourselves.'

'Jo, you do make me laugh,' giggled Sophie. 'The way you can get so cross about a poor inoffensive sandwich! A party would be great. You know it would.' She was all excited now. 'We'll keep Finn out of the way after lunch, don't worry. I'll make up some story about where you've gone. And I'll help you wrap everything tomorrow once they're all in bed.'

Jo gave Sophie a weak smile and got up to carry some dishes to the table. 'That'd be great. Thanks.'

Well, she'd got out of the 'bad doctor' thing but how was she going to pull off 'good mummy'? Two days until Finn turned ten, and she'd now have to come up with something wrapped and delicious for the birthday morning that would impress not just Finn, but everyone in the blasted house. This might take a bit of imagination. What on earth could she get down here that would justify this level of expectation? A bag of local fudge? Shit. She'd have to come up with something better, or it'd be *nul points* for her yet again.

She finished laying the table as Sophie poured squash, then went to call the kids who came bounding in, famished after their morning's exertions. But where was Imogen? Jo walked round the side of the house to see if she was out by the cars. Yes there she was, on her mobile, by the gate but with her back turned.

Jo walked over, her footsteps muffled by the grass, to semaphore that lunch was ready, but stopped short as she detected the strain in Imogen's voice. '... I wish you could have seen them, Guy. Hello? Are you still there? You've gone faint again. They were all so ... No, I just wanted to tell you about the ... No. Yes, I do realise. I just thought you'd like to hear ... Yes, all right. Yes, do that, please. What time do you ...? OK, whatever. Well, I'll be in all evening, won't I? Right, bye.'

What to do? She didn't want to catch Imogen

unawares so she quickly kicked a stone and sent it skittering across the driveway. Imogen spun round, and within a split second her face changed from distress to an over-bright smile. 'Oh, is lunch ready? Lovely. Just telling Guy about the children's surf lesson. He's so sad he missed it. He'd have been out there with his camcorder getting it all down for posterity. He loves to hear about what they've been doing.'

A stab of sympathy caught Jo by surprise, and she flicked her gaze away quickly. When she turned back, Imogen was re-tying her hair with a pink scrunchie she'd had round her wrist. 'I expect they keep him pretty busy at work, don't they?'

Imogen nodded wordlessly, her eyes suspiciously bright, and Jo continued slowly, not sure where exactly she was taking the conversation. 'Funny things men, though, aren't they? So single- minded. They compart-mentalise their lives so easily.'

Imogen seemed to address herself. 'I know he's busy, but one call to the HR department about Hong Kong can't take that long, can it?' She shook herself and went on irritably. 'Sometimes, he could be a million miles away from what's going on around him.'

Jo felt uncomfortable. She wasn't sure any response from her was necessary or wanted. 'Olivia seems all right now. I'll take a look at her foot later, if you like. But there was nothing that needed, you know … nothing I could have done that you couldn't.'

It was clear that Imogen wasn't really listening. As Jo watched, she squared her shoulders, then rubbed her hands briskly. 'Righto. Lunch then. Lead me to it. I do love Mexican food, don't you? Did you warm the taco shells, by the way? Never mind, won't take long. Then we can start making plans for your lovely boy's birthday.'

Here we go again. Jo shook her head slowly, and followed Imogen into the house.

An hour and a half later, Jo slouched out of the door to go shopping, rubbing her stomach. God, she'd eaten far too much again. But it had been such a challenge seeing how much you could stuff into a taco shell before it cracked in half. Maybe she could try it at home, with Finn. She got slowly into the car, winding down all the windows to get rid of the hot-apple-core smell – where had that got lodged? – and drove off moodily, heading for the big supermarket where she'd bought Finn's sandals. She hoped inspiration would strike there.

The results were disappointing. No doubt Imogen would have thought about presents months in advance, and have it all ordered, delivered and wrapped in plenty of time. This was now not so much a birthday as Judgement Day. No wonder communes had died out. Imagine all those poor old hippy mums having to parade their tie-dyeing and lentil-cooking skills for other families to scrutinise. Spotting a road sign for Tregant Bay, it suddenly hit her. Of course!

Jo struggled to find a parking space, and eventually squeezed between two VW campers. The shop door was open. Good. She unzipped her make-up bag – yuck, the lipgloss was warm and sticky – and touched up before she slid out of the car, smoothing the creases out of her short denim skirt. She saw him first, through a knot of customers trying on sunglasses. God, he looked fabulous. But she was gratified to see his eyes flash when he caught sight of her, then narrow again into his usual inscrutable gaze. She noticed him glance beyond her, presumably to look for the others, then when he realised she was on her own, he treated her to one of his teasing smiles. 'Dr Newman, I presume? To what do I owe this honour?'

To kiss or not to kiss? No, let him make the effort. She leant across the counter, allowing him a waft of her perfume. 'I am here on a mission. It's Finn's birthday on Wednesday. He's going to be ten.'

'God, I loved being ten. Having a party?'

'Oh don't you start too!' Then she smiled slowly. Should she? Why not! 'Yes, yes we are, as a matter of fact. In the afternoon. Would you like to come?'

Matt paused for a moment, and scratched his cheek. 'I'd love to,' he replied. 'Although it'll have to be later rather than earlier. I'll be busy with a class, but I'd go a long way for a piece of birthday cake. Where are you staying?'

Cake. Oh God, here was something else to think about. She smiled silkily, and gave him directions. Naturally, this involved standing rather close, and leaning over to write the details on a scrap of paper he tore out of a notebook for her, using a pen she took out of his shirt pocket. She could feel his eyes on her bare shoulders as she bent forwards and she smiled secretly to herself.

'Am I going to be able to read your writing? I could never have been a medic. My handwriting is terminally neat, I'm afraid.' He gestured to the hand-lettered labels around the shop. In a firm, stylish italic, they weren't what Jo would have expected. And the spelling and apostrophes were immaculate too.

She straightened up slowly. 'Here's the thing. I'd like to get him something and I was wondering if you could give me some suggestions. He says he'd like a surfboard. What do you think?'

Matt looked dubious. 'Well you could, I suppose, but I wouldn't really recommend it. I mean, it's not like you're going to be down here for long, and you won't get any use out of it at home. Not many rollers on the Serpentine, as I recall.'

Jo felt strangely crestfallen, as if she'd been dismissed as a dilettante, just passing through. And the fact that he was exactly right made it somehow worse. They stood in silence for a moment, Matt seemed to be thinking but Jo was quite blank. After a moment, he spoke again. 'How about his own steamer? He was going on about how cool it looked, and he can use it any time he goes in the sea. I've got some nice ones here, new in. If we get a ... let's see ... a size five, that'll probably do him for a bit. He's quite a scrap, isn't he? Most kids have to struggle to get into theirs, but not him.'

Jo bristled. What was he driving at? 'I do feed him, y'know.'

He stopped and turned round to look at her quizzically. 'Youch! Would you mind spitting my head out when you've finished biting it off? He's a skinny kid. Fact. Better that than fat. That's not intended as a reflection on you. Although ...'

Jo felt herself blush, as Matt's appraising eye swept over her. 'Although?'

He smiled slowly. 'Reflecting on you sounds like time well spent, now I come to think about it. Tell me, do you fancy having a go while you're down here? Shame to waste the opportunity. I'll take you out, if you want to have a try. Private session, on me.'

The time it took her to realise he was only suggesting surfing was fractionally too long to pass off, and she stammered, 'I'm … What do …? I don't think so. I'd be hopeless, probably. Isn't it hard to learn, as an adult?' Fortunately he had turned away and was rummaging in a pile of huge cardboard boxes with courier labels on them.

'Everything's harder to learn as an adult.' He squatted on the floor and opened one with a Swiss Army knife he took from his pocket. 'But if you really want something, you'll put in the effort. It's just tricky to find the time, when you're working.'

'I suppose you're lucky, then, doing something you really love.' She placed her hand lightly on his shoulder and leant over to admire the new wetsuits, still wrapped in plastic. 'That one's nice, with the turquoise panels.'

'Yes, I do love what I'm doing and I reckon that gives me a lot of energy for other things, but it's still hard to fit everything in. But don't you love your work? It must be amazing, knowing how you can help people. You're really making a difference. That's the only thing I question myself about, when things aren't going so well, I wonder what I'm really contributing. You can't be in any doubt about that, at least.'

Jo thought back to the morning and Olivia's foot and winced slightly. 'It's not always as straightforward as you might think.'

Chapter 10

Tuesday

Hot and bright, becoming
muggy and close later

Damn damn, bloody damn. Was she the *only* one who picked up towels off the sodding bathroom floor? The room smelt strongly of Jo's perfume, grassy and expensive, which annoyed Imogen even more. It was the type of fragrance she would never have had the confidence to buy. Imogen threw open the window, then sluiced out the bath, running a J-cloth soaked in cleaning fluid around the bottom, urging the stubborn grains of sand washed off the children's bodies last night down the plughole.

Standing up carefully, she glanced out of the window. The sun was serious already, and the sky was devoid of anything except a crisp blueness that could only intensify. The morning promised a perfect July day. Imogen wasn't feeling up to it.

She'd known she wouldn't feel up to it when she'd woken just after three, with that imperative one couldn't ignore that one had to get out of bed. Sure enough, a grope across the landing to the bathroom, including a stumble over Finn's discarded trainer at the top of the stairs, revealed that her period had started.

Like most irritations in life, Imogen viewed her period (or 'the curse' as her mother coyly referred to it) as something that had to be tolerated and in silence. She couldn't abide the sort of women who felt impelled to share the pattern and detail of their menstrual cycle with anyone who'd listen. No, Imogen prided herself on being discreet and stalwart, hiding her tampons in a tasteful washbag in the bathroom at home, to avoid Olivia's snooping. Plenty of time to explain all that. All she hoped was that the poor girl wouldn't inherit the pain that went with hers. She knew within a couple of hours she'd be bent double and feeling quite nauseous.

Naturally she'd never complained about it. Her mother used to tell her to 'scrub the floor, dear – works wonders for cramps'. As for Guy, anything to do with *that* kind of thing held no interest for him at all. It wasn't even that he treated it with disgust. The only time the subject was ever raised was when it precluded sex, or when, just after Archie was born, she'd had to ask him to buy some of those ghastly night-time sanitary towels. The experience of having to do the supermarket shopping at all has been enough of a challenge for him – her mother had held the domestic fort after Rory and Olivia's birth, but a nasty dose of shingles had kept her away for the third – and almost inevitably he had come back with incontinence pads instead.

Sitting down on the top step of the stairs, she hugged her knees to her chest. Some people really did make a fuss though. Some of her London friends, their birth stories now way back in the past and exhausted from the telling, had reverted back to period-talk, only this time chat about pre-menopausal symptoms was beginning to loom large. A couple of her posher friends had their own gynaecologists, like other people have personal trainers. The possession of one seemed to be the height of glamour and yet faintly indulgent, as if having your fanny inspected was less offensive if it took place in a consulting room near Harley Street with an oak desk and *Country Life* in the waiting room. It helped too if it was carried out by an avuncular figure in a three-piece suit and half-rimmed spectacles who called you 'm'dear'.

She yawned, from nausea more than tiredness. Best thing was to think about something else. Had Guy remembered Sandra, the cleaner's, money? Of course, she realised suddenly, Sandra wasn't working today, which was a blow because the children's rooms at home had hit 'disaster' on her personal Richter scale. As far as Imogen was concerned there was a fine line between creative mess and downright chaos, and she wasn't very comfortable with either.

Sophie's kitchen, on the rare occasions Imogen visited, was always strewn with school backpacks and ballet bags. Hugh's boots were always under the table and coats hung layer upon layer on the backs of chairs. The fridge – adorned with Sophie's photos, witty cartoons and wittier fridge magnets, Amelia's quaint drawings and family pictures – looked more like a piece of modern art and gave Imogen the vapours. She wanted nothing more than

197

to swipe her hand over it and clear everything away. Deep down she rather envied Sophie's laissez-faire – at school she'd tried for ages to decorate her five-year diary to look like her friend's, with hearts and David Cassidy stickers, but had given up when her innate sense of order would not permit the necessary element of anarchy needed for collage. She knew she wouldn't be able to tolerate Sophie's lifestyle for long. In fact, she wasn't sure that ten days living with it in this house hadn't already stretched her patience to the limit.

Her mobile buzzed in her pocket. Perhaps that was Guy now. He'd barely talked about Hong Kong again when he'd called last night, despite her proddings, and she had eventually handed over the phone to Rory so he could tell his dad all about the surfing. It didn't matter. She'd resigned herself to doing her own research about schools and places to live at an internet café she'd found in Wadebridge.

Her heart sank as she registered the caller's number on her phone. It was her mother.

And barely eight o'clock at that. Damn her for making the assumption that her daughter must be up and around if she was. And damn her again for being right.

'Darling! It's me. How is it? Daddy saw the forecast last night and it looked as if you were going to have some sunshine. Not as much as us of course. You should have come here – it's been idyllic, we've had to water the herbaceous borders like demons. What's the house like? Are the children enjoying it?'

'Woah, Mum, slow down there. One question at a

time. House is lovely. Weather is even better, and the children are exhausted but happy.' Well, that was putting one hell of a spin on it, but it was a necessity with her mother to paint each situation in a rosy glow, partly because she had not the slightest interest in catastrophe of any kind. During one rarely permitted phone call home from school, Imogen remembered, she'd made the admission to her mother that she was a teensy bit unhappy. For once she'd wanted to be one of the fragile ones, to be cherished and cosseted and, tears pricking behind her eyes, she'd run off a stream of woes.

'Bad luck, darling. You'll be fine,' had been the abrupt response, and her mother had moved swiftly on to another subject. Imogen knew now that she was guilty of painting every situation as beyond perfection because the last person in the world to whom she wanted to admit failure was her mother. Bastion of the Guildford bench and charity fundraiser par excellence, always dressed right for the occasion, her mother despised weakness in anything. And her daughter had long ago learnt never to show it.

'Sophie's down here as you know, with Amelia and Gracie,' she went on, '… you remember them. We had them over to lunch one day when you were staying with us and Gracie was just walking. Hugh's an architect. That's right. Blond as anything. Oh and there's a friend of hers here too with her son.' She could hear the next question before her mother voiced it.

'No, no husband. Just on their own. Guy and Hugh came down last weekend,' she hurried on, 'and are back on Friday. The children have been surfing,' and she began to detail Rory and Ollie's exploits, chatting swiftly to maintain her mother's interest.

'One thing I'll say for you, darling, you certainly keep them busy. You and your brothers used to be quite happy just pottering on the beach. They'll never learn to amuse themselves, you know, if you organise their every waking moment.'

'Oh, it's just a bit of fun,' Imogen muttered defensively, cut off at the knees once again.

'Now,' her mother drew breath, 'Edie Parkes lives close to where you're staying.' She sounded imperious, always seeming to know the 'right' people in every county. 'Somewhere a bit further down on the coast, I think. She'd love to see you and the children, I'm sure. Haven't seen her for donkey's years, since Ralph died in fact, but we exchange Christmas cards. Tell you what, I'll call her, shall I?'

Imogen stalled her, seeing her Cornish holiday being hijacked from Surrey. 'I don't think we'll have time really. Actually, Mother, while you're on …' and she diverted her with something right off the subject.

By the time she'd eventually got rid of her, and heaved herself to her feet, the stomach cramps had worsened. It was only a couple of hours since the last paracetamol so she would just have to ride it out for a while. A cup of tea might help, though the thought of breakfast made her want to gag. The kitchen was chaotic, the debris from the children's cereal and toast still strewn across the table, the butter pat decimated – smeared all over the dish – and Jo was alone amongst the detritus, pen in hand, writing a list. She looked up.

'Hello. Where have you been hiding? I thought you might have gone out to forage, when of course it's my turn to shop today. I've got to get stuff for Finn's birthday. Any last requests? I've put more loo-roll on already – those kids must be using it for some nefarious purpose, we're getting through so much – and I notice from your … rota list that it's pasta tonight so I'll get some fresh. Do you think they might eat prawns with it? I need to get a birthday card too. Hey,' she paused, midway through picking up her coffee cup. 'You're looking a bit green around the gills. Sit down. Hope it's nothing I've cooked.'

Imogen remained standing and put the kettle on, reaching for the teabags and the pot. 'I wish that were all. I've been talking to my mother on the phone, which is never the recommended way to start a day.'

'God yes, mothers. We holidayed with mine once.' Half-heartedly Jo started to stack the cereal bowls. 'It nearly ended our relationship for ever. By the time we parted at Victoria Station, I almost handed her over to the police for her own protection in case I strangled her.'

Imogen smiled weakly and flexed her fingers menacingly. 'I'd do the same to mine if she was near enough. What's yours like?'

Jo snorted derisively. 'A piece of work. She's had one relationship after another since my dad buggered off, and each man has been worse than the last. She's become a total doormat.' Fighting the urge to heave, Imogen made herself listen. This was more than she'd ever heard Jo reveal about herself and she was intrigued. 'Don't suppose your mum's like that, is she?' Jo asked, licking jam from her fingers.

'Ha! Mine's a professional Surrey wife and grandmother and mother-in-law. An all-round great big bully.' Gosh, where had that come from? She'd never really thought it consciously but smiled to herself when she realised she'd got it just right. She looked up just as Jo looked quickly back down at her list.

'You do look a bit peaky, though.' Imogen was surprised by the concern in Jo's voice. 'Bad night?'

'Bit, but hey it's your holiday and I know how you lot switch off out of surgery hours.' She'd made that all too plain yesterday on the beach.

'We'd never escape if we didn't, but forget that. This morning the doctor's in. Whassup?' And so Imogen found herself, rather falteringly, discussing her menstrual cycle with the last woman on the planet she thought she would. Jo asked a couple of pretty direct questions, some uncomfortably intimate but, as expected, her response was non-committal – she wasn't her patient after all.

'God, Imogen, I can't believe you've been putting up with this for over twenty-five years,' she said, patting Imogen on the arm as she reached for the smeary butter dish. 'There are no prizes for being a stoic, you know.' And she mentioned a couple of over-the-counter remedies to relieve the pain.

By the time everything was cleared away, and Imogen had run to ground the children's swimming things and chivvied them all into the cars, they made the surf class with only moments to spare. Finding Finn's sandals had taken the most time. He hadn't been sure where he'd left them, and Jo hadn't put them out before she'd gone to the shops, so there had had to be an all patrols' bulletin to search under beds and behind car seats. Convinced they must be in Jo's car, Imogen was not feeling well disposed towards anything or anyone.

'Hello, surfers,' Matt called across the beach, striding on long legs towards them. 'Oh Rory, carry that for your mother.' Rory meekly took the towels from Imogen's arms. 'Finn old mate,' he ruffled the boy's hair, 'how are you doing? Where are your sandals? I've got to make some calls later, so Dan the Man will be taking your group today. Now look sharp, cos he's no time for shirkers,' and the kids ran across the sand to Dan who was waiting at the water's edge with the boards.

'My turn to do a bit of perfect mothering this morning, Imo,' said Sophie, dumping her bags beside Imogen's in the sand. 'Come on, Gracie, Archie. Follow me for an innings of French cricket,' and she tiptoed off, with Archie dragging the bat behind him, making a wavy line in the sand in his wake.

Imogen shook out the fleecy rug – a typically practical Christmas present from her mother – and eased herself onto it, poured some coffee from the flask in her basket, and sat sipping it, watching the children at the water's edge. Rory was standing, hand on one hip, beside Finn, who had his arms crossed, but both were listening carefully as Dan demonstrated balance techniques. Olivia was hopping from one foot to another, never able to keep still. Perhaps it was cold by the water? Imogen cast about her for inspiration. There was nothing she could supply to warm her up that wouldn't be soaked within seconds. Over to her left she could hear Sophie shrieking in consternation in the distance as Archie bowled her out and danced with glee. She battled with the guilt that she should be over there with them. Archie might wonder why she was sitting on her own, something he'd rarely seen his mother do, but just now she didn't feel up to it.

'Bit of peace, hey?' She hadn't heard Matt come up behind her, but he plonked himself down on the rug, and rested his arms loosely on his bent knees. She found herself offering him a cup of coffee.

'Just had one thanks. I had to call work. Bit of confusion about some of next year's courses and they needed it settled for the students.' He looked over at the surfing group.

'Crumbs, that's working quite far in advance. I thought it was you who organised the courses, but I suppose details need to go up on the internet for next summer's bookings …'

He looked round at her quizzically, then his face lit up as he realised that they were talking at cross purposes. 'Oh no, not here!' He smiled broadly then looked back down the beach at the children, who were now wading waist deep into the waves. 'Nooo, this is just my summer beach-bum existence. I do earn an honest living the rest of the time. I even wear shoes, sometimes.' They both looked at his toes as he wiggled them in the sand. 'I love the summer down here,' he went on, 'with everyone so relaxed and in holiday mood.' I wish, Imogen thought. 'But I don't think I'd have many customers on a wet Wednesday in November and that wouldn't pay the rent.' He smiled at her, his eyes crinkling with warm amusement. What a lovely bloke, she thought.

'Here.' She dug out a packet of biscuits.

'Ginger nuts! Haven't had these since I was a boy – scrumptious!' And he stuffed a whole one into his mouth and grinned inanely.

'That's what mothers are for. Permanent distributors of biscuits. Now tell me what keeps you off the streets in November.' They chatted together for a while, or at least Imogen asked the questions and he supplied the answers. Matt had an easy, self-deprecating manner, and seemed quite unfazed by her customary interrogation. She didn't really think she was doing him justice at all, in fact, but the painkillers were beginning to wear off and she could feel the cramps increasing again. She knew too that she ought to find a loo. All she really wanted to do was to curl up at home, in London, on her own bed, or lock herself in her bathroom. Not in some over-populated holiday house with thin curtains and tacky furniture. She stood up carefully and began to gather her things together.

She glanced at Matt, who had stood up too and was now watching something over her shoulder. As she turned she spotted Jo, as he had, making her way through the families settled in little islands of beach rugs and cool boxes on the beach. It was unmistakable, his look of interest, almost fascination, as he watched her coming their way. Jo seemed unconscious of being watched, and her hips in a wrap-around batik-print skirt sashayed as she caught her balance on the moving sand under her bare feet. In one hand she carried her sandals and a carrier bag, and with the other she held up her skirt. Her hair was up under a little beanie hat, and her eyes were covered with sunglasses.

Half an hour later, Imogen slipped out of the hot seat of her car in a side street in Wadebridge, trying not to let any bare flesh touch the leather. She had almost changed her mind about coming to find the internet café at all, the lure of her bed had been so great but, after Jo's unexpected help, she had decided to take the detour. She had finally found the place and at first it had been quite a relief to sit under its cool fans, a cold lemonade to hand and a screen in front of her. But as she searched website after website to reveal what lay ahead for the family she began to feel jittery with anticipation.

The pictures were exotic, but strangely exciting: views of the city with skyscrapers lit at night and reflected on to the water of the harbour; cheery Oriental faces beaming out at her; prices in dollars the exchange rate for which she was clueless about, and all this wrapped in a veneer of glamour and perfection. So at odds with her sitting here in tracksuit trousers and a T-shirt on a sunny day in a café in Cornwall that smelt strongly of espresso.

The Hong Kong schools looked more like hotels. Guy, of course, hadn't mentioned schools. She'd have to ask whether his office could use some influence to get the children in. Would they settle? Would they have to learn

Chinese? Would they ever make friends? There seemed to be loads of choice and her mind became boggled. Then a sentence made her pause. 'A multitude of towering apartment complexes are what most ex-pat families call home.' Crumbs, it was hard enough containing the children with only a handkerchief-sized garden in Barnes.

'You holidaying there or some't?' said a voice beside her, and she turned to face a bloke marginally younger then her, and dressed in a yellow T-shirt and long grey shorts. From what Imogen could see, he was looking at sites to do with rock music.

'Um … no actually.' She tried not to be mesmerised by his pierced eyebrow and bottom lip. God, that must be painful, and she touched her own lips absently as if in sympathy. 'My husband's job is moving us out there.' The words sounded scary and final.

'Lucky you.' He turned back to his screen. 'Fantastic place. Lived there for a few months a while back. Great restaurants and nightlife. Bags of things to do, and lots of cheap shops selling fake Rolex.' He brandished his arm. 'Go on, see if you can tell the difference. Nah. You'll have a ball.'

'Oh that's interesting.' Imogen tried to keep his attention. 'What about schools and houses? Do you know anything about them?'

'God no. I dossed on a friend's floor most of the time, and I suppose there must be families somewhere, lots of posh ex-pats like er … you, but I never saw them.' And he turned his attention back to the screen.

Imogen disconnected and picked up her bag to leave,

her mind buzzing. Driving licences, visas. Would they need vaccinations? And shipping their stuff – would they do that? She'd have to make the mother of all lists. There was so much to think about, she thought heading out of the door. What she needed was a soothing diversion. Something to do while she thought it all through. Something to take her mind off the cramps. She paused and smiled. She knew the perfect thing.

When Jo arrived, the beach was hotting up, and she peered through the miasma of coconut-perfumed heat that hung over the acres of sand. The tide was right out so, despite the crowds now building steadily, it didn't feel full. The little denim hat she had bought was next to useless at keeping the sun off, but it worked quite well with the curls she had teased out from underneath, and she had slapped on plenty of sun cream.

She climbed onto a rock and slowly surveyed the beach, feet widely planted and her hand shielding her eyes. She had clocked Matt immediately of course, sitting next to Imogen on that rug. What were they talking about? she wondered. And why wasn't he taking the children's class like yesterday? She didn't want to go over to them straight away. Couldn't look too keen, but if he was working later he might have to leave, and then she'd miss him altogether. She really needed to get Imogen on her own, but she couldn't go over there and drive Matt away. He might not come back. Oh this was bloody exhausting. No wonder she never normally bothered to get involved with blokes. It was too much like hard work.

Imogen unintentionally came to her aid, getting up slowly from the rug and easing her back. It looked like she was making a move to leave. Matt had stood up too and was helping to gather her scattered belongings, and Jo felt a rush of warmth as she watched him stoop and pick up the thermos, then slip it neatly into Imogen's big straw bag. What a gent. She took her cue and sauntered over. 'Hello, sorry I'm a bit late. Took me a while to find what I wanted.'

Matt straightened up and greeted her casually. Point to him. She bestowed a smile and turned back to Imogen, 'Are you off? Shall I carry this bag back to the car for you?'

Imogen's look of surprise at this offer was a bit irritating, but she recovered herself and accepted, turning to say goodbye to Matt with a friendly smile. 'See you tomorrow, then, Matt. I've so enjoyed our conversation. I hope I haven't kept you from your phone calls. Take care.'

Matt headed up the beach with them for a little, veering off towards the café as she and Imogen headed for the car park. Jo held Imogen's bag patiently as she opened the boot, then dumped it unceremoniously into the immaculately clean interior. 'Now, Imogen, what we were talking about earlier,' Jo started without preamble. 'No, don't dismiss it. There's absolutely no reason you should have to put up with this level of discomfort. Why not sort it out before you go abroad? Now try this.' She produced from her bag a little brown glass flask. 'Fraxinus tincture. I know, I know. Alternative bullshit it may be, but it worked for me. A friend from med school, who's gone over to the dark side and is a full-time homeopath, recommended it. Drops in water – the dose is on the bottle. Give it a go.'

Imogen, her face stunned, took the tiny offering and looked at Jo, almost in puzzlement, staring as if seeing her for the first time. 'Thank you,' she said simply. 'I really … Thank you so much.'

'Well, er, you might as well get going, before Archie feels the tug on the old umbilicus. See you later.' Jo filled the awkward silence brusquely, and turned away, waving in an off-hand manner as she strode back down to the beach.

But Matt had disappeared back into his office. Jo pretended to fiddle with her sandal. Yup, she could definitely see movement in there. Well, she wasn't going to seek him out. She'd just have to wait. Now where was Sophie? Jo ambled back down to where Imogen had been encamped. There was the rug, forlorn without its chatelaine. Jo settled down and glanced about her, immediately picking out the children in their fluorescent surf vests in the water, visibly more confident today. And here was Sophie, skipping back, with Archie holding one hand and Grace the other, a bag of plastic beach toys bumping against her side as she galumphed ever closer.

Jo suppressed a smile. Good old Sophie never seemed to worry how she appeared to other people. She was just herself, and others could take her or leave her. Maybe that was, in reality, the epitome of cool – being unafraid of being uncool. Yet Sophie always looked fantastic.

Whatever it was that lit her from within, it was something Jo had never managed to achieve.

'Phew, I'm all cricketed out.' Sophie flung herself down on the rug. 'It never looks very hard work, does it, when you see it on TV? Quite sedate, really, but I'm baking. I bet my face is as red as a beetroot, isn't it?' Sophie wiped at the sweat on her face with the end of her T-shirt.

'More like raspberry purée,' Jo answered dryly. 'That's why I never do any exercise if I can possibly avoid it. Pilates is about as aerobic as I ever get, at least in public.'

'Ooh Pilates. How super duper trendy you are, Jo. I got a Pilates video once. Sent me to sleep. I thought the machine had gone wrong and it was on pause or something. "Zip up and hollow" indeed. It was like watching paint dry.'

'You want to go to a class,' laughed Jo, 'or even better do what my friend Becca does. She has this man who comes to her house and puts her through her paces. It's far trendier than having a tennis coach these days.'

Sophie snorted coarsely. 'I'll *bet* he puts her through her paces. How else could he tell if her pelvic floor was getting stronger?'

'Oh really!' Jo rolled her eyes. 'She invited me over to have a go once. It was all perfectly above board, I can assure you. Bit too earnest for my liking, actually.'

Sophie sat up and stripped off the pink T-shirt, then lay down on her back. 'Why doesn't somebody invent tits that don't disappear under your armpits when you lie down?'

'I think they already have,' Jo muttered, turning over on to her front and reaching back to undo the straps of her bikini. 'It's called silicon. I had a patient once with them. But d'ya know, I don't think most men could care less. It's availability they want, not quality. Or even quantity. In fact any "titty" will do.'

'But they can always find a new pair to take home. We're stuck with ours. Once you've had a baby, it all goes to pot, doesn't it?' Sophie looked down ruefully at her chest. 'Tits start the long journey south, and you get stretchmarks like a map of the London Underground, only less useful. Tummy all stretched out of shape, not to mention your fanny, and the start of varicose veins. Look at that, Jo,' she waved a leg in the air and gesticulated in the vague area of her flawless knee. 'It's downhill all the way from the moment sperm meets egg.'

'Darn tootin'.' Jo grunted. 'I'm the living proof.'

Sophie rolled on to her side, frowning in consternation, and missing the point entirely. 'Oh bollocks, Jo. You're gorgeous. In fact, you're the only genuine yummy-mummy I know. You must just be genetically glam. Have you any idea how irritating that can be?'

'Well, thank you – I think. You're not exactly the bride of Frankenstein either, y'know. But it still didn't do me any good, did it? Trevor took off as soon as that blue line appeared in the little box. He was like that bloke in *Jurassic Park*, running for his life from the terrifying Pregnosaur. Wish I had bitten *his* bloody head off.'

Jo tailed off, but Sophie was humming to herself. 'Typical man. God, I'm hungry. Is it time for lunch?'

'Yeah, just about.' Jo hadn't meant to even mention Trevor – what had got into her? – but the least Sophie could have done was show some interest. She glared at Sophie's unsuspecting back as she rummaged in the bag of food. 'Better leave some for the children,' she said cattily, then relented when Sophie turned indignant eyes towards her.

'It's all right, Jo. There's plenty. I packed it myself today. Imogen wasn't feeling too good. Reckon she's on the blob.'

In spite of herself, Jo guffawed. 'What a revolting expression! Is that one of your boarding-school slang things?'

Sophie giggled. 'No, we used to say "on the rag" then. Isn't that awful? When my girls start, I want to make it really special. Like a celebration. Not like when we were their age.'

Jo unfolded a bag of sandwiches and sniffed. Which was more revolting, peanut butter and banana or the idea of Sophie's menstruation graduation celebration?

'I know, Jo,' Sophie gabbled on. 'Why don't you invite Matt to come and eat with us? I bet he'd like to. He's probably just looking for an excuse to come and join us anyway. Go on.'

'Certainly not,' Jo hissed. 'No way am I going to invite him. And don't you either,' she warned as Sophie started peering up towards the café.

Sophie scowled. 'I don't understand you. If I'd played it that cool with Hughie, we'd never have got together. You've got to help men along, y'know.'

Jo looked at her, exasperated. 'Let's call it Newman's first law of emotion. In every relationship, there is one that does the kissing and one that allows him or herself to be kissed. Well, I've been the one that did the kissing in the past, and I'm never going to do it again.' What had made her say that? Maybe she'd had too much sun. She seemed to be discussing things she'd kept quashed for years. 'If Matt wants me, he knows where to find me,' she ended petulantly.

But she sneaked a sideways look up at the café as she forced down the chocolate-spread roll, throwing the Cheddar surreptitiously into the sand. 'Bloody hell, Sophie. This is disgusting. Will your kids really eat these sarnies? I'd rather put up with Imogen and her crisply ironed Tupperware than have to eat your peculiar combinations. Are you pregnant or something? There's no other excuse for these fillings. I don't think Matt would thank me for an invitation to lunch today.'

Putting her ham and fish-paste bap sadly back in its battered greaseproof-paper bag, Sophie sighed heavily. 'Sorry. But they seemed such a good idea at the time. Tell you what, let's get the kids something to eat at the caff. Sergeant Imo of the food police isn't on duty, and it will get us in close proximity to muscly Matt.'

Jo scowled, but only for a moment. It was a stroke of genius. The children were trailing up the beach, looking exhausted by their surfing efforts. She could imagine Imogen barking, 'Feed them quick before there's a riot.' She jumped up, leaving Sophie to stuff the food back into her squashed-banana-scented bag. 'Don't sit down, kids. We've decided to eat in the café today. Chips on me.'

An hour later, they took their leave of the whitewashed café, with its sandy wooden floor. Matt had (gratifyingly) joined them the instant they had entered. The meal, guzzled with their fingers, had been full of fun and laughter, and he'd kept catching her eye. As they left, they passed the bins, now drizzled with spilt juice and melted ice cream, and wasps were buzzing round avidly, so the children and Sophie, shrieking, rushed on ahead. Matt laughed softly. 'Not afraid of getting stung, Jo?'

She dropped her eyes, smiling slightly, then raised them quizzically to meet his. This game of double meanings had been going on all through lunch, and she was enjoying it. 'I reckon I'm immune,' she replied and shivered as he reached a hand out to brush sand from her shoulder.

'You don't look the thick-skinned type to me, but you talk as if you were. I'd say you're really very sensitive. Tender, even.' He laced his fingers with hers and pulled her closer. 'Delicate,' he breathed against her hair.

Jo swallowed. 'Not really,' she said, her voice a little unsteady. 'Tougher than I look, actually. And in a holiday state of mind. You know, just out for a bit of fun.'

Matt raised her chin with his free hand, and looked into her eyes appraisingly. 'Fun, huh? Well, you've come to the right place. I could show you a good time, if you've got some time, that is.'

She ran the tip of her tongue over her lips. 'Are you offering me a private tour?'

'Oh yes, very private. And very soon, I think, since you're on holiday. Don't want to waste a single day, do we?'

She paused. Was this what she wanted? A fling with a good-looking stranger? Yes, it bloody well was. 'Let's fix that up as soon as we can, then.'

He smiled in satisfaction. 'Whenever you like. I'm here for you, Jo.' And he kissed her, quite slowly on each cheek, grazing his lips a little closer to the corners of her mouth than he really should have.

Trying to avoid Sophie's incredulous look, Jo followed the others back down to the beach, and smiled ecstatically at the children. 'I know – let's work off those chips.' Within minutes she had planned a little obstacle course, complete with ditches to jump, buckets to fill with pebbles and shells to balance on spades. Finn was soon basking in her reflected glory as the other children vied to join in.

Jo was at the finish line, timing the children with Finn's function-packed watch when Sophie sidled up. 'My my, Dr Newman, anyone would think you'd been injected with monkey gland, or something. Is this what the promise of some hanky panky does to you?'

'I don't know what you mean!' said Jo innocently and played on.

But by mid-afternoon she had had enough. How the hell did teachers keep it going all day? 'OK everyone. Let's go back to the house, shall we, and have a shower. You're all so sandy, you look like starfish. I'll take the boys. Last one back's a slimy toad, Sophie. Eat my dust!'

'… I've got a song that'll get on yer nerves and I'm gonna sing it all day!' Jo joined in the rousing chorus as they raced back through the lanes, much to Rory and Archie's delight. Finn looked slightly embarrassed at first at his mother's lack of inhibition, but sang with his usual husky gusto. To Jo the landscape looked particularly beautiful in the fierce afternoon heat, and the water in the estuary shimmered with a dazzling dance of light.

'Listen, guys,' Jo confided as they turned in at the gate, 'your mum wasn't feeling too good this morning. She had a bit of a headache so let's try not to make too much noise. In fact, there'll be a prize for the quietest and I bet I'm gonna win.'

Jo congratulated herself as she managed to open the sticking door quietly and the children went in ahead of her. Things were shaping up nicely with Matt, she'd got Finn the perfect present for his birthday, and she would get a pile of fresh doughnuts for his tea party tomorrow; really make it nice. He'd be so chuffed. A squeal from one of the children brought her rushing to the kitchen, shushing frantically. Imogen might be trying to sleep, after all.

But Imogen wasn't suffering and asleep. In fact, she was looking positively radiant and before her on the kitchen table was a stunning 'creation'. There was no other word for it: a blue base, and an icing wave curving up at one end, the foamy edge picked out in white piped icing, and sprinkles of icing sugar on the tiny waves below. A yellow wafer surfboard was poised under the crest of the breaking wave, a figure made from coloured royal icing crouching on it with brown arms outstretched. It was the most perfect birthday cake ever.

Finn's eyes had almost popped out of his head. 'For me? Really for me? For my birthday? It's just sooo cool! I've never had anything like that before. Thank you, Imogen. Thank you. You're the best!' And Finn threw his arms round her and hugged her tight.

Jo backed out through the kitchen door. Sophie and the girls had just arrived and were spilling out of the car. 'Well, you beat us fair and square,' she laughed, 'but we'll get you next … Jo, what on earth's wrong? You're white as a sheet. Where are you going? Jo? You've only just got in. Have you left something at the …?'

Jo threw the car into gear and screeched out of the drive. A mile of twisting lanes later, she pulled into the first farm gateway she could find and, wrenching open the boot, lifted out a small white box. Breathing fast, she hurled it with all her might into the field, where it smashed against a trough of slimy green water. The cardboard split open, the garish yellow icing sticking to the metal, then slowly the little round birthday cake slid down the side of the trough and into the long grass.

Chapter 11

Wednesday

Distinctly chilly with strong winds

'Well, I'd like to have been able to tell you the good weather was set to stay, but I can't. That brief nice spell is over for a couple of days I'm afraid, and today will feel more like March than July.' Imogen flicked off the radio and watched the clouds racing across the sky. For once they seemed to be right. The rain might hold off, she peered out of the window and shivered, but it was touch and go.

What a pity on Finn's birthday. She'd hardly heard him this morning, but knew he'd been in with his mum first thing. Shame that. She'd have liked to see him open his presents with everyone like her children did – well, it was part of the birthday routine, wasn't it? Rory had been quite cross about his new friend disappearing and had taken it out on his siblings at breakfast until she'd booted them all next door to the sitting room to simmer down in front of what she hoped was suitable viewing, and not some 'I'm having my mother's boyfriend's child' confession show.

'Waaah!' Archie's wail crescendoed, and Imogen slammed down her cup on the table.

'Rory, have you done it again?' She stormed into the room, and gathered up the howling Archie, curled up on the sofa. Rory and, surprisingly, Finn were laid out in identical poses on their stomachs on the floor, both holding game consoles, oblivious to the noise above their heads.

'Rory,' she persisted, 'have you kicked your brother again?'

Rory didn't move but merely grunted. 'Wasn't me. It was Finn. Arch deserved it. He was annoying us.'

'Finn?' Imogen softened her tone slightly. 'Finn, did you kick Arch?'

Like his friend, Finn didn't move. 'Yup I did.' Imogen felt her anger rise, and something of her goodwill towards him after his enthusiasm about the birthday cake evaporated. This boy needed a firm hand and he obviously didn't get it from his mother. She knelt down in front of him and gently removed the game console from his hands. He let her, too incredulous to maintain his grip. 'Finn, I know it's your birthday but it is not nice to kick people, is it? If Archie is being annoying you come and tell me, or ask him to go away, but kicking is something horses do. What do you say to Archie?'

'S'rry.' He pouted ungraciously and he took the console back from her. She clambered up onto her feet, and taking Archie's hand turned back towards the door. Jo was standing in the doorway.

Imogen smiled. What was her mood now? She couldn't quite fathom what had happened yesterday. Only that Jo had left again, which seemed an odd thing to do when she had only just got back from the beach. She hadn't returned for over an hour. Jo had turned down the invitation for a cup of tea and a piece of homemade shortbread, and had gone into the garden by herself and sat under a tree with her book and her sunglasses. She'd barely said a word for the rest of the evening.

The look she gave Imogen now was inscrutable. 'I was just going to make some more coffee,' Imogen began. 'Would you like a cup?'

'I'll make some for myself later thanks.' Jo moved out of the way to let her pass, then followed Imogen and the red-eyed Archie into the kitchen. Imogen fetched Archie a drink of orange juice from the fridge and sent him back into the sitting room with a kiss on his head. She turned back to the coffee machine and started to fill it with coffee beans, aware that Jo was standing by the kitchen units, arms folded and was watching her. 'Sure you won't change your mind? It's no trouble.'

'No thank you,' her tone was cold, 'and I would prefer it if you didn't reprimand Finn. That's my job and you have no right to.' Imogen stopped pouring in beans and turned to the woman standing behind her. Her arms went cold with the fear of a confrontation, a challenge that devastated the façade of holiday spirit and close camaraderie. In a second Jo had shattered the illusion.

'Er ... well, I'm sorry, Jo. Yes of course. But you weren't around and Archie was crying. I simply told Finn that kicking wasn't nice.' Jo was motionless, her arms still folded over her chest. Imogen stumbled on. 'Perhaps it's ... perhaps it's that he's not used to interruptions when he's playing being the only one and all … mind you Rory hits out too.' She laughed mirthlessly to try and lift the mood. Jo's lips were set.

'It wouldn't matter if I had six children,' she said tightly. 'It's no one's place but mine to tell him off. You leave him to me, and concentrate on your own children thank you.' And she turned and left the room.

Imogen watched her back as she left, the bag of coffee beans still in her hand, and felt a rush of heat into her face. Oh God, now she'd really blown it. As usual she'd waded in, mother-hen fashion, trying to do it all the way she thought it should be done, and now any pretence of getting along had popped like a bubble. Jo really seemed to dislike her all of a sudden, but why, after everything she'd done? Turning back to the coffee machine, she tried to analyse the last couple of days. Jo had been so unexpectedly supportive about the blasted period pains, and buying her that stuff – whether it worked or not – was surprisingly thoughtful. A thought flashed into Imogen's mind – perhaps Jo was jealous that she'd been talking to Matt. She clearly fancied him. Oh how patently ridiculous. She was dumpy, hefty and clumsy. No match for Jo's slim brown curves and her gorgeous hair. The idea was laughable.

Pouring water into the machine, she switched it on. Perhaps I am bossy. She reached for a cup. But all I did was tell her wayward child not to kick my son. What the hell was wrong with that? Oh sod her.

By the time they finally piled into two separate cars and left for the surfing lesson again – this time it was

Amelia's shoes that had gone missing, and Sophie had spent an inordinate length of time brushing her hair – the wind was whipping up and Imogen's humour had departed almost totally.

'Steady on, old girl.' Sophie gripped the side of the car seat as Imogen swung a little too enthusiastically out of the way of a bespectacled urbanite in his khaki shorts and docksider shoes loading pasties and small children into a BMW estate. 'Have you been recruited by the fundamentalist arm of the Cornish Liberation Front to systematically rid the county of tourists?'

'Sorry – was a bit close, wasn't I? I'm just fed up of going into combat with this ruddy traffic. Rural bloody Cornwall and it's worse than Hammersmith in the rush-hour. Why can't they all find something better to do on a lousy day like today and just let me get where I need to go?'

'Ouch!' Sophie looked askance at her. 'Who rattled your cage this morning?'

Imogen let her shoulders droop, loosening her grip on the steering wheel. She dropped her voice so the children in the back couldn't hear. 'Oh I don't know. I just can't make your friend out. One minute she's nice, then the next she's ripping my head off.'

'Mmmm.' Sophie turned her head away and looked out of the window. 'She can be a bit tricky.'

'Yeah, I mean she hasn't even mentioned the cake. Not that I mind, you know I love to do that sort of thing and I thought it would be fun.' She could hear the incredulity in her voice and the pitch rising to an ugly level.

'Oh it was fab, and I'd have loved it for one of my girls – I mean I'd really love you to do one for Gracie's seventh – but Jo's not really like that. Jo doesn't go big on birthdays like we do.'

Imogen could see the glimmer of an opportunity to make amends. 'Really? Poor Finn. Tell you what, let's really make a splash. It'll be a treat for Jo too. Maybe she's just tired.'

'Well, I'm not sure what you—' Sophie started, but Archie interrupted, interrogating them from the back about what they were discussing, and they had to let it drop. They wound their way to the beach in silence. Perhaps they could talk more once they had the children sorted. But Olivia, who'd travelled with Jo, was at the window of her mother's car before it had even stopped moving. 'Hey, Mum, Matt wants to know if you'd all like a go surfing today. One family's gone home early cos of the weather and left some spaces.'

Ten minutes later and bowled along by Sophie's redoubtable enthusiasm, Imogen was dragooned into the surf hut with Jo and Sophie to be kitted out. She hadn't even been able to voice her knee-jerk reticence as the children squealed with delight at the idea of their mother joining them. She could have said she didn't have her swimsuit, but Olivia produced it with glee from the boot. She could have cried off because of her still-heavy period, but that would have elicited a deluge of questions from the children. She could have argued the wind was too strong, but Rory and Matt declared the conditions ideal, with 'off-shore winds and perfect lines stacked up to the horizon'. She'd even raised the important point that Archie and Grace couldn't be left alone on the beach, until she saw that Sophie had hitched them up with a very wholesome-looking woman in pink fleece and shorts with whom she'd made friends the day before. Her name was Abby apparently, and she had an air of Fulham about her. Her two similar-aged children were in sensible sun-protection suits and legionnaire hats, and were called James and Lily. Imogen reassured herself that people with children called James and Lily weren't usually child abductors, and she said a breathless thank-you as she pressed a bag of shortbread into Abby's hand.

There was no escape. Besides, how feeble would it have been to refuse when Jo and Sophie obviously wanted to join in? It would just confirm to Jo that she was truly pathetic. So it was she found herself standing in an orderly queue as Matt doled out wetsuits and booties. She kept well behind the others, and watched with mounting dread as he held one up against the other women's backs to check for sizing, then chivvied them off in the direction of the minuscule changing cubicles, partitioned off with faded curtains.

'Worn one of these beauties before, Imogen?' he asked, turning to her once Jo and Soph had disappeared to change.

'We have the odd depraved wetsuit orgy at home, but I tend to go for the deep-sea variety with the copper helmets …' she trailed off, aware of how weak her joke was, but he smiled.

'Yeah those ones do it for me too but the punters get

edgy.' Pulling a long-legged version down from the rail, he turned to hold it against her shoulders. 'Some of these steamers are still wet from yesterday, but I'll give you a dry one cos the wet ones are a bugger to put on. Pull it up to your waist before putting your arms in. Much easier.'

Sophie was giggling behind her curtain, and she could see elbows protruding through the fabric as she pulled up the zip. 'Corrr … I wish Hugh was here. He'd really go for me in this. It might take him a bit of time for him to get at me, but he'd really go for me!' And she roared with laughter, pulling back the curtain to reveal herself, swathed from neck to ankle in black rubber, a pink contrasting panel shaped down her waist to her thighs making her figure look boyish and sexy.

In the dim light behind the curtain, Imogen slipped off her clothes, the cold and damp of the hut making her shiver and her skin goosebump. Avoiding looking in the narrow mirror, she pulled on her swimsuit, and then followed Matt's instructions slipping her legs inside then, grabbing handfuls of rubber, wrenching the suit as hard as she could up her body. She tried to jump. It seemed to stick and stretch without moving up her legs. She tugged again, hoping it wouldn't ladder like a pair of tights, then endeavoured to heave the rolls of fabric over her bottom. Surely Matt must have underestimated the size? God, how embarrassing, she'd have to waddle out and ask for a bigger one in front of the others.

'Come on, Imo,' Sophie called from the hut door, 'we're all waiting for you so we can hit the rollers.'

'I won't be a moment. Don't wait. I'll be right there.' She listened till she heard their voices disappear. Feeling herself beginning to perspire gently now, and aware her face would be red and blotchy, she left the suit stretched over her bum, and inserted her arms into the sleeves, tugging as hard as she could to get it over her shoulders then, with one arm over her shoulder pulling and the other behind her back pushing in a kind of half nelson, she wrestled with the zip. She was panting with the effort and could feel tears pricking behind her eyes. Finally, the collar strangling her, she had the zip up to the top, and she turned to look at her image in the mirror in the gloom of the cubicle.

'My God,' she whispered, taking in her puce face, broad shoulders and thick thighs encased in the wetsuit, her bulges and curves somehow flattened into a great beefy mass, 'It's Tinky-Winky. I bet the sodding Chinese women in Hong bloody Kong don't look like this.'

The next hour was nothing less than excruciating. She knew it would be from the moment she came out of the surf hut to join the others and saw Jo from behind, her neat little buttocks encased in her wetsuit with room to spare. Attempting not to walk too much like the Michelin man, Imogen tried to concentrate on Matt's pep talk, then she picked up the ends of two surfboards – easier to carry that way in the wind he had said – strategically placing herself behind Sophie to avoid comparisons with black puddings. Carrying one under each arm, she made her way as gracefully as she could down to the water's edge, resisting the urge to give Rory a hefty shove when he snorted at his mother's new outfit. Keen to appear cool, he and Finn, resplendent in birthday wetsuit, then plunged into the waves, leaving Imogen to wade in tentatively.

'Jesus!' The water seeped into the suit, making her gasp as it reached the small of her back. 'This is torture.'

Matt, the water only reaching the top of his thighs, pushed over towards her. 'Chin up, Imogen. It'll get better in a minute.' He lowered his voice. 'It helps if you pee in the suit. Balances the body temperature and all that!' Then he roared at the disbelief on her face. 'We all do it!'

'And you mean someone's worn this wetsuit before me?' she shrieked. Five minutes later and she succumbed to what turned out to be excellent advice.

As for the surfing, well there had to be a knack but Imogen just hadn't got it. She battled to push the board out in front of her as instructed by Matt, who was shouting tactics across the swell, then to heave herself onto it on her stomach as a wave rolled towards her. It didn't help that she kept turning back to the beach to check that Archie and Grace hadn't been abducted, and each time she was whipped off her feet and submerged under the swell of an unexpected wave. The water filled her mouth, eyes and ears, making her lose orientation momentarily and, as she emerged again, choking after the third dousing, hair plastered unattractively to her face, her nose stinging from the salt, determined that enough was enough, she caught sight of Jo as she stood up triumphantly on her board for the first time.

*

'Right, Imogen,' muttered Jo, looking coldly at her own reflection in the mirror. 'You're not stealing my thunder this time, sweetie!'

With just an hour to go before the party tea, she had been effectively banished from the kitchen by Imogen's insufferable show of efficiency, all offers of help smilingly but firmly rebuffed. 'No, Jo,' she had said. 'Honestly, it's pretty much taken care of. Let me do the boring stuff – I have to admit I love it. Why don't you have a rest or go out somewhere with the birthday boy? After all, it's your celebration too. Really, it should be us mothers that get the presents, don't you reckon? For putting up with them this long!'

Jo had wheeled away, gritting her teeth, and stomped upstairs. Now she could hear Finn outside in the garden with the other children, refreshed after a warm shower and lunch. He clearly didn't need her either at the moment. She unzipped her daytime make-up bag, and ten minutes later stood back to appraise her image in the mirror. Yup, with a soft blush on her cheeks and a subtle gleam over her eyelids, she'd managed glowing and sun-kissed, but she'd have to lower her lashes to conceal that fierce glint in her eyes.

A short while later Imogen called gaily, 'Come on, everyone, party time!' then flung open the doors into the kitchen with a flourish, her face flushed and triumphant.

Everyone, well, almost everyone, murmured with delight and admiration at the transformation. Imogen had extended the seaside theme to take in every detail. Large round pebbles with place names written on them in specially bought aqua nail varnish anchored blue and green balloons to the table, and she had cut round the edges of paper plates to create scallop shells. A banner, in Archie's childish hand and decorated with cheerful-looking sea creatures, read: 'Happy Birthday, Finn – King of the Waves'. Jo felt sick. Finn, on the other hand, was speechless, his mouth hanging open as he stared around the room.

A camera flashed, before Jo had time to compose her features. 'Isn't it wonderful? I'll try and finish the film today,' Sophie promised, 'and get it developed tomorrow. Shall we sit down, Imo?'

There was a general searching for place names. Finn had been seated next to Jo, but she saw him and Rory, positioned in between his brother and sister, exchange conspiratorial glances. Boy, this was just getting better and better. 'Sit where you like, Finn,' she said, and quickly shrugged. 'Don't mind me.'

Imogen turned round. 'Oh, but I thought … Yes, of course, you are the birthday boy, after all.' She looked at her watch. 'I think that's everything. Matt said he might be a bit late, so we won't wait.' She undid her apron. 'Dig in, everyone, help yourselves. Squash, Ribena or my very own Mermaid's Delight?' She swiftly dispensed the drinks, then sat back down, only to bounce up again, on some other mission of vital importance to the fridge.

Jo leant back in her chair and crossed her legs, resting her ankle on her knee. Leaning behind the children's backs, she glanced over at Sophie. 'Psst, Soph. Fancy a glass of Chablis? Or how 'bout I rustle us up a Pimm's?'

Sophie's eyes rounded and she nodded vigorously. Jo pushed back her chair and set about it, aware of Matt's arrival as she washed the sprigs of mint before dropping them into the ice-packed jug. 'Here we are,' she said smoothly, carrying the tray of four clinking glasses. 'My very own Neptune's Narcotic!'

'Mmmm. What a lovely sight! Very tempting. Here, allow me.' Matt kissed her on both cheeks, then took the tray, handed a glass to each adult, then turned to tap his against Jo's.

Imogen demurred. 'Erm, bit early for me.'

Sophie took a healthy slug and sighed contentedly. 'What's wrong, Imo? Can't bear to be drunk in charge of a birthday party? You're missing a treat, y'know. Jo may not be much use in the kitchen but she can mix a mean cocktail – her mojitos have to be drunk to be believed.'

'Hardly "in charge",' Imogen protested. 'It's just that … Oh all right then, I suppose it is meant to be a holiday. Cheers everyone.'

'Meant to be, indeed,' muttered Jo darkly, topping up Matt and Sophie's glasses.

Matt sat down next to Jo in Finn's vacated seat, popped a sandwich into his mouth and took a handful of grapes, smiling round at everyone. 'Well, isn't this nice? It's years since I've been to a proper birthday tea. You forget how much fun they are, don't you? Finn, I hope you realise what a lucky chap you are to have such attention lavished on you. Better enjoy it while you can. Things go downhill fast when you're a grown-up.'

Jo smiled wryly. 'Ain't that the truth!'

'Anyway, are we doing presents yet, Jo, or should I wait?'

Jo shrugged and gave a tight smile. 'Better ask Imogen. She's the CEO.'

'Ahh.' Matt raised his eyebrows and glanced round the table. 'Later it is, then. Don't want to interrupt the feast.'

The children dived in, all of them fitting Hula Hoops onto their fingertips then eating them off as quickly as they could. Gracie made a flower shape on her plate with cocktail sausages for petals and a cherry tomato in the middle, and the piles of fish-shaped sandwiches were demolished by eager hands. Amelia made towers of neat little cheese cubes and Imogen gently admonished Rory for throwing grapes into the air and trying to catch them in his mouth – 'you'll choke, you silly twit'. Jo sat back and observed it all. They all seemed to be having fun.

Matt stood up. 'If I'm not stepping on anyone's toes, literally or figuratively,' he glanced down at Jo, and shifted his right foot so that it rested gently on her sandalled left one, 'I'd like to propose a toast. Everyone got a drink? Finn, thank you for being born on this particular day, ten – it is ten, isn't it? – years ago. Happy birthday, Finn. And may the years bring you perfect waves and no wipe outs.' Everyone laughed and followed suit as Matt raised his glass.

The rest of the party passed more easily with Matt's relaxed presence to leaven the atmosphere. Jo noted wryly that Imogen didn't turn down *his* offers of help, but at least that left her and Sophie to polish off the jug of Pimm's. Meanwhile iced biscuits in the shape of starfish and seahorses, and a huge bowl of strawberries and blueberries made their way to the table.

Matt chatted easily with the women in turn, allowing Jo the luxury of not speaking to Imogen – she wasn't sure she could have managed to without throttling her. Across the table, Finn was glowing with pleasure. He grinned seraphically across at her and, though Jo tried her best to smile back at him, she felt like she was sucking on a lemon. Maybe another drink would help.

At last, it was time for that cake. Even Matt waxed lyrical. 'Where on earth did you get it?' he asked Jo. She sat back heavily. Here we go. She could almost hear Imogen blushing as she spoke. 'Well, I made it, Matt,' she simpered. 'It wasn't that hard, once I'd got the idea.'

She couldn't keep the pleasure out of her voice, as Matt gasped in awe. 'Lucky Finn! I've never had a cake like that.'

Imogen sighed. 'I've always had a bit of a thing about birthdays. They were always such an anticlimax at school. Perhaps I'm overcompensating now.' She trailed off.

As Finn blew out the candles, to the tuneless strains of 'Happy Birthday', and everyone started cheering loudly, Imogen clapped her hands. 'Now, team. Time for pressies. Rory, can you get them, please?'

Jo stepped back. What next? A serenade by the New York Philharmonic? Sophie joined her. 'Wait till you see this,' she whispered in awe.

Rory came back into the room carrying a tea tray with green crêpe paper strands hanging from it like seaweed, mounded with little gifts all individually wrapped in shades of blue, green and aqua. Finn's eyes popped as Rory set it before him. 'For me?' he gasped, looking at Imogen.

Matt, who had popped out for a moment, reappeared and added a largish parcel to the pile. ''Fraid the wrapping doesn't match,' he said teasingly. 'Put it under the table, Finn, so it doesn't spoil the beautiful arrangement.'

Imogen nudged him. 'Honestly, you make me sound completely obsessive.' She giggled. Jo had a coughing fit and poured herself some more Pimm's. The onlookers watched as Finn threw himself into a frenzy of paper tearing. He opened Matt's present first, dropping the stripey orange paper to the floor.

'Cool! Thanks, Matt, they're brill!' He put the diving mask on straightaway and slid his feet into the flippers before continuing. There were juggling balls and a stretchy surf watch from Sophie and the girls; a surfing necklace, a book about a schoolboy spy, a copy of the *Beano* and some hideous joke teeth from Imogen and her children. He pulled off the mask when it steamed up altogether and fitted the teeth over his own, grinning inanely at his mother.

Jo forced a smile and turned to Imogen, now standing beside her, her face wreathed in a grin.

'Well thanks, Imogen,' she said curtly.

'Oh it was nothing. Such fun to do.'

'No, you misunderstand me. Thanks for hijacking my son's birthday.' Imogen whipped round, looking incredulous.

'Thank you, everyone,' lisped Finn, through the false teeth. 'It's all brilliant. It's the best party I ever had. *Thank you*, Imogen.' And he stood up, tripped over his flippers, and ended up in Imogen's arms.

Later, much later, Jo opened her eyes. She hadn't meant to fall asleep. She'd only sat on her bed for a minute while she waited for Finn to clean his teeth, but it was getting late now and all the children seemed to be in bed. She pushed open the door of the boys' room, but already Finn was sleeping, his head back and his mouth slightly open. She bent over to nuzzle his cheek, but in his slumber he stirred and moved away.

She felt oddly empty and unsatisfied, and realised it wasn't him that needed the reassuring cuddle. Stopping for a moment at the top of the stairs, she could hear Imogen and Sophie's voices floating up. She looked at her watch. Only eight forty-five. The prospect of the evening that stretched ahead filled her with despair. She wanted to be somewhere else, and she knew where. She went back into her room and looked around.

'Hello, stranger,' said Sophie knowingly, twenty minutes later, nursing a glass of wine in the sitting room. 'Feeling better? That Neptune's Narcotic's strong stuff for the unwary. You want to get into practice, like me. I've appointed myself Imogen's personal trainer, haven't I, Imo? And my rates are very reasonable.'

Imogen didn't look up, so Jo addressed her little speech to Sophie alone. 'I thought I should perhaps pop down to see Matt, thank him properly for Finn's present. It was so nice of him to go to all that bother.'

235

'Yes, you must thank *him* for all the trouble he went to,' said Sophie, peering up at Jo cynically. 'It would never do to be ungrateful for the kind things people do for you, would it, eh?'

Imogen had picked up a paper and was studying it intently. She certainly didn't seem to have registered what was going on across the room.

Jo looked innocently at Sophie. 'I'm just trying to be polite.'

'I hope you're wearing your best undies for this visit,' cackled Sophie, then broke into a belly laugh as she saw Jo flush under her make-up. 'Go for it,' she called after Jo's retreating back. 'But remember, only safe surfing – make sure he wears a wetsuit!'

Bloody Sophie. Jo closed the front door behind her and made for the welcome peace and privacy of her car. It was well past nine by the time she arrived at the beach, but she felt sure Matt would be there. He'd mentioned something about having to work late so perhaps he'd be in the shop again, like last time. She shivered in anticipation. She was sure he was interested in her, but maybe she should make a move on him if she wanted to really get something going – and she wanted to all right. She dug in her bag for her cologne, sprayed some down her front, and in her hair. She swallowed. It was now or never.

The sound of her car must have alerted him, and he appeared in the doorway before she was even halfway there.

'Well, hello! Feeling better? You looked a little bit stressed when I left.'

She smiled and raised an eyebrow and he came out to meet her. 'Stressed, yes. That about sums it up. I'm sorry I didn't say goodbye. I wanted to thank you for coming. It meant a lot to Finn, and for the present too. I had to prise the flippers off him before he got into his pyjamas. He'd have worn the lot, if he could have. Anyway, it was very sweet of you.'

'It was fun.' They were just inches apart now, almost face to face because of the heels she had chosen to wear. Matt smiled straight into her eyes and kissed the tip of her nose. 'You're looking very elegant, Dr Newman. Are you on your way somewhere?'

She hesitated. 'Nope, just coming to see you.'

'Then aren't I the lucky one? And me in my old red shirt again. Would you like me to slip into something less comfortable?'

'I think you'll do.' Jo returned his smile as he took her hand and led her into the office. Inside, his laptop was powered up, a dense screen of type visible.

'So, not playing Battleships then?'

He laughed softly. 'No, I don't have time to play games. Do you?'

'No, actually I don't.' This was it. She turned to him, placed her hand flat against his chest, moving in towards him. He tilted his head and raised an eyebrow quizzically, but slid his hand round her to rest near the base of her spine.

Jo shivered and he pulled her close. 'Matt, will you please kiss me?' she breathed.

Jo closed her eyes in anticipation, but nothing

happened. Oh God, don't let him be gay. She opened an eye to see him smiling. 'I was going to get round to it, don't worry.'

Then he raised one hand to cup her face and kissed her very gently at the corner of her mouth, brushing his lips back and forth against hers. His skin smelt of sunshine. The effect on Jo was electrifying. She could see white lights flashing behind her closed eyelids. There was no way she could play this one cool. With a shuddering breath she pulled him close, pressing her body against his and deepening the kiss. She felt him hesitate, then respond and he moved both hands to hold her shoulders, his fingers pressing into her flesh. She kissed him hungrily, little breaths catching in her throat.

She ran her hands down his back and pressed him hard against her, then, fumbling in her haste, she reached round for the buttons on the fly of his jeans, and started to pull at them, kissing him more deeply than ever. Abruptly, his hands released her shoulders, although he went on kissing her, and gently pulled her hands away from him, lacing his fingers through hers. She groaned in frustration, and tried to pull them free and push her body closer again.

He stepped back, leaving her trembling and gasping. 'Jo, slow down. What's the rush? What makes you think I'm that kind of man?'

She stared at him uncomprehendingly, then saw his slow smile and sighed in frustration. 'I bloody hope you are that kind of man. You're no good to me otherwise. C'mon, Matt.'

He looked at her appraisingly, and rubbed the back of his neck. 'Look, I've got to save that document. Give me a moment to shut down, then I think you could use a nice cool drink. I've got some beer in the fridge upstairs.'

Jo brushed the hair off her face, discomforted at his reaction. This was a new one on her. She cast around for something to say. 'Upstairs? Is this where you live then?'

He sat down at the computer. 'Well, it's not mine, obviously, but yeah. Where did you think I was staying?'

She shook her head. 'Dunno. I hadn't really thought about it.'

'Nice to know I'm occupying your thoughts,' he snorted. 'Why don't you sit down over there? I won't be long, but if I don't get this down, I'll probably forget it. I'll be as quick as I can.'

'Do you have a loo?'

''Course. Use the one upstairs. It's the door on the right through the sitting room. The light switch is outside, next to the bookshelves.'

She went carefully up the open-tread stairs into a large room with two long, mismatched sofas facing each other and a wide window overlooking the darkening bay. Lamps on low tables revealed the remains of a meal – some green salad, what looked like paella and a half-empty glass of red wine. There were cardboard boxes on the floor and it looked as though he had been rummaging through books and papers. She found the bathroom and went in. Her face in the mirror looked flushed, her eyes dark and heavy-lidded. 'God, you look like a slut,' she told herself severely. She checked her armpits, fine. She breathed into her cupped hands and sniffed. Fine. So what the hell was wrong with him? No one else had ever hesitated that way. Here she was offering it on a plate, and he was downstairs fiddling with his sodding computer. Oh God, maybe she was too old for him.

She washed her hands, trying to decide what to do. She had almost resolved to go back downstairs and leave while she still had her dignity, but when she walked out, he was at the top of the stairs.

'Now, sit down and let me get you that beer. Then maybe we can carry on from where we left off.'

Jo sighed with relief. Too nervous to sit down, she shifted from foot to foot while he tidied his plate away. He returned with two misty bottles and a bowl of macadamia nuts. 'Want some? They're my favourite. I brought a load back from the States.' He sat down on the lower of the two sofas, and pulled her down beside him, handed her a beer, picked a nut out for her. She opened her lips and took it with her teeth, then gently licked the salt from his fingers, gratified to see him swallow and hear the sharp intake of breath. He smiled slowly. 'Hmm. Yes, that's more like it,' he murmured. 'Look, Jo, can you stay? Do you have to get back? It's fine with me either way. I'll understand, but I really don't want to rush tonight. I want us to take our time. If you have to leave, let's just relax and arrange something else.'

Jo thought fast. Finn would be all right. Of course he would. He slept like a log. The others would hold the fort, just for a bit. She deserved this. It had been so bloody long since the last time and that had only been a fumble with a divorced friend of a friend. She reached across and took another nut from the packet, and fed it to Matt. He nuzzled into her palm and she felt his tongue probing gently between her fingers. 'Yes, I can stay. It'll be fine.'

Chapter 12

Thursday

Windy with heavy rain

Imogen woke with a start, her heart pounding. It must still be early, because the room seemed quite dark. She looked over at Archie beside her to be sure she hadn't woken him, then squinted at her watch on the bedside table. Six thirty-four. It should be lighter than this by now. Which, as Matt had predicted, could only mean the weather was crap. No surfing today.

Resting her head back against the pillow, she yawned. She'd slept fitfully, waking every hour or so. She knew she had been waiting to hear Jo, but she had managed to sleep since about four so perhaps she'd missed her coming back. Imogen could feel pain between her eyes from the weight of tiredness, but knew she had to find out if Jo had got back safely. Fighting the urge to get up straightaway she turned over onto her side, chastising herself. I'm not her ruddy mother, for heaven's sake, and there's no doubt what she's been up to. A vision flashed through her head of Jo having sex with Matt. With his physique and Jo's tanned figure they'd be beautiful together.

But what if Jo hadn't gone to see him? What if she'd got lost somewhere? Oh don't be so stupid. She's a grown woman. She closed her eyes, then a moment later opened them again and swung herself out of bed. She needed a pee anyway so she might as well check if Jo's door was shut.

It wasn't, and she could see the bed still strewn with clothes as it had been left last night. Jo clearly hadn't gone out on the spur of the moment. It looked like Imogen's bed had done before teenage parties, with outfits discarded and left tangled in a pile and, though she was knew she should find Jo's indecision rather endearing, instead she felt angry. How contrived. How divisive. Jo had behaved like a bitch on heat and she and Sophie had been left to babysit. She closed the door. Hopefully Finn would think his mother was still asleep.

Not that it seemed to bother Sophie, Imogen thought as she padded downstairs. (No point in going back to bed now.) But then nothing seemed to bother Sophie. She'd always been like that. Flown by the seat of her pants, and never considered what would happen if they missed the last bus back to school or stayed out after the main door to the sixth-form block had been locked. 'Oh gosh, is it that late really, Imo?' she'd breathe, her face a bit panicky. 'Bloody hell, Miss Hoskins will kill us.' Then, when Miss Hoskins had finished hauling them over the coals, Sophie would give her wide-eyed innocent look and it was Imogen who'd get the 'we don't expect this sort of thing from a girl like you, Imogen, how disappointing' lecture.

Crazy to be up this early. She should be making the

most of the lie-in. Isn't that what holidays were about? She could feel the effects of last night's wine, one glass too many, thanks to Sophie's insistence, but they had had a laugh in the end, and it had been such a relief to have Jo out of the way.

But now here she was, despite Jo's extraordinary remark at the party, once again doing her worrying for her. It was her own over-developed sense of responsibility, she supposed. The constant head prefect in her, thinking everything through and empathising with everyone's feelings. 'God, Imo, you'd worry for Britain if there was a medal in it,' Guy would tease. But this was the rub: who'd worry if she didn't? She could feel tears pricking behind her eyes and it hurt. Why did she have to think through what Finn would feel if he woke and his mother wasn't there? Perhaps he was used to his mother screwing around. But if he was, he shouldn't be. Not at just ten years old.

Something caught her eye outside and she craned round to see the nose of Jo's car come into the driveway. Seven o'clock almost on the nail. She had a sudden panicked urge to jump up and leg it upstairs so Jo wouldn't think she'd been waiting for her. Which of course she hadn't. But instead she sat tight, arms curled round her legs and waited, heart pounding again, to hear the door heave open. But shit. Jo wouldn't have a key for it. Should she get up? It was too late as Jo headed round to the back door, and spotted her sitting in the window.

A gust of cold air blew in as Imogen unlatched and opened the door. Jo's hair was wild and she looked as though she'd dressed hurriedly. Not her usual manicured self, she looked almost wanton. Imogen stopped herself from saying anything and simply turned around, leaving Jo to close the door.

'Oh hello.' Jo flattened down her wayward curls and pulled her jumper further round her. 'I'm going to have a shower,' and she moved hurriedly towards the door.

Picking up her teacup off the table, Imogen couldn't stop herself.

'We didn't know if you were OK.'

Jo stopped at the door and looked back. 'Well, I am, aren't I?'

Imogen's children weren't quite sure what had hit them when their mother stormed in to their rooms an hour later, fully dressed, her face set with determination.

'Rise and shine. The weather's dire so no beach today. Instead we're going to see an old friend of Granny's who lives down the coast.' Archie had been characteristically intrigued by the idea when he'd woken in her bed to find her getting dressed, but the sleep-swollen faces of Olivia and Rory registered first confusion and then dissent.

'Oh God, not some old lady,' Rory groaned, pulling the duvet up over his head. 'It's always old ladies.'

He maintained the same joyful outlook for most of the journey until Imogen had to tell him to be quiet. Edie Parkes had sounded very warm and welcoming when Imogen had called her just after eight, and didn't seem fazed at all by this impromptu visit, as if accommodating the daughter and children of an erstwhile friend for lunch at such short notice was an everyday occurrence.

But Imogen hadn't seen Edie for years and her memory of her was hazy, except of course that she was the widow of Ralph Parkes, an old golfing friend of her father's and, despite her parents' attempts never to voice opinions of their friends in front of their children, Imogen had gleaned at a young age that Edie was not quite like the others. Her mother referred to her as 'hippy'; her father as 'Bohemian', with that patronising little laugh he had when someone wasn't quite Eton and the Guards (though he himself was Charterhouse and National Service).

Imogen squinted again at the map quickly as she drove to confirm she was on the right road. No, Edie was deemed all the more odd because Ralph had been Magdalene and the City – several echelons higher up the scale than her parents both socially and intellectually – but a nice fairway and a five iron lowers most social barriers amongst the middle and upper-middle classes. Edie, however, was 'artistic' and 'creative', her clothes never quite right for the occasion, and there had been some talk of how Ralph had left his first wife – an A-list socialite – for Edie whom he'd met at a reception at the Royal Academy and with whom he'd fallen 'madly in love' – a concept Imogen's mother made sound like contracting cholera.

'It's going to be sooo dull. Can we leave like straight after lunch?' Rory's face was beseeching.

'We'll see. We'll go as soon as it's polite to,' Imogen compromised, not even sure herself that she hadn't condemned them all to a dreadful day, but anything had to be better than spending it cooped up in the house with Jo.

Edie's house was built somewhere between the wars. It was surprisingly large and, even more surprisingly, ugly. Set down a short drive on the road out of a smallish fishing port, it looked bleak and unwelcoming in grey stone and she caught a glimpse of the garden round the side, full of hardy shrubs like hydrangea and hebe being blown ferociously in the wind. Imogen's heart filled with foreboding. She wouldn't even be able to gush about how lovely it was, to pass the time.

'Right, everyone,' she barked as she pulled up outside. 'Best Granny and Grandpa manners. Archie, no dirty fingers on anything and a quid to anyone who remembers their pleases and thank-yous. Let's go.' But no sooner were they out of the car than the front door opened and Edie stood on the doorstep.

'Imogen, my darling. And looking so like your mother.' Edie, in faded jeans and a striped navy-blue T-shirt, her figure as slight as ever, held her at arm's length, her eyes dancing with pleasure. Her face, still beautiful, was now lined and interesting. 'But with your father's height. You are like a fine thoroughbred.' An observation so tactfully put that Imogen loved her for it. 'Come on in quick. It's quite ghastly out here,' and she led them into the hall. It was as ugly as the outside, with a heavy mahogany staircase going up to the left and a window looking out onto the drive, but every square inch of the walls was covered in paintings. Watercolours, signed in scrawled pencil to 'darling R and E', and small oils of the sea in heavy frames. 'That's better.' She ran her fingers through her white, bobbed hair and the bracelets on her arms jangled. 'Now, who are you? Let me have a look at you all.' She turned to look at the children, lined up inside the front door, struck dumb by the effusiveness of this sparkly woman who, Imogen was prepared to bet, didn't match up to Rory's expectations at all.

'You must be Rory.' Edie had him entirely in her gaze. 'My, what a man. Let me guess, you must be eleven soon. I can remember your granny writing on one of her Christmas cards that you'd been born. And ...' She paused for a split second. 'Olivia. You must look like your dad, because of that colouring. And Archie?' He hid his face in Imogen's leg. 'About six or seven? Am I right?'

He smiled shyly. 'Not bad for an old bird with no children, am I?' And she laughed a deep, throaty laugh.

'Very impressive,' Imogen ruffled Arch's hair. It had to be said now before she lost her bottle. 'What a lovely house, Edie—'

Edie's snort interrupted her. 'Lovely? Good God, girl, it's hideous.' She roared with laughter again and turned to open a door to the left. 'No, there was only ever one reason to buy this monstrosity ...' and she pushed back the door to reveal the sitting room.

Imogen gasped. The room was filled with light despite the weather, and packed with squelchy-looking sofas and chairs, covered in tapestry, but in front of them, beyond an enormous grand piano, was a massive plate-glass window looking straight out to a lawn, which fell away to the ocean beyond.

The children looked in wonder. 'On a clear day I can see the Empire State Building!'

'Seriously?' said Rory, his mouth open unattractively in awe.

'Well almost!'

Archie wandered over to the piano and began to put his fingers on the keys.

'Uh uh,' Imogen said quickly. 'Don't touch, Arch!'

'What else is a piano for if you can't touch it?' admonished Edie, going over to heighten the piano stool for him. 'Just don't bash the poor thing too hard though. It's even older than me.' So while Archie plinked on the keys, Imogen took in the rest of the room: the frayed silk and tapestry mismatched cushions in jewel colours. The oak dresser with huge church candlesticks and large ceramic plates, obviously one-offs. Bits and pieces collected over years of mixing with creative people. And above the stone fireplace, a large oil of Edie, painted when she was about twenty, sitting on a window seat, her legs pulled up, wearing a colourful silk shirt with birds and flowers. Her hair was fixed up on her head with combs, and her face, clear and beautiful, was gazing dreamily out of a window.

'Now it's too wet for football, isn't it, boys? But if you go up the stairs, all of you, and go into the first room on the right after the bathroom, I think you'll find something to do while I get your mother a drink.' The children looked to Imogen for her approval, uncertain if it was all right to do what Edie suggested, but Imogen smiled and they ran off, pounding up the stairs.

'Clever you. I've never seen them move so fast.' She followed Edie's retreating back through the hall again and into a warm kitchen with its mish-mash of free-standing furniture, and an old duck-egg blue Aga, the walls above which were covered in hundreds of postcards, mainly of early twentieth-century paintings and most faded and curled at the edges. The overall impression was of clutter, the huge kitchen table covered in correspondence, address books and diaries. Imogen noticed a catalogue from a London gallery exhibition, and something else from a mixed media show in St Ives. She knew the whole room would offend her mother, who was so proud of her immaculate custom-built maple units, with matching tea and coffee jars and colour-coordinated tiles, and she smiled.

Edie turned and clapped her hands together. 'Now, a drink!'

'Coffee would be lovely.'

'Coffee my foot. I think we both deserve something a little stronger, don't you?' She smiled wickedly. 'I'm so thrilled you've come.' Imogen sat herself at the table with a glass of wine, whilst Edie bustled around the Aga, pulling a pan out of the bottom oven. 'Your mother phoned to alert me to the fact that you were up the coast.' Imogen could have sworn there was a hint of a tease in her voice. 'But I have to say I put it right out of my head. Couldn't imagine you'd want to visit me, but I'm delighted you have. Especially when you're about to disappear to foreign shores I gather. How exciting that sounds!' She put a heavy pan on the hot plate – please

God may it not be soup, thought Imogen, the kids won't touch it – and, putting down the oven glove, came to join Imogen at the table. 'The children will love it.'

She took a dainty sip of her drink and sighed with satisfaction. 'Now your ma also tells me you're sharing a house near Padstow. How's it going?' Her face was so open and her question so direct, Imogen forgot the flannel she was going to give and told it like it was.

Edie listened in silence then shook her head slowly when Imogen had finished. 'Well, what do you expect, darling? Two women should never share a kitchen, let alone three. A kitchen should be like a dictatorship, run by one person with anyone else acting on orders. There is no room for democracy over the gas ring. Why do you think all those awful TV chefs are such tyrants?'

'Gosh, you're so right,' Imogen breathed. At last someone understood her irritations. 'And this wretched Jo woman never empties the dishwasher and I find towels on the bathroom floor the whole time. Sophie, well I thought after all this time I knew her. She leaves the teabags in the sink, and is always feeding the kids rubbish. Then,' Imogen leant forward getting into her stride, 'I really thought it would help if I made Jo's son a cake for his birthday, because she didn't seem to be going to do it. In fact, I had to arrange a whole tea party, or there wouldn't have been one and there wasn't a word of thanks from her. In fact, she accused me of hijacking it!'

Edie looked at her, a half-smile on her face. 'Can't people be annoying?' Imogen nodded her head vigorously in agreement as she took another sip of her drink.

'Holidays do show you the other side of people, don't they?' Edie continued. 'Those funny little irritations. I remember Ralph and I went on holiday once to the South of France with another couple we thought we knew well, and this chap used to read bits out loud from the paper over breakfast. I nearly stabbed him with the butter knife.' Imogen laughed in pleasure that at last someone knew where she was coming from. 'But his wife! By the end we called her Polly Plumper. All we wanted to do was lounge about but she planned everything. Every time you stood up she'd plump up the cushion and tidy away your glass. Very unrelaxing.' Edie glanced up into Imogen's face, a gentle knowing smile on her face, and Imogen had to smile a bit sheepishly.

'It's about compromise I think,' Edie continued kindly. 'Letting everyone do things their way for a couple of weeks isn't such a big sacrifice really, is it? And making a cake, darling. How would you have felt if she'd done that for Rory?' Imogen looked down into her drink, the tears pricking behind her eyes. 'I hardly know you, sweetheart, but I suspect you are like your mother. Immensely capable, but in a way that makes the rest of us feel rather inadequate. You know when Ralph and I used to take our afternoon walk – we used to do it everyday until he was too poorly.' She glanced down briefly. 'We'd end up on a bench by the harbour, and he used to sit me next to him and hold my hand and say: "Faces up to the sun, old girl." And he was right, you know: it's important to stop and just let it all go for a while.' There were tears in her eyes, but she leant forward, and winked. 'But I

252

know what you mean about the towels.' And she smiled broadly. 'Now let's see what those children are up to,' and she stood up, only to be pre-empted by Rory storming through the door, his face lit up with glee at the 'cool' toys they'd found upstairs.

The rest of the day was a joy. Imogen was right – it was soup. A thick broth of chicken, carrots, potatoes and beans, but the children (Arch and Ollie dressed in Edie's vintage cast-off clothes) demolished it, mopping it up with hunks of homemade bread. Brown, for goodness' sake! The rain stopped for long enough after lunch for a trip down the steep steps to the cove beneath the house, and Edie taught Rory to skim stones and helped Olivia find interesting shells. Then they came back for a cup of tea in mismatched china cups, and Edie challenged the children to shove halfpenny with real halfpennies on a deep brown board, glass smooth from years of love and polish. In between times, she asked Imogen about her life, coaxing her into revealing things Imogen had never thought she'd end up saying.

Edie talked little about herself, but she did mention Ralph's name whenever possible.

'Do you miss him?' Imogen asked, kicking herself for such a crass question.

'Every second of every day,' said Edie, without looking up from her game with Rory. 'I poured all the love I had into him – very unhealthy.' She laughed self-deprecatingly. 'But I didn't have children, did I? Just wasn't to be. So he got all that unused maternal love too, poor man!'

By the time they'd said their goodbyes and pulled away from the drive, it was nearly six, hours later than Imogen had anticipated. 'That was fun, wasn't it, kids?'

'She's well cool,' said Rory, and Olivia just stroked dreamily the old feather boa Edie had handed to her as they left.

Jo woke with a jolt and that awful feeling of not knowing where she was or why. After her shower earlier she'd sat on the bed and had only meant to close her eyes for a moment. Now, staring around her in confusion, she felt as though someone was there that shouldn't be, or someone wasn't that should be. Weird. She sat up and shook her head a few times, to clear it. Waking as dawn broke and finding herself in Matt's bed, she'd felt a surge of panic – she hadn't meant to fall asleep with him at all. She had to get back to Finn! Immediately she'd slid out from under the weight of his outstretched arm, retrieving her clothes from the floor where he'd let them fall.

He'd undressed her so slowly the night before, brushing her hands away when she tried to reciprocate or hurry him. But, in the cold grey light of morning, she'd pulled her cold, limp jeans and top back on briskly and silently, shuddering slightly at the feel of yesterday's clothes, before tiptoeing back down the stairs, glancing at the evidence of last night's abandon as she went. The empty beer bottles that never made their way back to the kitchen. His red flannel shirt.

She had hoped no one would realise she'd stayed out. But thanks to Imogen lying in wait for her in the kitchen, like a suspicious mother, that had been blown. She'd had no right. It was none of her business, and only a bit of fun. And what fun! She smiled silkily as she replayed a moment from the night before. Her body was still aching but it had all felt so good. She'd been right – it was just what she'd needed. She shivered and, letting the damp towel slip from her as she foraged for clean clothes from the pile on the bed, she looked down at her naked body. Had she been all right for him? What he'd been expecting? And then there was an unfamiliar feeling: had she given too much? Been too passionate? It was like some awful game where the rules changed every time you played, but she knew it was a long time since she'd responded to a man like that.

Now from downstairs she could hear the sound of plates crashing together and the TV turned up too loud. Imogen must be losing her grip. She selected some clothes at random, fixed her hair and face minimally and plodded downstairs.

'Turn that telly down, for God's sake, Finn. And why aren't you eating at the table? Look, you've dropped crumbs all over the sofa. Imogen'll wig out.'

'Chill, Jo,' he placated. 'She's not here. None of them are. They've all gone to see a friend of her mum's, or something. Rory didn't want to.' Finn couldn't conceal the pride in his voice. 'He wanted to stay here with me and make a den in the garden. Can he come and stay when we get back to London? Can he?'

Jo was slow on the uptake. 'What do you mean, they've all gone? I can hear Sophie in the kitchen.'

Finn sighed long-sufferingly. 'Yes, *they're* still here. Bloody girls. They drive you mad. I think Gracie *fancies* me. She keeps following me. Gross! Can we go and see Matt today? He can't be busy, cos the weather's so bad. Can we, Jo?'

Backing out of the room, Jo wondered if a large coffee would help. She'd forgotten how full-on Finn could be. All those questions. All those demands. And he never bothered to wait for the answer. He'd been so much better here, with Rory to absorb some of that excess energy. Without him, he'd be bouncing off the walls soon. Coffee.

An apocalyptic chaos greeted her in the kitchen. Sophie was muttering crossly, crouching down to squint at the coffee machine, and there were beans and grounds scattered over the work surface. A strong smell of burnt toast filled the air, despite the fact that all the doors and windows had been thrown open. Amelia and Grace were flicking Coco Pops at each other and a pool of chocolatey milk was starting to drip off the edge of the table.

'Oh there you are at last!' exclaimed Sophie crossly. 'Can you work this sodding machine? Nothing seems to be coming through. I've tried everything. And the frigging toaster has a mind of its own.' She straightened up and eased her back, giving Jo a searching look. 'And what time did you get in, you dirty stop-out? I tried to wait up but I was knackered. Or pissed perhaps. I bloody well hope you're going to fill me in on the details as payment for babysitting.'

Jo gave her what she hoped was an innocent stare, then

tried to divert her by prodding at the coffee machine. But Sophie was not to be deflected. She lowered her voice. 'You pulled a fast one there, you old trollop. Imogen was frantic. Well, as frantic as a woman who's drunk two-thirds of a bottle of wine and the dregs of a jug of Pimm's can be. She was all for calling the police, y'know. Had you dead in a ditch by eleven.'

'Look, it's just this switch here. Ow!' A blast of scalding steam shot out, and Jo leapt back, nursing her wrist then, cursing, shoved it under the cold tap. The coffee started to trickle through. 'Imogen usually does this, doesn't she?' she commented glumly. 'Oh God, did she really freak out? For goodness' sake, I'm quite grown up now.'

Sophie fished two clean cups out of the dishwasher. 'Grown up?' she asked pointedly. 'You were behaving more like a teenager. Of course she freaked out, she's a natural-born worrier. At least give us some warning next time. I presume there's going to be a next time?'

Jo felt as if she'd been sent to stand in the corner. 'Don't know,' she replied sullenly. 'I doubt it.'

Sophie frowned. 'That doesn't sound like Matt. What did he say?'

'Well …' Jo sipped the scalding coffee. 'Oh Sophie, this coffee's vile. How much did you put in? He didn't really say anything. I … er … sort of left early and there wasn't much time.'

'You didn't!' Sophie thumped her mug down on the work surface, slopping the murky brew over the sides. 'You bloody did, didn't you? You did a bunk! Was he even awake?' In response to Jo's evasive shrug, she threw up her hands. 'You are the limit, really you are. What's the poor man going to think?'

'That I'm uncomplicated and don't want to get involved beyond a bit of mutually satisfying rumpy-pumpy?' Jo suggested hopefully.

'No, Jo. Think it through. He'll probably assume that you wished you hadn't stayed, you don't really like him, that you think he has a tiny willy and you had to fake. Is that what you want?'

Jo frowned. She hadn't thought of it from Matt's point of view. 'Well, no. Not really. But I didn't mean to stay in the first place. I just fell asleep afterwards.'

'Well at least it wasn't during!'

Jo felt herself blush uncharacteristically. 'No danger of that,' she murmured quietly. 'Oh Soph, it's not like we're dating or anything. He won't mind – he'll probably be relieved.'

Sophie glanced irritably at the squealing girls, who were on all fours under the table, chasing each other round and tugging on the table cloth. 'Girls, buzz off, would you? Go and watch telly with Finn and quieten down, please. We'll think of something to do in a bit. Maybe go out to that doll's house shop, but only if you're good.'

The girls emerged, their pyjamas studded with soggy nuggets of cereal. 'Finn told us to sod off when we went in,' Gracie lisped. 'That's a bad word, isn't it?'

Jo tutted. 'Well, you tell Finn from me that if he doesn't let you watch whatever you want, I'll take *him* to the doll's house shop as well.'

The girls trotted off, and the women replaced them at the table. Sophie looked round at the debris in disgust. 'It never seems to be like this when Imo's here. I don't know how she does it. Does she spend all her time cleaning or something? This is going to take ages to sort out.'

'I never thought I'd say this,' said Jo with a rueful laugh, 'but I almost miss her obsessional behaviour.'

Sophie sat silently for a moment, looking at Jo carefully. 'Y'know, you could cut her some slack. I realise she trod on your corns a bit yesterday with the birthday party thing, but she was doing it for the very best motives.'

'What? To make me feel inadequate? C'mon, Soph. You know that über-hausfrau thing isn't me. Why should I feel bad about that? I work bloody hard, y'know. I haven't got time for all that crap.' Jo stared at the table, tracing patterns in the spilt milk, looking up only when Sophie leant forward to squeeze her arm.

'I *know* you work hard. I *know* that tiggy-winkling isn't your thing,' she said firmly. 'We all know that. We also know that it *is* Imo's thing. She loves it and she does it bloody well. Why should you feel threatened by that? Women can't be expected to do everything though, God knows, we seem to expect it of ourselves.'

'Well,' Jo said tightly, 'Finn said it was his best party ever. He seemed much happier to hug her than me. And she took over completely. I might as well not have been there.'

'Jo, you're his mother. He needs you more than he needs anyone else. He needs you far more than he needs a cake, for Christ's sake. But everyone likes to feel special occasionally.'

Jo closed her eyes, thinking of the way Matt had gently pushed her hair off her face as she lay on the pillow, the snack of toast and tea he had brought after they had made love for the first time. Special.

Sophie's voice brought her back with a start. 'Imogen certainly doesn't think any less of you because you don't make cakes. Why should you think less of her because she does?'

Jo sat up and rubbed her eyes. 'Y'know what? Why don't you and the girls go out to your doll's house thing. We'll stay here and clear up a bit. I'd like to spend some time on my own with Finn. It'll be good.' She smiled briskly. 'Go and get dressed now. Go on, or the day'll be half over. Any idea if the weather is going to pick up?'

'Why don't you listen to the weather forecast?' Sophie grinned wickedly. 'The radio's tuned in to the right station.' And she padded from the room. 'Girls? What are you doing to poor Finn? Let him up. Oh for goodness' sake! Untie him at once …'

While Finn went to shower and get dressed, Jo started in on the kitchen by emptying the dishwasher. She noted wryly that Imogen had left her own family's crocks neatly piled up on the side, but still dirty. By the time Finn reappeared, his hair shiny and ringleted with wax, she was finished.

The little boy glanced round at the restored order hopefully. 'Oh, is Rory back?'

'Nope,' Jo snorted. 'I did this all by myself, without a

safety net. I was thinking, Finnster, would you like to go out somewhere, just you and me? We haven't done much of that these hols. Maybe drive along the coast, see if there's an indoor pool somewhere, go into Newquay?'

He brightened up. 'There's a zoo at Newquay, and Matt said there's a pool right next to it with flumes and stuff.'

This was beginning to look like a plan. 'Okey-doke. Get your swimming gear and we'll give it a go. It's ages since I've been to a zoo.'

Finn started off up the stairs, then turned back. 'Could we ask Matt? He says there's a red panda there that's really friendly. Is that right, Mum, is there such a thing as a red panda?'

Jo carefully ignored the first half of his question. 'Red panda? Sounds a bit glam. Maybe red is the new black in the panda world. Well, there's only one way to find out. Let's take the camera, just in case. We'll have lunch out somewhere. Go on, move it!'

By the end of the afternoon and a massive margherita pizza devoured by Finn, they were both tired and happy. They held hands and ran to the car, then headed for home, Finn chattering nineteen to the dozen then abruptly falling asleep, his mouth open and his head jolting with every turn. Sophie's car was in front of the house, but no sign of the über-frau. Strange. She knew Finn wouldn't be thrilled his new best friend wasn't back yet – and he'd be lumbered again with the doe-eyed adoration of Gracie. Jo turned off the engine and Finn blearily opened his eyes. His hair had gone mad, drying without the calming effect of any product. As they walked into the house, Amelia raced downstairs in her pyjamas, then stopped in horror to stare at him. 'Finn, your hair has exploded. You look like a golliwog.'

Jo winced and waited for Finn to react. His hair was his pride and joy, and he lavished hours and most of his pocket money on styling products. 'So?' he grunted aggressively. 'You look like a stupid doll *all* the time.' And he stomped off upstairs.

Jo followed him up and the mood there was no better. Sophie emerged from the bathroom, her hair frizzy from the steam and her face a deep shade of purple. She was muttering darkly under her breath. From behind her Gracie's sobs rent the air, crescendoing as she ascended the foothills of Mount Tantrum.

'Christ, Soph. Sounds like the Iranian Embassy Siege in there. Want me to summon the SAS?'

Sophie shuddered. 'I doubt even they would be able to dissuade her from using my John Frieda conditioner on her sodding Barbie! Is Imogen back yet?'

Jo shook her head and walked into her room to dump her bag on her bed. 'Nope,' she called over her shoulder. 'Can't you tell? There's no delicious smell of frying onions.'

'Too right there isn't,' Sophie shouted back from retrieving Grace's pyjamas. 'It was my turn to cook and I forgot. I hope to God they've eaten on their way home. It's slim pickings for us, I'm afraid. There's some of the girls' supper left in the pan I think.'

Half an hour later, Grace had been placated and Finn,

his hair now tamed back into ringlets and a look of disgust on his face, was sitting a safe distance away from the two sisters as they watched *Powerpuff Girls* on DVD.

'Mmm, this is delicious,' said Jo with heavy irony as she steeled herself to take another forkful of tinned novelty pasta with little sausages coated in tomato sauce. 'I wish I'd nicked more of Finn's pizza now. I can't believe Imogen put this muck on the shopping list.'

Sophie looked up sheepishly. 'Sorry. Guilty. It was the best the late "nite" shop at the garage could come up with.'

Jo abandoned her bowl and threw down her fork. 'Well, not even your girls would eat it and they're pretty omnivorous, aren't they? Doesn't that tell you something?' She rubbed her stomach. 'I'm starving. How long does it take to make bread in that machine of Imogen's?'

Sophie too abandoned any pretence and scraped the contents of her bowl into the bin. 'Gosh, I wouldn't dare touch that! Look what happened with the coffee machine this morning.'

Jo groaned miserably. 'There's only one solution. One of us will have to go for a kebab. Best of three at stone, scissors, paper?'

It was then that they heard tyres on the drive outside, and moments later, throwing themselves at the front door, a beaming Rory, Olivia and Archie tumbled in, followed by Imogen. In her hand she was balancing a huge, flat package.

'Hope you haven't eaten yet,' she gasped breathlessly.

'Found a gorgeous deli close to Edie's, and couldn't resist this steak pie. The children scoffed one in the car, but it won't take a second to reheat this one. Any takers?'

Chapter 13

Friday

Sunny and dry with warm sea breezes

'Well, that's a nuisance,' Imogen sighed. 'We're all itching to see you. What time do you think you'll get here tomorrow?'

She could hear the tension of the day ahead in Guy's voice. 'I should be able to get an early flight. I've asked Polly to look into it now. But it's been a bugger of a day already and it's not even eight thirty.'

'How's things at home? Did you remember to water the tomatoes?'

'Thanks, David, tell him I'll call him back.' Guy's voice came back on the line. 'Sorry? Oh yes, tomatoes. Well, I've forgotten a couple of times, and they look a bit wilted but they should pick up. House is fine. Hardly been there really.'

'Have you remembered to feed them too?' She'd nurtured those ruddy plants from seed and she wasn't going to have them killed by negligence.

'OK OK, I'll try and remember before I come down.'

'Any news on Hong Kong?' She knew nothing she was saying couldn't wait, but she wanted to show she was interested, and talk to him before the business of the day lured him away. 'I've taken the chance to look at some websites while I've been here and found out a bit more stuff.' She could hear interruptions in the background and muffled voices as Guy had obviously put his hand over the receiver. Talking to him at the office was hell at the best of times, but worse in the mornings when the markets were still open in the Far East. Her heart sank. It had been like this throughout their marriage and, she suspected, it was going to be worse than this when they were out there. People she'd spoken to – well, didn't everyone know someone who knew someone who'd lived in Hong Kong? – had hinted that you worked hard and played hard, which didn't sound much like the lifestyle she knew. In Barnes, with friends round the corner to drop in on for coffee and the civilisation of Wimbledon Common or Kew Gardens not far away, one could almost kid oneself one was living the life of a country wife. Well, she could dream, couldn't she? How at odds it would all be with life in a high-rise.

'Look, Imo darling, I've got to go. Things are a bit hairy here. Re: HK, Graham wants to talk to me later about it so I should have a firmer idea of things tomorrow. I'll call this evening.' And the phone went dead. Poor man, thought Imogen, work really was hassle hassle hassle. I hope to goodness Hong Kong has its compensations.

Coming out of the back door, she was surprised to see Jo already sitting at the garden table, cup of coffee in hand, her legs pulled beneath her. She's so graceful,

Imogen heard herself think. *I can't quite imagine her in work clothes ministering to someone's haemorrhoids, but perhaps she works in one of those trendy inner-city practices where it's OK to dress how you like.*

Imogen looked warily at her, wondering what sort of climate the morning had brought.

'Thanks for the great pie again,' said Jo after a pause. 'It was a lifesaver.' Imogen, encouraged, could feel herself start to gush.

'It was rather scrummy, wasn't it! They must put wicked things in that pastry.' Jo nodded, then indicated the phone in Imogen's hand.

'Sounded like trouble?'

Imogen sighed dramatically. 'Oh men! Work. Cancellations. Same old story!' She wasn't going to show her disappointment to Jo. 'Guy'll have to get a flight here tomorrow because something's come up at the office. It's all a bit frantic before our posting.' She smiled broadly, and went on, 'So I'm afraid we'll both be feeling like gooseberries tonight!' She jerked her head towards the house and raised her eyebrows in mock despair.

Jo shuddered exaggeratedly. 'Count me out. I think I'll see whether the Finnbar wants to try out some of those lovely chips at the harbour, then we can throw the soggy ones to the seagulls and drive the residents mad!' *But you probably won't,* thought Imogen, smothering a feeling of disappointment at being knocked back again, and unable to suppress the uncharitable thought that Jo's devil-may-care attitude was all posturing. *How pointless.*

'Oh well.' She shrugged, as if she couldn't give a

monkey's what Jo and Finn did for the evening, but knowing there would be fall-out from Rory. Then an idea came into her head. 'I think I'll take my lot to the cinema in Wadebridge to see that new sci-fi nonsense. The boys will love it,' and getting up from her seat, she walked inside.

God! What was it about that woman? Imogen threw sandy beach shoes into the bag with unnecessary force. It was a case of permanent shadow boxing, and she was almost ashamed of herself at playing Jo back at her own silly game, but what else could you do when the blasted woman was so changeable?

'Right!' she hollered up the stairs. 'Five minutes till off for surfing, and anyone who's late is cleaning the loo!'

They drew up in the beach car park with time to spare, having left Jo back at the house. She'd promised to do the afternoon shift with the older ones while 'you girls prepare Babette's feast for the menfolk', as she had put it. At first Imogen couldn't make out Matt amongst the mêlée on the beach. With it being the last session of the week's course, there was plenty of enthusiasm oozing out of the group of small children who were bouncing up and down in their little black wetsuits, with a handful of young instructors trying to corral them into some kind of order for the lesson.

'Looks like old lover boy's not here.' Sophie dumped her beach bag and towels next to Imogen's pile. 'I'm quite jealous really. Can you remember in the early days when your heart used to go pitter patter when *he* called or took you out?' She looked dreamily out to sea.

'Well, from what I *hear* you don't seem to be doing too badly on the romance stakes even now.' Imogen gave her a well-meaning poke in the ribs.

Sophie rolled over onto her stomach and started idly to smooth down the sand with her hand. 'Oh I still fancy the pants off Hugh, but it's not quite like the old days, is it?'

'Be grateful for that, old love. For the rest of us the pitter patter of your heart was fast replaced by the pitter patter of tiny feet and we all know what those little darlings do to romance ...' She laughed hollowly. 'Perhaps Jo's got it right doing it alone.'

'Oh, that wasn't by choice, I can assure you,' Sophie whispered confidingly. 'She's not as hard as she looks and it's all bravado. I don't really know much about what went on with Finn's dad. She just clams up. She's never had anyone serious since I've known her and that must be getting on for five years. But it's probably difficult with Finn around. Bit of a passion killer.' Imogen's ears pricked up at this information – it hadn't stopped her the other night – but Sophie, now poking her finger into the sand and watching the grains pour down into the little holes, seemed to have gone off on another tack. 'Can't imagine what it must be like doing it all on your own. I'm glad I've got Hughie beside me. And you feel that too, don't you?'

'Oh of course I do! Guy may work idiotic hours, be as good as useless at the weekends and not be entirely sure where the children go to school, but at least he's home most nights and there's someone to wake me with their snoring.'

There was a contented pause. 'Are you looking forward to your big Far East adventure?'

'Do you know – I think I am, especially now I've found out some more details. The kids will love it and it will be a whole new experience!' A shadow fell across her and she squinted up into the sunlight to see who it was.

'Matt!' Sophie said delightedly. 'Not on duty today again, you part-timer? Have a Hob Nob,' and she delved into her bag.

'You women are worth coming over to see for your biscuit supplies alone!' He laughed, helping himself to the outstretched packet.

'Well, don't pretend it's because you want your young helpers to think you've pulled us chicks. We know your motives!' and Sophie got slowly to her feet. 'Right, Imogen, by way of a thank-you for your sterling work last night with the meat pie, I shall sacrifice my snooze on the beach and entertain Arch and Gracie,' and she waded through the soft sand to where the two children were playing.

Imogen turned back to Matt. 'Playing truant today, are you, or is it more work hassle?'

'The latter I'm afraid. Summer's just started but I feel like the pressures of the real world are looming already. So I thought I'd let my little band of helpers keep the surfers occupied this morning and I've been on the phone half the time.'

'People always talk about the "long vac" don't they, and when I was a kid it used to go on for ever, but before you know it now September's here and it's new shoes, haircuts, sharpened pencils and back to the fray.'

'Sign of getting old, I suppose.' His eyes crinkled in a smile. 'I was the third of three boys, so it was always hand-me-down uniform and my mum was even known to pass on their shoes! No wonder I've picked a job where I don't have to wear a tie!'

She laughed. 'I'm stretching it all out for one more term, and Rory will have to make do with a blazer that's far too small.'

'How come?'

'Oh I thought Jo might have mentioned it,' she paused, 'though I suppose there's no reason why she would have. It's their last term in that school for a while. We're off to Hong Kong for two years, probably at Christmas.'

Matt looked round at her, his eyes wide. 'Wow! What an opportunity! I've been there a couple of times myself, in fact. It's cookin' is Hong Kong, and the kids will be able to surf!'

Imogen was the wide-eyed one now. 'Never!'

'Oh yes.' He smiled broadly. 'Tai Long Wan or Big Wave Bay's the place. And it's clean, which isn't something that can be said about all bits of water round there. It's hell at weekends though, but that's when the ex-pats come out to play.'

'Oh Matt.' Imogen couldn't believe her luck. 'Rory will be thrilled. He is so against going at all, but I'm working on him, and this might swing it.'

'He'll be the proverbial pig in clover. I tell you what, I'll get Lucia to talk to him.'

'Lucia?'

'Yeah, the little darling. She gives me a hand when I'm short-staffed and I had to enlist her help this morning. She might even be taking Rory's group today.' He put his hand up to shield his eyes and looked down the beach to the group of children larking about in the water. 'Yeah, that's her with the ponytail and the turquoise stripe down her wetsuit. She's been out to HK a couple of times too – once with me – and she'll have a slightly younger perspective on it, I reckon!'

Imogen's curiosity was piqued as he talked about this pretty young woman at the water's edge, and the trip they had taken. 'Oh yes,' he enthused, 'we had a ball. She took me to places a man of my age shouldn't ever go near! Still, it keeps you young, hey!'

'I hope Guy doesn't get any ideas!' Imogen laughed uncertainly, trying to imagine Matt with this girl who must be twenty years his junior. This was a side of him she hadn't imagined.

'Jo's been there too, I think,' she said suddenly, aware that she was fishing for information about the two of them. Hell, Jo had scuttled home at the break of dawn from his bed, hadn't she? What was the point in pretending?

'Really? I wouldn't know,' he said slowly, a closed expression on his face. 'Have you known her long?'

'About three days longer than you. Why?'

He squinted out to sea again. 'Oh, I see. It's nothing really. It's just … she's a hard one to read, isn't she?'

Disarmed by his comment about a woman with whom

she'd assumed he was having some kind of relationship, she didn't quite know how to respond. 'Er, well. She's a friend of Sophie's really. But, yes, I can't really work her out.'

He turned and smiled cynically at her. 'Well, it's nice to know I'm not the only one around here. I was getting paranoid!'

'You like her though, don't you?' Matt didn't reply for a moment and she wondered whether he'd heard her.

'I thought I did.' He turned to face her. 'But I'm beginning to think she could be high maintenance and I'm not sure I've got the energy for it.' He looked at the children, now cavorting with Lucia in a game of chase. 'Those are the only kind of games I'm prepared to play now. Nice, uncomplicated ones.'

Imogen followed his gaze, disappointed that perhaps any hope of playing Cupid between Jo and this man, who'd seemed so ideal for her, looked doomed to failure. Though why the hell she should be helping out Jo she didn't know. They watched the children's antics with Lucia in silence for a moment.

Imogen sighed. Who could blame him? 'She is lovely, Matt.'

His eyes crinkled at the corners. 'Yes, she's terrific. I'm as proud as hell of her,' and, with Imogen's gentle encouragement, he began to talk about the woman whose happy laughter was carrying across the beach to them, until Rory suddenly lunged into Imogen's line of vision, dripping wet but his face alive with excitement. He was followed swiftly by the others.

'That was fab. Mum, this is Lou. She's great and she showed me how to carve a wave.' Imogen turned to welcome the open-faced young woman now standing beside Rory, with Olivia's arms draped around her. Her dark, shiny hair, still wet from the surfing, was held back in a wind-blown ponytail and, when she smiled broadly, she revealed small white teeth.

'Hello, Lou. I've just been hearing all about you. Fancy a coffee to warm you up?'

Once everyone had left the house for the beach, Jo flopped into a chair, exhausted, and sighed deeply. She'd been drawn into the vortex of fannying about to get everyone ready, and it would have been impossible simply to sit down and read the paper. That would have required more single-mindedness than even Jo was capable of. Now, had she been a man ...

She'd seen it time and again with boyfriends and friends' partners. That completely blinkered view of the world that would allow a man, with no apparent pangs of conscience, to opt out of all decision-making, preparation or involvement with the day-to-day running of house and children. She'd even witnessed one particularly gormless bloke ask his wife, while she was simultaneously feeding the dog, worming the cat, helping two recalcitrant boys with homework and a third to make a Santa sleigh out of a shoe box, if *she* thought he needed a hair cut. Men! Honestly! She was better off without one and no mistake.

Jo shifted in the armchair. Men. Yes. She was quite

pleased the other two had jumped at her offer to take over childcare at the beach after lunch, leaving them free to prepare for the weekend. What they didn't know was that she was dreading seeing Matt again and what he might have to say about her dawn bolt. A morning on her own would give her breathing space before she faced him.

Jo had to admit that she was also dreading the arrival of Guy and Hugh. Inevitably they would disrupt the balance of the house – however uneasy it was – with their noise, their clutter and their habits. They had a perfect right to be there, of course, but somehow everything changed the minute they put their bags down in the hall. As eagerly awaited as the Messiah, they would arrive on clouds of glory, unlikely saviours in chino shorts and docksiders. They would punish the unworthy and reward the just – well, shout at the children and buy ice creams for everyone. And once again Finn would be thoroughly left out.

Unable to sit still any longer, she pottered about, trying not to keep checking the wall clock. She really had nothing to be nervous about, after all. Then, with an hour to spare before she was due to relieve the others, she popped back upstairs to shower, change and fix her make-up before setting off. The early start paid off and, surprising herself, she was down at the beach in plenty of time.

This time she could feel Matt's presence before she even saw him. Some kind of tingly sixth sense told her that he was behind her and she quickened her pace slightly in spite of herself.

Imogen looked up. 'Ah, Jo.' She smiled abstractedly. 'Good. Sophie and I will get going right away if you don't mind. Oh, Matt. Thanks for coming back, but Jo's here now after all. Did you manage to get through?'

Jo turned around, but not before she had composed her face into a look of casual disinterest. 'Oh hi, Matt. All right?'

'Yes thanks, Imogen. It's all sorted out.' He turned and looked briefly at Jo. 'Hello. I gather you're on the second shift today.'

Jo could feel herself tense up. God he looked fantastic, all self-contained, lean and sun-bleached, but his expression was unreadable and she knew straightaway she'd screwed up badly. Sophie had been right, she shouldn't have left while he was still sleeping. He deserved better than that. Could she salvage something? Would he understand why she'd had to go, or would he be like all the others, with no time for the time she had to make for Finn?

She didn't really want Imogen overhearing this conversation but, luckily, she was engrossed in packing her belongings. 'Yeah, I had a few things to do this morning, calls to make. You know, keep in touch with home.' Jo fiddled with her bag, looking down as she spoke. 'So now it's my turn so the others can get ready for the weekend.'

Matt nodded. 'Right, yes. The weekend.'

'Er, where are the kids?' Jo blurted, looking hopefully down the beach as she sidled away from Matt. 'Has Finn been OK, Imogen?'

'He's been great,' answered Imogen, warmly. 'They've all done really well, actually. Matt was just saying, weren't you, Matt? He's done some certificates for them, so we can have a little graduation ceremony in a minute, if they like.'

Jo laughed nervously, glancing over to Matt who was standing with his arms folded, looking down the beach. 'More crap to clutter up Finn's bedroom! Just what I need.'

Imogen's eyes flicked over to Matt, frowning. 'Well, I know my two will be delighted. What with that and the photos Sophie has been taking all morning, they'll be dying to show their mates when we get home. And I'm encouraging them to start a scrapbook before we go to Hong Kong, so they'll remember all their friends. I'm sure they'll want to stick it in there. Oh, that's an idea! Let's have a group photo when they get back, shall we? I think Sophie's going to round them up now, so we can say bye bye.'

Jo grimaced. In this wind, her hair would look an awful mess. She was aware of Matt staring at her, but ignored him, shielding her eyes from the sun as she scanned the beach. After a moment, he turned away and stretched out a hand to help Imogen to her feet. 'Where are they now, Imogen?'

Imogen scanned the beach pointing out each child's location. 'I'll rally them. They've all eaten well, Jo, so that won't be a problem, but if you could just reapply the sun cream – here you are – if the little ones go in the water? Thanks so much! I've got stacks to do for tomorrow – want to make some fresh pasta for a start. Just as well Guy isn't coming tonight.'

Imogen set off determinedly across the sand. There was an awkward silence between Matt and Jo. Then they both started to speak together. 'Are you …?' 'About the other …'

Matt nodded at her. 'You first.' He watched her narrowly.

'I just wanted to thank you for a nice, er, evening.'

He stared at her, clearly waiting for more. After a while he gave up. 'Yes, well. Obviously I enjoyed it too. Wasn't so keen on the morning, though.'

He was looking at her as though she'd emerged from underneath a rock, and she could hear a whiny, defensive tone creeping into her voice. 'I thought you'd be busy. I wasn't sure …'

He shrugged. 'I thought that kind of behaviour was supposed to be the preserve of the less savoury type of man. I *thought* that kind of thing went out with Cro-Magnons. But maybe I'm out of touch. Is that how you do things now in London? Fuck and run?'

Jo winced. She felt like she'd been thumped. To him, her behaviour must have looked like old-fashioned, hit-and-run, one-night-stand, wham-bam, unreconstructed sexist crap. 'Matt, it wasn't like that. I had to—'

'Come on.' Imogen's jolly voice collided with her stammering explanation. 'Can I use your super camera, Sophie? Rory and Finn, you stand at either end, girls in the middle. Matt, Jo go on, closer.'

Matt hung back, still looking accusingly at Jo. Rory

was looking round in puzzlement. 'Where are Lou and Dan? Can we get them in too?'

'They left straight after lunch, I'm afraid,' Matt shrugged apologetically.

'Oh that's a shame, we can't say goodbye,' said Imogen.

'I'm seeing Lou later, so I'll pass on the message. Look, why don't I take the photo and you join the others? Sophie, just show me what to press.'

Jo could feel Imogen muscle in beside her. 'Are you planning to see Matt this weekend?' she said in a conspiratorial voice. 'Only I was wondering if you'd like to invite him to have dinner with us on Saturday evening?'

Jo panicked. 'Ooh, no. I don't think so, really.'

'I'm sure he'd love to come. Let me invite him. I've got a lovely recipe for fresh lobster ravioli, and its just as easy to do for six. Matt,' Imogen raised her voice before Jo could stop her, 'Matt, why don't you and Jo join us old marrieds on Saturday night?'

Jo, her face aghast, frantically nudged Imogen and hissed at her to be quiet.

'Smile!' Click. Matt reappeared from behind the camera, handed it back to Sophie and, though Jo couldn't quite overhear, she was pretty sure he was making his excuses for dinner. Why couldn't Imogen butt out for once? Matt turned away to help the others with their bags. 'Let me take those for you,' he offered, and walked up to the car park with Sophie and Imogen, who threw a slightly anxious glance back over her shoulder. Left alone,

Jo kept an unobtrusive eye on his movements, but after he waved them off, he went straight back to his office. If it hadn't been for the children scattering back to their games, she'd have turned tail and fled.

Damn it. She sat down again and dug into the sand with her toes, flicking her glance between the two groups of children, contentedly absorbed in their respective games. The minutes ticked by, but still Matt didn't return. God! He was acting as if she had the plague, or something. She smiled mirthlessly. Whereas the other night, he'd been all over her like a rash. She spied him briefly at one point deep in conversation on his mobile, scuffing at the step outside the office with his foot, before he disappeared again inside.

An hour must have gone by, and she'd tried pathetically to concentrate on her book, glancing up from it every now and then to scan the beach and check on the children, but she'd eventually thrown it aside. She shifted her bottom to find a more comfortable position, took off her T-shirt then promptly put it back on again. Nothing felt right.

'I was having some tea,' said a cool voice behind her. 'Thought you might like one too.' He handed her a mug, but remained standing and she had to crane her neck to look up. She took a deep breath.

'Look, Matt, about the other night. I know I should have left a note or something, of course, but I wasn't really thinking it through. I'm not used to … I'm not really …' Jo could hear herself babbling and sighed. 'The thing is, I didn't mean to stay the whole night because I didn't want Finn waking up without me there. And when I woke I panicked and …' Well, she'd said it.

'Ohhh,' he said slowly, and she could see an amazed relief spread over his face. 'Oh, right. Well, of course, that's different. When you said you could stay, I assumed you meant … yes, I see.' Now he seemed to be the one feeling uncomfortable. 'I should have thought about it.' He paused and smiled teasingly. 'A note would have been nice though.' He crouched down. 'I thought perhaps you didn't enjoy yourself.'

She could feel herself blush. 'Did you …? Ooh, no. Not at all. Quite the contrary, in fact.'

He sat down beside her now. 'Hmmm. Would you like to do something this weekend, maybe? Not necessarily supper with the others, though. I did get your message back there.'

'Weeell, Finn's going to the cinema tonight with Imogen and her brood,' she lied quickly, grasping the moment, 'and I don't really want to get stuck in Snogsville again, so if you were free …'

Matt frowned. 'Er, tonight? No, sorry, it's difficult. I've already got plans. How about tomorrow afternoon? How about …?'

Imogen had looked pleasantly surprised when Jo had asked if she could join in their cinema jaunt and later that evening, leaving Sophie and Hugh chatting cosily while their girls ran around unchecked, she followed Imogen's car along the road to Wadebridge. At the quaint little one-screener, Finn and Rory went off together, looking at posters for the upcoming films, with Archie tagging along behind. Finn was particularly taken by one for a teen frat movie – certificate 15 – featuring bikini-clad girls draped over the gormless heroes. 'Cor, look at the bazongas on her,' he stage-whispered to Rory, and they giggled furtively.

Jo saw Imogen trying to signal to Rory to come back over to her and stood up quickly. 'Anyone fancy popcorn?' She was surrounded in an instant and, to make up for her imposition, bought them medium packs, rather than the small ones Imogen was promoting. 'My treat,' she said, 'and how about drinks? I hate having to get up in the middle of the movie, so I always stock up before. Coke, anyone?'

'Not for Archie, if you don't mind. I'd sooner they all had orange juice. Or how about some bottled water, Ollie?'

With the children eventually satisfied, they waited in the queue to go in. There was a silence between them. 'Jo, I hope you don't mind me asking, but you've travelled a lot. Are there any health issues I should be worrying about in Hong Kong?'

Jo shook her head slowly, relieved they had something they could discuss. 'Not really. Not in the hallowed portals of the ex-pat community, anyway. There are some fantastic doctors out there, excellent hospitals. If you went into mainland China, it might be different, of course. Nah, I reckon Hong Kong will be OK. Though there are definitely some places I wouldn't take children.'

'Oh?'

'Well, I have patients who take their children all over

the place and the poor little buggers have to take these awful malaria pills. They can be vicious and the side-effects can be very unpleasant. Mind you, better than catching it. Personally, I wouldn't put Finn through it or take him to anywhere with hepatitis, or those other nasties – river blindness, bilharzia, dengue fever.' Jo smiled at the mounting horror on Imogen's face and patted her arm. 'You'll be fine in Hong Kong.'

Imogen laughed uncertainly. 'Perhaps we'll stick to Padstow for holidays.'

When the lights came up after the film, Archie was looking decidedly green. Maybe he'd have been better off with a small popcorn after all. And Imogen clearly thought so too, to judge from her slightly told-you-so demeanour as they made their way to the car park. She'd insisted Archie go in her car, though, so at least Jo wouldn't have to deal with any puke. But when they drew up outside the house, he'd already fallen asleep. Imogen carried him inside, shushing the others in front of her as she went.

Jo found Sophie and Hugh slumped on the sofa in the sitting room. 'Oh hi! How was the flicks? I meant to say, I got the photos developed this afternoon. There are some lovely ones of Finn's birthday. Let me show you.'

Jo flicked through Sophie's glossy prints. As usual the composition was perfect. The children looked exquisite and happy, and there was a fantastic one of Finn at the beach, taken when he was concentrating hard on digging sand, his curly hair whipped across his face by the breeze. In the one at Finn's party, Jo looked like she'd swallowed a wasp. But worst of all was the last – the group photo Matt had taken at the beach in the afternoon. They all look distracted. Imogen with her mouth open, Rory and Finn scuffling, Sophie yawning. She stared, horrified, at the image of her own face. She looked so old. So bad-tempered. So tense. Was that what he'd seen when he looked through the lens? God! No wonder he hadn't wanted to take her out tonight.

Chapter 14

Saturday

Hot and sunny, with thunder in places.
Cooler later

It felt like one of those mornings when you were a child and you woke up with an excited feeling in your stomach and you couldn't work out why. Then you remembered that your best friend was coming over to play *all day*. Imogen rolled over and realised that she felt happy because it was Saturday and that meant Guy was coming. She was far too self-contained to show the sort of exhilaration Sophie demonstrated, practically diving into Hugh's arms the minute he was out of the car last night and smothering him in kisses, but she had to admit she was looking forward to Guy's arrival.

What I want, she thought as she gazed up at the underside of the four-poster bed canopy (realising fleetingly how horribly dusty it must get up there), what I want is to be able to hand over to him, to have him pour the drinks, share my interest in the weather, understand everything without my having to explain it. And she was especially wanting to finalise the plans for Hong Kong now he'd have spoken to Graham.

She swung out of bed, determined to have a delicious shower, slap some cream on her legs (which were beginning to brown nicely), and blow-dry her hair, something she hadn't done all holiday. Well, what was the point when by evening it was matted with sand and salt? It was seven thirty now – gosh, quite late for her, the holiday effect must at last be kicking in – and she wasn't sure what time he was arriving.

He'd phoned yesterday evening but Rory had intercepted her mobile and, in his chat to his father, had neglected to ask what time the plane landed at Newquay, muttering something about 'coffee time'. With a bit of luck she'd be able to get some bread baked, and get down to the deli for some pâté, ham and olives for lunch. No, better still, she thought as she stepped under the hot water of the shower, she'd go to the fishmonger's and get some fresh crabs. He'd love that, especially if she made mayonnaise. Lucky she'd brought her very special olive oil.

Hot after the shower and with the day already promising to be a scorcher, she put on a pink vest top and chino shorts. OK so they made her bum look big but what the heck. 'Pssst, Arch,' she hissed round his door. She could see he wasn't sleeping but didn't want to disturb Rory or Finn, who was lying on his back, his mouth open and the sheet thrown back to show his brown body, bare save for a pair of boxer shorts with a bright Lichtenstein cartoon pattern on them. Even his underpants were precocious.

Archie sat up and rubbed his eyes. 'I'm off to the deli

to get lunch for Daddy. Want to come?' she whispered again.

'Yeah. He flung down his rabbit onto the bedclothes and padded out to her, looking so small in his short-legged PJs with his ruffled hair. She gathered him to her and rubbed her cheek against his, and he put his arms around her neck, squeezing her tight. God how she loved this child. Her baby.

'What does crab taste like?' he asked as they set off down the road a little while later, with a promise of a warm croissant from the deli for breakfast.

'Sort of meaty but fishy. Very, very delicious.'

'Sounds yuk.' Archie was resolute and, having passed judgement, looked out of the window at the bright, sunny morning. 'Do they have crabs in Hong Kong? What do they eat there?'

'Well,' she said slowly, knowing she was on dangerous territory here, 'I suppose they eat Chinese food, like Daddy and I have sometimes. Rice and stir fry.' She could see the horror mounting on his face. 'But,' she added quickly, 'we can cook what we like in our own house. Just buy the ingredients like we normally would and have all your favourite things.'

'Will they have sausages and baked beans and things like that?' he persisted.

'Oh I'm sure they will.' And if they don't I'm having them imported, she thought, as she pulled up outside the deli.

'*Voilà!* Warm croissants, pains au chocolat, and a couple of Danishes.' Half an hour later back at the

287

kitchen table, Imogen emptied the contents of the paper bags onto plates in front of the children, who dived on them. She screwed up the bag and lobbed it into the bin. It was a lovely morning, the room smelt of coffee, she had bread in the breadmaker, crab in the fridge, shaved legs, blow-dried hair, and Guy was coming. Not even Jo was going to dent her mood.

In fact, there was little sign of Jo, and Imogen cleared away the children's mess – again – and sat taking a moment to finish her coffee and read the food pages of the weekend paper. Then, putting on her apron, she collected together the ingredients for mayonnaise. The eggs were super fresh and, even though they probably hadn't, she imagined they came from plump, happy Cornish hens who'd only ever breathed fresh sea air and had not seen the inside of a chicken house in their feathery lives. She turned on Radio Four and some easy Saturday-morning chat kept her company as she whisked, slowly adding the oil drop by drop until a whitish, creamy mixture began to appear. It was like alchemy, transforming one thing into another with the whisk of a whisk. She added salt, pepper and some crushed garlic, then dipped in her finger, scooping up a delicious blob into her mouth and wiping off a drip that had landed on her chin. Divine.

'Mum.' Olivia marched in through the kitchen door, in her hand a huge bunch of cow parsley, honeysuckle and ox-eye daisies, and plonked them down on the counter. 'These are for you, Mum.' And before she could escape, Imogen grabbed her and swung her around, holding her close, until she wriggled out of her mother's arms, giggling, and skipped outside again to join the others.

Two cups of coffee later, and a major assault on the chocolate biscuits, Imogen had begun to wish she had insisted she go to collect Guy. She looked at the clock again, and picking up the dishcloth, she wiped the already immaculate work surfaces and tidied up after herself.

'Is he here yet? What time's he coming?' Rory wandered into the room, bored and listless, his baggy three-quarter shorts not exactly contradicting the image. 'You said he'd be here this morning.'

'It is still the morning officially, and you were the one that spoke to him! Come here and give me a hug. You look like a sloppy teenager.' Rory's face lit up at this news – result! – and he let himself be folded into his mother's arms. Imogen could feel the softness of the skin on his bare back against her hands. He'd always had beautiful skin and she dreaded the day when it became muscly and, oh perish the thought, acned. He's still a little boy, just for now.

'Should be any time now I expect. Won't it be lovely to see him?'

'S'pose.' That was a yes. 'I want to show him the den Finn and I have fixed up in the garden. It rocks!' And with that he left the room and Imogen smiling after him.

When Guy did pull up in a taxi three-quarters of an hour later, Imogen forgot how twitchy she'd been and gave him a warm hug.

'You look tired.' She took his bag from him. 'Rory, get Dad a cold beer and I'll shove this upstairs.'

'Yup, pretty bushed.' He ran his hands over his eyes as if to prove it. 'I was with Graham last night until about eight, and then had loads to finish up in the office. In fact,' he put an uncharacteristic arm round Imogen's waist as they went inside, but made the familiar apologetic face she'd seen a thousand times before, 'I may have to get the earlier flight back tomorrow. Things have gone a bit pear-shaped.'

'Things are permanently pear-shaped. What's up now?'

'Oh, I'll tell you about it later,' and he let go of her to ruffle Archie's hair when he careered out of the door to greet his father.

Imogen dismissed it – well, he hadn't sounded too worried so it couldn't be anything awful – and bustled in the kitchen, while Guy had the cold beer and chatted to Hugh outside on the terrace. She could hear Hugh's guffaws of laughter in that hail-fellow-well-met way men have when they are a bit nervous about seeing one another again. Even Jo, up and about now, seemed keen enough to cooperate with the laying of the lunch table outside and, when Imogen came out bearing the tray with the crabs laid out on the huge platter, garnished with lemon and rocket, she smiled with joy at the yelps of delight from the assembled crew.

'Cor, Imo. You've surpassed yourself!' Sophie rubbed her hands in excitement, and they all dived in, even the children, who enthused about cracking the claws with the implements Imogen had found in the cutlery drawer, and then, once they'd sniffed the crab meat and turned up their noses, packed baguettes with ham and salad, and filled their faces with those instead. All except Finn who, Imogen saw with delight, picked up his now-empty crab shell and licked out each corner with his tongue, then put it down, revealing a broad grin on his mayonnaise-covered face.

The day was warm and the sunshine intense, with a white light bouncing off the terrace, and Imogen could feel her face getting even warmer as she sipped her second glass of white Burgundy far too quickly. But sitting back in her chair, replete with rich crab meat, mayonnaise and crusty brown bread, she surveyed the table, with everyone chatting and licking their fingers and thought, this is how I wanted it to be. All of us sitting around the table, as if we were in Provence, and surrounded by the debris of a delicious meal, with everyone full and happy.

The children had wandered over to the lawn and Rory was bowling balls at Finn, who was using a stick as a wicket. The girls were in the Wendy house and Arch was fiddling around somewhere. Imogen felt sleepy in a slightly boozed sort of way, and wanted very much to close her eyes and drift off. She let the conversation between Sophie and Hugh waft over her. Guy was quiet but perhaps he was tired. Jo put in a comment here and there, but they were arguing about some famous golfer who'd run off with a fluffy 'It' girl and it wasn't really Jo's milieu. Imogen couldn't be bothered to think about what *was* Jo's milieu, and her mind wandered to the Hong

Kong country clubs she'd been told about. Would they spend afternoons there like this, swimming and playing tennis in the humidity?

Her imaginings were interrupted by Sophie, who finally rose to her feet and started to clear up the fishy plates. She held her hand up as Imogen made to stand up. 'Absolutely not, Imo, old thing. You made it, we clear it. Isn't that one of your famous rules? And anyway you had better get used to being waited on hand and foot in HK.'

They all laughed at this, except, Imogen noticed, for Guy, who frowned. Perhaps he didn't like the idea of his wife getting lazy, though that was the last thing Imogen could ever imagine being accused of, but she stood up anyway and picked up the salad bowl and some side plates.

'Gosh, wouldn't do to get too used to that!' She tried to sound light-hearted. 'I'll come and dig out the ice cream. Many hands make the heart grow fonder,' and she carried her load inside.

Jo had stayed nursing her glass of wine at the table, but between the four of them there was light banter as they loaded the dishwasher. Hugh hovered over it, rearranging plates as they were dropped in so they went just so.

'Oh for God's sake, Hugh!' admonished Sophie. 'We've coped very well without you all week. Stop being so anal. It's only the sodding dishwasher.'

'No, these things matter and I'm a highly focused male who can be trusted to complete this challenging task to perfection,' he replied imperiously.

'Highly focused? Yeah right,' Imogen snorted. 'Unable to do more than one thing at a time more like! Only a man could have fiddled while Rome burned. He couldn't do that *and* call the fire brigade!' Sophie giggled loudly and Hugh flicked a bit of crab off his fingers at her. Imogen glanced at Guy but he didn't seem to be listening. He was rubbing his face, something he only did when he was stressed.

Feeling a little uneasy now, Imogen loaded Sophie and Hugh up with a bowl of summer fruits, and a tub of homemade brown-bread ice cream. 'Right I'll get the coffee on, and bring out the spoons. I'll need to wash a couple,' and she started to get down cups and lay them out on the tray. Sophie and Hugh gingerly made their way back out to the terrace, Hugh picking up the papers from the table and balancing them on the ice cream as he went.

Guy wiped the work surface ineffectually behind her as she fetched coffee mugs from the cupboard. It was strangely silent in the room after the laughter.

Guy cleared his throat. 'Imo, plans have changed. It's going to be Jakarta.'

Imogen spun round to face him, a mug in her hand, not really sure if he was still talking about something to do with her Nero joke. 'Sorry?'

But there was no joking in his face. 'They are posting us to Jakarta.' His hand stopped on the dishcloth. 'The bank made a takeover bid for a local Indonesian bank, and we've just heard it's been successful.' He looked at her, excitement in his eyes, perhaps encouraged by her lack of response. 'I suspected something was going to happen this week – I mentioned it, didn't I? – but it was only finalised on Friday night – hence the talk with Graham. They want me to manage the integration.' He beamed at this, thrilled by his announcement. 'Imo, the package is great!' He came over and held her by the upper arms, looking intently into her eyes as if to drive home the greatness of it all. 'You should have seen me! I had Graham over a barrel, darling, because we both knew I was the right man for it. I know that market inside out, so it was really a question of naming a price.' He mentioned a figure that caused Imogen to raise her eyebrows, her mind flying.

He bundled on, the words pouring out and his eyes alight. 'It'll mean we'll get a great apartment, much better than we'd have had in Hong Kong,' and in Imogen's mind she mentally deleted the picture of clubs and tennis and replaced it with … with what? She'd known little enough about Hong Kong. She knew precisely nothing about Jakarta.

'Well,' she faltered, knowing he was willing her to match his enthusiasm, 'the money sounds good, but how much have you found out about it? Did Graham fill you in?' Guy looked a bit sheepish.

'To be honest, love, we only really talked about the job. It's an exciting proposition and they want me out there as soon as possible. By September really.'

'Oh gosh, so soon. What will we do?'

Guy turned away at this. 'Well, sweetheart, I really need you to sort out a place for us to live as soon as you can, though there will be relocation people to help obviously,' he added quickly. 'I won't have much time for the apartment-hunting and stuff, and you're so good at that kind of thing.'

'Oh Guy! I've got everything sorted for Hong Kong. Now I'll have to start all over again! And what about schools, Guy? Do they have good ones? And is there time to get them in? These things need to be sorted.'

He paused and leant back against the sideboard opposite her. He looked at her for a long time. 'Imo, love, we can't take them with us.'

Everything around her went still and quiet. Her stomach lurched and she felt nauseous.

'What do you mean? I don't understand.'

'It's just too dangerous. There are already Foreign Office warnings on areas close by and there's been some nasty stuff out there.' He made it sound like a bit of harmless argy-bargy amongst the natives. 'It'll be fine for you and me, of course – all the ex-pat areas are compounded but, listen, part of the package I negotiated was the bank paying the fees for schools here.' He hurried on, seemingly finding confidence in the fact that she hadn't interrupted. 'In fact, I called the head at Dunsters this morning. Nice chap. He said they'd have no problem accommodating Rory at such short notice – I think it helped me having been head boy!'

Imogen was aware her mouth was hanging open. 'But what about Olivia and Arch? He'll only just have turned seven at the end of August, for goodness' sake, Guy.'

His eyes looked bright. He'd clearly thought this

through. 'I was wondering if you could have a word with the head at your old place about Ollie. These schools are very used to this sort of thing and pretty helpful in an emergency, you know.' He made it sound as if he had wide experience in the field. 'And Arch can probably go to my old prep school. He'll be fine, love.'

Imogen looked down at the mug in her hand. Had she been going to make coffee? 'I know it's not what we planned, darling,' he came over to her, his voice gentle and persuasive, 'but it's such a good opportunity. The kids will be fine. We survived it, didn't we?' He laughed, then he added with urgency, 'And, Imo, this is important for me. It's a big move. A fantastic challenge. If I turn this down, they'll never offer me anything like it again.' He paused. 'I need you there with me, sweetheart.'

She looked up at him now. She felt cold and short of breath. 'But—'

And broke off as Sophie stumbled into the kitchen. 'Oi, who d'ya have to fuck round here to get a spoon?'

Jo scraped the last bit of ice cream from her bowl and glanced at her watch. She still hadn't let on that she and Matt had an arrangement – certainly not a date – for the afternoon, and she hadn't told Finn yet for fear he'd blab. The last thing she wanted was a barrage of questions over lunch and silly innuendo from Guy and Sophie.

She cleared her throat and looked at the throng around the table. 'I was thinking of taking Finn along the Camel Trail later on.'

Finn sat up. 'Camels? Like that time in Morocco?

Cooool!' The gust of laughter that greeted his comment had him red-faced and scowling in an instant.

'Bikes, babe,' said Jo quietly, regretting now that she hadn't briefed him before. 'You can rent bikes.' He hated to be wrong-footed and would probably respond by sulking for ages – until he discovered Matt was included in the plan, that is.

All heads swivelled her way, Finn still looking mutinous, the others intrigued. 'Blimey, Jo. That's a bit organised for you, isn't it?' laughed Sophie. Imogen, who'd been unnaturally quiet and pale throughout pudding, suddenly looked up, an almost panicked expression on her face. 'But I thought we were doing that on Wednesday … I mean I was going to suggest we all go on Wednesday, perhaps. Although there's no reason why you shouldn't do it today … Mind you, do you think you'll be able to get bikes on a Saturday without booking ahead?'

'Hmmm, maybe not,' improvised Jo. 'Well, perhaps we'll do something else.'

'Muu-uum,' Finn complained. 'Wanna go with Rory.'

Jo gave him a warning look, completely ignored, and she could see all the signs of a major strop on the horizon – no need for the long-range forecast for that. She crossed back to his side of the table and leant over to speak quietly to him under the guise of a cuddle. 'Look, don't say anything, but Matt's invited us to do the bikes then go out on a boat with him. OK?'

Pointless to expect discretion from a ten-year-old. He whooped and sat bolt upright. 'Is it Matt's boat? Has it got sails or an engine? Can I catch a fish?'

There was a silence, then Sophie's clear ringing tones. 'You crafty old bag! You've gone and got yourself a date, haven't you?' Then the other children broke out in a clamour of complaints and questions. Jo tried to make her escape in all the confusion, pausing only to grab Finn and hiss, '*Nul* bloody *points* for discretion. There's not enough room on the boat for this lot. Now come on, let's pack a bag quick before a riot breaks out.' She made for the kitchen door, mouthing an awkward, 'Sorry' at Imogen on the way out, but was met with a blank expression.

'Um … sorry. Yeah right, have a great time,' Imogen eventually muttered distractedly, then seemed suddenly to come to. 'Do you want to take a picnic? I'm sure there's something in the fridge.'

That would just be too weird, having this escape plan catered by Imogen. 'Er, no thanks. We'll improvise I 'spect.' And Jo hurried out, her face still hot, with Finn trotting alongside undaunted, asking endless questions.

What was it with Imogen and Matt? They were the last people you'd imagine hitting it off – him with his faded jeans and flip-flops, and her all posh schools and Peter Jones – but yesterday they had looked so comfortable chatting together on the beach. Imogen seemed able to talk to anyone and Jo had felt like she was butting in. It was a relief, it had to be said, that Imogen had eased up on the Cupid business – but Sophie was now doing more than enough for both of them.

Not that any of it mattered. Come next week she'd be back at her desk and it would all be forgotten. He'd probably have moved on to the next yummy-mummy to throw herself at him, she thought grimly as she parked the car in Wadebridge. But hey, it wasn't as if she was expecting any more, though she couldn't ignore a stab of something that, if she hadn't known better, she'd have taken for jealousy. Ridiculous.

Finn, who had subsided into sulky silence in response to her discouraging answers and had spent the journey picking at a scab on his ankle, was on the alert again as he spotted Matt leaning against a fence, chatting amiably with a family of holidaymakers.

'Hi, Finn, old mate, Jo.' He ambled over to them, quickly wrapping up his conversation. Jo felt an unexpectedly strong surge of pleasure at the sight of him, all lanky and relaxed, heightened when he leant down and kissed her. God, he smelt good, and there was just enough stubble on his face for her to go on feeling the brief contact on her mouth as they walked over to the hire shop. There didn't seem to be too many bikes left and Jo glanced anxiously at Finn. He'd be so disappointed if this expedition had to be abandoned. But Matt, as usual, knew the form. He'd clearly called ahead, and seemed to know the youth at the desk who quickly fitted all three of them out with distinctly superior-looking bikes and a helmet for Finn. Jo had tried to pay, but he'd waved her away firmly and with a quizzical look that made her wonder if she'd insulted him. They wheeled their bikes towards the roundabout and the boy who'd dealt with them shouted his farewell. 'Have fun, Doc. Don't worry 'bout getting back before closing.

Gimme a call on me mobile, and I'll open up for you.'

Jo turned round and gave a distracted wave. 'I don't recognise that kid at all. It's amazing where you can run into patients. The worst is when they start coming up and telling you the latest on whatever it was you were treating them for. Or asking advice for their aunties. Ugggh! Drives me crazy.'

Matt scooted his bike along with one foot on the pedal, then swung his leg over, heading for the gateway underneath the road bridge where the trail began in earnest. 'Yeah, I know what you mean. It's the last thing you want to be doing in your spare time.'

Concentrating ferociously, Jo clicked at her gears then fell into place beside him as the trail sank between hedgerows studded with tiny wild flowers. 'No way! Really?' She snorted incredulously. 'People ask you for surfing tips when you're out and about?' Aware of his amused stare, she glanced across at him and wobbled unnervingly. 'What? Finn, not so fast, you maniac. That horrible bloke who sold me the wetsuit won't give me a refund if you end up in traction, y'know. Oh you stinkers! Come back, the pair of you! I can't go that fast.'

Laughing uproariously, Finn and Matt tore off together down the trail, slowing only as they emerged into the sunlight again where it opened out and they had their first uninterrupted view of the estuary. When Jo caught up with them, they had stopped and were sharing a drink that Matt had produced from his rucksack. Jo accepted gratefully, and the zing of lemon hit her tongue. 'Real lemonade! Cor, did you make it?'

Matt screwed the lid back on and handed Finn the bottle to stow in his pack. 'I'm a bit of an expert. We used to make it in Australia all the time.'

'I suppose you can surf there all year round,' Jo commented, licking her lips. 'I'm surprised you ever came back. C'mon, Finn, let's see if we can get all the way to Padstow without any contusions. Your knees are a real mess, mate.' Slipping back onto her saddle, Jo pulled out behind Finn and in front of Matt, leaning forward just a little to increase the gap between the top of her baggy stone-coloured shorts and the bottom of her vest top. There you are, she thought to herself. See if you can resist that, Surf Boy. Sure enough, he cycled behind her for the next ten minutes at least, while she and Finn traded mild insults and stupid knock-knock jokes.

The tide was in when they reached Padstow, but the tide of visitors was against them, most making their way in the opposite direction along the trail to be back for the five o'clock closing time. Jo felt comfortably superior as Matt led them down to the harbour then round and out along the other side to where the pleasure boats were moored. Chaining their bikes to a bollard, they followed him over to a handsome-looking vessel tied up at the water's edge.

'Wow,' gawped Finn, his eyes wide, and even Jo had to admit she felt excited. It was years since she'd been on a boat.

The Skylark, its name written neatly on the bow, appeared to have both sails and an outboard motor, but wasn't big enough to have a cabin. It wasn't fibreglass like the boats around it, but timber-built, varnished on the inside to a rich, deep brown, while the hull – she thought that was what it was called – was aqua blue, the rolled-up sails a faded orangey-brown. The man on deck hailed them and beckoned Matt, who jumped down onto the deck with practised ease. Jo couldn't hear their exchange, but the man turned to look at her with frank curiosity and at her legs with undisguised admiration, before picking up his bag and climbing up onto the quay.

With everyone safely aboard, Matt handed out buoyancy aids, and helped them tighten their waist straps. He fired up the outboard motor and slowly steered them up the estuary, pointing out landmarks as they went – the Doom Bar, the cottages at Hawkers' Cove – then he cut the motor, and put a terrified Jo in charge of the tiller while he hoisted the sails and, quite suddenly it seemed to Jo, the land fell away behind them and they were out in the swell of the Atlantic.

They had been sailing perhaps only half an hour, with Finn conscientiously playing crew, hauling on sheets and using all the jargon Matt taught him, when Matt started to manoeuvre the boat back in towards the coast again. 'It takes for ever to get to this bay by land,' he said. 'Hardly anyone bothers. But it's probably my very favourite place in the whole world.' Jo pretended to look at the view, but she couldn't keep her eyes off him. He was standing, squinting in the strong light, and his tanned hand was lightly holding the tiller behind his back. He was chatting to Finn, but beneath the banter his eyes were vigilant and his look serious and, what? Competent. She wasn't quite sure what to do with herself and tried to stay out of the way, hardly daring to even touch a rope, but looking for something solid to clutch on to. Where, she wondered fleetingly, had he learnt to do this? Suddenly she wanted to know more about him.

She watched fascinated as they hauled in the sails and Matt pulled hard on the starter of the outboard motor again. He chugged in as close as he could to the crescent of white-golden sand, then cut the engine and dropped the anchor. There was silence, except for the 'ting ting' of the stays against the mast. The water beneath them was so clear, Jo had no way of telling how deep it was – the pebbles might only just have been out of reach – but when Matt slipped himself over the side of the boat, it reached well above his knees. 'Do you want a piggyback? The water's pretty cold.'

The idea of clinging on to him tightly was too tempting. Jo caught her breath and looked away. 'If you take Finn, I'll take the backpack.' He smiled ruefully but carefully helped her to slither into the water, laughing and pulling her close when she gasped at how cold it indeed was. Finn passed her the pack, which was heavier than she'd anticipated, then clambered onto Matt's back, and leant his dark little head over next to Matt's to stare down into the water.

On the shore, Matt pulled a towel out of the bag and rubbed Jo's legs vigorously, pretending to chafe the life back into them while she rolled back and fended him off unconvincingly. The legs of her shorts were soaked but, in the shelter of the bay, soon dried off in the sunshine and, when Matt produced a frisbee from his seemingly bottomless bag, all three threw themselves into a frenetic game, hurtling across the sand for seemingly irretrievable shots. By six o'clock even Jo, stuffed with crab only a few hours earlier, was ready to eat and Matt let her unpack his picnic with delighted curiosity.

'Not up to Imogen's gourmet standards, I fear,' he said cheerfully and with no trace of apology. Jo inspected the doorstop sandwiches of granary bread: bacon and egg with no butter for Finn – his favourite. How did Matt know? Wedges of cheese, tomato and chutney for them. Pouring still-scalding coffee from the flask, she sighed with contentment. 'Yeah, but you're a bloke, aren't you? And this is a perfect blokes' picnic.'

'Glad you noticed.' Matt reached out and took the cup from her, had a sip of coffee and handed it back. 'Ouch! Too hot.' He put his hand up to his burnt lip. 'I'm suffering. What do you advise, Doc?'

'Oh don't *you* start!' she laughed.

Finn had wolfed his sandwiches and was wandering off collecting driftwood, singing to himself. Matt rolled over onto his side and leant towards Jo, nuzzling her hair.

'You could make my lips feel better, you know you could …' She glanced over to where Finn was, before quickly kissing Matt, pulling away before it became too intense. The sunshine and the cold water had set her whole body tingling and, if Finn hadn't been there, she'd have had trouble keeping her hands to herself. Matt sat up, smiling at her deflection, and watched the little boy, his eyes crinkling up at the corners as he smiled.

'Does it make you uncomfortable, kissing while Finn is around?'

'Erm, gosh. I dunno, really. I hadn't thought about it. It hasn't really arisen before.'

'You are joking, right?' Matt looked at her sceptically. 'I mean, you do see people in London, don't you?'

'Well, yes, of course I do. Loads, in fact,' she blustered. 'Just not normally when he's around.'

'What about the ones that get serious?' He looked away, craning his neck round to watch Finn scrambling up a rock. 'Then do you talk to him about it?'

'Well, it's not really his business, is it? And serious isn't really my style.' She scanned his face, expecting to see at the very least a glimmer of relief. But there was none there, though there certainly was an odd expression on his face. He turned back with a brisk smile and patted her knee in an almost brotherly way.

'Yeah, well. Probably best to keep it that way, if that's what you prefer. Now,' he delved into the rucksack, 'I've got a bag of cherries in here. Hope they've survived the journey. Why don't you tuck into them while I try, probably in vain, to vindicate myself in another game of kamikaze-frisbee with your implausibly fit son?'

He hauled himself to his feet and ran across the sand to Finn, whistling shrilly to get the boy's attention. Jo, watching them playing and laughing easily together, frowned as she nibbled at a cherry, turning the stalk this way and that before she tugged it off with her teeth. What had just happened back then? He'd seemed offended, as though she'd brushed him off. Had he been asking, in a roundabout way, if she wanted to get more involved? This was new. She spat a cherry pip into the sand and watched as the soft red flesh that still clung to it began to dry up. Their lives were so different. How on earth could it ever work?

Chapter 15

Sunday

Hot and humid

Out of the window Imogen watched a woman walking down the lane, a fussy little terrier pulling on the end of a lead. In her red shorts and boatnecked T-shirt, the woman looked too seaside to be a local. Nothing betrays a holidaymaker more than those boatnecked T-shirts, but this one oozed the confidence of a Cornwall regular. She stopped every now and then to let the dog sniff at the hedgerow and lift its leg, before moving on. Imogen wondered what was going through her mind as she walked. She was certainly out very early, but she looked as though early mornings were the norm, not the result of being unable to sleep. Perhaps she was wondering if there was enough bacon for breakfast in her large rented house, probably scattered with slumbering teenagers in sleeping bags who'd been partying all night. She certainly didn't look as if *she* was grappling with a bombshell.

Imogen had been up since four thirty grappling with hers. All the delicious anticipation she'd felt yesterday morning had evaporated. After a fairly low-key supper with Sophie and Hugh, during which Sophie had been chatty as usual and Imogen had let her natter on about nothing very much, Guy had taken her in his arms but hadn't persisted when she'd made it clear sex was the last thing on her mind, even if she hadn't been off games. He'd barely mentioned Jakarta either, as if sensing that he'd said enough and she'd need time to regroup.

She got down from her curled position on the window seat, slowly unravelling her leg, grown stiff from being sat on, and emptied the dregs of her third – or was it her fourth? – cup of tea into the sink, then set about unloading the dishwasher. She was past caring that it had fallen to her to do it yet again – she needed to get her head straight about things.

Jakarta. Throughout the night, while he'd slept beside her, she'd run through what Guy had said again and again. And as the hours had gone on, and she'd had time to think about it from all angles, her devastation had slowly given way to reason. Surely he must be wrong about the danger thing? Jakarta had been a posting for ex-pats for years. She'd had a boyfriend at university whose dad worked there, she was sure of it. There was bound to be a big ex-pat community and international schools.

She'd make it all right. She'd persuade Guy that the children could come.

As she put clean mugs back into the cupboard on automatic pilot, she began to feel almost elated. It was out of the question that the children wouldn't come, for goodness' sake. Nothing was impossible and she'd find a way around it. In the meantime, she'd be enthusiastic about the whole venture – after all, the money sounded fantastic – and try to forget all the tantalising information she'd stored in her head about Hong Kong. Next stop Jakarta. Rejuvenated by the thought, she accelerated her dishwasher-unloading speed and decided she'd make Scotch pancakes for breakfast.

It was a good move, and the children demolished them as she knew they would. She was still in her pyjamas and on her third batch of batter, trying to meet demand, when Guy emerged downstairs, his hair wet from the shower, and kissed her cheek.

'Mmm, good smell. Enough for me to have one?'

'You'll have to be quick. This lot are showing no mercy.'

He went to pour coffee, and said quietly, 'I tell you what, boarding-school is going to be the making of Rory. I've just been into his room and it looks like there's been urban warfare in there. He'll have to learn to put his stuff away.' Imogen winced but didn't say a word. As with the children when something they wanted seemed impossible, like a warrior outfit or a tree house, she'd keep quiet until she sorted everything out. OK so he'd already called Dunsters about admitting Rory at short notice – an action she found so out of character as to be laughable. Nothing was confirmed, was it? She'd just call and cancel.

'So where did Dr Dolittle disappear to yesterday afternoon?' Guy stuffed a pancake into his mouth. 'She didn't waste much time finding a bloke, did she?'

'Sssssh,' Imogen admonished. 'The chap who does the surfing. He's lovely. I thought there was a romance, but now I'm not so sure.'

'A beach bum?' Guy poured cereal into a bowl, not disguising his relief at his wife's cheery mood. 'Well that figures.'

'Stop being so quick to make assumptions, you bigot.' She poked him affectionately on the arm and started ladling more circles of batter into the smoking pan. 'Now, do you want bacon with your pancakes? I bought some delicious stuff from the deli – not that watery nonsense you get in packets – and I've got a piece of beef for lunch – local stuff and I thought we could maybe go for a walk while it's cooking. What do you think?' She turned to face him.

The answer was already on his face. 'I've got a seat on the one-thirty flight, darling. I'll have to be there before lunch. I did say I had to go. I'm so sorry.' He took her in his arms and she could feel her throat hurting with the effort of not crying from disappointment. 'But can we do the walk after breakfast instead?'

The children's initial moaning dissipated as they got into the mood and ran down the lane towards the beach. Finn came too, but Grace and Amelia stayed at home, which was a relief because walking with Amelia was a pain. She always had a ruse – a stone in her shoe or her flip-flop rubbed – and Sophie always seemed to stop for her, holding them all up. It was warm already, and Imogen could feel the heat on her shoulders, and the sunshine was dappled as it penetrated through the trees on to the warm tarmac of the road. Guy was walking ahead of her, talking with Archie, or at least Archie was chatting and Guy was listening. His hand slipped into his father's and Imogen held her breath. He kept it there for a moment and then let it drop, ruffling his son's head instead. He'd never been one for hand-holding.

'Muum,' Rory bellowed, 'can we have an ice cream?'

'You've only just had breakfast,' she hollered back. 'Later maybe. On the way back.' And she smiled. That boy's stomach was bottomless. God help her when pubescent growth-spurts really kicked in. She watched her son as he lolloped ahead of her. She reckoned she knew every inch of his body, but just now he seemed like a stranger. Scary how, all at once, something you have created grows bigger than you are. Dr Frankenstein must have felt that about his monster.

Despite her crushing disappointment at the ruined day, the hour they spent at the beach was a happy one. The kids ran about and Guy, obviously guilt-ridden and on his best behaviour, got involved in their games, helping Arch and Olivia build a tower of stones. Imogen wandered the tide lines picking up mussel shells and pulling up bits of string and scraps of white plastic beakers that poked out of the sand, making a small pile of them to put into the bin later. Then she sat on a rock and watched as families came down on to the beach for the day; fathers laden down like Sherpas with rugs and cool boxes, balls and windbreaks, while fat-legged mothers in shorts strained to navigate buggies through the sand. Once they found their spot, they'd drop everything and stand hand on hips looking about them, before faffing about unloading their bags and setting up camp for the day.

She watched large dogs cavorting into rock pools with excitement and then running over to their owners to shake off the water, provoking shrieks of dismay. Here too were toddlers in large nappies and sun hats crouching over buckets, filling them with sand then patting them down with their spades, before tipping them over clumsily in an attempt to make castles.

And every now and then Imogen squinted to find her family, over there busy with their beach projects, and felt huge waves of love for them. This boarding-school thing was nonsense. They didn't need to go. She'd sort it out.

Guy left at around noon with an 'I'll call when I get there' and a 'we need to crack on with things. Can I leave it to you?', and they settled down to the beef and buttery new potatoes. Sophie had thoughtfully put in the joint while they were out – 'you've bought it all, why don't I cook it?' – but Imogen was certain she wouldn't have basted it, and opened the oven door on the quiet to scoop spitting fat over it when no one was looking. More frustrating still were Sophie's pitiful attempts to make gravy – Bovril indeed! By the time she put on the French beans to cook and promptly left the room, Imogen was in a lather of distrust and, five minutes later, couldn't resist the urge to poke them with a knife to check they weren't overcooked. Just as Sophie walked back into the room.

'Oi! Bugger off! I'm doing them.'

Imogen dropped the knife as if it were red hot. 'Oh, I wasn't sure where you'd gone. I was just seeing if they were OK.'

Sophie jokingly barged her out of the way. 'I do know how to cook, you know, Imo,' she said with a smile, but her annoyance wasn't completely veiled. Edie's words about kitchen democracy came into Imogen's head. Point taken.

'Mind if I slip away this afternoon, Soph?' she asked, after they'd dispatched deli-bought treacle tart and ice cream and were sitting having coffee outside, the dishwasher humming contentedly in the kitchen. Jo had plans apparently to take Finn off to the beach and was upstairs titivating.

'Off to meet your lover already?' mumbled Sophie, her eyes closed. Hugh was lying out in the grass, the newspaper over his head. 'Crikey, Guy's barely left!'

'Actually I need to go and find something. Can you handle my lot?'

'Sure thing. If we're not here when you get back, we've either gone down to the beach or sold them all into the slave trade and left for the Caribbean.'

'Sounds an inspired idea,' and Imogen levered herself out of her chair, her legs sticking painfully to the plastic in the warmth of the afternoon sun. Her car seat was even stickier and she turned up the air-conditioning as high as she could. The passenger footwell was now covered in a layer of sand, a discarded bucket lying on its side and rolling to and fro with the movement of the car. It all smelt deliciously of seaside.

Once she'd found a parking space in Wadebridge, she walked determinedly up the road, ignoring the colourful shops hoping for Sunday custom. She didn't even stop to look at the little boutiques with their shapeless clothes made in India that looked so appealing when you were on holiday, but were so out of place in the wardrobe once you got them home to London. Instead she made her way straight to the internet café, which, she was relieved to see, was open. She hadn't made provision for it not to be. It was quite quiet and she settled herself in front of a screen, not bothering to buy a drink this time, and began to type in the address for the Foreign Office. It would tell her about Jakarta in a sensible British way.

'Hello again. Weren't you here before?' She turned at the voice of the man beside her. He was even wearing the same yellow T-shirt he'd had on last time she'd been in, and he looked as dishevelled and unkempt – though thankfully with no more piercings. Well, visible ones anyway.

She smiled. 'Hi there. Do you live here or something?'

He looked wry. 'Seems like it. Me girlfriend works in the supermarket and she doesn't finish till four, so I have a muck-around here till I pick her up. So what you lookin' for this time? Searching Hong Kong, weren't you?'

The page now loaded, Imogen clicked on the country area. 'No, bit of a change of plan actually. My husband's just been told we're off to Jakarta.'

The man's face fell and he sucked the air in through his teeth. 'Bloody hell, luv. Rather you than me.' He screwed up his eyes and grimaced.

Imogen's arms went cold. 'What's wrong with it?'

He laughed rather patronisingly. 'Jakarta? Bloody

trouble spot. I thought everyone knew that. Terrorism. Don't you remember the bombings? I'd stay well out, luv. Stick to Hong Kong.' And he turned back to his computer game.

With a feeling of increasing alarm, she found the right page on the website and read. And read and read, her eyes frantically scanning the page. 'We strongly advise against ... we continue to receive reports that ...' Oh it can't affect us, her rational brain told her, but then she scrolled further down the page. Street crime, westerners harassed, passengers robbed on highways. The implications slowly seeped into her brain. Earthquakes, floods, dengue fever. What was this? It sounded like the Apocalypse. Then the final horror: 'Medical advice should be sought regarding malaria.'

Oh bugger. Buggeration.

Sophie came out of the loo to find Jo at the bottom of the stairs. 'What? You're not going out as well? Honestly, I'm starting to get a complex.'

Jo looked up from the embroidered bag she was stuffing with towels and goggles for Finn. 'Imogen gone too? I didn't know she was going anywhere this afternoon. Did I miss it in the five-year-plan, or is this a dangerous outbreak of spontaneity?'

Sophie shrugged. 'She just asked me if I'd keep an eye on the kids and off she went, so I'd say the latter, probably.'

'Did she seem all right?' Jo straightened up, smoothing her hair back, and slid her bare feet into the flip-flops

Matt had given her. 'I thought she seemed a bit tense this morning.'

Sophie pretended to reel back in astonishment. 'Now I know I'm entering the Twiglet Zone. First Imo going AWOL – if I may use an anachronism – now you acting all doctory out of hours. The universe as I know it is falling apart. Aaargh!'

'Very droll, I'm sure,' snorted Jo. 'We'll know we've really entered a parallel universe when a night passes without you and Hugh bonking loudly into the wee small hours. Have you no shame, woman?'

Sophie stretched smugly. 'Nope! And I hope I never will.'

Jo pretended to retch. 'Soon as Finn's changed his clothes, I'm leaving this den of vice. Now for goodness' sake, woman, try to keep your hormones under control, just for this afternoon, eh?'

Sophie shrugged resignedly. 'So where are you and the Finnster off to? Let me guess?'

'No need,' Jo answered serenely. 'We're going to see if Matt's at the beach today. I said I'd pop over for a drink later, but the weather looks so nice now, seems a pity to waste it. Oh, there you are, Finny-Finn-Finn. Hop in, mate. I'll join you in a sec.'

Sophie looked narrowly at her. 'You're looking suspiciously chipper, Dr Newman. What's put that smile on your face?'

'Well, not the same thing as for you, that's for sure,' Jo replied archly. 'We had a very nice, very chaste, very wholesome time yesterday, rounded off with a big bag of

316

chips when we got the boat in. Well, I told you all about it when we got back, didn't I?'

'Yeah, but not the juicy details. Go on – give! Do you like him?' Sophie shuffled closer, looking intrigued.

Jo hesitated, wondering whether to tell Sophie just how much he'd surprised her and she'd surprised herself. How being with Matt yesterday had revealed that he was different. How he seemed to listen to what she said and really think about it. How he remembered things – even little details. How he was so considerate when Finn was around, helping him and making sure he felt included. No, better not to say anything. Yet. Jo felt a shiver run up her spine, but shook her head impatiently.

'Gerroff, Sophie! You blissful marrieds are all like this. Desperate to pair everyone off, just to relieve your own boredom. Matt's fine. He's nice. But it's just a holiday thing, OK?'

Sophie mimed cowering away from Jo, hands raised defensively in front of her. 'Youch! Prickly, aren't we? Don't worry, Jo, I'd never try and pair you off – I know you're determined to preserve that famous independence of yours. And I reckon it'd take a braver man than Matt, so don't worry. You're perfectly safe with him. Give him a kiss from me, though, won't you? He is a bit gorge. If I didn't have my Hughie, you'd have to wrestle me for him. And I could take you too. That's right, run away …'

Jo could hear Sophie's teasing voice float after her as she joined Finn in the over-heated car. He was lying in the back, skinny legs propped up on the seat, reading a comic. He didn't look up. 'What did Sophie mean?' he asked distractedly. 'There *is* no one braver than Matt, I bet. I think he's really brave – and cool. Ollie had a wasp in her hair, and he got it off her, no bother. And you know what? He can lift his toes up, one at a time, make them do like a Mexican wave. It's brill. Wish I could do it.' He hauled off one of his sandals and started practising. Fortunately for Jo, this challenge occupied him most of the way to the beach but, from the occasional muffled curses from the back, it didn't sound as if he was progressing very well.

The beach car park was packed when they arrived. Jo swiftly checked her reflection, and dabbed at the moisture beading her forehead with the sleeve of her cotton wrap-over top. Glowing was good but shiny certainly wasn't. They scrunched over towards the beach, bags bumping against their bare legs. Jo looked smugly down at the flip-flops. She hadn't worn them since that first night – first date, really. Would he notice? Probably. That was one great thing about Matt – he was so observant. Far more than most men. Deep breath. Should she have called ahead, to let him know she was coming? Nah, better to surprise him. Better to make it look casual. She'd just loiter decoratively around with Finn then, when the moment was right, she'd stroll over to the café maybe. No, it might be better if she let him come and find her.

The tide was going out so she changed tack and steered Finn towards the newly exposed rock pools. He followed on docilely enough, still staring down at his toes with a concentrated frown. There was an animated game of cricket going on in the middle of the newly washed sand, with gangly teenage boys in oversized shorts throwing themselves around with unnecessary zeal. Jo edged her way round them, amused when a boy who should have been fielding was hit a glancing blow on the shoulder by the ball as he turned to look at her legs. This skirt was definitely a winner.

She continued past the barricades of striped windbreaks and staked a claim on a spot where she and Finn dumped the bags. She straightened up and twisted this way and that, surveying the scene. Finn wanted to change into his wetsuit straight away and was all for going up to do so in Matt's office.

'No, babe. He's probably busy at the moment. We'll go and say hello later on, maybe. Here, put your bathrobe on and change under that. No one'll see your manly parts – such as they are. Oi! Stop that. Kicking sand isn't nice.'

Finn laughed. 'You sound like Imogen when you say that. She's always saying things are "nice" or "not nice". She never says things are nasty … except spitting. Me and Rors were spitting on the girls from our bedroom window the other day and she said it was nasty and disgusting.'

Jo held out a towelling robe. 'Well, she got that right. It is gross. Who's idea was it, anyway?'

'Dunno. It was a laugh though.' Ready now, Finn shrugged off the robe thoughtfully and slid his arms into the wetsuit. 'But, Mum, if they didn't like it, why did they stand right underneath and yell? Girls are weird, aren't they? Don't think I'll ever get married, well unless I make a baby with someone.'

'You don't have to, hon. I didn't.' Jo smiled tightly, reaching round to do up the zip at the back of his wetsuit, taking care to hold his hair out of the way when she reached the top.

Finn bit moodily at a hangnail before replying. 'Yeah, I know, but … it'd be quite cool to be a dad. Maybe not one like Guy or Hugh, though. I'd be cooler than that. If I had a kid, I'd want to be with him all the time. I'd take him sailing and everything.' Finn looked slyly at Jo. 'That's the best kind of dad, doncha reckon?'

'We're pretty good on our own, though, aren't we?' Finn looked wary. He was used to hearing this as a statement rather than a question, and Jo cursed herself for allowing that chink of doubt to creep into her voice. 'Oh, come on. Get this snorkel on. I want to see you do your thing. I'll walk along next to you, if you like, but I'm not going above the knees. It's bloody freezing in there.'

With another quick glance back up at the café, Jo slipped off her skirt to reveal her bikini bottoms and kept the vest top on. Surely that would get him down. The water was icy, the hot sun making the contrast even more excruciating, but she stuck it out, trying to look as picturesque as possible. Finn kicked along just under the surface of the water, turning his head from side to side very deliberately – although there didn't seem to be anything to look at. She checked again. Where the hell was Matt?

Wading deeper into the water, so that it lapped the tops of her thighs, she moved out beyond Finn and turned to face the shore. Jo shivered, then glanced down at Finn, who was swimming in tight circles round her legs, grabbing on to her knees to help propel himself round. He was so brave – always ready to try something new and, although he had inherited her horror of looking stupid or even looking as if he didn't know what he was doing, he didn't let it stop him.

Jo tickled the back of Finn's neck. He squirmed and rolled over on his back, his face breaking through the surface of the water, glistening and creased in a grin. 'It's brill, Jo,' he enthused as he struggled to his feet and pushed the mask up. 'Bit scary at first, cos you almost can't believe you're going to be able to breathe, but the more you relax the better it is. D'you wanna try? You won't drown, I promise. You've just got to be brave and go with it.'

She hugged him impulsively, drenching her top, and tasted salt on his chilly, wet face. OK, she thought. I can be brave too. I'm going to haul him out of this bloody cryogenic water, walk straight up to the office, and ask for another date. Time to take a little risk, Newman.

She kissed Finn's nose. 'Do you know, I think you're right, my love! What about we go up to the café and I get you a hot Ribena and some chips to warm you up? How would that be? And I could do with a coffee. It's tiring work watching you swim, y'know.'

They waded back to the shore and Finn pulled the mask and snorkel over his head, pausing to help Jo gather up their bags again. The teenagers were still playing, and had managed to involve some girls in the game. Jo hesitated before braving the crossing – play had become a little wilder since the girls joined in – and she squinted through the flailing tangle of long brown limbs up to the door of the café. A flurry of movement caught her attention. Was that …? Was it …?

From around the side of the building, a girl in shorts and a tight black T-shirt came running full pelt, closely followed by Matt. She spun round to face him, fending him off with both hands. Her dark hair was in a loose ponytail, whipping round her face as she laughed, throwing her head back. Matt lunged forward and grabbed her round the shoulders and they both fell to the ground. Jo felt as though she was looking through the wrong end of a telescope and the chill she'd felt moments before was replaced by a wave of heat. There was a rushing sound in her ears. She couldn't hear it, but could imagine their laughter. She had to get away before he saw her.

Finn – thank God – was trying to engage the bowler in conversation, hoping to get himself invited to play. Matt was sitting up now, leaning against the wall with his hands resting on his knees, his ripped, red check shirt hanging open over a T-shirt. The girl crawled up beside him on all fours, then sat next to him tilting her head to smile at him.

The sun was in their eyes. Matt looked like his were shut. It was now or never. 'C'mon, Finn,' she snapped. 'I want to get out of here. I'm bloody freezing and I've got a stinking headache.'

Finn looked round, puzzled. 'But I thought we were going to have chips.'

'Yes, well, I've changed my mind, OK? Come on, I need to go now. Don't you want to see Rory, anyway?' Head down, she started up the beach, unable to prevent herself from glancing over again. The girl was now passing Matt a mug of something – probably tea – and he was smiling up at her. Goddamn him. And her – bitch.

One of Jo's flip-flops came off as she stormed up towards the car park. Barely pausing, she pulled the other one off and hurled it at the dunes backing the beach. 'Good sodding riddance,' she hissed, and rushed on, then stopped, agonised by the sharp stones that formed the path. Tears rushed to her eyes and she gasped with pain. She hobbled on, aware of Finn trailing sulkily behind, willing him to hurry.

'But I wanted to see Matt,' he whined.

Jo clenched her jaw. 'He's not around this week. He's gone to London or something. I can't really remember. Come on, get in.' The little boy tutted and threw himself into the back seat, still dripping and encased in his wetsuit, confused and muttering under his breath. 'But I need a towel.'

Finn struggled in silence to change into the clothes she'd thrown into the back, while Jo drove aimlessly around the lanes for ages, breathing fast and checking in her mirror as though searching for something, but she didn't know what.

This feeling was familiar, too gut-wrenchingly familiar. All those years ago. It had been January, sleeting and so cold. Driving round Highbury in the middle of the night, completely out of control, too tired to sleep, desperate and hanging onto the steering wheel as though her life depended on it. Driving round, just looking and looking for Trevor's car, for confirmation of what she already knew – as if knowing where he was could bind him to her, bring him back. And when she'd found his car, parked not near the house she knew he was in, but a few streets away, she'd double-parked next to it and just stayed there, waiting and watching – until she must have fallen asleep. The milkman had woken her up, cross once he saw there was nothing wrong with her. He's said she was stupid – she could have died of cold. And she wished she had. She'd driven back to the flat they'd once shared, shivering and numb, her hands almost too cold to put the key in the lock, and had thrown herself on her bed, their bed, and cried until she had no tears left.

She couldn't go through all that again. She'd promised herself that at the time, and she'd kept her word – almost eleven years. How could she have let herself weaken? How could she?

The petrol warning light came on now on the dashboard. Finn was still silent in the back. Jo turned the car around and headed back to the house.

Chapter 16

Monday

Humid with very mild winds

She was in a lift in a high-rise apartment block somewhere foreign. She knew she was abroad because she couldn't understand what the man in the lift was saying to her. He was wearing a loud Hawaiian shirt and was measuring up the dimensions of the doors, but when they finally opened he told her, in plain English, to mind the gap. The lift led into the Top Dorm at school, and Archie was bouncing on her bed. She shouted at him to stop and he cried. Then there was Sophie in a gym slip asking if she should take the washing out of the machine. 'Oh for God's sake,' Imogen snarled at her. 'Just bloody do it.'

Her eyes snapped open. She felt fiercely hot, her heart was racing and she had a terrible sense of something being badly wrong but she couldn't think what immediately. She kicked off the duvet. The air felt still and humid and she struggled for breath. Pulling herself upright, she picked up her watch from the bedside table. It wasn't as early as she'd thought. Almost the time to get herself a cup of tea, but somehow she couldn't move. She just wanted to lie there, and tears pricked behind her eyes.

Hugh had been departing when she'd got back from the internet café yesterday and Sophie had been hugging him on the drive by the car when she'd pulled in. She had waved him off girlishly and sniffed dramatically as he disappeared out of the gate. This irritated Imogen and, rather than tolerate another evening listening to Hugh's virtues being expounded, she'd gone up to have a bath. She'd even poured in some of the bath oil she found on the shelf – she didn't recognise the brand name but the bottle looked classy and it smelt delicious. A little bit gone wouldn't be noticed.

Imogen had slid into the hot water and gently slooshed it over herself. Little blobs of oily water had sat on her boobs, the top half of which were tanned now. The swell of her stomach, still white from lack of exposure to the sun, stuck out in a slight mound above the water, and she'd rested the sponge on it so she didn't have to look, fed up with being the one of the three who didn't have that appealing little expanse of flat stomach to show off between shorts and T-shirt.

Lying in bed now she felt sweaty and ungainly. Her pyjama top wasn't strappy and sporty like Jo's or feminine and frilly like Sophie's. It was very definitely a T-shirt. So she'd got it wrong. Again. She always got it wrong because for her it was never quite right. She'd been the one in the sensible little Start-rites when everyone else had been promoted to Dolcis. She'd been the one who arrived at the party in high-necked, long Laura Ashley, when all the other girls were in short, black dresses and high heels. She'd always been high street, practical, sensible, value for money, but when a glamorous school friend had very generously offered her the chance to borrow her favourite suede boots – oh, the height of sophistication – Imogen hadn't even been able to get them over her calves.

As if in reflex Imogen pulled up her legs now and curled herself into a ball at the shameful memory. She didn't have the legs for boots anyway. Too chunky. Too sensible. Too fat. She'd never been the girl she wanted to be: the one with the right pencil case, the one with the bum that looked right in Levi's, the one whose nose wrinkled up cutely when she flirted with the boys.

And now she wasn't the woman she wanted to be either. She was about to commit the crime she had sworn she never would. She was going to let down her children, when she'd promised herself, and them, she'd always be there.

She'd given up her job insurance broking, as soon as she knew Rory was on the way, and had never worked again, and it wasn't just because she hated the City and they could afford for her not to go back. She would have been there for them whatever. No Eastern Bloc nannies for her. No nurseries from seven thirty in the morning until six at night. No way. She been the one who'd read Penelope Leach over and over again, and battled through mastitis, determined to breastfeed Archie despite the agonising pain, for as long as she had the other two. She'd been the one who'd carefully stewed up organic vegetables and frozen them in ice-cube trays so there would always be 'some for later'. She was always the first figure at the school gate, or feeling sick with rising panic if she was held up in traffic and her face wasn't there for them as they poured out of the classroom. She knew she over-mothered them – Christ, she'd breathe for them if she could – but wasn't that her job? The whole reason for having them? Was it possible to over-mother anyway? Everyone needed their mother, and now she'd be on the other side of the world when they fell over, got bullied, felt ill or sad.

She could feel the unbearable grief rising and, determined not to let it overwhelm her again as it had throughout the night, she got up and forced herself to get going with the day. Her eyes were small and puffy. God, she couldn't even cry elegantly. She splashed cold water onto her face almost violently as Archie padded in, thumb in mouth and rabbit held against his face.

'Hello, Mama,' he mumbled and held his head against her towel as she wrapped it around herself. Be brave, be brave, she urged herself, as she gently rubbed his soft hair. He'll survive. I'll survive. I survived before.

Neither Rory nor Olivia were quite as cute, however, and by the time she had urged them downstairs for some breakfast they were at each other's throats.

'It's my turn to have the free gift out of the Rice Krispies,' screeched Olivia, despite Imogen's shushing that she'd wake everyone else.

'Who cares? Olivia always gets it and it's my turn.' Rory slammed down the milk carton, splashing it all over the table and started to shovel in his cereal like a builder shifting gravel.

'Rory, be careful. Olivia, share it with your brother and come and sit down. It'll be forgotten and in the bin by ten o'clock anyway. Arch, I've told you to leave those felttips, sweetheart. It's breakfast time.' Joining them now were Grace and Amelia, shortly followed by Finn, but not another adult in sight. What do those women think this is, thought Imogen, chucking bread into the toaster with one hand, and pouring orange juice with the other, a bloody crêche for their children, while they lounge about getting their beauty sleep?

'Get up and get the jam yourself, Gracie dear,' she said through tight lips. 'You've got legs, haven't you?'

Half an hour later and Sophie strolled in, sleepily poured herself the first cup of tea from the pot Imogen had just made, and popped a crust in her mouth from one of the plates abandoned by the children before the exodus to the TV. 'Did Amelia have something, did you notice? She doesn't eat enough.'

Imogen could feel her shoulders tensing. Why didn't you get up in time to see then? she snarled in her head. 'Plenty I think.' She smiled beatifically, and carried on unloading the dishwasher.

Jo followed shortly afterwards, looking surly but still fragrant, and, rather than take a clean mug from the dishwasher, got one down from the cupboard and poured herself a cup of tea from the pot. Plonking herself down at the table, she pushed the used bowls out of the way and, rejecting the half-eaten loaf, sliced off the crust from the crisper, fresher one.

'What's on the agenda today then, Imogen?' Sophie

329

said brightly. 'What excitement do you have lined up for us?'

Ignoring her, Imogen, hand suspended between cutlery basket and drawer, watched Jo intently. I know she's going to do it, she thought, waiting for the inevitable. I just know it. She always does. And sure enough, Jo picked up a clean knife and started to scrape butter from the pat, making a smooth crater in the top. Imogen felt herself burst inside with the anger, the irritation, the frustration at everything. She knew it was petty, unnecessary, childish but she couldn't stop it bubbling to the surface.

'For God's sake, Jo,' she snapped, 'why the fuck do you have to massacre the butter like that? Can't you cut it properly?'

Jo looked up astonished, and seemed about to say something, but it was Sophie who slipped in first. 'Oh get over yourself, Imo. It's not a crime!'

Imogen clenched her fists out of sight behind the counter. She just wanted to get out. 'Oh never mind. Well, I'm taking my lot for a picnic on the beach—'

'Great idea, might be cooler there,' Sophie enthused, sounding glad the momentary tightening in the atmosphere had been dispelled. 'This heat is vile. What's the weather going to do?'

Imogen realised that she had no idea. In her distress last night she must even have forgotten to listen to the six o'clock forecast. How could she have? Now she might be caught off-guard. Uncomfortable at having to throw herself at the mercy of the climate, she set about putting together a picnic, determinedly making Rory his very favourite cheese and Branston sandwiches, and grimly seeking out a perfect banana with not a blemish to put off Olivia. She even threw together quickly the ingredients for some chocolate brownies – everyone's favourite – which were baking nicely in the oven when her mother rang. Oh great.

'Hello, Mother,' she said shortly, and went to sit on a garden seat, out of earshot of the others. Trying to keep the annoyance from her voice, she half-listened to her mother's report about her latest golf round and imparted a few brief details about the holiday, putting her usual spin on things. She told her too about the visit to Edie, refusing however to be lured into a bitching session when her mother enquired if her house was as 'chaotic and artistic as usual'.

'Now about Hong Kong, darling,' her mother carried on, barely drawing breath. 'I've been talking to Sylvia Peckton-Davies – you remember her from the golf club. Lots of blond hair and a revolting Yorkshire terrier called Meldrew. Well, she has a son who works for Nat West over there apparently – and she's called him, and he says his wife can't wait to meet you and show you round, so I've given her your number—'

'We're not going.'

'Don't be silly, dear!'

'We're not going.' There was stunned disbelief at the other end, and Imogen took a deep breath and told her about the change in events, keeping the information as factual as possible. 'So,' she finished, trying to stop her voice from cracking, 'the children will be going to school over here.'

'Oh simply perfect idea.' She could hear the pleasure in her mother's voice that at last her daughter had seen sense and surrendered to the logic of the boarding option. She'd always believed boarding-school was the only acceptable form of education, knowing nothing else and deeply suspicious of day schools (private, of course, state education had never featured on her radar). 'They'll have a lovely time – never did you any harm, sweetheart – and then you can fly them out for holidays.'

Like freight. Imogen had a vision of the children sitting on a huge airline seat, feet sticking out in front of them, and labels round their necks, and the grief rose unbearably again inside her. She dispatched her mother as soon as she could, past caring that she'd soon be imparting this latest news to her father and anyone else in the county who would listen.

She could sense Sophie hovering in the doorway behind her. 'Are you all right?' she said cautiously, placing a cup of steaming coffee on the garden table in front of Imogen. 'Was that the Gorgon of Guildford I detected you talking to? Is there trouble on the lush fairways of Godalming?'

Imogen ran her fingers slowly and distractedly over the phone keys. 'Who did we go and see when we were sad?'

Sophie sat down next to her. 'Come again?'

'At school I mean. Where did we go when we were homesick?'

'Oh, I was wet as water and had everyone looking after me, don't you remember? They appointed that

332

sixth-former to keep an eye on me.' She giggled naughtily. 'I hammed it up terribly – did my little blond girl act. But you were fine, weren't you? I don't remember you ever throwing a wobbly. You were always looking after everyone else.'

Too right, thought Imogen. That's me. Big, fat and reliable. 'We had mates though, didn't we?' Sophie went on, taking a sip of her coffee and pulling a face. 'Oh! Do you remember Elizabeth Sergeant telling us about the facts of life when we were about ten in D dorm? She was so hugely grown up at fifteen. Huge knockers!' She put on a posh, girly voice. '"It will hurt a bit, but you let him do it and then he goes all stiff and the seed comes out."' She laughed uproariously. 'Cor! I bet she's an Ann Summers rep these days!'

Imogen's heart contracted. Perhaps she should hurry to tell Rory the facts of life now, the right way. The way she wanted him to learn, before some boy lent him a porn mag and told him that's how it was. Oh God, he'd be a man by Christmas, and have it all wrong and she'd have missed it. She turned away from Sophie to hide the tears in her eyes.

'It was dire though sometimes, wasn't it?' Sophie was off now. 'All that bloody Saturday-morning letter-writing home. "Dear Mummy and Daddy, I am fine. I played lacrosse today. Please send two pounds for tuck." Hah! I bet it's all mobile phones and credit cards these days, lucky buggers. No lacrosse and stringing out your tuck.'

Imogen was right back there, almost able to smell the linseed oil on the lacrosse sticks in the pavilion, and the sweet stench of her tuck box with its half pack of stale Ritz crackers and tube of cheese and prawn spread. She was there on a long Sunday afternoon, sat on her bed wondering where all the other girls were.

'Ha!' Sophie laughed. 'Did your mum used to send you back with yoghurts? Yoghurts, for God's sake, and no fridges! Do you remember, we used to wait until the lids were all tight and raised then punch a hole in them so the contents sprayed everywhere? It used to taste all fizzy. Good dose of healthy bacteria I reckon. It never did us any harm. Who needs those fancy probiotic ones!'

Imogen smiled bitterly. It never did us any harm.

Sophie paused, then giggled thumping Imogen's arm in her rush to share the memory. 'And bloody weekend afternoons and spending our allowances at that funny little shop in the village. Christ – crème eggs! We used to eat them with a needle to make them last!'

They sat now in silence, both lost in their own memories: Sophie in the fun of it; Imogen in despair. 'And the days out!' said Sophie suddenly, remembering something else. 'We had a weekend at home once every half of term, do you remember? They come home every weekend now I'll bet!'

Not when you're on the other side of the world they don't, and Imogen got up from her seat and went inside as fast as she could before Sophie could see the tears streaming down her face.

In Jo's experience, there came a moment in every holiday when you wished it was all over and you could just go home. This was her moment. All she wanted to do was curl up in a nice dark room and obsess on how bloody stupid she'd been, and yet here she was stumping along this sodding lane – again – on the way to the sodding beach – again – bringing up the rear – again – lugging a picnic lunch that would sink a sodding battleship – again! This wasn't a holiday, it was *Groundhog Day*. Only instead of her life getting steadily better, it was going down the tubes, and at top speed.

The only, absolutely only, good thing in all this crap was that she hadn't made a public fool of herself. But that was only luck. If she hadn't seen Matt with that … that little tart, she might easily have marched straight in there and … ugh! Despite the sultry heat of the day, she shivered to think of how it might have turned out. The embarrassed silence, the horrified expression, the awkward excuses, the reassuring pat on the arm; even, God forbid, the promise of a pity fuck! It had been a narrow escape, all right. Whatever angel protects women from wholesale humiliation had been on her side – for once. How could she have let her guard down with him? *How?*

Jo grabbed a stick from the hedge and started to slash viciously at the wild flowers growing there, unrepentant as petals and leaves scattered to the ground. And, of course, the girl had been – just that – a girl. From what Jo had been able to make out, she was the right side of thirty, maybe even closer to twenty, with everything nice and firm and pert. Jo shifted her shoulders irritably, trying to free the thin cotton sticking to her sweaty skin.

It was such a cliché! She'd thought Matt was better than that – but she'd forgotten that crucial detail. Matt was a man, and therefore innately crap.

Well, gravity would take its toll on that bloody girl eventually. And then she'd see. There were some things that not even Lycra and hugely expensive skincare could defeat, and motherhood, particularly single motherhood, was one of them. Hurtling towards forty at around the speed of light was another. She'd see, she'd bloody see. But would Matt see? Probably not for years. Maybe never. He'd just get more lined and craggy and everyone would think he looked 'interesting', and he'd go on pulling stupid, gullible, desperate women for years and bloody years.

Jo glared up the straggling line ahead of her. No one wanted to walk with her. And why would they? She knew she'd been vile all morning – in fact, she'd been vile with Finn since yesterday's debacle, barely talking to him as she'd driven along the coast road and back again, aimlessly taking turnings that led nowhere, having to back up terrifying little roads to let other cars through. If it hadn't been for the shortage of petrol, they'd still be there doing it now. When Finn cautiously asked if she had her period, she'd snapped at him so fiercely, he'd shut up straightaway and sulked in silence. Poor kid hadn't even got his Gameboy with him.

Back at the house, she'd refused to let him answer Matt's calls to her mobile to find out why she hadn't turned up for their planned drink. He'd left a message, and he'd called three times in all. At least that had given her some satisfaction.

And she was only here on this ruddy route march to the beach out of guilt at what she'd put Finn through. She looked ahead to where he and Rory were talking now, with their heads close together, although Finn was so much shorter Rory had to stoop to listen. No doubt Finn was complaining about what a bitch his mother was. She'd always thought they got on pretty well. More like mates than mother and son. But even Finn didn't seem to want or need her now. And what was there to want? Crap mother, crap cook, old, badly organised, bad-tempered, unable to produce birthday parties with a simple wave of a magic sodding wand, incapable of keeping a man. All she was good for now was refusing to sign scripts for antibiotics to overweight, chain-smoking hypochondriacs with sniffles, hell bent on bleeding the NHS dry.

Surely they must get to the beach soon. This walk seemed to get longer every time. True to form, Imogen gave a hearty wave as she breasted the final hill. 'Look, everybody! I can see the sea!' Same tired expression every time, and today more than ever Imogen seemed to be trying to create something special out of the whole experience – make it more than it was. Well today more than ever Jo wasn't going to be bossed around.

After what seemed like an eternity, Imogen selected a spot for them to set up camp. All very sensible with rocks behind for drying towels on. Why did she have to make this fuss, everywhere they went? Jo dropped the baskets she had been lugging with an audible sigh and flung herself down on the sand. Sophie helped Imogen to spread the ever-present rug.

'Have I got time for a nap before lunch, I wonder?' Sophie asked no one in particular. 'This holiday's so relaxing I could just sleep all day. And this heat doesn't help …'

Jo rolled her eyes silently as Sophie lay back on the rug and closed her eyes. Imogen on the other hand had slipped off her trousers and top and was sitting bolt upright in her swimsuit, watching the children with intense attention.

'So, Imo,' Sophie yawned, 'is Guy coming down again before we leave to help clear up?'

'Er, what?' Imogen barely turned towards Sophie, her gaze still fixed on the children, who were chasing each other with handfuls of seaweed. 'Guy? I expect he will.'

'I can't believe this is our last week, can you? I wish this holiday could go on for ever!' Sophie stretched luxuriously, kicking over the basket of towels. Imogen, strangely, didn't rush to rearrange them, but started rummaging in her capacious zip-up beach tote.

'Did I put enough sunblock on Archie?' she muttered. 'Perhaps I'll just …' Slightly clumsily, she arranged a brightly coloured length of material around herself so that it covered her from boobs to knees, knotting it as securely as she could, then got gingerly to her feet and, with a tube of thick, gooey factor 50 and a legionnaire's cap, stalked off down to the water's edge.

Jo was perfectly aware of Sophie turning round to look at her, but wouldn't meet her eye, focusing instead on the patch of sand between her bare feet, which she was smoothing and patting with exaggerated attention.

'Isn't it amazing? We've been here over two weeks already. Feels like no time at all. I'm so relaxed now. I don't think I'm ever going to be able to get revved back up to London speed. I don't know how I'll cope with working again – but I have to say, I can't wait!'

Jo grunted, non-committally. She recognised small talk when she heard it, and she just couldn't be arsed today. But Sophie wasn't satisfied. 'Oh for goodness' sake, Jo. You two are a barrel of laughs. Cheer up, can't you? It may never happen.'

'That's just what I'm afraid of,' Jo replied bleakly.

'Oh well, if you're going to talk in riddles, I can't be bothered. Why don't you go and see Matt if you're feeling so grumpy? He'd sort you out in no time.' Sophie rolled onto her back and put her sunglasses on, thus missing Jo's most contemptuous glance. She just didn't understand and probably never would. In Sophieworld, love was a law of nature – fixed and eternal – and Jo certainly wasn't going to offer up her failed attempt at it for dissection by anyone.

Up to her knees in sea water, Imogen was trying valiantly to smear the children again. It looked rather like trying to baste live chickens, and she clutched awkwardly at the strip of cotton draped round her, now heavy with sea water at the hem and threatening to fall off.

'That sarong is sooo wrong,' muttered Jo, smirking a little.

'Oh for goodness' sake, Jo,' Sophie snapped, sitting bolt upright. 'If you can't say something nice, don't say anything at all. It's easy to sneer if you just sit on the sidelines all the time. You may not ever make a prat of yourself, but you miss out on a lot of fun too. At least Imo's trying.'

'Yes, very bloody trying,' Jo retorted tartly. Even Sophie was picking on her now. What was Jo even doing here? All she wanted was to be left alone to lick her wounds – and plan the rest of her miserable life. Sophie tutted loudly and brushed irritably at the flies buzzing round her face.

'You know what the real problem is, don't you? It's the weather. It's so still and humid. My hair's gone completely bonkers, which is a sure sign that there's rain on the way. I almost wish it would hurry up. At least it would clear the air and God knows it needs clearing,' she added meaningfully.

Imogen was plodding back up towards them, fiddling with the top of her wrap and turning back every few steps to look at the children. Jo watched her narrowly. 'Don't tell me *you're* getting obsessed with the weather now, Sophie? Please don't say it's contagious.'

'Contagious? Something I should know about?' Imogen lowered herself onto the rug, anxiety creasing her brow. 'Is it something the children might catch?'

Jo looked down as Sophie glared at her. 'No, Imo, it's just Jo being daft about something. Just ignore her.'

Imogen made a play of rearranging the lunch boxes. An edgy silence fell, soon punctuated by Sophie's gentle snoring. Thank goodness Jo had thought to bring a book. She couldn't have stood to make polite conversation today, and fortunately Imogen seemed to have the same idea. Jo sneaked a couple of looks over the top of the page to see her following the children's every move again with her eyes, her fists clenching and unclenching on the thick material of the rug. Didn't she ever let up? Sure enough, a few minutes later she was up on her feet again and, picking up an armful of spades and buckets, heading determinedly down the beach to join them, only coming back when the kids' hunger drove them to lay waste the immaculately packed feast.

Jo had lost her appetite but picked at the crusts Finn discarded and dissected a mini Scotch egg, eating the centre and tucking the rubbery pink meat in the rubbish bag. She was too hot to have a cup of steaming, milky coffee, mixed in a flask by Imogen that morning but served, naturally, in dinky china cups she'd painstakingly wrapped (individually, of course) in kitchen towel. Jo's phone chirped inside her bag, with some infuriating polyphonic ringtone she didn't recognise.

'Finn, I thought I told you to leave my phone alone.'

He shrugged sullenly, but hopped up to answer it before she'd even got to her feet. His face registered delight. 'Oh, hi, Matt. We're at our beach. Where are you? Oh, right. Cool. Yeah, I hope so. She's right here. Hang on.'

'Fiiinn!' she hissed in annoyance. This was one call she wouldn't have taken – and he knew it. Within a minute, she'd dismissed Matt briefly but thoroughly and turned the phone off with a flourish before dropping it back into her bag. She ignored Finn's confused stare, his trembling lip, and turned to face down the others, who all suddenly busied themselves eating up the scraps.

'Stop that, Rory. I've told you before not to do that and, anyway, you're wasting the ones you drop.'

Rory looked defiantly at his mother and threw another blueberry into the air, shifting his head to try and catch it in his mouth. Success! He tossed up another one, and threw his head back, mouth wide open and in it plopped. But suddenly he doubled up, a horrible gasping noise coming from his throat. Imogen jumped to her feet and started towards him.

'For goodness' sake, don't you ever listen!' And she started to thump him between the shoulder blades. But the gasping continued. No amount of thumping seemed to shift it. Suddenly the mood changed. The child was in trouble. Jo jumped to her feet too. Oh my God – she really ought to take action but she'd only ever done the Heimlich manoeuvre on a mannequin at a training course years ago. What if it didn't work, and, God forbid, she had to do a tracheotomy? That she was damned sure she'd never done, and certainly not with a picnic knife. Quickly she looked about her, hoping that an heroic A&E consultant might jump up from his picnic beside her, like Clark Kent, disguised as a mild-mannered holidaymaker.

Rory continued to fight for breath, and she steeled herself to wade in. Here goes, and she put her hand on Imogen's shoulder to move her out of the way. But to her amazement, and not a little indignation, Imogen rebuffed her hard with her elbow and, with the aplomb of a seasoned paramedic, grabbed the choking boy from behind and thrust her clenched fists upwards towards his diaphragm. The offending blueberry was propelled out whole onto the sand at Rory's feet.

There was stunned silence. The children were agape at this sudden violence, and Archie started to cry uncertainly, while Rory drew a shuddering breath, coughing and trembling. Imogen wilted onto the sand, gathering her boys to her, murmuring soothingly and stroking their hair. Olivia ran up to join them, nuzzling in to find a place on her mother's lap. Jo watched in silence and turned away, affronted and superfluous.

No one seemed to want to stay on after that and, once Rory had recovered (and Jo had done what she knew how to do, felt his ribs and put her ear to his chest), and the other children had been reassured that Imogen hadn't been inflicting some arcane punishment, they packed up and left, all very subdued. Jo hung back but Imogen seemed to be making a point of avoiding her eye, fussing with the children and the bags and repeatedly asking Rory if he felt OK now. Jo shook her head. Bloody amateurs. Lucky she hadn't broken his ribs.

But from amongst her uncharitable thoughts, a little voice piped up: You didn't know how to do it, did you? Jo shrugged it away. At least Imogen's layman's skills had saved her from risking a personal injury suit.

Dark clouds were massing inland, although the sun was still beating down more fiercely than ever. Jo had never been happier to see the house, but the atmosphere in the kitchen was even more oppressive than the sticky heat outside.

Nothing seemed right. Jo put the cool box on the

kitchen floor by the fridge, and Imogen moved it pointedly, tutting, over to the back door. Sophie started to make tea by chucking teabags into mugs, only to find that Imogen had already made it in the pot. The normally spacious room suddenly seemed claustrophobic and they edged round each other like boxers in the ring. It didn't help that Sophie, presumably in an attempt to dispel the atmosphere, was wittering on about nothing in particular. Jo and Imogen maintained a chilly silence.

A sharp cry from the garden made them all look up. Gracie came running in, curls bobbing. 'I saw a big caterpillar. It was *deegusting*. Come and look, Mummy.'

Sophie, who had just sunk into a chair with her cup of tea, groaned. 'Oh sweetie, Mummy's just resting. Don't make a fuss. Just leave the caterpillar alone, darling. Soon it'll turn into a beautiful butterfly.' Gracie ran out disappointed. Jo sat down next to Sophie and smiled cynically. 'Don't worry, Soph. Next year she'll be old enough to go out and clean chimneys and you can start making a few bob out of her. Failing that you could pack her off to the Foreign Legion!'

They both jumped as Imogen slammed a tray down on the counter behind them. 'What did you say?' she hissed, her eyes narrowed in fury. 'What did you say? How could you be so insensitive? How could you say such a stupid thing?' Imogen was advancing on Jo now from around the counter, her face red and blotchy with anger. 'She's a baby. That's all she is, and you think it's funny to make comments like that, do you? How can you be so bloody cold all the time?' Jo stared at her in bewilderment. Had she lost her mind? Where was this coming from?

'It was a joke, for God's sake! Lighten up, can't you?'

Imogen was almost leaning over her now. 'Everything's a joke to you, isn't it? Do you think I haven't noticed you sneering at me? At everything I do. You've contributed bugger all to this holiday and all you can do is take the piss out of people who have!'

Jo stood up, she could feel her face pinched with anger. 'It's hard to get a look in when every second of your day is planned in advance for you. Christ, Imogen, we almost have to ask permission to go for a pee!'

'Well, if it was left up to you we'd be eating sodding spare ribs and sitting on our arses in complete squalor.'

'At least we might have a laugh occasionally. You're just a fun-sucker, Imogen. A boot camp would be more of a holiday than this.'

Imogen sneered sarcastically, her face twisted with loathing. 'Take yourself off to one, then, and do us all a favour. I'm fed up of having to pussyfoot around you and your moods. You think you're so clever, but you don't know the first thing about living with other people. All you know about is taking care of number bloody one. It's time you thought about someone else for a change.'

'Steady on, you two.' Jo could hear Sophie's voice weakly in the background.

'Thanks for your precious advice, Imogen. You know best of course.' Jo spat out the words. 'Because you know best about everything, don't you? Even how to cut the bloody butter. And you just can't resist showing us.

Perfect little wife. Perfect little mummy. Perfect little party hostess. You make me sick.'

'Well, at least I'm there for them.' Imogen was shouting now. 'Not leaving other people to look after your child, while you disappear off all night like a bitch on heat!'

Jo gasped. 'How dare you speak to me like that?' she said slowly through gritted teeth. 'You sanctimonious cow! How dare you judge me? You don't know the first thing about me. I work bloody hard and I'm not answerable to anyone, especially you. Some of us aren't lucky enough to live in leafy suburbs supported by our oh-so-important husbands. The sooner you bugger off to Hong Kong with your perfect little family, the better!'

Almost in slow motion, Jo saw Imogen draw back her hand then, before she could dodge it, she felt the hot sting as it slapped across her face. Then, agape at what she'd done, Imogen turned and crashed through the door, slamming it behind her. They could hear noisy sobs as she thumped upstairs.

The silence she left behind her stretched out between Sophie and Jo. They stared at each other mirroring astonishment. Sophie spoke first.

'Fuck me!' she said quietly. 'Are you all right? I've known her the best part of thirty years and that's the first time I've heard an outburst like that! What's wrong with her?'

'She's certifiable that's what.' Jo rubbed her cheek slowly.

'No, no, it's more than that.' Sophie shook her head,

puzzled. 'If you learn one thing at boarding-school, it's that you avoid confrontation and Imogen was always the world champion at it. Something must be terribly wrong for her to have said all that.'

'Too bloody right it is. I'm not putting up with any more of this shit.' Jo strode over to the garden door and called out. 'Oi, Finn! Come on. We're outta here.'

Chapter 17

Tuesday

Humid and sticky, with thunderstorms
brewing in the South West

Imogen woke feeling as if she'd never slept. The air was stiller than ever, and even with the sash windows thrown wide open, there wasn't a breath of wind to ease the oppressive heat. It was like the inside of a tumble dryer. She had a headache right across her eyes as if she had a hangover. She'd had a drink all right – God, she'd needed one – but not that much and certainly not enough to get drunk on. Brushing off Sophie's gentle and well-meant overtures, she had made her excuses and gone to bed.

The pain in her head now was from waking throughout the night to get water for Archie and then weeping herself back to sleep. Heaving sobs that bunged up her nose and made her fight for breath until she was almost sick.

She'd been aware, too, of Finn pottering about between the bathroom and his mother's room long after they'd eventually come in at ten o'clock. Imogen had gone to apologise straightaway for her unforgivable slap at least, but Jo had turned her back, fussing over getting Finn ready for bed. The poor child would be exhausted today, but that wasn't her problem. Jo could deal with the fall-out this time. She'd made it quite clear Imogen's interference wasn't wanted.

Her feet too hot for her to bother with slippers, she started to pad downstairs, hoping for an hour's solitary recovery time – it was still early after all – and perhaps five minutes or so in front of the open fridge door to help her cool down.

Jo sliced the last orange in two and pressed each half in turn down onto the electric squeezer. A handful of ice cubes and it would be just perfect. 'Here you are, hon. That'll help cool you down.'

Finn yawned theatrically. 'Thanks, Mum. I'm not hungry, though.'

'Me neither. In fact, my tummy was so full last night, I couldn't even get to sleep,' Jo sat down at the table next to him, and tickled the back of his neck. It was damp with sweat already. 'Then there was that little matter of your hundred-decibel snoring. You can keep *Rory* awake all night, tonight, if you like. Don't worry if you're not hungry. I thought we'd go out for brekkie later. Sound good?'

Finn grunted, and started to sip at the fresh juice, surreptitiously crunching the ice cubes as he went. ''Lo, Imogen.'

Jo stood up and went back to wash up the juicer, but did not turn round. Time to leave. 'Don't worry,' she said briskly, 'we're going out for breakfast.'

Imogen put the kettle on and Jo noticed her wipe up the drops of juice left on the counter.

'It's your kitchen too. Don't feel you have to go out.'

Yeah right. 'Come on, Finn, finish that up. We'll go and get dressed and then we can get going.'

And she swept past Imogen with barely a glance.

'Did she say if she was joining us?' Sophie asked yet again, as they laid out the beach rug, with the practised skill now of synchronised divers. 'She looked awful when we passed on the stairs this morning, but then you don't look too great yourself. They must have had lunch out. This ruddy heat. It makes everyone arsey. Even Gracie.'

She stood up and polished an apple on her front. 'Ouch my boobs are killing me. I must be retaining water like mad – like a camel! But what about you, Mrs?' She took a bite from the apple and pointed it accusingly at Imogen. 'What the bloody hell was yesterday all about? Are you just not going to talk about this?'

Imogen dug out Olivia's hat for her and watched as her daughter ran off to play, then she dropped down onto the rug. 'I really don't want to. I've got a lot on my mind.'

'Oh come on, last night wasn't about "things on your mind". This is me you're talking to here. Come on, choke up.' She took another bite out of the apple.

Imogen hesitated. 'I'm sorry. I know it was unforgivable. It's just there's been a change of plan that needs a bit of sorting.' She laughed tightly. 'Typical Guy. He's gone and got himself posted to Jakarta instead.' There it was, out in the open.

'What Jakarta, as in "she went of her own accord"? Or is that Jamaica? Ha!'

350

How could she be so up about it? 'Well, I'm not going of my own accord.' Imogen smiled thinly. 'I'd got Hong Kong really sorted in my head and now it's all gone pear-shaped.'

'Oh you'll cope. You always do. Sounds wonderfully glam. I bet it's one of those places that sells fab fake Chanel bags. It'll be all cocktail parties and gin slings on the veranda at sundown. I know, we could all come out and visit. Is it very hot there? D'you know, I don't even know where it is. You'll probably have to slather old Arch in factor 100, won't you?'

'Well, actually—'

'Oh look there's Jo come to join us after all. Now behave, Imo. No more tanties if you please.'

'There – are you satisfied now?' Jo thrust out her hand for the bag Finn had been carrying. 'You might as well go off and play with him. Go on. Get lost.'

Finn glared at her. 'Well, I certainly don't want to stay here with *you*. You've been a cow all morning. I never wanted to go out, anyway. You made me!'

'You ungrateful little wretch. That's the last time I take you out to eat.'

'Good!' He stamped off across the sand to join Rory and the others, who were kicking an inflatable ball around, listless in the heat. Jo nodded at Imogen and Sophie, who had turned to watch her approach. She hoped they hadn't heard that little exchange. She didn't want to give Imogen any more ammunition. Much more self-satisfaction, and she'd explode out of her over-stuffed chinos.

'I've got a bit of a headache,' she lied. 'Think I'll sit in the shade over there. Maybe see you a bit later.'

Ignoring Sophie's concerned protest, she walked briskly back up the beach, negotiating her way irritably around lolling sunbathers and sodding windbreaks, to where there was welcome shade under some overhanging rocks. What a relief. She settled down with her book, putting on the sunglasses she'd managed to buy that morning in Rock, before Finn's sulk at being separated from Rory got too much to ignore. He was lucky. If it had been up to her, she'd have packed their bags last night and left.

'That's enough, Arch. Drink any more water and we'll run out. Everyone's going to be thirsty so just take sips.' Imogen could feel the sweat making its way down her cleavage and under her boobs. God, it really was too much. She'd never expected this sort of stiflingly warm wind on the Atlantic coast. The house had been unbearable at lunchtime and she'd hoped the beach would have brought some relief. If she couldn't stand this, what the hell was Indonesia going to be like?

Up behind the dunes she could hear the familiar sound of an ice-cream van pulling into the car park – a jangle that she hadn't heard for years but which took her right back to her childhood. It was one of those unmistakable noises that meant reassurance and normality.

'Oi!' she yelled at the rest of the little group bent intently over a three-legged crab that was circling around

352

frantically in the sand. 'Leave that poor thing alone. Now who's for an ice lolly to cool you down?' She blocked her ears to the response. 'Right, let's go and get them.'

'I'll guard the camp,' said Sophie and pulled her sunglasses back over her eyes and lay down.

'I'll help you, Mum,' said Arch, putting his small hand into Imogen's, and behind her the other children followed in dribs and drabs, making their way over the soft sand and skirting other families playing and sunbathing, to the car park above the dunes. In their excitement at the sight of the van they ran over towards it.

'Is Finn on his way too?' she asked Rory as he scooted past her.

'Just coming. Can I have a Magnum?'

Imogen sighed – always the most chocolatey option. Mind you, the fruit lollies bore no relation whatsoever to any fruit she'd ever encountered. 'We'll see what they've got by the time this queue's gone down. Wait here with me and you can take one for Finn, if he doesn't get here first.'

Jo glanced up from the pages of her book – it was getting quite exciting and she'd devoured three chapters almost without stopping. The beach was getting a bit too crowded for comfort now. People were swarming like bacteria in a Petri dish. They'd probably all come here to escape for the afternoon from the people with whom they'd foolishly agreed to share a holiday house. Maybe it was time to extract Finn and move on.

She jumped as Imogen appeared at her side, tentatively extending a lemonade lolly, a half-eaten Mivvi in her other hand. 'Thought you might like one of these. There's a van in the car park.'

'Oh, right. Well thanks. How much do I owe you?' Jo took the lolly. Was it intended as a peace offering? She peeled off the thin paper wrapper in strips and scrumpled it into her bag. There was silence between them but Imogen made no move to walk away. 'It's hot, isn't it?'

'Certainly is. I'm not sure I'll be able to stick it out much longer. Maybe we should round the kids up and take them back.'

Jo looked carefully at Imogen over her sunglasses. She was clearly nervous, and looked as uncomfortable as Jo felt. Could they just pretend yesterday never happened? No, they'd both said way too much. A return to their previous veneer of holiday camaraderie was out of the question and they both knew it. How should she take it from here? She stood up slowly, brushing sand off the back of her skirt.

Imogen took a deep breath, as if about to say something … then, 'Rory, why are you eating two lollies? Didn't Finn want his?'

Rory guiltily licked the ice cream dripping down his arm. 'Couldn't find him. He said he was going to put that crab back into a rock pool. 'Spect he's over there somewhere.' He gestured vaguely across the beach with the Magnum hand, flicking melting ice cream as he did so.

Jo casually scanned the beach, narrowing her eyes. Imogen was telling Rory off, in a low-key way, saying he'd have to queue up again to get Finn another lolly. Oh there he was! No hang on, wrong trunks. Was that him paddling with a group of older boys? She inhaled sharply. Where was the little beast? Her eyes flicked quickly from group to group, then she started again, methodically this time, going from right to left. He shouldn't be exactly inconspicuous among the hordes of blond children, blotchy with sunblock. He couldn't be that hard to spot. She stood on her toes and started again.

'Can you see him?' Imogen asked.

'Oh, he'll be around. He loves to wander off. Perhaps he's over with Sophie and the girls. That's where he'll be.'

Imogen's eyes darted over. Not only was Finn not there, neither was Sophie. 'Amelia, darling,' she started to walk over to them, 'where's Mum?'

'She's gone for a wee. We met her on the way back from the car park.'

'Did she have Finn with her?' Without thinking Imogen crouched down and wiped some ice cream from Gracie's chin.

'Don't think so.'

Imogen stood up again. 'Rors,' she called airily to her son, who was frantically licking the melting ice cream now from both arms, 'could you be a love and go back up to the car park. See if Finn's waiting for us there.' He started to wander in the direction of the dunes. 'Oh and darling, check out the Gents for us, could you? He might have gone in there for a pee.' She watched her son's slow progress through the sand then went back to stand with

Jo, who had positioned herself on a rock, her hand shielding her eyes as she scanned the crowded sand.

'Any luck?'

'Not yet. Perhaps I'll take a stroll down by the water's edge.'

Imogen glanced at her watch. Should she mention it? 'Er, Jo,' she called after her, 'do you suppose he'd go round the headland?' Plenty of time. No need to alarm her. Jo shrugged and carried on walking towards the water. Where the hell was Sophie?

Imogen turned to see her friend walking towards her. 'Hi, I was bursting for a pee, sorry. I've just seen Rory. So Finn's done a bunk, has he? Little bugger!'

'Soph,' she said quietly, 'stay with the children, can you? I'm going to have a quick look round the headland. The tide's coming in. Rory!' He came back over, shaking his head, the ice creams now dispatched. 'No sign? Right, you head over to the path up to the golf course. Have a look and see if he's playing on the dunes there, but come back straightaway and don't talk to anyone.'

Jo didn't realise Imogen had come down to the water's edge too until she was standing right beside her, with her hands on her hips. Jo could tell that she was scanning the sea as well.

'I had a look round the headland … you know, just in case.' Jo's stomach clenched at the urgency in Imogen's voice. She forced herself to sound nonchalant.

'He's got a very good sense of direction. Um, I was just wondering if he'd met some kid with a body board and

356

decided to have a go. You know how he likes to try new things.' She could feel her lips going dry.

Imogen slipped her phone out of her bag surreptitiously. No need to worry though. Jo was over on the far side of the beach now, scanning the hill that abutted it for signs of Finn playing in the bushes. Damn, poor reception.

'Soph – can you keep an eye on my lot too? I'm just going up to the car park again. Might have a word with the man in the kiosk. You never know.'

'You don't think …?' Imogen shot her a warning look. The last thing she needed was the children spooked.

Up at the car park and a couple more bars on the phone. No, the attendant hadn't seen anyone, but then he hadn't seemed very interested in her question. The ice-cream van was long gone.

Imogen looked at her phone again. Should she, or was it overreacting? Not nine nine nine. She was sure it wouldn't come to that.

She looked at her watch. Oh Lord, it must have been an hour and a half by now since the ice creams. She punched in some numbers. 'Hello, I want a number in Wadebridge, Cornwall.'

Jo approached yet another group of people, a red-faced man with his fat, ugly wife. Again, their initial bewilderment at being approached by a total stranger on the beach was soon replaced with a show of concern. They shook their heads. No, no, they hadn't seen a little mixed-race boy in red shorts. Well, maybe earlier, but not for a hour at least. She cringed at the feel of their sympathetic looks following her, soon to change, no doubt, into smug relief once they'd located their own children safely. There but by the grace of God, hey?

She glanced over at Imogen, bending down to ask a family on the far side of the sand. Jo watched as she shook her head, shrugged and moved on. Had she missed anyone?

Where was he? Where the hell was he? He must be worried by now. Maybe he was hungry?

She went up to some youths, larking about, stubbing out roll-ups on the sand. What would they care? ''Scuse me. Have you seen a little boy, mixed race, about ten – but small …? He looks younger …'

One of them jumped up. 'Is he lost? We'll help you look, if you like. When did you last see him?'

Public schoolboys, you could tell by the accent. Sod her prejudices. She nodded gratefully. 'That would be wonderful. Thanks. It must be at least an hour. It feels like longer.'

The tallest one took over. 'Tris, Ed – why don't you guys take the dunes?' He turned back to her. 'Have you asked the car park bloke? He might have seen something.'

Jo took a shuddering breath. There was a pain in her stomach. She couldn't bring herself to contemplate what 'something' might be. The boy was getting into his stride. 'Might be an idea to call the coastguard. Have you got a mobile?'

She turned away. Oh shit, oh shit. Surely that wasn't necessary? He'd turn up. Any second now, he'd appear, grinning that lopsided grin, wondering what all the fuss was. She felt a wave of cold sweat. There was Imogen coming towards her. She'd know what to do next. Jo stared at her face, willing her to smile, to say everything was going to be all right. But the set of her mouth said it all.

Jo felt the fear sweep through her body as if she had been injected with it. She spun round and screamed at the top of her voice, 'Fiiiiinn! Fiiiiiin, where are you? Come back! Please, come back!'

'He's about four foot tall. Yes, his skin is dark – coffee-coloured really, and he's got tight curly hair but it's quite long, especially when it's wet.' The policeman leant down over his booklet. 'We last saw him about two o'clock.'

'Can I ask you what he was wearing?'

Imogen looked over at Jo again, beside her standing hunched and hugging herself. She didn't seem capable of answering. 'Er, I think it was a blue T-shirt, isn't that right, Jo? You know, light blue and—'

'Red shorts,' Jo mumbled. 'And it says "Surf Maniac" on the front of the T-shirt in big yellow letters, with a sort of squiggle.' She gestured a shape vaguely with her hand. The policeman's radio burbled something.

Out of the corner of her eye, Imogen spotted Sophie gesturing hesitantly, trying to get her attention. She put her hand on Jo's shoulder. 'I'll be back in just a second,' and moved over to speak to her.

'The children are getting hungry. Do you think I should take them back up to the house?' Sophie whispered. 'Anyway, someone should be there in case he turns up, shouldn't they?'

'Good idea. Get Rory to help you carry the bags, and I'll bring the rest later. And, Soph … keep your mobile on.'

The beach was emptying now, with people making as much fuss about packing up as they had unpacking hours earlier. Even the public schoolboys had given up the search. Jo stared around frantically. It must be getting late. How could everyone just walk away like that as if everything was normal? And why did they have to keep on glancing back at her as they rolled up their stupid beach mats and closed their cool boxes? People always stare at policemen, hoping to see something bad. Vultures. This would give them something to talk about in their hot, sandy cars on the way back to their caravans, their children fractious in the back. Fractious but safe.

There was debris left on the sand and Jo, vaguely registering it, looked around in distaste. She closed her eyes. So many questions. When were they going to get on with looking for him? Thank God Imogen was answering them for her. She couldn't have. She took a step away. This couldn't be happening to her.

'Mrs Newman, can I ask you?' The younger of the two policemen approached her. 'Has your son been acting normally to you? Was there any reason for him to be upset?'

Jo's throat tightened. It hadn't really been a row. It

wasn't worth mentioning. Maybe they would think it was her fault. Maybe it was her fault. Maybe they wouldn't look for him if they thought he'd gone off in a huff. Dear God, she'd told him to get lost. 'No, nothing. Please can you just look for him? Why all this waiting? Why aren't there more of you?'

'We're waiting for the Coastguard.'

Jo dropped to her knees in the cooling sand. 'Oh God no.'

The policemen crouched down beside her. 'It's just normal procedure, madam, this close to the coast. Your son might have wandered onto the rocks and got himself in a bit of a fix. Now is there anyone he might have gone to see? Any friends?'

'Oh for fuck's sake,' she sobbed. 'We're on holiday! He's never been here before in his life.'

Imogen put her hand gently on Jo's shoulder and crouched down beside her too. That vanilla perfume of hers that Finn liked so much suddenly seemed quite reassuring. 'Jo,' she said gently, 'what about Matt? Shall I call him?'

She shook her head frantically. No, no. He was the last person she wanted to witness this. What would he think? She couldn't bear to be shown up in front of him for the crap mother she was. The last thing she wanted to see was the pity on his face. The other policeman took Imogen aside and was speaking to her quietly. Jo could feel herself trembling but couldn't seem to stop it. She strained to listen but all she could hear was his radio crackling with static and indistinct voices.

'Mrs Newman, why don't you let us take you and your

friend back to your house and have a nice cup of tea? We'll look after things here.'

'No. I can't. I can't go. He won't know where I am.' They mustn't take her away. She had to stay where she was and make sure that they were searching hard enough. 'He won't be able to find me. He'll be so frightened.' She felt Imogen's arm around her shoulders gently urging her away.

Imogen punched the buttons of her phone, relieved at having the surf-school number programmed in. He answered instantly. 'Matt, Imogen here—'

'Sorry, Imogen. I'll have to call you back. There's a kid gone missing and I've been asked to go out to help—'

'Listen, Matt, it's Finn.' There was an awful silence and she hurried on, anxious to get the details over as quickly as she could. Matt seemed to know most of it already but, attentive as ever, asked a few brief questions and she could hear him transmitting the answers to someone else. 'How did you hear about it? Oh I see ... About four hours now ... Yes, I'm sorry I didn't call before ... Bit complicated. No, Matt, don't come here. Just do what you can.' She hung up. He'd sounded brisk and businesslike and reassuring. She turned back to the house, her shadow long across the lawn now.

She looked at her watch again and went back into the kitchen where Sophie was half-heartedly trying to organise a game of Mousetrap, but the children were sitting, unresponsive, in a muted little group. Rory was slumped, pale under his tan, and looking younger than his years. Gracie was sniffing miserably.

'I'll take Jo another cup of tea,' Imogen said. 'She needs something to occupy her.'

Sophie looked up. 'Anything?' Imogen shook her head quickly, but smiled bravely at the children. 'Come on, cheer up. He'll turn up soon, you'll see.' But what if he didn't?

'But what if he doesn't?' Gracie's eyes looked huge and moist.

Sophie clutched her daughter to her. 'Oh course he will. He has to.'

In the sitting room, Jo was on her knees in front of the silent television, tidying up DVDs. Putting the cup down on a small side table next to another full, cold mug, Imogen joined her in her strange task, matching the disk to its box.

Jo sat back on her heels. 'That's better.' Then she got up quickly and, leaving the room momentarily, came back with the laundry basket from the kitchen, full of wrinkled clothes from the dryer. Casting aside the other children's clothes, she carefully selected Finn's things and, smoothing them with her hand, folded them and piled them up neatly on the arm of the chair. Task completed, she cast around for something else to do, and pulling the clip from her hair, tied it back again carefully.

How can I end this suffering? Imogen asked herself, watching Jo's shaking hands and ceaseless movement. 'We'll find him,' she mumbled inadequately.

'Will we?' Jo looked at her with manic intensity. 'Will

we? What if we don't? What if we don't?' Her eyes flooded with tears, and they began to roll down her face. 'Where's he gone, Imogen? He was so tired. I shouldn't have kept him out. You were right. He does need more sleep. He has to come back right now. He needs to … he needs …' She grasped painfully onto Imogen's arm. 'Find him for me. My baby!' She threw back her head and howled. 'My baby, he's all I've got.' Instinctively Imogen enfolded the sobbing woman in her arms.

Jo could hear an animal. It sounded as if it was in pain and she wished it would stop howling. Why wouldn't it stop? It wasn't until she heard Imogen making comforting, hushing noises in her ear that she realised the sound was coming from her.

Imogen looked at her watch again. There could only be an hour now before the light failed. She could hear the throb of the helicopter. It was a bad sign. She knew they wouldn't stop until they found him – found something. She shivered. The police control centre had been updating them all afternoon, and the gentle voice of the officer at the other end of the phone had reassured her that they would use thermal imaging if they didn't find him before dark – but she'd rather not have heard that helicopter coming over again. They had been calling in more and more people, he'd also told her – local people, expert in searching the terrain. If he'd hoped that would reassure her, he was wrong. It smacked of desperation.

Gently she tried to shift her position. She didn't want

to give Jo the impression she was shaking her off, but her back had gone stiff and she felt sticky in the stifling heat.

Each time she had moved even the slightest bit in the last hour Jo had looked up, startled, and Imogen had had to reassure her that she wasn't going anywhere. At least she had stopped that heart-rending keening noise. Occasionally Sophie had popped her head around the door, and now Imogen could hear the floorboards creaking upstairs as she bathed the children and cajoled them into their pyjamas. The door was pushed open again, but this time it was Archie, rabbit in hand and thumb in mouth, whose head appeared around it. Imogen extended her other arm out to him, and gathered him to her side.

His little face was deadly serious as he leant over to kiss Jo on the cheek, then handed her his rabbit.

'Here you are,' he whispered. She took it gently from him and he stroked her arm softly with his forefinger. 'He'll need a big cuddle when he comes back, won't he?'

Jo smiled weakly. 'Yes, darling,' said Imogen, handing him back the rabbit. 'Now run along and ask Rory to read you a story.'

'But he always does silly voices.'

'I don't think he will tonight.'

The phone's shrill on the table next to her made all three of them jump. Imogen snatched it up and waved Archie out of the room, blowing a kiss.

'Hello?'

'Hi, darling, it's me. Just got home. I've had a hell of a day. How's things?'

'Guy, I can't talk now. I'll call you back.' She put down the phone. An explanation would have to wait.

The tension abated after a moment, but she could feel despair and disappointment radiating from Jo. Then they both went rigid again. Was it? Yes, it was definitely a car on the driveway. A door slammed, and a deep voice called through the open doorway.

'We're in here,' Imogen called back eagerly, and they both stood up as the older of the two policemen from the beach came cautiously into the room.

'Mrs Newman.' No one bothered to correct him. 'No news yet, I'm afraid. We are getting concerned, but I just wanted to reassure you that we have drafted in a further ten officers to help look for your son—'

'Oh God, Oh God.' Jo's breathing became ragged. 'He'll be so frightened … are you sure you've looked everywhere? You might have missed something – I should be out there helping. ' She started to make for the door, but he gently put his hand out to stop her.

'Mrs Newman, we've called in a specialist rescue group who know the area like the backs of their hands, and our search coordinators are working with everyone to make sure we are thoroughly combing the area—'

Sophie pushed open the door with a tray. 'Here. I thought you all might like something to drink,' she said softly, placing it on the table and pouring out a cup from the teapot for the officer. He accepted it, and the four of them sat down, Jo planting herself almost hip to hip with Imogen on the sofa. There was a long silence broken only by Jo's rapid breathing.

She jumped up suddenly making them all start and began to scrabble through the clothes she'd neatly piled up. 'When you find him, he'll be cold. Here, take this.' She grabbed a red fleece and tried to push it into the officer's hands, her voice rising with panic. 'It's his favourite. He even—'

'Ssh, Jo.' Imogen placed her hand on Jo's arm, a finger to her lips, and strained her ears. Had she imagined it? No, there it was again.

'Please, he'll need it,' Jo continued until Imogen had to stand up and shake her shoulder urgently, her face intent. 'Sssh, listen.'

'Jo-o, I've got him. Jo-o, it's all right. He's here. He's safe.' Matt's voice grew louder as he came through the front door, shouldering it further open, Finn's slight form held close in his arms.

Barging the policeman out of the way, Jo stumbled into the hall. There he was. 'Oh my darling. Oh my God, my baby ... are you OK? Let me see him,' and she almost snatched him from Matt's arms, slipping down onto the hall floor, cradling him to her across her lap, raining kisses on his face and rocking him. Finn's face was screwed up against the light, and tears rolled down his cheeks as he and Jo talked to each other incoherently, each simultaneously reassuring the other that they were there; they were really there.

Unable to bear the intensity of the tableau, Imogen looked across at Matt standing now with his arms limply by his sides, his face pale and drawn. 'Where was he?' she mouthed.

'Tucked away out of sight under a gorse hedge on the golf course. I just caught sight of his T-shirt,' he said loud enough for Jo to hear if she was ready to, then he managed a tired smile. 'He was fast asleep.'

From the floor Jo sobbed a half-laugh, half-cry at the absurdity of it, and stroked Finn's head as he struggled to explain.

'I thought you'd all gone,' he sobbed. 'I put the crab back and I stayed for a bit to see if he was all right and then I couldn't see anyone. I couldn't find you. I thought Rory was bringing me a lolly, and I waited, but then he didn't come and you'd all gone. You left me behind.' He struggled to sit up now in her arms.

'Ssh, darling, we were looking for you. You know I'd never leave you.'

'But then I tried to take a short cut back to the house, but it didn't look like the way we've been before. So I sat down and waited.' Imogen saw Matt look up the stairs, alerted by a noise, and following his gaze she saw five faces peering round the top of the banister. She nodded at them, and they hurtled down the stairs, questions tumbling out to Finn, who was now bolt upright, cross-legged on the floor, beginning to realise he was the hero of the hour.

'Wait right there!' Imogen held up her hand to halt them. 'Finn, love,' she crouched down beside him and Jo, 'you missed supper. Fancy something to eat?'

An hour later, everyone had left and Jo was ensconced in her room with her son. She had sat with him on her knee and watched him eat cereal and toast, following every spoonful into his mouth, and had then bathed him like a baby, wrapping him in a towel and drying him with care. Content now that she was strong enough to be left, Imogen phoned Guy and explained, failing to come even close to describing the horror of the afternoon.

It wasn't until she herself went up the stairs to bed around midnight, the house quiet now save for the first faint rumblings of thunder in the distance, that Imogen thought for the first time in hours about what loss the future held for her.

Chapter 18

Wednesday

Fresh after the storm, with temperatures
getting warmer later

In bare feet, Imogen tiptoed past Jo's bedroom. The door was ajar and she could see Jo still asleep, her body curled around Finn's like spoons in the narrow single bed. She was protecting her son with her arms even in her deep sleep – and it must be profound because, Imogen knew having passed on her way to bed, that she hadn't stirred all night despite the fearful thunderstorms. She paused outside the door watching them, feeling a bit like a voyeur yet unwilling to look away. She'd never imagined she'd see such vulnerability in Jo, or such tenderness.

Yesterday had seemed to last for ever, and during the long hours of waiting she'd seen the raw person emerge from behind that cool exterior. There had been no place for artifice. All the niggles of the last two and a half weeks, all the appalling insults they'd hurled at each other, had been swept away and everyone had focused on getting Finn back. What would today bring? Imogen wondered, as she watched the rise and fall of Jo's breathing. Would the shutters be up again? Would they be back to snarling over discarded teabags and sculptured pats of butter?

She carried on down the stairs, feeling shamefaced at her pettiness. The dishwasher was full of little other than mugs – none of them had eaten but had survived on cups of tea and coffee all yesterday afternoon. She supposed the children must have been fed at some point – Sophie must have taken that in hand. Well, they'd survive one day on jam sandwiches and yoghurts, for heaven's sake. It all seemed very trivial now.

'Mum, is Finn OK?' Archie stuck his little face around the kitchen door, and sidled up to her, resting his head on her thigh. She sat down and scooped him onto her knee at the table as the kettle boiled.

'Yes, darling. He's safe with his mum now.'

'That was scary, wasn't it? I thought he was lost for ever. He must have been frightened.' Archie looked into her eyes. 'I'd be frightened if you weren't there.' Imogen took in his wide gaze, the smattering of freckles on his nose from the sunshine, the round softness of his face, and then she couldn't see, for tears were blurring her vision. 'Don't cry, Mummy, I'm here.'

To stop herself from sobbing out loud – that wouldn't do at all – she gripped onto him and listened to the rising hiss of the kettle as it came to the boil, until, unable to bear it any longer, he wriggled in her arms. 'Oi, Mum, you're squashing me. Can I go and watch TV?'

Imogen laughed snottily, glad of her son's prosaic words. 'Fickle youth. Rating me below the Chuckle Brothers,' and she tapped him on the bottom as he ran out laughing.

Pushing open the door of Jo's room carefully with her

hip to avoid spilling any tea, she wondered whether she should leave it beside the bed – would Jo wake before it went cold? – but there was no need to worry. Jo was already propped up on one elbow and was staring down intently into Finn's still sleeping face beside her. Her eyes were roving over him, taking in every inch. She looked round as Imogen approached the bed and smiled sleepily.

'Hello. That's kind of you. Just what I needed,' and she put a bare arm out to move books out of the way to make room for the mug.

'I made it strong,' Imogen whispered back. 'I've noticed you like it that way first thing.'

'Mmm lovely. Haven't you brought yours up, or have you had one already on your usual dawn patrol?' Imogen wasn't sure if the tease was meant kindly, but could see a warm smile in Jo's eyes.

'Oh yes well, I am a bit of an early riser. Always have been.' She tentatively sat down on the other bed, not sure if she was imposing, but not wanting to lose the moment.

Jo lay back against the pillows and yawned. 'God, I should think you need the time on your own with your crew around you all day,' she said quietly. 'It's all I can do to cope with one, and even that's pretty intense at times.' She smiled wryly, and Imogen looked away. Yes, she'd witnessed something of that intensity yesterday.

Her glance skimmed over the clutter of the room, and she realised she hadn't been in here at all since the first day they had arrived. Although it was strewn with discarded trousers and T-shirts, it smelt softly fragrant like clean linen and yesterday's perfume. God, it was small though. Downright poky in fact. She couldn't have put up with it.

'You got the short straw a bit with this room, didn't you?' Imogen smiled apologetically, and Jo laughed softly.

'It's fine. I didn't have a husband to accommodate, just this little newt,' and she looked down lovingly at her son, dropping a kiss onto his bare shoulder without waking him. 'Well, I suppose I ought to have a shower ... I feel all grimy this morning and probably look like shit.'

Imogen made an indistinct noise in her throat. 'Like you ever do.'

'That's all smoke and mirrors. You'll see.'

Noticing Jo's hesitation, Imogen wasn't sure if she should ask the next question. She didn't want her to think she was fussing. 'Listen, would you like me to sit with him while you're in the shower?'

Jo's eyes lit up as she swung slowly out of the bed. 'Would you? Just in case he wakes?'

'Go on. He'll be fine. But I can't guarantee I won't drink your tea.'

When Jo had left, Imogen curled her feet up under her on the bed, and rather wished she had brought her cup up with her. Jo's shower sessions could be epic – she'd drained the hot-water tank more than once since that first day – and she might be in for a long wait. She took the opportunity to look round the room again as if it might reveal some clues about its occupant. Her eyes ran over the piles of intertwined, wrinkled clothes on the floor and the suitcase spewing out T-shirts and sweatshirts, then she saw the dressing table. Tucked behind the door, it had been out of sight before, but now she could see it was crammed with neat rows of bottles and jars.

Imogen squinted to see some of the labels. There were brands she recognised, some she'd never heard of but they all looked as exclusive as the bottle of bath oil she'd used in the bathroom. There were exfoliation creams, body scrubs, expensive sun cream and body milks (an idea Imogen had always thought sounded faintly disgusting) all standing tall in tubes or bottles at the back. At the front, squat white jars in various sizes, with apricot-coloured lids; small bottles of foundation and tinier jars of eye cream. Tubes of mascara, at least three different makes, lay beside them, with a palette of eye shadows that looked as inviting as a child's paint set. Beside this lay eyelash curlers, eye liner in a tube and what Imogen assumed was an eyebrow pencil judging by the brown lid. A small zip-up make-up bag was open to reveal a couple of bottles of nail varnish, one in deep red, the other palest pink, an emery board with a pattern, and one of those sticks for pushing back cuticles. Jammed in too was a blue wiggly rubber contraption for separating the toes.

Well, well, well, Imogen smiled in amazement. Smoke and mirrors, indeed. It reminded her of a dressing room at the theatre. So this was Jo's stage paint. Creating a character and hiding behind it. All at once she felt a stab of sympathy for this lonely, insecure woman.

Finn stirred without waking and rolled over on to his back taking the space his mother had occupied. Imogen studied his face, like Jo's in many ways but transplanted onto a brown skin. The unrecognisable features – his eyes, his mouth, of course his hair – he must have inherited from that missing part of the jigsaw, his father, and Imogen tried to imagine what he must have been like. Finn had certainly inherited his mother's obstinacy – she'd seen it manifest several times over the holiday – but he had an incredibly gentle and enthusiastic side too, demonstrated when they played a game on the beach or she suggested somewhere to visit. Was that from this missing man too, or was it a streak Jo had, but just wouldn't show?

Before she could stop herself Imogen sneezed, and Finn's eyes opened slowly. He looked for a moment as if he wasn't sure where he was, then turned towards the noise that had woken him.

Imogen leant over to him and gently stroked his hair.

'Morning, you.' She smiled, hoping she sounded reassuring. 'Mum's in the shower. She won't be a minute. How are you feeling?'

'Orright,' he replied croakily and rubbed his eyes with both fists. 'Where's Rory?'

Normal service resumed, she thought, relieved. Oh, the resilience of children. 'He's downstairs, love. Watching telly, I expect. That's a pretty safe bet, wouldn't you say? Are you hungry, sweetheart? Would you like a plate of pancakes, just for you?'

Finn nodded sleepily, and rolled over, pulling the duvet around him tightly, just as Jo reappeared at the door, wrapped in a towel, droplets of water on her shoulders. Record time, Imogen thought wryly as she went softly downstairs again.

'What are we doing today, Mum?' Olivia enquired through a mouthful of toast half an hour later.

'Yeah, can we go pony riding?' Gracie asked eagerly.

Sophie leant back in her chair, stretching languidly. 'Oh please no, Gracie. Can't we just stay in and watch *The Lion King* again? I can't move today.'

Imogen looked at her friend over her coffee cup and shook her head impatiently. 'You lazy old trout.'

'Either that or you need some vitamins, my girl,' mumbled Jo from behind the cereal. 'Or less Chardonnay.'

'But I didn't have any yesterday in all the excitement.' Sophie leant forward earnestly. 'Maybe that's my problem. Is it too early for one now?'

The others groaned. 'Actually I haven't thought of anything special for today – you'll all be surprised to hear,' Imogen said pointedly. 'But if you're desperate, Sophie, I'll take the children up to the fields behind the house to those standing stones while you put your feet up, you poor lamb. There's quite a nice walk, I think, then we'll come back for lunch.' She glanced at Jo. 'Want me to take Finn?'

Jo blinked rapidly. 'Er … I think I'll join you all. A walk would be good.' She paused and added quietly, 'Just not the beach, hey?' Imogen looked at her face, reading the message written there. She looked vulnerable and young. In fact, she'd emerged from the shower all scrubbed and glowing, her face clear of make-up – a bare look that Imogen had never seen before – and she'd kept it that way through breakfast. She looked natural and tanned. Facially nude. Imogen was about to say something, but thought better of it. Bit too personal to point out such a significant step.

After a brief contretemps with Rory, who insisted on wearing a thick surfing hoody for the walk, they set out in a crocodile along the lane from the house, partly so the little group could walk until they reached the footpath without fear of being squashed by aggressive holidaymakers in four by fours. But partly, Imogen couldn't help thinking, so Finn was protected front and back, however unconscious that was.

The morning was fresh and breezy after the storm, the clouds scudding across the sky but white and fluffy, without bringing any threat of rain. The crocodile wound left into a footpath, a green tunnel of overhanging trees between two cottages, with barely enough width for one person. Wet wildflowers brushed their legs, and the odd 'watch out for the bramble' came from the largely silent group as someone held back a spiky branch of flowers and green, unripe berries for fear it would spring back into the face of the person behind. The path began to curl around and to enter a steep incline, and Imogen, bringing up the rear, urged Archie on as his legs became tired, pushing him gently in the back.

He was just starting to complain more forcefully, Amelia was launching into a fuss about her shoes, and the gap between the heartier walkers and the slowcoaches was beginning to widen, when they burst out into a field of deep lush grass and, out of breath, turned to look behind them at the view down over the houses and cottages, to the beach and out to the estuary and the sea beyond.

'Wow,' Rory marvelled, surprising his mother who'd always believed views were lost on children.

'Something else, isn't it?' She stood beside him, panting slightly from the exertion. Rory, red-faced too, peeled off the hoody. 'Can you hold this, Mum?'

'Why should I carry it? I told you you'd be too hot if you wore it.'

'Ah Muuum. I can't run about with Finn and stuff,' and he pressed it firmly into her arms and ran off.

Sighing, she tried to tie it round her waist and, realising the sleeves weren't long enough, threw it around her neck like a cricket umpire. Following Rory and Finn's lead, the other children ran on ahead too, towards the stones, the massive expanse of space in front of them meaning they could be clearly seen, and Jo fell into step beside Imogen.

Finding herself as good as alone with Jo again, she suddenly couldn't think of a single thing to say. Should she sound trite and make small talk or acknowledge the unravelling of the holiday that yesterday had precipitated? She took a path she hoped was somewhere down the middle.

'God, I don't know why I bother issuing warnings. I suppose I should just let him find out for himself the consequences of wearing a sweatshirt when it's warm. I'm always doing it though: insisting he takes a coat, or has a biscuit in case he gets hungry or wears more comfortable shoes. But it's weakness really. It's so much easier to do his thinking for him – saves him being uncomfortable and me having to put up with the whinge.'

'It's quite nice to have to mother them sometimes, though, isn't it?' Imogen hadn't expected an answer like that. She waited to see what Jo would say next, but for a moment Jo turned to address the view, brushing out of the way the hair that the wind had blown across her face. 'In no time,' she went on, 'they won't need us at all.' She paused for an age and Imogen thought that was an end to it. 'But I need him,' she blurted suddenly. 'I didn't realise just how much until there was the danger he wasn't going to be there.'

Imogen held her breath and waited.

Jo was aware of Imogen's encouraging silence but she looked down, embarrassed at showing what she felt, again. Hadn't she done enough soul-baring yesterday? They walked on for a while until they reached the stones, where the children were already busy, inventing rules to a game they had just made up. Imogen bent down to feel the grass, then laid out Rory's sweatshirt.

'Shall we sit here for a bit and watch them play?'

Jo settled herself cautiously against a standing stone. It had been warmed slightly by the sunshine already and she started to relax, relishing its solidity as she tilted her head back. She could hear Finn laughing at something Grace had said. He seemed completely unaffected by yesterday's adventure and unaware of all the panic that had followed. Better it should stay that way.

By the time Matt had appeared at the door with Finn in his arms, she'd been beyond desperation. She'd snatched her son away and held on tight, unable to let go in case he disappeared. In bed, she'd held him close, staring at him through the darkness until he'd squirmed irritably out of her arms in his sleep. She'd thought she'd never get to sleep herself but had soon plunged into a dreamless oblivion, the scent of his skin on every breath she took. Thank God, thank God.

Jo shivered and opened her eyes to see Imogen looking sideways at her. She smiled wanly.

'How're you feeling now?' Imogen's voice was soft.

'I feel completely knackered, to be honest. As if I've been through a mangle. Sitting here's helping – I feel as though I've relaxed at least by a notch – y'know, like letting a belt out when it's too tight. But I reckon it'll be a while before I can let him out of my sight again.'

Imogen tutted good-naturedly. 'What would you know about tight belts?'

Jo frowned and tried to think it through, realising that she'd stumbled across the perfect image. 'Well, it's weird. In a way I feel like I've been wearing one for years. Like I've been holding my breath for ages and I've only just let it go.'

There was a brief silence. Then Jo felt as if she wanted to talk. Was Imogen still listening? She glanced sideways at the other woman. Imogen was watching her, nodding slightly. 'That must feel strange.'

Jo closed her eyes tightly and took a deep breath. 'Y'know, I haven't cried like yesterday in years. Not since … since Trevor, Finn's dad, since we broke up, well, since he ditched me actually.' She trailed off. It was strange. Bastard, coward, cheat. She'd described Trevor as all these, but, she realised now, she'd never actually admitted before that she'd been 'ditched'.

'That's a long time to be wearing a tight belt, Jo,' Imogen said quietly.

So she was listening. Relief cascaded over Jo, and she sat up and crossed her legs. 'It feels weird,' she said. 'And apart from the fact that my eyes look like piss holes in the snow, I think it might have done me good. I felt so scared yesterday. I really thought – well, you know what I thought, but today it's as if I've been given another chance.'

'You really did go through it, didn't you? I can't imagine how it must have felt. Well, a little bit, but not when you thought he might …' Now Imogen trailed off and Jo nodded gratefully. Even now she didn't want to hear the words said out loud. She fought the urge to go and grab Finn and hold him close. She wondered how long it would be before she would stop feeling that way. Would she ever even let him go to the corner shops near the flat again?

She looked down and tugged idly at the grass in front of her. 'Did I make a real fool of myself?' she asked at last. 'Am I going to have to apologise to everyone in the county for acting like a complete loony?' She forced a tight smile. 'I'd probably better take out a full-page ad in the local paper. All those people on the beach! All those policemen, coastguards! Matt! Oh God! I must have looked like a crazy person.'

'Oh come off it!' Imogen retorted. 'He's your son. I'd have been on my knees within minutes. Just the idea of being separated from your own children, not knowing where they are or if they're all right. Being so far away.' Imogen looked away quickly.

Jo tilted her head back once again, feeling the warmth of the sun on her skin. She hadn't put on any sunblock today – or even any make-up, come to that. She probably looked about a hundred, but somehow it didn't matter. She opened her eyes as a ladybird landed on her arm, and watched as it laboriously made its way to the tip of her index finger, before spreading its wingcases and taking off in a blur of movement. 'That's it. Fly away home. What are you doing leaving your children on their own?' She shivered again. 'God, I'm so lucky.'

She heard Imogen take a breath, as though she was about to speak, and turned to look at her. Imogen's face was serious, but when she spoke at last, she sounded hesitant. 'Jo, what did happen with Finn's dad? You don't have to tell me if you'd rather not. Was it really awful?'

Jo shook her head and gave a bitter little laugh. 'Pretty awful, yes.' She paused. 'I will tell you – if you really want to know – but stop me if I get boring. Usual stupid story. I wanted him, he wanted to – er – fuck around, basically. So we weren't terribly compatible.' She laughed harshly, and turned to Imogen with a cynical half-smile. 'That's it, in essence.'

Imogen turned to face her and folded her legs beneath her, her expression serious. 'Come on, Jo. I really am interested, y'know. Don't push me away.'

It pulled her up short. Imogen laid a hand lightly on Jo's bare arm. 'I'd like to know, if you want to tell me that is.'

Jo could feel something unlocking in her, as though the belt was slipping yet looser. Whatever else she thought about Imogen, she was no bullshitter. She bit on her lower lip, and thought about how to start, then took a deep breath. 'I met him at a friend's house. I think it was a bit of a set-up, really, and it certainly worked. He was gorgeous, an actor, really exciting and intense. He had the most fantastic head of really fine dreadlocks and he used to push them back from his face. He had these expressive hands – theatre training, I suppose – and these eyes. So like Finn's. Anyway, he was the centre of attention at this dinner, everyone was hanging on everything he said. I couldn't believe he was interested in me. But everyone else started leaving, and it was just me and him, and I don't think I'd ever fancied anyone so much. He wasn't all that tall, but he had a kind of intensity that just made me feel like I was the only person in the room. I was desperate for him to make a move on me, and eventually he did. It was just mind-blowing when we were together.'

Jo stopped. Would Imogen be shocked? She didn't look it. Jo pushed her hair back from her forehead and went on. 'Within a couple of weeks we were living together. I was still finishing my training, doing my rotation, working my arse off. I was really ambitious then and so was he. He would often work late too at the theatre – he was in the West End at the time – and we'd sleep in, then go for breakfast in Brick Lane, meet up with his friends. I thought it was for ever. I'd never loved anyone like that before.' She could feel that familiar lump in her throat but she was empty of tears after yesterday. 'We didn't discuss it, of course. We were both far too cool for that. But I couldn't imagine that he felt any different to me – I mean, how could he, when I felt so strongly about him? Some of my friends didn't like him – which is always telling, isn't it? He could be cutting, and I think he thought they were a bit boring. Some of them said things. I got angry. Gradually, I stopped seeing anyone but him and his friends. Just work and him – that was all I wanted.'

There were renewed squeals from the children as Finn and Rory found the others hiding behind a bush. Jo stopped and looked over at them, then looked away. 'There were probably signs I should have noticed. I don't know. I suppose I just ignored anything I didn't want to see or hear. We'd been together for almost a year – I guess I thought it was normal that it wasn't quite as intense as before. Anyway, it was getting on for Christmas. He had to go to New York for an audition and, while he was away, I found out I was pregnant. I thought he'd be so pleased. I'd got it all planned, how I was going to tell him on Christmas Eve. I'd got him all these presents, and I'd done the tree while he was away. Bet you never imagined I'd do that!' She stopped and shook her head. Christ, she'd even lit candles all over the place and made the flat smell of cinnamon and pine needles.

'When he got back, he wasn't interested in any of it.

He hadn't got the part and he was in a really bad mood. Nothing I could say would cheer him up. I ended up telling him anyway and he just stared at me …'

Jo swallowed painfully and Imogen rubbed her gently on the arm.

'He was so cold. He said, "You're a doctor, you get it sorted," and he just left. He hadn't even brought his bags in from the car and I realised he'd been planning to leave all along. I found out a couple of days later he was seeing someone else. Another actress. Petite. Blond. Usual crap.' She shook her head ruefully. 'I made a complete fool of myself, actually. Quite on a par with yesterday. Calling him up in the middle of the night, trying to see him at the theatre, looking for his car all night, until all hours. What an idiot I was.'

She remembered the pitying look of the bloke at the stage door, obviously uncomfortable with having been asked to brush her off. Probably not the first time either. God, what a coward Trevor had been – why hadn't she realised? She closed her eyes, feeling a stab of fresh pain as she thought of Matt and that girl.

Imogen prompted her gently. 'What about the pregnancy? How did you cope on your own? It must have been so hard.'

Jo shrugged and split the blade of grass she was playing with. 'I went into complete denial about it. Didn't tell anyone, didn't even get the normal antenatal checks. Some doctor, huh? For about two weeks, I didn't even go back to the flat. Just slept on people's floors – well, the few friends who'd stuck by me – I had my toothbrush wrapped in a bit of foil in my handbag and I bought a new T-shirt and a fresh pair of knickers every day.' She winced. 'I still hate talking about the pregnancy and the birth and all that. For most women, it's one of the happiest times of their lives. For me, it was a nightmare. And the delivery!' She glanced at Imogen and laughed bitterly. 'Let's just say, natural it wasn't.'

'Go on,' Imogen urged gently.

'I had an emergency section at thirty-four weeks, he went straight into special care. I thought I'd lose him then. When I held him, I was so afraid. He seemed so tiny, and I just didn't know what to do with him. Everyone thought cos I was a doctor, I could cope. But I couldn't. And there was no one I could ask. I couldn't admit that Trevor had dumped me, that it had all been a huge mistake, that I'd been such a fool. You know, I even pretended to my mother that we were still together. She wasn't really interested. She'd got some new bloke and the last thing she wanted to be was a granny, particularly to a little "wog" as she called him.' She shifted her body on the hard ground. 'I've been a crap mother right from the start. He's so great. I love him so much.' She could feel herself gabbling. 'He deserves a better mother than me. I'm so crap. Being on my own with him terrifies me. It always has. There's no one else to ask. No one else is really interested in him – they may pretend to be, just to be polite. But it's all down to me, all the bloody time. And I'm so afraid of getting it wrong again.'

Silent tears started to pour down Jo's face and she rocked slowly back and forward. 'I thought I'd lost him,

I thought I'd lost him. I've been so afraid to let myself really love him. I thought I could protect myself from being hurt.'

Imogen slipped her arms round Jo and pulled her close, as she had the night before, and Jo gradually relaxed into the other woman's warmth, her tears flowing freely. Not choking sobs this time, but healing tears from saying what she had kept hidden for so long, and not feeling judged for it.

Imogen was murmuring into Jo's hair. Soothing words, nonsense words, as though comforting a child. Jo allowed herself to relax into it, but only for a moment. Suddenly she pulled away and wiped her nose on her sleeve. There was even more stupidity to own up to about Matt, but she couldn't face that quite yet. She'd have to lie. She continued slowly.

'It's so lonely, Imogen. It can be so hard. When Trevor left, I promised myself I wouldn't risk it again. I wouldn't get involved or let myself trust again. And that's why ...' She sat back, leaning her face in her hands with her elbows resting on her knees. 'That's why I couldn't get really involved with Matt. I know you like him, and you think I've been hard on him. But now, well surely you can see why I can't get involved. I probably shouldn't have spent so much time with him, but – well, I thought it would just be a bit of fun. I know I should go and thank him for finding Finn. And I will, of course. But, do you think you could come with me? I don't really want to face him on my own. Not after what's happened.'

Imogen nodded, a look of concern on her face. 'Of

course, Jo. Don't worry. I don't really understand why you should feel that way, but of course I'll come with you. I do like him, I'll admit, and I'm sure he likes you, but if you really feel that strongly, then …' Imogen stopped as the children came drifting over towards them.

'And, Imogen, there's one more thing. I'm so sorry about everything I said on Monday. I was a complete cow.' She put her hand up to stop Imogen interrupting. 'No, hear me out. This holiday would have been awful without you. We'd have starved for a start … and Imogen, yesterday.' She stopped and swallowed. 'I couldn't have coped without you.'

Imogen blinked rapidly but any reply was curtailed as the children arrived beside them. Their appetites had put an end to the game, and they groaned when they realised there was no picnic ready to hand. Jo scrubbed at her face with her fists to restore some order, pulled her jumper back on, and helped the children gather their discarded sweatshirts and fleeces, grateful for the distraction. She felt wrung out. She wasn't in training for all this emotional honesty. But thank goodness Imogen hadn't pressed her about Matt. There was a limit to the amount of stupidity any woman could admit to in one day.

Back at the house, Sophie looked better for having had another nap, but she hadn't done a thing about starting lunch. Jo noticed Imogen roll her eyes, and went to try and help her in the kitchen, or at least unload the dishwasher while Imogen whipped up fluffy, golden Spanish omelettes. Sophie laid the table, and kept up a running commentary as they worked. '… and I meant to say, Matt came by, Jo. He brought you a bunch of flowers. Isn't he sweet? I didn't unwrap them, just stuck them in some cold water in that bucket.'

Jo stiffened. That was thoughtful of him, and if she didn't know better, she'd have read it as romantic concern. She nudged the bucket with her foot, and peered at the tightly furled apricot roses – at least two dozen – surrounded by cream freesias. Imogen glanced at them too. 'They're lovely, Jo. Would you like me to put them in a vase for you?'

'Thanks, yes.' Jo shot her a grateful look. 'I'll serve up, shall I?'

The children had been sent to wash their hands and Jo laid the bowls of cherry tomatoes and sliced baguette on the table while Imogen cut the stems of the flowers with her sharpest kitchen scissors. 'Oh, what's this? There's a note.'

'Put it over there, would you? I'll look at it later,' Jo said over her shoulder.

Imogen shrugged, arranged the flowers loosely in a vase and placed the little envelope on a shelf. 'Are you really sure about him, Jo?' she said quietly, joining her at the table with a jug of pink lemonade. 'He does seem a nice bloke.'

Jo shook her head. 'I'm sure he is, but I happen to know he has other things on his mind than me.' She shrugged and lowered her voice even further. 'I might as well tell you. Last weekend when I went down to the beach with Finn, I saw him with a girl. And believe me, they were more than just good friends. As much as I'm grateful for all he did yesterday, I'm quite certain he's no more interested in taking this any further than I am, and I'd rather just leave it at that.'

'A girl?' Imogen repeated, jug suspended in mid-air. 'What girl? Rory, sit down, for goodness' sake.'

Finn came and wrapped his arms round Jo's waist. Jo teased her fingers through his hair and answered quietly, 'Oh I don't know. I didn't see her close up. Dark hair, tied back in a ponytail. About twenty-five, shorts. Classic gorgeous surf-bunny.'

Finn looked up. 'That's Lucia! Was she wearing a necklace? I want one like that. I asked her where she got it, and she said Matt brought it back for her from Australia.'

'You've met her?' Jo looked down incredulously. 'He introduced you to her? Well, isn't that just terrific? Honestly!'

'Oh Jo,' Imogen shook her head in mock despair, 'you really are the limit!' And she threw her head back and roared with laughter. Oh God, what was this?

Imogen wiped her eyes. 'Lucia's his *god-daughter*. He's known her since she was a baby. She's Jack's eldest. You know, the Jack who owns the surf shop. Matt told me all about her the other day. She's at college in London doing fashion design, apparently, but is spending the holiday down here with her parents.'

'Oh my God!' Jo slapped her forehead, and pulled Finn towards her, shock slowly giving way to a smile.

Imogen shook her head and laughed again. 'Honestly,

Jo, what are you like? Finn, pour your mother some lemonade. Or maybe she needs something stronger. I'll get that note, shall I?'

Chapter 19

Thursday

Clear and bright with a slight risk of rain

It had been like the old days, Imogen thought as she pulled herself out of bed the following morning, except the characters had been different. Then it would have been Sophie who sat on her bed late into the night after Matron had stopped her patrol and they'd have talked about boys and bras and what they wanted to do when they grew up. But last night it had been Jo who'd slipped off her shoes and curled up on the end of the four-poster, bringing in the smell of the summer night with her.

Imogen and Sophie had had a quiet supper, then Sophie had pleaded fatigue and disappeared upstairs at about ten with *Hello!* magazine, leaving Imogen to tidy up and wipe down the sides in the kitchen, and to think about what a fag it was going to be packing up to go home. Sophie barely mentioned Finn's disappearance and Imogen had found herself holding back about Jo's outpouring at the standing stones.

Of course Sophie may have turned in early so she would have enough energy to cope with her husband and his famous libido when he turned up tomorrow for the last two nights of the holiday, but Imogen was past caring. It was Jo's love life that was interesting her much more. After the revelation about Lucia – Imogen still smiled about that – Jo had ummed and aahed until Imogen had practically pushed her out of the door at about six to go and find Matt ('No she wouldn't take her eyes off Finn', 'Yes it was OK to go out, she didn't mind'). If Jo didn't find him now and get things straightened out, she'd lose a good man, and judging by the fact that she hadn't come in until late, Imogen had deduced that she must have found him.

That Jo had come home at all had been a surprise. Imogen had had in her mind a image of some serious making-up, which left her, she had to admit, feeling pig sick with envy but hey, Jo deserved a break. However, at about eleven thirty, while she'd been battling with another chapter of a rather self-indulgent travel memoir, Imogen had heard Jo come in and, rather than go into her own room, she'd appeared in Imogen's doorway, left wide open in case Finn called out.

'Wotcha?' she'd leant against the door jamb, arms folded, in a short faded denim jacket, pretty skirt and a rather self-satisfied smile on her face. One which she made no effort to cover up.

Imogen had dropped her book onto her knee. 'Are we to assume from that smug expression, Doctor, that you've sorted out a few things?' She realised she wanted Jo to stay and talk for a while, so she smiled encouragingly, hoping that would make her venture in from the doorway.

It had worked. 'Well, he seemed pretty pleased to see me,' she'd pushed away from the door jamb, and sat rather tentatively on the edge of the bed, 'and I've had chapter and verse about Lucia!'

Imogen had snorted gently. 'You really read him wrong, didn't you? He's such a great bloke, and any fool can see he's smitten with you.'

Jo had shrugged and picked absentmindedly at the drapes around the bed, then seemed to notice them for the first time. 'God, these are vile.' She'd looked around the rest of the room. 'This is like a passion palace. I'm surprised you didn't allocate it to Mr and Mrs Bonkmeister. Much more their scene, don't you think?' And she'd grinned broadly.

'I don't think Soph pays too much attention to her surroundings. In fact, I'm convinced she went to bed early to build up her strength for Mr Bonkmeister's return.'

Jo had groaned. 'Oh God, I really don't want to know! I had no idea about this side to their marriage. Has she always been like this?'

'Well, there wasn't much in the way of males when we were at school except for the caretaker's son – Colin, I think his name was. A wan, spotty youth as I recall but he became a figure of lust of Donny Osmondesque proportions, simply because we had no one else to ogle at. In fact, thinking about it, he was at the receiving end of the hormonal surges of about two hundred and fifty nubile schoolgirls. I wonder whether the poor boy ever recovered. He's probably still in rehab.'

'Or gay.' Jo had been wide-eyed. 'Christ, no wonder Sophie's a nympho. Making up for all those years of repression.'

'Didn't have the same effect on me.' Imogen wasn't sure how she should ask the next question; it was far too nosy. 'While we're on the subject, I'm quite surprised to see you back so early …'

'Not as much as I am.' Jo had pulled her legs up and rested her chin on her knees. She'd laughed. 'In fact, it's quite something for me really. I've always been the get-'em-into-bed-then-bugger-off-home-before-it-gets-awkward sort of girl. But tonight. Well, it didn't seem the right thing to do somehow.'

'No,' Imogen had said, trying desperately to imagine what it must be like to lead a sex life like that. She'd only had two serious boyfriends before Guy, and both of those she'd kept hanging for months before she slept with them. 'No, Matt's a bit different, isn't he?'

'I'm so glad that he found Finn yesterday.' Jo had looked hard at Imogen. 'It just feels right that it was him. I think he really cares about Finn.' She paused. 'Oh I don't know. It's only been two weeks, for goodness' sake. Perhaps I'm kidding myself.'

'Jo, you'll never know unless you take the risk.' She hoped she didn't sound too like her mother.

Jo laughed. 'You sound just like my mother, but you are right of course, oh wise one. That's why I didn't stay tonight I suppose. For once I took the risk that he might like me for other reasons than just my irresistible body.'

'Oh I think he might be able to find the odd redeeming feature.'

There had been an awkward pause for a moment, and Imogen had thought Jo was going to say goodnight. Instead she'd curled her feet under her and looked faintly embarrassed.

'My towering intellect won't be one redeeming feature though. Oh God!' She slapped her hand against her forehead. 'I keep thinking about things I've said to him and I had no idea.'

'Idea about what?'

'Well, I can hardly bear to tell you, but while I was there tonight I saw this letter on the side in his flat. It was addressed to Dr M. Rowlands. Well, sort of being nosy I said, "Who's this?" and he said, "Me." And, oh God, I said, "Don't be stupid!"' Smiling broadly, she'd closed her eyes in disbelief at herself. 'Anyway he said, yes it was and you didn't have to be able to diagnose angina to be called a doctor – and do you know, Imo, he's not a full-time surf bum at all?' She had put her hands to her face in horror. 'It all makes sense now. That boy at the bike hire who called me Doc was talking to him not me! He's only a bloody university lecturer in History of Art!'

'Something of an expert on Rothko, I gather.'

Jo had looked at her in disbelief. 'You knew?'

'Yes, I knew. We talked about it on the beach one day. Jo, how come you didn't? What *did* you two talk about, for God's sake?'

Jo laughed quietly and shrugged her shoulders. 'Evidently not a lot.'

'Would it have mattered if he'd been just a beach bum?'

'Maybe at first, yes. I'm a bigger intellectual snob than I thought.' She'd looked thoughtful. 'But it seems to matter less now I know what he really is. Or perhaps that's just the beauty of hindsight!'

But what I want is foresight, thought Imogen this morning as she got out of bed and pulled on T-shirt and shorts. She looked out of the window at the fields rolling down to the golf course and the sea beyond, and felt a massive wave of sadness that the holiday was so nearly over and ahead of her was the appalling prospect of the schools, Jakarta, no children with her. No children.

She could feel her throat tighten. She had to think positive about this. Slipping into her flip-flops, she pulled a brush through her hair and headed for the bathroom. No, boarding-schools were fine these days. No way would it be army blankets and press-down bathtaps; washing your socks with handsoap and wrapping them around the radiator to dry, only to peel them off the next morning stiff and twice as long. Hell no. She brushed her teeth with vigour. It's probably all mollycoddling: duvets, laptops and mobile phones to call home every five minutes to ask your parents to pay the credit-card bill. Her own parents lived close by for emergencies, didn't they? And they had tons of friends who'd gladly have the children to stay. She spat out the toothpaste with determination. Time to get on with it.

As she whipped around the kitchen gathering her bag and something to write on, Jo gave her an enquiring look. 'You're turbocharged. What's going on?'

In all the drama of the last two days, there hadn't seemed to be the right moment to mention it. 'I've just got to nip out. Won't be long. There's been a change of plan with the posting – we're off to Indonesia – and I've got to do some emergency boarding-school research. You wouldn't approve,' she laughed, glancing back over her shoulder, but the concern on Jo's face was not what she'd been expecting at all.

Two hours later and, hotfoot from the internet café again, she was getting back into her car in the car park in Wadebridge, with ten sides of notes on A4 paper stuffed in her bag. The three websites she'd scoured, from Guy's prep and senior school, and her own boarding-school, had been quite an eye-opener. They were a shameless exercise in marketing, seducing parents with copy that oozed warmth and friendliness. Everywhere were pictures of hearty-looking, well-bred kids playing rugger on immaculate playing fields or having a ball in the science lab. Words like 'pastoral care' and 'nurturing environment' were bandied about with abandon. All promised endless extra-curricular activities, the pursuit of excellent academic results and the guarantee that they would spew out a 'well-rounded, interesting child' at the other end.

What more could you ask? Imogen thought briskly, putting her keys in the ignition. The children in the pictures all looked healthy and happy enough; all three schools were tucked neatly into the Home Counties so not too far from Heathrow. Ideal.

'Can't see the point in having them, just to send them away.' Imogen pushed away Jo's dismissive words that kept ringing irritatingly in her head. Imogen and Sophie had been reminiscing about school over dinner one night and Jo had snarled her left-wing disapproval of the private system. But even she would have to agree Jakarta was out of the question. There were terrorists; there were tsunamis; there were tropical diseases. There was no option.

Winding down the windows to cool down the inside of the car, Imogen punched in the private number Guy had given her last night for the headmaster of Dunsters. Guy had taken her there once, when they were going out, to show off his Alma Mater and, as the phone rang in her ear, she could remember the quad, the Victorian brick-built chapel with its rolls of honour to ex-pupils killed in the wars, and the all-pervading smell of boys.

'Hello?'

'Mr Hamilton? Imogen Fogg here. Guy Fogg's wife. I'm ringing about Rory.'

By the time she'd finished talking to all three schools a little while later, she'd covered another ten sheets of paper. All three heads had been effusive in their enthusiasm, had given her reams of information about uniform requirements (or the phone numbers of people who could help), and had promised a mid-holiday visit in a couple of weeks to show the children round. 'It'll all be closed up and very quiet, of course,' laughed the horsy-sounding head from St Mary's, 'but I'm quite sure you'll be able to tell Olivia all about it,' pnarff pnarff. 'Changed a bit though since your day, Mrs Fogg, I expect!'

The call to Painswich, the Dunsters' feeder prep that Guy had suggested for Archie, was the hardest of all. The head, who introduced himself as Tim Sayers-Reed, sounded wet and chinless, and kept talking about Ginny, his wife (Imogen envisaged plump and hearty) in a smug fashion that got right up her nose. Her enquiries about dormitory sizes and bedtimes – a ruse to try and ascertain what sort of love and care the boys would get – met with an 'Oh he'll be fine' response, which, in her sensitive state, she interpreted as 'You are bloody lucky we can squeeze him in at all at this late notice'. He mentioned several times the need for her and Guy to appoint legal guardians, and when he finished with 'we'll look after the little chap, don't worry', she had to put an end to the call very quickly.

Back at base, Olivia threw herself into Imogen's arms as she got out of the car, to find solace after a blazing row with Grace, which Sophie described as being like the Battle of the Somme with Barbies. Rory had made Archie cry by snatching his beloved rabbit and running off around the garden with it, showing off in sensational manner to Finn, who was egging him on, and Amelia had been stung by a wasp, an injury that she managed to milk for all it was worth.

'Vinegar,' said Imogen, watching Sophie dab the sting ineffectually with a wet tissue, and extricated herself from her sobbing youngest son for a moment to go to the cupboard. 'Malt not balsamic. Rory, will you stop riling your brother and lay the table? Olivia, you are hungry. Get those pasties I've bought out of the bag and put them on that baking tray. The quicker you do it, the quicker we'll eat.'

Order restored, stomachs filled, the women sat back over coffee.

'Cycle up the Camel Trail in a bit, and an ice cream in Padstow?' Imogen wanted to busy her head. All she could see was an image of Archie's bed at school, and a letter from her on the side in an air-mail envelope from the Far East, delayed in the post and horribly out of date. Perhaps she could email him? She'd forgotten to ask Tim Chinless-Weed.

'Finn and I have already done that with … er, Matt of course.' Jo looked sheepishly sideways at Imogen.

Sophie, lying languidly in her garden chair feet up on the one beside her, wrinkled up her nose in distaste. 'Listen, girls, I've a much less energetic plan. Hugh's due to arrive in an hour or so. Why don't I promise huge favours if he babysits for us tonight and we go out and have something to eat? What do you say?'

Neither Imogen nor Jo responded immediately. Imogen knew she was making excuses in her own head – Arch didn't know Hugh that well and six kids was quite a tall order for anyone to cope with – and she also knew that Jo would be loath to leave Finn.

'Um, I don't know Soph. Be better to stay here wouldn't it …?' she answered lamely.

'Oh come on,' Jo sounded resolute. 'If Hugh's happy to, why not? I can't keep an eye on Finn permanently, and it'd be nice to have a break from them all, wouldn't it? That's if you can stay awake long enough, Soph.'

Gathering the children to her and summoning up lots of motivating enthusiasm, Imogen had them all on bicycles up the Camel Trail for the afternoon. By the time they got home and downed supper with gallons of ice-cold lemonade, their faces were glowing and their legs felt satisfyingly tired. Hugh, his normal jovial self, was now in shorts, stretched out on the lawn, shaking off London tension and stress, and saying that he would gladly babysit.

'Come on then, Arch. Time for a cool bath,' Imogen called out of the kitchen door to her son who was sitting thumb in mouth in the doorway of the Wendy house.

'Where's my rabbit?'

Imogen felt her heart sink alarmingly, and cast her eyes around the kitchen. 'Where did you last have him?'

'Don't know.'

'Go and have a look upstairs.' Archie slowly made his way up, followed by Imogen, aware that her concept of looking for something was not in the same league as her son's.

His bed had been stripped, as had hers, Rory's and Finn's, the laundry basket emptied and even the insides of Imogen's slippers investigated, but still no rabbit could be found. She'd even checked the airing cupboard, the cupboards in the attic and the toy chest. Her sense of unease rose to match Archie's growing panic.

'Where is he, Mum? I can't sleep without him. Where is he?'

'Right,' Imogen yelled, pounding down the stairs. 'Action stations. Rory, you cover the car and I mean under the seats and everywhere. Even the glove compartment. Olivia – behind the radiators in the bathroom and the bedrooms. Gracie, can you look in your room, under your beds?'

As she spoke she was pulling out the contents of the beach bag, throwing towels and goggles behind her. Damn. Not there.

'What can I do to help?' Sophie was waving a glass of wine airily.

'Help me find the blasted rabbit.'

'Where did he last have it?'

She turned on Sophie. 'I don't fucking know, do I? If I did I would have found it by now. Amazingly I don't know everything.' She turned away. I will not cry. I will not cry. What if he lost his rabbit at school? Would they even let him have it there? And would he be teased?

'He's lost, isn't he, Mama?' he sobbed. 'What shall we do without him?'

Imogen gathered him up into her arms. 'We'll find him, darling.' She stroked his hair, simultaneously rushing from room to room pushing cushions off chairs and books off shelves in her vain search, as Jo walked into the house from the garden, snapping closed her mobile phone as she did so.

'What's the kerfuffle? Olivia and Amelia are turning

out the Wendy House like one of those TV life laundry shows.'

'It's the rabbit. We can't find him. I don't know what to do.' Imogen knew her eyes were full of tears but she couldn't blink them away.

'Hey, Imo, calm down. Now let's think. Weren't Rory and Finn playing with it before lunch and winding up Archie?' Without even thinking what she was doing, Imogen stood up and hugged her.

Sure enough, once Rory's memory had been jogged, the rabbit had been retrieved from the hole in the tree, brushed down and restored to its placated owner. Imogen took stock. Where the hell had her over-reaction come from? As Archie sat in the bath, trickling water onto his knees from the sponge, she perched on the closed loo seat and watched him, thinking hard. She thought about Guy and his promotion. She thought about Rory, growing so fast and learning so much. She thought about Olivia and discovering what it was like being a woman, and she thought about this little boy in the bath here, innocent still to all the world would throw at him one day. And she thought about herself, the girl she'd been and the woman she was now.

'Right, mate.' She lifted him out into a towel, and held him close. Then she rubbed down his hair and helped him slip into his pyjamas. 'Run off and play for a minute. I've got a couple of phone calls to make.'

'Shift over, hon.' Jo gently shoved Finn out of the way with her hip and positioned herself in front of the mirror.

'Have you moved back in here, then? Doesn't Rory want you as a cell mate any more?'

'As if! Rory's my best mate. It's just – well, Archie really pisses me off. All that fuss about a stupid rabbit, for God's sake, *and* their dad's coming down tomorrow and they're getting all funny about it again. Anyway, I wanted to read my new *Beano* in peace. Look, there's a packet of Haribos on the front. Can you cut it off with your scissors, so it doesn't tear?'

She finished towelling her hair dry and combed it back off her face, then delved into a make-up bag and tossed a pair of nail scissors onto the bed beside Finn. She applied moisturiser with brisk practised movements, then paused, looking carefully at her reflection. No, she just couldn't, no matter what Matt had said the night before about preferring her without the war paint. Tinted moisturiser at the very least, and some mascara – otherwise she'd actually look scary. Not so bad. Maybe she could get used to this new minimal routine, and it would certainly save time. She looked round. Finn was lying stretched out on his bed, shoes on, chomping loudly at his sweets and laughing occasionally at the comic he was reading so intently.

'Finn, could you look at me for a minute?'

'Wha'?' Finn looked up startled, clearly assuming he was in trouble.

'Do I look different to you?'

He frowned and looked at her hard for a moment. 'Nope.' He returned to the comic. 'You look just the same as ever, only not quite so shiny. And not so tired.'

Shiny and tired. Interesting. Well, that settled it. He glanced up to watch her putting in the silver shell earrings Matt had given her earlier. 'You going out with him, then?'

'I was, but I'm not now,' she said slowly, watching for his reaction in the mirror. The sudden scowl said it all. 'Actually, I'm going out with Imogen and Sophie tonight, just the three of us.'

'So who's looking after us, then?' He turned over another page.

'Well, Hugh and … we did have another offer, but I wasn't sure what you'd think.'

Finn looked questioning.

'Matt said he'd come over and keep Hugh company.'

'Yesss!' The little boy punched the air. 'Result!' He jumped up and started to tidy his clothes away. 'Maybe he'll read me a story.'

Jo kissed the top of his head, hoping that Matt could live up to Finn's expectations, then applied a squirt of cologne and slipped from the room, going downstairs to join the others.

Imogen was alone in the kitchen, covering dishes with clingfilm and arranging them in the fridge. She jumped as Jo came in and started to explain, rather apologetically. 'I thought the chaps might enjoy some dips, so I just made a quick guacamole and some salsa. I'd better go and change. Are Hugh, Soph and the girls back yet?'

'No, but I don't expect they'll be long. Hugh may well be able to smell the garlic in that salsa from the beach, and he won't be able to resist. I rather wish I could stay in and babysit now. Whatever we have to eat, it's not going to be a patch on one of your creations.' At Imogen's urging she dipped a carrot stick into the guacamole, groaned in ecstasy and closed her eyes. 'OK, that's one you're definitely going to have to teach me. Drink?'

'Er, yes. I think I will. Could I have a G and T, please?'

'Need a stiffener because of the bunny business, eh?' Jo winked broadly as she dropped ice cubes into a glass. 'Honestly, Imogen, after the way you coped with everything the other day with me and Finn, I'd have thought it would take more than a stuffed rabbit to stuff you.'

Imogen shook her head helplessly and sat down at the table. 'So would I, but it just seemed to sum everything up. Thanks.' She took a healthy swig of the drink Jo handed her and shrugged. 'Archie's still such a baby and it made me realise how much he needs me – and I need him.'

'Well, Amen to that,' Jo agreed, sitting down opposite her. 'But a rabbit? How's Archie going to manage if he loses it at school? ' she said gently. 'More to the point, how are *you* going to manage on the other side of the world? Are you really sure about this?'

'Wait till Dad gets here, you little git.' Rory and Archie burst into the room. 'Mum, Archie keeps hiding my trading cards. Tell him to stop, or I'll take his precious rabbit again and flush it down the loo this time.'

Archie wailed in anguish and hurled himself at Rory, who side-stepped neatly and tripped the little boy up.

Imogen jumped to her feet and bellowed, 'Rory, you beastly child, you stop that at once, or I'll flush your blasted Gameboy down the loo.'

In the stunned silence that followed, there was a sudden commotion in the hallway, and Sophie and her lot walked in, accompanied by Matt. 'Hellooo,' she called. 'We found this waif coming along the road, so we've brought him back for a few drinks. OK?'

Rory fled and Imogen sat back down with a thump, Archie clinging to her legs, while Jo rushed around to greet the newcomers. 'Drinks, everyone? Imogen and I thought we'd get a head start but feel free to catch us up. What can I do you for, Dr Rowlands?'

Matt gave Jo an appreciative once-over, before pulling her close and planting a noisy kiss on her lips. 'Don't you want to get going? It can get busy at Gaetano's. If you give us our instructions – simple, mind – we'll get the children to bed then we can have something once they're asleep. I must admit, it's been a while since I did any babysitting – since *Lucia* was little, actually,' he smiled pointedly at Jo, 'but I'm hoping Hugh knows the form.'

In under half an hour they were all ready, Imogen looking tanned and glowing in a pale blue linen shift dress, and they were pushed out of the door by Matt and Hugh, who pretended to cover their ears against the barrage of last-minute advice the women insisted on giving them. The children were all waving wildly from the upstairs windows, none of them looking remotely sleepy.

'You do realise, don't you, that we're going to come

back at midnight to find all the kids still up and playing poker?' laughed Sophie.

Imogen shrugged. 'Maybe they all need a little dose of anarchy. I know I do, for one.'

Jo stared at her in astonishment. Something must definitely be going on in Imogen's head. She'd like to have finished that conversation they'd started earlier. They made their way to the restaurant – a popular Italian bistro with scrubbed wooden tables and bright, abstract paintings – to be greeted by the vivacious owner who recognised 'the three lovely ladies from Matt's description' and gave them the best table outside in the late-evening sunshine.

'Cor he's worth knowing, your Matt, ain't he!' Sophie scanned the drinks menu. 'What's this? They've got a cocktail called a Jellybean – shall we have one each? If it's nice, we can get a jug.'

Jo looked at Sophie narrowly. She had a hint of an idea, and decided to act on it. She held up a hand. 'Since I'm designated driver tonight, I won't thanks. But, Sophie, you've had a fair bit of sun today – why don't you have some juice instead?'

Over huge salads and a bottle of Italian white, they started to chat, initially sticking to safe topics, as if by prior arrangement. But with the pasta course, Imogen hesitantly and jokingly referred to the rabbit crisis.

'It really isn't like me to cry, y'know. I know it seems absurd, but – well – after Finn, and everything, it just made me think about how vulnerable they still are. And how everything can change in an instant.' Imogen drained her glass and tried to get the waiter's attention to order another bottle.

'Where's the bugger gone?' Sophie tried to peer into the restaurant. 'I'll try metaphor.'

Jo laughed. 'A metaphorical waiter's no good at all, but wave your arms anyway, hey Soph.' She looked over at Imogen, hoping to share the joke, but she was thoughtfully tucking her hair behind her ears.

'I didn't even cry in front of people at school, y'know. Not once. Not the whole time I was there.' Imogen looked as if she was somewhere else entirely. 'I always felt as if it would be letting the side down, as if I had to be strong for everyone. And it's stuck! Good old reliable Imogen, that's me.' She shook her head.

Jo fiddled guiltily with her napkin. Now the holiday was almost over and, after the whole Finn episode, she couldn't believe how worked up and resentful she'd felt towards Imogen, time and time again during their stay. It all seemed so trivial compared to what they'd had to deal with in the last few days. And now here was Imogen having to face packing her children off, while she followed Guy wherever his blessed career took them.

Sophie once again had missed the point entirely. 'Perhaps it's hormones, love. I must be due on, I'm knackered.' She yawned as if to illustrate just how knackered. 'I feel like the dormouse in *Alice in Wonderland*.'

Jo snorted. 'What does that make us, then? The Mad Hatter and the March Hare, I presume. Which one is which?'

'Well,' Sophie grinned like the Cheshire Cat, 'now you come to mention it, you've both been acting a bit bonkers this holiday, if you want to know the truth. I was afraid that disgraceful display the other day was going to turn into a real knock-down drag-out. How would that have been? Two of my muckers slugging it out, with me in the middle as referee. That's what it's felt like, y'know.'

Jo started to retort, but stopped and took a deep breath, then smiled ruefully. 'Yeah well. I hope we've made our peace. We have, haven't we, Imogen?' She looked across the table anxiously.

'Oh I think they can call off the UN. I have to say, Jo, I've never slapped anyone before but God it feels good!'

'Not to me it didn't! But heck, I probably deserved it and it was lucky for you that you got in first!' She ran her finger around the rim of her glass. 'I know it's a bit late in the day, but I might as well admit it. Right from the word go, I've felt really envious of the way you make it all look so bloody easy. One minute you're whipping up hot chocolate, the next it's wipes and plasters in your handbag – not to mention the cooking. Christ, you can even do the bloody Heimlich manoeuvre better than me.'

Imogen smiled a little. 'I did a course. You can't—'

'Be too careful?' Jo laughed. 'It's just really intimidating being with someone as competent as you.' Jo sat back, feeling strangely relieved to have off-loaded all that. But Imogen was staring at her, frowning. Oh hell. Had she said too much again?

'What? Me? Intimidating? Jo, I've felt intimidated by you from the moment you got here.' Jo was stunned. 'Well, *look* at you. You're slim, you wear fantastic clothes, you always look gorgeous, men stare at you wherever we go, you've got a great career. You've even bagged the dishy surf bum *and* the art historian. Next to you, I feel like a boring, lumpy, frowsy old bag!'

Jo mirrored the puzzlement and disbelief on Imogen's face, then a low chuckle rose from her throat and she shook her head slowly. 'What have we been doing to each other? This was supposed to be a holiday, not a form of torture.'

'Not been on many family holidays, then?' Sophie giggled.

'Holidays full-stop,' said Imogen with feeling, and both Jo and Sophie looked at her in surprise. 'Well, let's face it, that old thing about travelling hopefully being better than arriving is never truer than when you're off on your hols.'

'But Imo, you're always so up-beat. So optimistic.'

'Perhaps I'm finally wising up. If it's self-catering, it's just the same shit, different kitchen. If it's in a hotel, you're constantly fretting that the kids are getting on somebody's nerves. I've been on enough holidays to know that if you haven't got plans B, C and D covered plus a wet-weather contingency, it can all come unravelled pretty quick and then everyone's miserable and like an idiot, I blame myself. We seem to cram a year's worth of expectation into a few precious weeks, and what do you end up with? Sunburn and a few tacky souvenirs.'

'Well, it looks like Jo picked up the most interesting souvenir!' Sophie nudged her theatrically. 'That Matt's a bargain – what's going to happen with you two? Go on, dish!'

Jo looked down and started carefully shredding her napkin. 'Well, I really like him.'

'Oh tell us something we don't know,' groaned Sophie.

Jo paused while the waiter cleared away their plates. 'I think he likes me. When I went down yesterday evening, we just talked for hours and I found out all about him – you know, he was married for a while, when he was working in the States. They got divorced, though, because she couldn't get used to living over here. And he's a lecturer – isn't that amazing?' Jo trailed off and looked sideways at Imogen. 'But then you knew that already!'

Sophie tutted. 'I expect you were too busy playing it cool to even ask, weren't you? Honestly!'

Jo sat back in her chair. 'And I thought I had everything under control!'

'Join the club,' said Imogen with feeling.

Sophie gestured with her spoon and dug into her chocolate fudge brownie. 'Well, I think you're a pair of idiots. You're both as bad as each other!'

Jo and Imogen exchanged outraged looks. 'Don't hold back, Soph. Tell us what you really think!' Jo growled.

'OK I will. Why would you even want to be in control all the time? What a waste of energy!' Sophie was getting into her stride, a smear of chocolate around her mouth. 'You two are more alike than you think, you know. That's why I knew you'd get on, though it was touch and go for a bit there, wasn't it? You're both so busy trying to make things happen, you miss out on the things that really are happening around you. You're too busy worrying to ever really enjoy yourselves. You've only got one crack at life. So what does it matter if your soufflé doesn't rise or your mascara runs?' Jo wondered for a moment if Sophie was talking in semaphore again. 'And what does it matter if someone looks better in a wetsuit than you,' Imogen looked startled, 'or someone makes better birthday cakes? We're all different and, if we're sensible, we can all help each other.'

There was silence. 'Bloody hell, Soph, that was quite a speech.' It must be the hormones talking, thought Jo, but maybe there was something to it. She'd almost blown it with Matt because she was so worried about looking needy. Perhaps, after all, she should give this one her best shot. 'You may be right about me, Soph, but look at Imogen. There she is grabbing life with both hands and off to the jungles of South-east Asia, with nothing but her credit card for protection to follow the man she loves. You can't say that she's missing out.'

Imogen took a deep swig of wine, freshly poured by the waiter. 'Actually, I need to tell you both something. Guy won't be coming down before we leave on Saturday and – erm – well, I'm not going to Jakarta with him.'

'What?' Sophie dropped her spoon with a clatter. 'You mean he'll be going there all alone?'

'Er, yes, Sophie. That would be it.' Imogen picked wax

off the candle, and held it close to the flame until it dripped. 'I've decided I just can't leave the children. I don't want to be apart from them. They need me – and I need them. It should be me taking care of them – not someone who's paid to do it. You were right, Jo. That's not why I had children – to send them away.'

Jo too had stopped, mouth open, her spoonful of tiramisu in mid-air. 'Hell, Imo, you don't want to go listening to me. What did Guy have to say?'

'He wasn't too happy about it, obviously.' Imogen smiled grimly. 'In fact, he had a major sense-of-humour failure when I called him this evening. He was in a late meeting, and for once I interrupted it. I've never done that before, but I knew this was more important than anything else. But he couldn't see that. He actually told me not to be irrational and tried to persuade me.' She shook her head, still angry with him. 'But he's a man, isn't he? I mean an adult. He can fend for himself. The children can't and, after all, he's chosen to go there, for his career. The children would have no choice in the matter and I don't see why I should impose that on them.' She paused again. 'Do you know, he even told me I'd have a cook out there? As if that would clinch it! I sometimes wonder if men ever really listen at all.'

'But what about schools and stuff? I thought you had it all fixed up?'

'I'd already called them and cancelled the places. They weren't too chuffed I can tell you. But tough! I'm not going to change my mind. Mind you, I haven't told my mother yet. That'll really be fun.' She shrugged, then forced a brave smile. 'She'll think I've taken leave of my senses. We're so different – that's something I hadn't realised before. She's wife first, mother second. For me it's the other way around.'

There was quiet in the car as they headed for home, the darkness broken only by the oncoming headlamps of the occasional car. Imogen's bombshell seemed to have silenced them all.

'Do you think I'm mad, Jo, doing this parenting thing on my own?' Imogen muttered after a while. Jo glanced quickly at her in the passenger seat.

'Anyone who puts themselves in that position voluntarily has got to be two-thirds bonkers, but I don't see that you have any real choice.'

She gave a short laugh. 'Ironic, isn't it? I'll be joining the ranks of the single parents and you're now in a couple! Any tips for me?'

'But, Imo, you're not a single parent. Guy's still their father. And you're still married to him. It'll just be a hell of a test for both of you.'

'I know, I know, but perhaps, Soph, you were right. This is something I can't control and I'll just have to trust that our relationship is strong enough to cope.' She laughed quietly again. 'This is something new for both of us, hey? You've got to trust enough to be with Matt. I've got to trust enough *not to be* with Guy. So any more words of wisdom on that one, Soph? Soph?'

Pulling up outside the house, both Jo and Imogen looked back at the blond curly-haired woman now lying curled up across the back seat of the car. She was snoring gently. They looked at each other and exchanged a complicit grin.

'God, I didn't know I was that boring. Are you thinking what I'm thinking?'

'Bloody serves them right!'

Chapter 20

Friday

Warm and sunny with a promising outlook

'So what happened to you last night, Rip Van Winkle?'

Bleary-eyed, Sophie skulked into the kitchen, her hair standing on end and a hooded sweatshirt thrown over her pyjamas, to face Imogen, Jo and Hugh, drinking coffee amongst the usual detritus of the children's breakfast.

'God, I'm so sorry.' She ran her hands through her blond curls, a gesture that helped not at all to improve her look of general dishevelment. 'It was so warm and cosy in the car, and I just *couldn't* stay awake. Terribly sorry, girls.' She plonked herself down next to Hugh, and rested her head against his shoulder, closing her eyes again. She yawned. 'And I'm sorry, darling, if you were hoping to ravish your wife. I was dead to the world. Must have been the Pinot Grigio. Or I'm getting old and can't take late nights any more.'

Imogen put down a cup of tea in front of her. 'Well, it's only a hunch, old girl, but I think you'd better get used to them cos Jo and I think you're in for some sleepless ones pretty soon.'

'What do you mean?' Sophie looked quizzical, and Imogen exchanged a glance with Jo.

'Oh, come on, Soph.' Jo sounded as if she was talking to a small child. 'You're up the duff or my name's Hamish.'

Imogen wasn't sure she had ever heard something human actually squeal, but there was no other description for the noise that emanated from Sophie at Jo's supposition. Her hands flew up to her cheeks, her eyes wide with disbelief.

'You're joking!'

'Well, only you can tell, sweetheart,' said Jo, 'but you seem to be showing all the signs: sore boobs, tiredness, peeing constantly, not to mention the unspeakable sandwich fillings!'

'For heaven's sake, Sophie. You must know. You've had two babies already.' Imogen was incredulous. She knew Sophie was fairly ditzy, but to not notice changes in your body, especially third time round!

Sophie looked at her husband, from whose face the blood seemed to have disappeared completely. 'I suppose I am late, though I've never been very good at remembering. Oh God, darling, I think they're right.' She paused in stunned silence. 'How the hell did that happen?'

Jo coughed loudly. 'Er, perhaps you could discuss that between yourselves later. I'm not sure Imogen and I need to be a party to that kind of detail. In the meantime, you need to lay off the vino, hon.'

Imogen smiled then laughed. 'Welcome to the world of the three-child family!'

Sophie remained stunned, looking at Hugh who appeared to have lost the power of speech entirely. 'Oh God-diddly-od. How on earth am I going to cope with another one? Imogen,' she looked up her eyes wide with horror, 'you're the expert. How the hell do you manage with three?'

'Well, all I'll say is God-diddly-od only gave us two arms for a reason! Get yourself a new car, an au pair, and a house nearer to your mother's, and you'll manage in your blissfully chaotic way.'

'Better pee on a stick anyway, just to make sure.' Jo heaved herself up from the table. 'Meantime, when have we got to sling our hooks tomorrow?'

'Ha! You see? Where would you be without me? My legendary efficiency is useful after all,' and Imogen pulled out the sheet of house details supplied by the letting agent. 'By ten. Crumbs, that's not going to give us much time. We'd better start removing a layer of sand and grime from the bedrooms today.'

While Sophie and Hugh went for a walk together, still in deep shock about their news, Imogen spent the first half of the morning pairing up shoes and picking up DVDs from the sitting-room floor, organising them into piles depending on who they belonged to. Then from the open window of her bedroom, where she was starting to fill a suitcase with fleeces and trousers, she could hear the children playing and screaming, and stood up from time to time to look at them as she worked. All of them had tanned nicely and their hair was shot with streaks of blond, with the exception of Finn of course.

Perhaps she had been too cynical last night. They were holidayed – would the Americans call it 'vacated'? – relaxed and comfortable with each other. The prospect of the rest of the summer in a stifling London suddenly depressed her. She'd been so focused on the move to Hong Kong that she'd dismissed London now. Put it out of her head and shifted her life-path to an apartment in a foreign country, with the challenges of new friends to make, new places to discover. She was still up for the challenges all right, she thought as she folded up a skirt, but not with the loss of the children as the price she had to pay for them.

She rummaged in the back of the wardrobe for her high heels, never worn thanks to Archie putting the kibosh on the evening at the seafood restaurant and, pairing them neatly heel to toe, placed them in the case. Come to think of it, when had she last worn them? The school ball in early May, she supposed. Oh heavens, there was a thought. She'd have to ring the old schools today and try to reinstate their places. Then, as she leant into the wardrobe again, another thought occurred to her. Why did they need to live in London at all now?

She sat back on her heels to explore this. They would be able to sell the Barnes house for a fortune and, instead of play-acting rural life with trips to the common and shopping in the 'village', as South-west Londoners are wont to call it, they could do the real thing. Could she really have a house a bit like this one, with a decent-sized garden? Even find a school they could walk to? Could they look over fields and buy a paper at a village shop instead of a corner shop? She could feel the excitement growing in her. Her phone rang on the bedside table.

'Hi, darling, it's me. How are you enjoying your last day?' Guy sounded up-beat, trying hard to be chatty and friendly. He'd been so disappointed yesterday, crushed even, but she hoped that this wasn't going to be some misguided attempt to soft soap her and try to bring her round again.

'Just starting to pack actually, so you aren't missing much, then we'll maybe go down to the beach later. You know, make the most of the sunshine before the drive back tomorrow.' Her heart sank as she thought of the logistics of the journey, packing up the car, fights over who would sit in the front, the inevitable queue at Chiswick Roundabout. She wouldn't tell him now that she'd been thinking about leaving London. That should wait for a face-to-face conversation when the impact of her decision not to go to Jakarta had lost its sting.

'Are you sure you aren't going to come with me?' She was surprised at his uncharacteristic directness.

'Yes, darling, I'm sure.'

'But why, Imo?'

'Guy, we talked about this yesterday.' She really thought she had convinced him then. 'I don't want them at boarding-school and us on the other side of the world.'

She could hear him sighing. 'They'd cope, love. We did and we're pretty OK, aren't we?'

'Are we?' she implored him. 'Are we better for having been sent away from home and our parents? Have we benefited from having to cope on our own? I'm not so sure. But Guy, it's more than that. Being that far away from the children would break my heart. I can't do it. I couldn't cope with being that unhappy. I'd miss the changes in them as they grow and those stages in their lives would be gone – bouff – before we knew it. I want to see Rory becoming a man, not have a snapshot of him in the holidays and some house-mistress telling me things about my son I didn't know. Ollie and Arch, they need to be able to ask *me* those questions children ask and be able to say something stupid without someone judging them or, I don't know, not taking them seriously. I don't want to have a relationship with them like I have with my mother.'

Unexpectedly the depth of her feeling came tumbling out and the tears rolled down her face. She couldn't remember the last time she'd cried in front of Guy. 'They are our babies, Guy, and we need to be there to help them and love them. OK, so it will only be one of us, but one parent's better than none, isn't it? For you to go is important, I can see that, but for me to go as well is just selfish.'

His voice was low and quiet. 'But you're my wife, my partner, Imo. I need you there with me.'

An uncontrolled sob burst from her. 'We'll have to learn to survive it, the being apart, because we shouldn't have had children if we are going to leave them behind.' She wasn't going to tell him not to go. It was a side of him, his career and his ambition, that she couldn't begin to understand. What she did know, however, was that if she held him back, though he would never say so out loud, he would never forgive her. He'd married her to raise the children; she'd had the children to raise them herself. Something would have to give.

There was a long pause. 'Let's not do this over the phone. We'll talk tomorrow when we get back. And,' she laughed, sniffing inelegantly, 'if my tomato plants have died, you'll follow!'

'Died?' He sounded outraged. 'They've even got little green fruits growing on them already.' They laughed. So he had listened. 'And Imo, just before you go, I do … I do love you.'

'Me too. Bye, darling.' She clicked off the phone, in wonderment that he'd said that now (how long had it been?), but itching to know if he'd said it in front of everyone else in the office. She threw back her head and smiled broadly. Now that would be something.

Jo was reading the newspaper as Imogen walked into the kitchen. Aware her eyes were red, she tried to scoot past quickly to empty the wastepaper basket she was holding, but Jo looked up and groaned.

'Oh Lord, has the great clean-up started already? I can't face it frankly. Hey, you all right? What's up? Been talking to Guy?'

'Got it in one.' Imogen put down the lid of the bin and pushed the hair out of her face.

'Is he putting on the pressure?' Jo asked gently.

'No, he's just confused by my decision. I don't think he'll ever understand, but that's the difference between men and women, isn't it?' From the boiler cupboard, she pulled out a cardboard box and, opening one of the kitchen cupboards, started to fill it with the contents.

'Hey,' Jo came to crouch down beside her, 'you've done what felt right for you despite the pressure it will put on your relationship with Guy, and that's brave, Imogen. That's very brave. You don't always have to do things just because that's what's expected of you. Nor,' she added, taking a jar out of Imogen's hand, 'do you have to do all this packing on your own. Tell me where you want it all and I'll help.'

Imogen waved her hand airily, all at once embarrassed by the wealth of ingredients crammed into the cupboard. She'd only brought all this stuff because she wanted to make things right; to have everything she might need so she could produce a meal that would make everyone happy. Now it looked fussy and silly and over the top.

'No, honestly, Jo. I'll just stuff it in this box and take it home,' and she tried to empty the cupboard as quickly as she could before Jo could see. But it was too late and already Jo had picked up a bottle and a packet from the shelf.

'Mushroom ketchup? Star anise? What's all this?' Imogen could feel her face flush with embarrassment. 'I've never heard of half this stuff. How do you know what to do with it all?' Imogen looked at Jo suspiciously.

'Are you taking the piss?'

'God no!' Jo was delving further into the cupboard. 'This is like a whole new world to me. There's stuff here I've only ever read on a menu!' She'd opened the next cupboard before Imogen could stop her, and was pulling out the slicing mandolin, the bobble whisk, the pestle and mortar, the potato ricer, the electric hand whisk and – Imogen could hardly bear to look – her blow torch for caramelising tarts.

'Bloody hell!' Jo's voice was high with incredulity. 'This is a mixture between the potions lab at Hogwarts and an Ann Summers stock room! Have you used even half of this stuff?'

'Well, yes, as a matter of fact,' she said defensively. 'The hand whisk is great for pancake batter and the bobble whisk—'

Jo held it up suggestively, wiggling her eyebrows. 'This looks more like something Sophie and Hugh would use!' Imogen could feel the laughter bubbling and, with overwhelming relief at the decision she'd made about the children, the thought that she might, just might, be able to escape London, and with a massive sense of her own ridiculousness, she let the laughter take her over until she and Jo were bent double with the pain of their hysteria, and the sound of their shrieking made its way into the garden.

Archie came flying in, desperate concern all over his face at the noise his mother and Jo were making. 'Mama, what's up?' He smiled uncertainly. She enveloped him in her arms, unable to speak, the tears of laughter pouring down her face.

'Everything's fine, Archie my love,' Imogen gasped. 'Just fine. I think Jo and I are at last getting in the holiday mood.' She held her sides, struggling for breath. 'Now, here's my medical advice: sod this, the packing can wait,' and taking two wine glasses out of the clean dishwasher, she made her way over to the fridge, and filled them with chilled white wine.

'But Imogen, it's only eleven thirty!'

'Who cares? Follow me,' and, balancing the glasses in one hand, she took Archie's hand in the other and the three of them made their way out of the kitchen door.

'Jo, sit yourself down, this one's for you. Arch, you'll have to share mine.'

'Yeuch,' Archie made a face.

She sat down on the other bench, put her arm around her son and closing her eyes, tipped back her head back. 'Here we are, Jo. We've managed it. As my *other* wonderful new friend, Edie, would say, "Faces up to the sun, old girl. Faces up to the sun."'

'Well, I'm stuffed!' Hugh stood up from the table, stretched the waistband of his shorts to ease his discomfort and gave his belly a scratch.

Jo looked up from emptying the dishwasher. 'Coming out in sympathy, are we? You'll be getting morning sickness next. You can take this new man stuff too far, y'know.'

Sophie laughed derisively. 'New man? That's a total fallacy. Scratch the surface and they're all grumpy old men. Hugh's just like his dad – always has been, in fact, haven't you, sweetness?'

Jo shuddered theatrically as Sophie nuzzled her husband's neck. Handing Matt a pile of clean plates, Jo glanced at him, trying to gauge his reaction, then rolled her eyes. 'You need a pretty strong stomach to be round those two for any length of time, I'm afraid,' she whispered.

Matt tilted his head to one side and watched them, clearly amused. 'Oh, I don't know. They're rather sweet about it all, aren't they? Wouldn't you like it if I was like that?' Taking Imogen's glass cloth in both hands, he looped it over her head, pulled it taut round her waist and pulled her slowly towards him, smiling suggestively.

'Eeeuch!' She pretended to pull away, and protested, not very convincingly, while submitting to a little nuzzling herself. It felt fun, for once, to be in on the joke rather than on the outside looking in and, despite her complaints, a little frisson of pleasure sneaked through her. She kissed him quickly and pulled away.

Just in time too, as Imogen came back in from organising the bags for the outing. The last thing she needed was to see everyone else in happy couples, but when Jo looked at her carefully, she seemed the same as ever. If she was under a strain, she was hiding it well, but then, Jo thought ruefully, old habits are hard to shake off. No, if anything, Imogen seemed to be in her element – constantly on the go, checking and packing everything to her satisfaction, calling instructions and encouragement to the children every so often. How could Guy ever have imagined that a life of indolent luxury, far from her brood, would appeal to her?

Jo put away the last of the teaspoons and looked around. They were nearly ready and it delighted her to see everyone so excited by her suggestion for their last afternoon together. Matt had brought his portable barbecue and had smilingly submitted it to Imogen's scrutiny. The remaining food in Imogen's stockpile couldn't stretch to a beach party, so they'd given in and bought some more. Now sausages, chicken breasts and skewered kebabs were double foil-wrapped and packed away, along with marinades and dips, napkins, plates, cutlery, wipes and everything else Imogen considered mandatory for a casual beach barbie later on. Jo wasn't sure she'd ever get the hang of this whole food thing, but at least she was guaranteed a feast. The catering was something she'd certainly miss about Imogen although – she eased the waistband of her combats – maybe a little less feasting would do her good.

She suddenly shrieked, her eyes falling on a large vase of dried grasses and Chinese lanterns on the mantelpiece. Had Imogen lost her mind? 'Where the hell did they come from!'

'Oh those.' Imogen looked up from her task. 'They're just one of the many tasteful items I censored and hid away before you arrived on the first night, to prevent lasting damage to our aesthetic senses, and now restored to their rightful place. Wait till you see the horse brasses in the sitting room! Right! Ready now. Who's going with who?' She dried her hands on a dishcloth and zipped up the last bag.

Jo glanced up quickly. Imogen's voice suddenly sounded a bit wavery. What was she thinking? The casual assumptions of the past weekends, when the families slipped back into their cosy nuclear structures and Jo had felt left out in the cold, had been blown apart. If anything, Imogen was the odd woman out now and Jo felt a surge of compassion for her. Matt seemed to read her mind.

'We can probably squeeze into two cars, can't we?' he said. 'The three of us and the three boys? And Sophie and Hugh can take the girls. I'm quite happy to take the Jeep – that way you two can both relax and have a drink. You all deserve a treat.' Jo squeezed his hand before she could stop herself. He'd made it all sound so logical and easy – typical Matt. She felt a tightening in her stomach and turned away, pretending to fiddle with her watch.

'Come on, let's get going, shall we? We can take all the stuff down and let the kids play until they get hungry, then get the barbie going – OK?'

Matt looked at her intently for a moment. 'Jo, I do understand that you're new to this, but you can't rush these things, y'know? They have a natural progression – well, if they're going to be successful, anyway.' Jo was startled for a moment. Had he read her mind again?

'Yep!' He leered theatrically. 'The flames are spectacular, all right, but it's the glowing embers you want. Unless you prefer your sausages burnt on the outside and raw on the inside, that is. It's got to be lit well before the kids get hungry, or we'll probably have a mutiny on our hands!'

Jo laughed ruefully. Damn him for being a step ahead, once again. For someone so used to hiding her feelings, this was turning out to be a rather disconcerting relationship. She got her revenge by loading him up with bags and bustled him out to the cars, then went to help Imogen round up the children, who were almost incoherent with excitement at the prospect of a night-time barbecue.

Except, that is, for Grace, who was standing on the landing sobbing, tears pouring down her face and clutching her doll.

'What on earth's the matter, Gracie love?' Jo asked, crouching in front of her.

She inhaled jerkily. 'Rory says we're cooking Barbie for supper …'

Jo tried desperately to stop herself smiling. 'Oh sweetie, they meant a barbecue. Aren't they rotten those boys? Come on and take my hand. We'll give 'em hell.'

'Will it be dark?' Grace asked anxiously, her warm, sticky little hand in Jo's. 'We won't get lost, will we?'

From nowhere, Finn appeared and took Gracie's other hand. 'Nah! Don't worry. I'll look after you,' he said. 'I'll take my torch, and anyway Matt knows his way round. I bet he could take us there with his eyes shut,' he reassured her with a calm air of superiority, and Gracie looked up at him, her eyes wide with adoration.

As their shadows grew longer and afternoon stretched towards evening, the beach began to clear. Jo pulled a fleece from the bag and remembered last time she'd stood on the sand. Thank goodness no one had suggested going back to the same place – she'd see it in her worst nightmares forever! No, this was a cove Matt knew. He said it was almost exclusively used by locals, as opposed to DFLs – Down From Londons – like them, he laughed with mock superiority. Matt and Hugh had settled them down, then gone back to fetch the rest of the bags. Finn had run back with them, anxious to be part of the men's team and Rory, looking slightly miffed, had gone with him. It certainly made a nice change to be waited on by the children!

As she pulled her fleece on in the cooler night air, Matt appeared at her side, helping her to untangle the sleeve. 'Having fun?'

She smiled and nodded. 'It's a lovely way to end the holiday – and it certainly keeps the kids out of the house, now we've more or less tidied everything up. Do you want any help getting that monster lit?' She nodded at the cast-iron griddle he'd balanced on a pile of stones.

'I've got the strangest feeling you don't believe I can cook, Dr Newman. I am capable of a couple of things other than surfing, y'know.'

Jo blushed. 'Oh, don't remind me! You must have thought I was such an idiot.'

'Nope. I thought you were a woman with other things on her mind. And you were, weren't you? But I got your attention in the end. I just hope I can keep it.'

She looked down to conceal the dopey grin she could feel spreading across her face. 'Just hurry up with that food. I'm hoping you're functional as well as decorative. That's what'll swing it for me!'

He pretended to look worried and, producing a lighter from his shirt pocket, lit the charcoal and the pieces of dry driftwood the children had collected earlier. 'What if

I get stage fright and burn everything? Will you still love me then?'

Oh God, the L-word. Jo shot him a terrified look but Matt simply smiled and put a gentle finger to her lips. 'Plenty of time for that,' he said quietly. Imogen saved her from having to respond by coming over with two glasses of icy white wine and a beer for Matt and, in comfortable silence, they watched as Hugh, benign referee to a motley football game, tried, once again, to explain the off-side rule to Amelia. Let's hope they have a son this time, thought Jo, so the poor man won't face a lifetime of having to watch Arsenal on his own.

'Imogen, you're making me nervous,' Matt said after a while. 'And Jo's as good as said she'll dump me if my cooking isn't up to scratch, so bugger off, why don't you? Hugh's got the kids under control, so why don't the three of you go round that headland now the tide's gone out? There's a fantastic little bay there, completely secluded. You could even have a swim, if you're feeling brave.'

Jo and Imogen shrugged a 'why not?' at each other and went to lever Sophie up from where she had flaked out on the sand with all her possessions around her. Imogen stopped to pick up a few towels and they walked side by side, Sophie in the middle, along the newly washed and deserted sand towards the setting sun. For a while no one spoke. The laughs and shouts from the football game grew gradually fainter as they neared the headland, to be replaced by the soothing rhythm of the tiny waves, frilling the water's edge. The earlier breeze had died down, and the air was warm and soft. Jo could almost feel the tension seeping from her body. Had she undone the belt by another notch?

'So this is it,' breathed Sophie at last. 'Almost the end of the holiday. I can't believe it's been three weeks already. It seems to have flown past.'

'Not all the time,' Jo put in, wryly. 'I can think of a few hours that seemed to last for ever.'

She could hear Imogen's intake of breath as she nodded in agreement. 'But we're all here to tell the story, thank God. In fact, there's one more of us than when we started, thanks to you and Hugh, Soph. I feel jealous in a way.'

'Don't! I keep forgetting – then something happens or someone says something and the whole thing comes flooding back in on me. Of course, I'm delighted. Or at least I will be soon. But this was not part of our plans, let me tell you.'

Jo laughed. 'I think all our plans have gone a bit awry lately. If anyone had told us what was going to happen on this holiday, I reckon we'd have cancelled.'

There were protests from the other two. 'Well, I must have been preggers before we came away, so it wouldn't have made any difference to me – although if I'd known I was going to be such a wet lettuce, I might have cancelled anyway.'

'I don't think cancelling would have changed things between me and Guy,' said Imogen quietly. 'Jakarta would still have happened and I'd have had to find a way of coping somehow. And anyway, it's been good training being without him.'

They rounded the headland and gasped as the little bay opened up before them. The low sun made the dunes glow and the still-damp rocks glisten like rubies.

'Do you regret coming here, Jo?' Sophie's question was so direct, Jo stopped walking for a moment.

She spoke slowly. 'I'd give every penny I have for Finn not to have got lost, but ...' She hesitated. 'It did make me think about what's really important to me. And of course you don't meet many surfers with an intimate knowledge of abstract expressionism down the Mile End Road.'

Sophie inspected the rocks until she found some that were reasonably dry. 'Come on, I simply must sit down. I'm so worried I'll get varicose veins this time. Hugh'll never fancy me again.'

They all perched on the rocks, padding them as best they could with the towels and jackets they'd carried with them.

'You will get them, just you wait,' growled Imogen. 'You may have skipped through your first two pregnancies like a little bunny rabbit on Prozac, but believe me, this one will knacker your pelvic floor good and proper – or such was my experience.'

Jo laughed. 'Don't listen to her, Soph. You'll sail through this one, just like the other two. And in a few weeks you won't even be tired any more, just annoyingly glowy and blooming, and your Hugh won't ever be able to keep his hands off you.'

'Just think, Soph,' Imogen put in, 'next year, it'll be five of you on holiday and sand in the nappy.'

Sophie scratched her nose. 'God what a thought! I'll tell you what though, if this holiday has taught me anything it's that I never want to holiday with other families again. Next time we're on our own.' The other two turned round, startled.

'Well,' Imogen started defensively, 'it seemed a good idea in January …' Then she snorted and they all laughed.

A seagull waddled towards them and they sat watching it in an amicable silence for a moment.

'You'll be walking like that soon, Soph,' commented Jo.

'Well, I'd better make the best of it while I still can,' Sophie yawned. 'I know – let's have a swim. It's bound to be freezing but I think we have to, just to say goodbye to the sea. C'mon. I'm in charge for once!'

She was already stepping out of her trousers and knickers. Imogen looked aghast. 'But we haven't got our swimsuits.'

'Who cares? Last one in's a rotten egg. Oh come on, you two.'

Imogen and Jo exchanged a glance and started feverishly throwing their clothes down onto the sand before they lost their nerve then, holding hands, ran down after Sophie, who had gone in as far as the tops of her thighs and was now hesitating.

'Don't go weak on us now,' Imogen shouted. 'This was your damn fool idea. Just go for it.'

Jo flung herself forward into a wave and felt an icy blast that lifted her off her feet and carried her gently back to shore. Muffled screams told her the others had joined her. Again and again, they hurled themselves back into the exhilarating swell, losing their footing then finding it again. After what felt like hours, but was probably only ten minutes, they emerged from the water, arms companionably linked, shivering but elated. With the towels Imogen had brought, they rubbed themselves until their skin glowed and dressed again, feverishly tugging their knickers and trousers over still-damp skin, sticky with salt.

'Hang on,' Sophie rummaged in her basket. 'I've got my camera here. I'll set the timer and we can get a group photo.' She stood it on a rock, and squinted at the others through the viewfinder. 'You both look brilliant – like wild women or something. Hang on, I'm coming.' She ran round next to Jo and they huddled in together.

Just at that moment, waiting for the camera to flash, Jo had the strongest sense of being absolutely present. Exactly where she wanted to be. No doubts, no fears, no regrets. Just pure being, and for that moment everything was perfect.

Then the flash burst into brilliant light, leaving them blinking and laughing. From round the headland, they could just hear Matt's voice carried on the breeze, calling everyone to eat.

They picked up their stuff again, turned their backs to the setting sun and went to join the others.

Acknowledgements

Many of the incidents explored in this book are based on our own holiday experiences, but any similarity to yours is entirely intentional. However, we did need help with some details and for that we thank Liz White at Knight Frank; Françoise de Saint Germain; Philip Okell; Priscilla Chase; Susanna Wadeson; Sharon Newman, Cornwall Police Headquarters; Stuart Elliman, Watch Officer, Marine Rescue Sub Centre, Brixham; Philip Skevington, Standard Chartered Bank; Lady Tombs; Chris Martin (no, not that one); Lucia Griggi and Ben Ridding, Cornish super surfers; Denise Perry-Dehainey; Gabrielle Edwardes, homeopath; Rosie Clementi; Dr Helen Gunton; Dr Kate Crocker; Craig and Mark Spence, Aztec Watersports, Evesham; Jackie Wheatley and the RTs. Thanks particularly to Jane Wood and Sara O'Keeffe at Orion, and Mary Pachnos, for her support and enthusiasm. And, of course, Cornwall. We love you really.

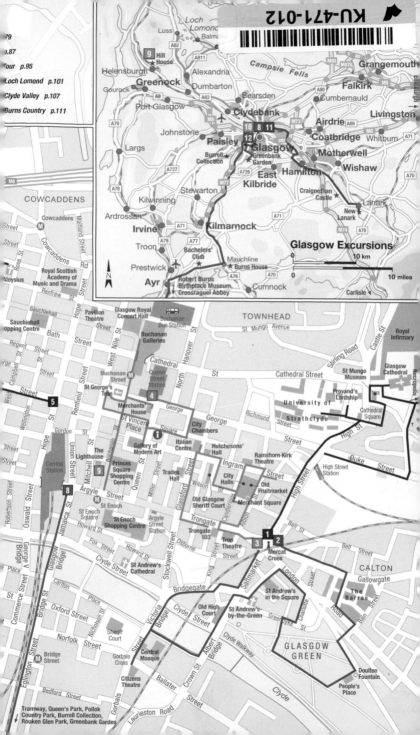

Glasgow's Top 10

From Glasgow's dazzling variety of art and architecture to the wild natural beauty of the surrounding countryside, here, at a glance, are the top sights and activities of this fascinating Scottish city

▲ **Kelvingrove Art Gallery and Museum** *(p.72)*. Discover the wonders of Victorian civic endeavour at this red-sandstone museum filled with compelling exhibits.

▲ **Shopping**. Choose from swanky designers at Princes Square *(p.56)* or quirky boutiques in the Merchant City *(p.45)* and West End *(pp.69 & 83)*.

▲ **Loch Lomond and the Trossachs** *(p.104)*. It's adventures galore in this national park, dipping into Britain's largest lake, trekking and visiting beguiling villages.

▶ **Glasgow culture and nightlife** *(p.10)*. With its myriad music scenes, cutting-edge theatre and nightspots, Glasgow caters for everyone.

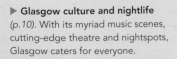

▲ **Cathedral and Necropolis** *(pp.20 & 22).* Glasgow's impressive cathedral was founded in 1136, while the Necropolis provides spine-tingling moments amid crumbling temples and monuments.

▲ **Riverside Museum** *(p.74).* Glasgow's award-winning new transport museum features buses, trams, trains, bikes and cars.

▲ **Burns Country** *(p.110).* On the trail of the Scottish bard, visiting Alloway Kirk's graveyard, Burns Cottage, and the Robert Burns Birthplace Museum.

▼ **Pollok Estate** *(p.89).* A splendid mansion, riverside walks, biking trails, and the world-class Burrell Collection make for a memorable Southside day.

▼ **New Lanark** *(p.109).* David Dale and his son-in-law Robert Owen's model factory town is now a fascinating Unesco World Heritage Site.

▼ **Glasgow arts scene** *(p.66).* The Glasgow School of Art and assorted galleries give the city one of the world's most vibrant contemporary art scenes.

Overview

The Art of Reinvention

Glasgow is a city continually in flux: its vibrant culture, and its grand architectural splendours of sandstone and steel make it sparkle despite dark urban realities

Glasgow is something of a Renaissance city. Like a proud fighter who refuses to be knocked down, this vibrant, bustling, rumbustious Scottish city is once again busy reinventing itself. Born as a fishing village on the slopes

above the meandering River Clyde, Glasgow has been, in turn, a market town, an ecclesiastical centre, a seat of learning, a city of merchant adventurers, a gateway to the New World, an industrial powerhouse of the British Empire and a European cultural capital.

ARCHITECTURE

Approaching from the south, first impressions are not great. However, despite some misguided 1960s urban planning – Brutalist tower blocks and the M8 motorway which rips through the heart of the city – Glasgow is an architectural treasure house. Its mix of Victorian, Georgian, Venetian and Art Deco equals anything in Europe.

The city retained its grim face until well into the second half of the 20th

century, when the New Glasgow Society – a loose collection of early eco-warriors – led a rearguard action against the City Corporation's policy of 'If it's old, knock it down'. Victorian tenement homes were stripped and refurbished instead of being demolished, revealing honey-and-red sandstone wonders and striking detail. The defining moment in Glasgow's recent past was its selection in 1990 as European City of Culture.

ECONOMY AND RENEWAL

Today the city is once again reviving its fortunes with the bold regeneration of the inner-city riverbank. In 2011, the Zaha Hadid-designed Riverside Museum added to the shimmering riverside scene. Meanwhile, the Merchant City's abandoned warehouses continue to be transformed into swanky apartments, businesses and restaurants. The Trongate 103 arts centre is at the centre of a plan to regenerate run-down streets and connect the city with the Clyde.

Glasgow boasts some chic shopping centres, such as Princes Square. High-profile events like the biennial Glasgow International Festival and preparations for the Commonwealth Games in 2014 are reinvigorating the city. Its reputation as a dour, violent slum is finally being shaken off and Glaswegians are generally proud of the transformation.

Above: Glasgow's skyline reveals its rich mix of architectural styles. **Below**: the riverside is packed with striking buildings, such as the Science Centre.

LOCATION

The city lies in the wide strath, or plain, of the River Clyde and is sheltered to the north, east and south by high, open ground; it's possible to be in rolling countryside 20 minutes' drive from the city centre. Glasgow is about 26 miles (40km) from the sea at Greenock, and the Clyde starts to widen into the Firth just below the Erskine Bridge at Old Kilpatrick. North of the city, the Campsie Fells rise to 1,900ft (600m) and are dramatically visible from many areas.

CLIMATE

The Gulf Stream warms the whole of the west coast of Scotland, and Glasgow is a beneficiary of more temperate weather than might be expected from its latitude. Winters are generally mild (between 0°C/32°F and 6°C/43°F) with more rain than snow, though cold snaps of as low as -24°C (-11°F) have been known. Summers, in common with the rest of Britain, appear to be growing warmer, with temperatures of up to 25°C (77°F).

However, the prevailing westerly winds which blow across the Atlantic bring with them their fair share of rain. A day which offers glorious sunshine in the morning can become a depression of drizzle by the early afternoon. Go prepared.

Above: the doomed ocean liner RMS *Lusitania*, pictured here in 1907, was built in the Glasgow shipyards.

Above: the grand Merchants' House *(see p.58)* in 1874.

HISTORY OF TURMOIL

Glasgow was inhabited as long ago as 4000BC, when hunters pushed north in the wake of the retreating ice. Roman general Agricola found hostile tribes in the area in AD80 and threw up a chain of forts across the narrow waist of Scotland. The retreat of the Romans led to centuries of turmoil between warring tribes of Scots, Picts, Britons and Angles.

St Ninian began missionary work in Strathclyde in the 4th century, but St Mungo is credited as the founder of the city in AD543, although only legend bears witness to his arrival. Glasgow Cathedral was founded in 1136 on the site of St Mungo's Church on the banks of the Molendinar, a pretty *burn* (stream). But, although the city was seen as a respectable seat of learning (Glasgow University was created in 1451) with strong religious traditions throughout the Middle Ages, all the political and military action took place in Edinburgh, Falkirk and Stirling.

INDUSTRIAL AWAKENING

The British Empire spawned Glasgow's development as an important port city. John Golborne's ingenious plan of the

🕝 The People

Glaswegians have a way with words, even if visitors have difficulty understanding them. The patter, sociologists argue, is a mix of native sharpness, Highland feyness, Jewish morbidity and the Irish *craic* (witty story-telling). Much of Glasgow's story has been harsh, and, in the past, raising a laugh served as an antidote to adversity. The shipyards of the 1960s, for example, have provided plenty of material for Glaswegian-born comedian, Billy Connolly.

Above: Glaswegians are generally very quick and funny.

1770s – to build piers along the banks and allow the river to scour its own bed – turned Glasgow into a serious contender as an Atlantic port.

The 'Tobacco Lords' were the first major merchants; many of their houses still stand. They created not only the tobacco trade with Maryland, Virginia and North Carolina, but a merchant class. Their need for iron tools, glass, pottery and clothes to trade with the colonies was the impetus for the city's awakening to the Industrial Revolution.

Glasgow became a cotton town in 1780. Within a decade, scores of mills were using the fast-flowing Scottish rivers to power their looms, and immigrants from Ireland and the Highlands were flooding in. Glasgow's population exploded, from 23,500 in 1755 to a peak of 1,128,000 in 1939. The metal-bashing industries – shipbuilding, ironworks, armaments – were complemented by textiles, chemicals and manufacturing.

During the 20th century, Glasgow shared in the spoils and misfortunes of the industrialised world. There may be no more belching foundries or clanging, but recent city administrations have pragmatically courted private finance to unlock the city's post-industrial potential. New developments and attractions are sprouting everywhere, bringing with them a new sense of civic pride. Glasgow is flourishing once again.

Find our recommended restaurants at the end of each Tour. Below is a price guide to help you make your choice.

Eating Out Price Guide

Two-course meal for one person, including a glass of wine.

£££	over £45
££	£25–45
£	under £25

Guide to Coloured Boxes

🅴 **Eating**	This guide is dotted
🅵 **Fact**	with coloured boxes providing
🅶 **Green**	additional practical and cultural infor-
🅺 **Kids**	mation to make the most of your visit.
🆂 **Shopping**	Here is a guide to
🆅 **View**	the coding system.

Entertainment

PERFORMING ARTS

Glasgow is a thriving centre for the arts, mixing the old with some of Scotland's most cutting-edge scenes. When it comes to variety of music events, art shows and nightlife, few cities in Britain can compare. For full details of performance times and dates, check in the local press (*The Herald* and *The List* are the best), or visit www.seeglasgow.com.

Theatre, dance, opera and comedy

The Citizens Theatre (tel: 0141-429 0022; www.citz.co.uk) in Gorbals Street combines iconoclastic drama with stunning design. **Tramway** (tel: 0845-330 3501; www.tramway.org) is an exciting arts centre and theatre space, home of Scottish Ballet.

Below: the Art Deco Glasgow Film Theatre champions arty fare.

Above: the iconic Clyde Auditorium, popularly known as the Armadillo.

The **Tron Theatre** (tel: 0141-552 4267; www.tron.co.uk) shows hard-hitting Scottish drama, concerts, comedy and pantomime. Comedians Billy Connolly and Dave Gorman appear at **The King's Theatre** (tel: 0844-871 7627) in Bath Street and **Pavilion** in Renfield Street (tel: 0141-332 1846).

Scottish Opera and Scottish Ballet mount major productions at the **Theatre Royal** (tel: 0844-871 7627). Modern dance productions, musicals and plays are also staged here.

Classical music and gigs

The **Glasgow Royal Concert Hall** (tel: 0141-353 8000) hosts regular performances by the **Royal Scottish National Orchestra** (tel: 0141-225 3561; www.rsno.org.uk). The refurbished **City Halls** and the **Old Fruit Market** in the Merchant City area are home to the **BBC Scottish Symphony Orchestra** and the Scottish Music Centre (tel: 0141-353 8000). **Henry Wood Hall** (tel: 0141-225 3555), at 73 Claremont Street, is a beautiful venue in a former church, mainly used for classical events.

The **Scottish Exhibition and Conference Centre** (tel: 0141-248 3000) and the adjacent **Clyde Auditorium** – dubbed the 'Armadillo'

– stage high-profile classical concerts and big rock and pop gigs. Jazz, Blues and Country gigs are held at City Halls, Old Fruitmarket and the Royal Concert Hall. For a closer look at the music scene and venues *see feature, p.66.*

Film
The first stop for arty, independent film is the wonderful **Glasgow Film Theatre** (12 Rose Street; tel: 0141-332 6535; www.glasgowfilm.org). Both the **Centre for Contemporary Arts** (**CCA**) and new **Trongate 103** arts centres screen indie films and flicks for kids. For more mainstream releases, try **The Grosvenor** in the West End (Ashton Lane; tel: 0845-166 6002) and **Cineworld** (Renfrew Street; tel: 0871-200 2000).

NIGHTLIFE
Pubs and bars
Drinking has always been a serious business in Glasgow. For sophisticated drinking and eating head to the Merchant City. Sauchiehall Street is mobbed by barefoot stiletto-wielding youth at weekends. The West End is popular with students and arty types.

Some of the best hostelries include **Babbity Bowster** (Mon–Sat 11am–midnight, Sun 12.30pm–midnight) at 16–18 Blackfriars Street, home to a heaving bar that attracts an eclectic mix of media types and local worthies, and **Blackfriars** at 36 Bell Street (daily noon–midnight), which has a friendly bar, a range of real ale beers and is a comedy club and music venue at night. The **Captain's Rest**, at 185 Great Western Road (tel: 0141-332 7304), is great for indie gigs and fun events including Disco Bingo. For traditional Scottish whiskies, try **DRAM!** at 232–246 Woodlands Road (Mon–Sat noon–midnight, Sun 12.30pm–midnight), with more than 75 varieties on offer.

Clubs
Glasgow's club scene is eclectic *(see also Gigs, opposite)*. **The Arches** (253 Argyle Street, tel: 0141-565 1000) offers big-name DJs, while **The Buff** (142 Bath Lane, tel: 0141-248 1777) hosts an eclectic mix of music from indie to Motown. **The Flying Duck** (142 Renfield Street, tel: 0141-553 3539) presents indie club nights, oddball cultural gatherings and gigs, and the **Sub Club** (22 Jamaica Street, tel: 0141-248 4600) is the home of the excellent Optimo – rare grooves and stompers for Sunday music hedonists.

🅕 Festivals

Celtic Connections (www.celtic connections.com) in January celebrates Celtic musical culture. The biannual Glasgow International Festival (www.glasgowinternational. org; Apr–May) showcases the latest visual arts. The West End Festival (www.westendfestival.co.uk) has lots of fun events and concerts in June. Also in June is the Glasgow Jazz Festival (www.jazzfest.co.uk).

The Glasgow Comedy Festival (www.glasgowcomedyfestival.com) is in March and the arts-focused Merchant City Festival (www. merchantcityfestival.com) is in July. Glasgay! (tel: 0141-552 7575; www. glasgay.co.uk) in Oct–Nov is the UK's largest gay-lesbian arts festival.

Above: revellers in Ashton Lane at the West End Festival.

Tour 1

High Street

This half-day, 1-mile (1.6km) walk takes you from the gritty old traders' hub Mercat Cross up to the spiritual and spooky realms of the Cathedral area and Necropolis

Mercat Cross was the visible evidence of a burgh's right to hold a market, the domain of traders and merchants, making this area Glasgow's traditional centre of social and economic life for many centuries. There is no clear evidence of exactly where the original **Mercat Cross ❶** stood, and the squat octagonal building with a unicorn-topped pillar that now stands on the intersection at Glasgow Cross is a replacement erected in 1929. The Mercat Building located behind it is, despite its Chicagoesque appearance, a warehouse erected in 1925. The new arts centre Trongate 103 and the Tron theatre (*see p.41 for both*) are slowly revitalising this part of the Merchant City area.

Highlights

- Tolbooth Steeple
- Barony Hall
- Provand's Lordship
- St Mungo Museum of Religious Life and Art
- Glasgow Cathedral
- Necropolis

TOLBOOTH STEEPLE

Starting our walk here, the cross is dominated by the **Tolbooth Steeple ❷**, which lies stranded in the middle of busy traffic where the High Street passes into Saltmarket. The Tolbooth was once an integral part of civic life in Glasgow and has occupied this site in various forms since the earliest days. Its

Preceding Pages: Bells Bridge and the 'Armadillo'. **Left:** the Necropolis. **Above:** the Tolbooth Steeple.

functions were manifold, from a meeting place for the town council, to a tax collection point, courthouse and jail.

The square tower was part of a five-storey building which extended west along the Trongate, towards the steeple of **Tron-St Mary's** (see p.41), and its buttressed crown houses the latest of a fine carillon of bells which, in the 18th century, played out a different Scottish melody every two hours. The present bells, installed in 1881, were tended by hereditary bell-ringers, the last of whom, Jessie Herbert, rang the bells until 1970. Their annual high point was, of course, marking the Hogmanay celebrations which saw vast crowds welcoming the New Year in boisterous fashion. The Hogmanay party now takes place in George Square, to the sound of rock bands.

HISTORICAL HIGH STREET

The High Street runs north past Victorian tenements (1883), with shops below on the left and new flats converted from old warehouses

on the right. The street names offer clues to the past: Blackfriars Street, from the 13th-century Dominican monastery; Bell Street, after Provost Sir John Bell (1680); and College Street, denoting the **Old College** which was sited here until the middle of the 19th century. The University of Glasgow was established by Bishop William Turnbull in 1451 and flourished for the next few centuries in a pleasant environment between the High Street and the Molendinar Burn. It was here that Adam Smith, author of seminal work on laissez-faire economics *The Wealth of Nations*, was appointed Professor of Moral Philosophy in 1752.

The university moved westwards in 1870 (see p.80), and the site was sold to the City of Glasgow Union Railway Company, which demolished it and erected the College Goods Station, which has now also gone. However, the area is currently undergoing substantial redevelopment.

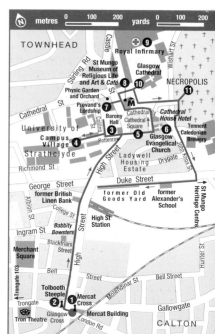

Above: Barony Hall was designed in the Scottish Gothic Revival style and is a popular venue for weddings, as well as the site of graduation ceremonies.

On the left, opposite the High Street Station, is the shell of the old **British Linen Bank**, which has a statue of Pallas, goddess of wisdom and weaving, and a plaque on the corner recalling that the poet Thomas Campbell frequented a coffee shop on the site. Close by, on Nicholas Street, is the Old College Bar, Glasgow's most ancient pub (est. 1515).

Crossing George Street and curving up the hill, the street is flanked by restored tenements with crow-stepped gables, turrets and balconies. On this hill, the Scots freedom fighter William Wallace – glorified by Hollywood and Mel Gibson in the film *Braveheart* – fought a running battle with English forces in 1297.

UNIVERSITY DIGS

On the corner of High Street and Rottenrow is **Barony Hall** ❸ (Sat–Sun), the first major building of the Cathedral complex, which opens out onto Castle Street. It was built in 1889 from beautiful red sandstone and graced with slender stained-glass windows and a grey Gothic spire. It is now owned by

the University of Strathclyde, and on graduation days the street teems with begowned students and tutors making their way to the hall to receive and bestow degrees. Rottenrow is one of Glasgow's earliest streets, and its name has never been adequately defined,

Below: the Mercat Building (see p.14) on the Trongate.

with suggestions as far apart as *route du roi* (king's way) to *vicus ratonum* (street of rats). It leads to the university's **Campus Village ❹**, a pleasing and colourful student quarter built over the past two decades, proving that not all modern architecture is unsympathetic.

AROUND CATHEDRAL SQUARE

Opposite Barony Hall is **Cathedral Square ❺**, guarded by a rather imperious equestrian statue of William of Orange, which was resited by the Provincial Grand Black Chapter of Scotland in 1989 from the Trongate, where it suffered terrible indignities each Hogmanay. It is said that the tail of King Billy's horse was broken off by a reveller and replaced with a ball and socket joint, with the result that on particularly stormy days, the tail can be seen to wave in the breeze.

On the south side of the square is the 1960s Ladywell housing estate, built over the medieval well of that name and the former Duke Street jail. The east side is bounded by the **Glasgow Evangelical Church ❻**, which features life-sized statues of the Apostles. Just to the north, more worldly pleasures can be found at the **Cathedral House**, a small hotel housed in a red sandstone building dating from 1896, which has an interesting three-level bar and is reputedly haunted.

The oldest dwelling-house still standing in Glasgow is **Provand's Lordship ❼** (tel: 0141-552 8819; www.glasgowlife.org.uk; Tue–Thur, Sat 10am–5pm, Fri–Sun 11am–5pm; free). It lies opposite Cathedral Square and was built in 1471 by Bishop Andrew Muirhead to house the master of the hospice of St Nicholas, who looked after a complement of 12 old men.

The house was saved and restored in 1906, with financial aid and period furnishings supplied by Sir William

Above: a sign indicates the oldest Glasgow house still standing, Provand's Lordship, which is now a museum portraying medieval life in the city.

⑤ Gruesome Tales

If spirits haunt any part of Glasgow, it should be here. Men and women were hanged outside the Tolbooth, and alleged witches and miscreants scourged. The original building had spikes on the walls for the decapitated heads of felons. When the justiciary decamped to the river end of the Saltmarket and the council moved west, the main part of the Tolbooth was lost; only the steeple and its winding stone staircase remain.

Above: the Tolbooth has a long and gruesome history.

Burrell *(see p.90)* in 1927, and is now run by Glasgow Museums. Behind it lies a **Physic Garden**, in tribute to St Nicholas. The sound of the traffic gives way to medieval calm here, among the herb plantings and knot gardens. Behind the wall, towards the Strathclyde campus, is a small but ambitious orchard, where students convene under the spring blossom and try to ignore the M8 just up the road.

RELIGION AND MEDICINE

Back across the High Street – traffic is always bad here – is the **St Mungo Museum of Religious Life and Art** ❽ (tel: 0141-276 1625; www.glasgow life.org.uk; Tue–Thur, Sat 10am–5pm, Fri and Sun 11am–5pm; free), which caused some controversy before it was opened in 1993 over whether it was an architectural pastiche. The honey-coloured stone building stands on the site of the medieval Bishop's Castle and houses works of art from the main religions – Buddhist, Christian, Hindu, Jewish, Muslim and Sikh – as well as minor ones. Religious rites are explained alongside intriguing relics and there are gorgeous views from the top floor.

Above: a restored room at Provand's Lordship depicts medieval living.

Inside the Gallery of Religious Art there are powerful images of religious figures and rites to explore, including an imposing figure of the Hindu god Shiva, Lord of the Dance, and the Mexican Day of the Dead skeleton, which celebrates the victory of life over death. Illuminating the poignant images are some truly stunning stained-glass windows showing Christian saints and prophets. The museum's pleasant coffee shop backs onto an attractive Zen-style garden

ⓢ Quirky Shops on the High Street

Along this sweep of handsome red-brick tenements – between the pubs and fish-and-chip takeaways – there are dishevelled shopfronts aplenty. But tucked in among the intriguing and slightly unsettling array of shops – from beauty/massage parlours and hairdressers to religious missions and a butcher or two – lies **23enigma** (258 High Street; tel: 0141-553 1990), bubbling with spell books, talismans and crystals. It even offers alternative therapies including hypnosis and reiki.

Above: tarot cards are just some of the spooky wares on offer at 23enigma.

Above: the St Mungo Museum of Religious Life and Art has won awards for its fascinating exhibits and attempts to promote inter-faith understanding.

designed by Yasutaro Tanaka, another unexpected haven of peace in this busy street.

The cathedral precinct is fronted by a statue of the Scots missionary explorer David Livingstone *(see p.107)* and provides an excellent foreground for the massive bulk of the **Royal Infirmary ❾**, which was completed in 1915 and commemorates the 65-year reign of Queen Victoria, whose solemn presence looms above the entrance. The Royal, which

has been operating since 1794, has made a proud contribution to world medicine: Lord Lister pioneered antiseptic surgery here in the 1860s; Sir William Macewen established his reputation in brain surgery and osteopathy here in the 1890s; and his matron Mrs Rebecca Strong introduced the world's first systematic training for nurses. In the early part of the 19th century, its resources were considerably stretched as it sought to cope with epidemics of cholera, typhus

Above: the Royal Infirmary has been the site of many medical breakthroughs.

Above: Barony Chapel, in the crypt of Glasgow Cathedral, is so named because it was used by Barony parishioners for their worship.

and dysentery. Today, it has one of the busiest casualty departments in Europe, coping with Glasgow's still prevalent weekend bouts of random and inventive violence. One casualty surgeon remarked that it was one of the few cities in Europe where patients still came in with sword wounds.

GLASGOW CATHEDRAL

At the east end of the precinct lies **Glasgow Cathedral** ⑩ (tel: 0141-552 8198; Apr–Sept Mon–Sat 9.30am–5.30pm, Sun 1–5pm, Oct–Mar Mon–Sat 9.30am–4.30pm, Sun 1–4.30pm). The tides of history have washed over this important ecclesiastical site since Glasgow's early days. It was founded in 1136 on the site of St Mungo's Church and has always been a focus for Christian learning and culture in Scotland. It has stood through the supremacy of the bishops, the War of Independence and the upheaval of the Reformation, and began to take the shape

which we see today around the middle of the 14th century. Its blackened stone illustrates the colouring of many Glasgow buildings before stone-cleaning became widespread.

Below: Glasgow Cathedral is the best-preserved medieval church in Scotland.

Above: the cathedral is known for its magnificent stained-glass windows.

Attempts have been made to clean it up, but it was felt that it would cause too much damage.

The visitors' entrance is flanked by a memorial to the Hutcheson brothers and George Baillie, who 'divested himself of his fortune to endow institutions devoted to the intellectual culture of the operative classes'. The grounds are surrounded by gravestones. Blue-robed custodians belonging to the Society of Friends of Glasgow Cathedral give fascinating little impromptu tours.

Music enthusiasts and anyone interested in the labyrinthine history of this colossal building will be keen to find out about the latest recitals and lectures held in the cathedral. Completing the warm welcome given to visitors and incredible resources available to the curious, there is the Congregations' Library, which is situated in the Cathedral Hall in the basement of the nearby St Mungo Museum *(see p.18)*. It is open on Wednesday afternoons from 2pm to 4pm.

Architectural features
The main structure is a rectangle with a cross surmounted by a tower and steeple. A lower church opens up underneath the choir. Damaged by fire, the original cathedral building was succeeded by a larger one, which was consecrated in 1197. Major 13th-century rebuilding by William de Bondinton (1233–58) can be seen in the Quire and the Lower

F St Mungo

Legend has it that a century after St Ninian dedicated a Christian burial ground at Cathures (later Glasgow) Kentigern arrived, popularly known as Mungo. Kentigern hailed from Culross in Fife (Glaswegians may be taken aback to learn that their patron saint was in fact a Fifer) where he was trained as a priest by St Serf. He accompanied the corpse of a holy man, Fergus – carried on a cart by two oxen – to the St Ninian's burial ground in Cathures where Fergus was buried.

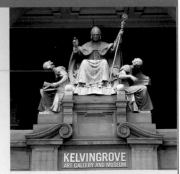

KELVINGROVE
ART GALLERY AND MUSEUM

Above: images of St Mungo, Glasgow's patron saint, adorn the city.

Church. Check out the doorways of the sacristy (Upper Chapterhouse) and of the Lower Chapterhouse; these date from the mid-13th century. Extensive work enlarged the nave in the 14th century – for a closer look at these developments seek out the southwest door and the entrance to the Blacader Aisle, where the body of Fergus is said to have been buried by St Mungo *(see box p.21)*.

Other intriguing architectural and social developments occurred after the Reformation to allow three different congregations to worship in different spaces, reflecting rank and class divisions. From 1595, the Barony Parishioners worshipped in the lower church (crypt), while from 1648 the High Kirk congregation worshipped in the choir itself, and the nave was used by worshippers from the eastern part of the city. Ask one of the robed custodians for interesting tidbits from this period.

NECROPOLIS

At the south side of the Cathedral is a bridge which spans Wishart Street and leads to the **Necropolis**  (7am– dusk; free) an impressive ornamental garden cemetery modelled on Père-

Lachaise in Paris. It is full of crumbling temples and monuments, many of which are in a sorry state of repair, which only adds to the chilling atmosphere, especially on dreich days.

In 1831, John Strang, Chamberlain at the Merchants' House, wrote *Necropolis Glasguensis* ('Thoughts on Death and Moral Stimulus'), which included an outline of city plans for the hilly site that had been previously known as Fir Park, which he considered to appear 'admirably

Ⓥ Views Between the Tombs

The splendid views from the hill housing the Necropolis not only give some idea of the imposing grandeur of the Cathedral in medieval times, but also stretch as far as Ben Lomond to the north-west and the Cathkin Braes to the south. Roe deer can be seen roaming between the monument obelisks and haughty headstones. The combination of wildlife and monumental Victorian display and decay – with a skyline backdrop of lines of high-rise flats and churches – is strangely spine-tingling.

Above: situated on a hill, the Necropolis offers wonderful views.

Above: crumbling memorials in the Victorian Necropolis.

adapted for a Pere la Chaise, which would harmonise beautifully with the adjacent scenery, and constitute a solemn and appropriate append-age to the venerable structure (the Cathedral) in front of which, while it will afford a much wanted ac-commodation to the higher classes, would at the same time convert an

Below: a Celtic cross adorns a grave in the Necropolis.

unproductive property into a gen-eral and lucrative source of profit, to a charitable institution'. It was to be 'respectful to the dead, safe and sanitary to the living, dedicated to the Genius of Memory and to extend religious and moral feeling'.

Architect David Hamilton, Stuart Murray, Curator of the Botanic Gar-dens, and James Clelland, Superintend-ent of Public Works, produced a fea-sibility study for forming the Glasgow Necropolis, and in 1828 the commit-tee of Directors of Lands and Quar-ries agreed to the proposal. Then in 1831, a competition for converting the Fir Park into a cemetery was launched, with five prizes up for grabs of £10–50. As the burial ground was intended to be interdenominational, the first burial in 1832 was fittingly that of a Jew, Joseph Levi, a jeweller. Extensions into quarry ground in the 1860s and 1870s give us the present-day dimen-sions of 37 acres (15 hectares).

A walk around the graves
Some 50,000 burials have taken place at the Necropolis and most of the 3,500 tombs are about 14ft (4m)

Above: one of the Necropolis's elaborate tombs.

deep, with solid stone walls and brick partitions. Some of the Necropolis tombs on the top of the hill were blasted out of the rock face. Many of the monuments were designed by major architects and sculptors, including Alexander 'Greek' Thomson, Charles Rennie Mackintosh and

Below: a stone angel on one of the Necropolis's monuments.

J.T. Rochead, which makes a walk around the sprawling site a fascinating insight into both Victorian and Edwardian styles and tastes. The administration and maintenance of the Necropolis was handed from Merchants' House to Glasgow City Council in 1966.

The Necropolis's grand bridge was built by the Merchants' House of Glasgow to 'afford a proper entrance to the new cemetery combining convenient access to the grounds' and views of 'the venerable Cathedral and surrounding scenery'. Paths lead in circles round the hill past gloomy, ivy-clad, marble-pillared tombs and sombre obelisks. The Victorians took themselves as seriously in death as in life. The crowning monument on the summit is to John Knox, the austere father of the Reformation in Scotland, which 'produced a revolution in the sentiments of mankind'. Knox still keeps a suspicious eye on the city below. The Friends of Glasgow Necropolis (www.glasgownecropolis.org) is a superb organisation which runs tours of the site and various cultural events.

BACK TO GLASGOW CROSS

Leaving the cemetery in Wishart Street, this tour continues past the huge steel tanks of the **Tennent Caledonian Brewery**, which supplies a commodity as welcome to many Glaswegians as Loch Katrine's water. At the foot of the street the modern flats and high-rise blocks on the right stand on the site of the Drygate, one of the original streets of old Glasgow.

Turning right into Duke Street, past the former Alexander's School, now a business centre (adorned with busts of the heads of Shakespeare and other luminaries on its frontage), the road follows along the wall of the old College Goods Yard.

To return to Glasgow Cross, turn left at the traffic lights and head into the High Street.

Above: the tanks of the Tennent Caledonian Brewery stand in close proximity to the Necropolis tombs.

E Eating Out

Babbity Bowsters
16–18 Blackfriars Street; tel: 0141-552 5055; daily lunch and dinner.
Housed in a handsome Adam brothers-designed building, this popular hangout has the Schottische restaurant serving hearty portions of Scottish classic dishes with a Gallic twist here and there. The homely pub serves decent ales and malts to a live folk music soundtrack. This place is popular with a diverse crowd. £

St Mungo Museum Café
St Mungo Museum of Religious Life and Art; Tue–Thur, Sat 10am–5pm, Fri and Sun 11am–5pm.
This museum café serves predominantly simple, honest British grub, as well as some pasta dishes, heaped salads and good-value soup of the day. There is also an attractive garden where you can enjoy your meal in good weather. £

Above: Babbity Bowsters.

Tour 2

The Barras to Saltmarket

This short 2-mile (3.2km) walk takes in the banter and bargains of the Barras, Glasgow Green's delights and a short stroll south to the Clyde

If the High Street walk *(see p.14)* uncovers layers of Glasgow's history, this tour, which takes in the lively Barras, is where the city's working class past meets modern struggles and endeavours. This walk is a real eye-opener and is bound to deliver some memorable, oddball stories, encounters and scenes.

Although at first glance this busy marketplace is tatty and run-down, the area is full of life and colour, and bargain-hunters flock to it from all over the city and beyond. Down towards the Clyde and over the bridge there are old and new popular Glaswegian institutions – including the People's Palace museum and the handsome Winter Gardens at Glasgow Green – as well as the Citizens Theatre and

(see p.14)

Highlights

- The Saracen's Head
- Exploring the Barras
- The People's Palace
- Glasgow Green
- Doulton Fountain
- St Andrew's Parish Church
- Central Mosque
- Citizens Theatre
- Clyde Walkway
- Saltmarket

Central Mosque. Round the corner from historic folk music pubs there are notorious locations etched on the Glaswegian psyche, like Nelson's Pillar, sight of many a public hanging.

Left: one of the riverside developments on the banks of the Clyde. **Above:** the Central Mosque (see p.34).

Saturday or Sunday are the best days to undertake this tour, as the majority of shops around the Saltmarket are open.

ALONG GALLOWGATE

Starting the walk from the **Mercat Cross** (see p.14), head east up the **Gallowgate**, which is generally accepted to have the macabre meaning

its name implies. However, the late historian George Eyre-Todd suggested that it meant the *gait*, or way to, the *gia lia*, or sacred stone of Celtic times, which would make it one of the oldest roads in Scotland. Social raconteur Jack House recalls days in the 1930s when the street housed 60 pubs and he 'never ventured there without an occasional *frisson* disturbing me'.

The road leads under a bridge, passing a row of discount shops, as well as Moir Street and Charlotte Street, after which you reach Glasgow's oldest chippie (1884) at Little Dovehill and then Great Dovehill on the left. According to legend, this is where St Mungo was preaching to his flock when someone at the back complained that he could not see him, whereupon he commanded the adjoining ground to rise up in the air.

A little further along, you will come to **The Saracen's Head** ❶ (Sat 11am–11pm, Sun 12.30–11pm), or 'The Sarry Heid', a pub whose glory days are most definitely behind it. It lays claim to being the first real hotel in Glasgow, built in 1755 from the ruins of the old bishop's castle, and takes its name from a 12th-century

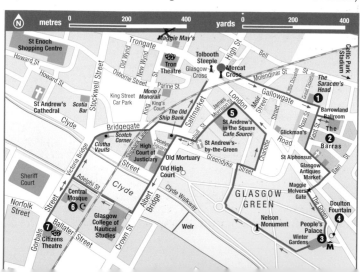

Above: the Barras market takes its name from the Glaswegian dialect for 'barrow'; in the market's early years, the traders sold their goods from handcarts.

inn in London frequented by Richard the Lionheart. The first mail coach from London arrived here in 1788, and it was a haunt of Scotland's judges as they progressed round the western circuit from Edinburgh.

THE BARRAS

Crossing the road to Kent Street, **The Barras** ❷ (Sat–Sun 10am–5pm) originated as a street market consisting of hand-barrows hired out by the McIver family to traders too poor to have their own. The covered market

came into being in 1926 and, after a spell in the doldrums in the 1970s and 1980s, it has been revitalised and is now said to be one of the biggest markets in Europe.

Second-hand furniture and clothes predominate, although in keeping with the times, DVDs, computer games and CDs, whose legality is continually challenged by trading standards officers, now feature. Slightly further along the Gallowgate from the Kent Street entrance is the **Barrowland Ballroom**, a dance

❻ Sarry Heid's Colourful Patrons and Relics

The old inn has been visited by an impressive list of patrons, including Robert Burns, John Wesley, James Boswell, William Wordsworth and Adam Smith, who was allegedly ejected after a swearing match with Dr Samuel Johnson. It houses the 1760 Saracen's Head punchbowl and the skull of Maggie, the last witch to be burned at the stake, which the title deeds demand is to be passed to the People's Palace if the pub is ever demolished.

Glasgow's first
PUB - MUSEUM

See the *Skull of Maggie* the last witch to be burned at the stake. Read a poem in *Rabbie Burns*' ane handwriting.

Above: the Sarry Heid's inn displays a range of quirky artefacts.

Above: the Barrowland Ballroom is a popular venue with a variety of local and high-profile international acts, who praise the acoustics and atmosphere.

hall which was the focus of the 1960s Bible John murders – when three women were killed by a man with a penchant for quoting Old Testament texts to his victims – but is now one of Glasgow's largest live music venues, staging gigs by local bands like Camera Obscura and international stars, including one of Dumbarton's finest sons, David Byrne.

In case you are wondering about the green-and-white-striped men often seen staggering along the Gallowgate, chanting musical ditties, these are fans of Celtic Football Club. Among the many bars to and from **Celtic Park Stadium**, a 15-minute walk east of the Barras, is Baird's Bar, next door to the Barrowland

Ballroom. It is a well-known Hoops haunt and pre-gig watering hole. Pop your head in to see an eye-opening afternoon karaoke session, or if you are on the way to a game at Paradise, Celtic's home ground (for fixtures and tickets go to www.celticfc.net), this is a good spot to soak up some local banter and gauge the mood of the local support.

Kent Street leads through to London Road, and, turning left, you'll see St Alphonsus Church. Next door is **Glasgow Antiques Market** (tel: 0141-552 6989; Sat–Sun 9.30am–4.30pm), which has a café attached. Proceed down Bain Street, through the Maggie McIvers Gate, and into **Glasgow Green**. Through the trees you will see the exotic coloured-brick frontage of the old Templeton's carpet factory, an enthusiastic copy of the Doge's Palace in Venice, designed by William Leiper in 1889. The factory is now a business centre.

PEOPLE'S PALACE

Turn left for the **People's Palace ❸** (tel: 0141-276 0788; www.glasgow life.org.uk; Tue–Thur and Sat 10am–5pm, Fri and Sun 11am–5pm; free), a museum presiding over one of the

Left: shopping for fruit and veg at the Barras; a farmers' market is also held here on the last Saturday of the month.

tree-lined avenues of Glasgow Green and a favourite with Glaswegians. It was built as a cultural centre for workers in 1898, who were living in some of the most abject conditions of the Industrial age. Lord Rosebery outlined the purpose of the grandiose civic project: 'A palace of pleasure and imagination around which the people may place their affections and which may give them a home on which their memory may rest'. He then declared the building as 'Open to the people for ever and ever'.

Originally, the ground floor provided space for reading and recreation, with a museum on the first floor, and a picture gallery on the top floor. Since the 1940s it has concentrated on the history and the way of life of the working class as well as kings and cardinals. Exhibits range from a ring that belonged to Mary, Queen of Scots to comedian Billy Connolly's 'banana boots'. The

Above: an exotic and colourful flower at the Winter Gardens.

red-sandstone building, with its domed roof and pillared frontage, was completely refurbished for its centenary in 1998 and now uses the latest computer technology and film to tell its story.

On the top floor is a powerful series of paintings by artist and Glasgow

Above: the Winter Gardens hosts exhibitions and events throughout the year.

Above: the Winter Gardens café is a pleasant place to spend some time, particularly on a cold or rainy day.

School of Art graduate Ken Currie, who was commissioned to mark the 1987 bicentenary of the massacre of Glasgow's Calton weavers, Scotland's first trade union martyrs. The series of eight paintings adorns the splendid dome: the cycle begins in 1787 and ends with a vision of the future. It traces the development of the Scottish labour movement through Currie's powerful imagery. **The Winter Gardens** (daily 10am–5pm), a huge conservatory housing tropical palms and ferns, butts onto the back of the Palace. After a serious fire in 1998, it has now reopened and houses a café-cum-bar.

GLASGOW GREEN

In 1450 Bishop Turnbull gave the common lands of **Glasgow Green** to the people of the city, although its previously rural vista is now bounded by the high-rise flats of the Gorbals, across the river. Bonnie Prince Charlie mustered his armies here, and the Glasgow Fair, instituted in 1190, is still celebrated in the park in the last fortnight of July. Turning right past the palace, a 144ft (44m) needle erected to commemorate Lord Nelson dominates the western end.

In front of the People's Palace, the magnificent red-terracotta **Doulton Fountain ❹**, gifted by the Victorian china manufacturer to commemorate Queen Victoria's Golden Jubilee of 1887, has recently been restored with investment from the National Lottery Fund. Its five-tier, 46ft (14m)-high and 70ft (21m)-wide display of imperial pride makes it the largest terracotta fountain in the world and a mesmerising insight into Glasgow's prominent place in the British Empire. It was first unveiled at the Empire Exhibition held at Kelvingrove Park in 1888 and then moved to Glasgow Green in 1890. Walk around it to get a closer look at extravagant figurative groups representing India, Australia,

Ⓚ Saturdays @ the Palace

On selected Saturdays, usually once a month, at 2pm the People's Palace holds a family-friendly event that is aimed at entertaining and engaging children with the museum's exhibits. The talks are often themed, from the history of World War II to Scottish royalty, or may reflect the time of year, such as a day of Halloween fun.

Above: the splendid People's Palace and Doulton Fountain on Glasgow Green.

Canada and South Africa. Seek out national flora and fauna (South Africa's ostrich, Australian sheep and Canadian beaver), alongside military and naval figures including a kilted highlander. Completing the array of dizzying decorations are gargoyles, coats of arms, lion masks, and young girls pouring water over the figures below. Topping the whole Imperial enterprise is a lifelike statue of Queen Victoria.

Ⓢ Independent Shopping

It may have the Barras and some scruffy old markets, but this area is not renowned for its upmarket shopping. However, a few excellent independent shops and specialist outlets have opened in recent years which are well worth seeking out. **Monorail** (12 Kings Court, King Street; tel: 0141-553 2400; Mon–Sat 11am–7pm, Sun noon–5pm) is run by Pastels front man Stephen Pastel, and is a must for musos and vinyl addicts. They have a great vegan-friendly café and a space for cultural events, cinema screenings and other cultural get-togethers.

Just north of Monorail is Glasgow's best comic shop, **A1 Comics** (35 Parnie Street; tel: 0141-552 6692; daily 9.30am–5.30pm, Sun noon– 5pm), which has some fine toys for kids and objects for geeky adults alongside piles of Marvel and DC editions. Just off the London Road is **GOOD:D** (11 James Morrison Street; tel: 0141-552 6777; daily 9.30am–5.30pm, Sun noon–5pm), which is full of quirky modern design pieces.

Above: the music shop Monorail is heaven for vinyl lovers.

Above: Nelson's Pillar (1806) was the first civic monument in Britain to commemorate the Admiral's victories.

ST ANDREW'S IN THE SQUARE

Returning north to London Road, along Charlotte Street, is Glickman's fabulous confectionery shop (est. 1903), a sweet-tooth's paradise. The tour continues towards Glasgow Cross and left into James Morrison Street and St Andrew's Square, which is home to **St Andrew's Parish Church** ❺ (now known as St Andrew's in the Square), the oldest church in the city after the Cathedral. It was modelled on St Martin-in-the-Fields in London, and its massive pillars and stone ornamentation illustrate the grand tastes of the 18th-century Tobacco Lords. It now stages musical and other cultural events, and houses the excellent Café Source (*see p.37*).

The south side of the square passes the district courts, where minor offenders are daily chastised, and, turning left and then right into Steel Street, the route leads to the Saltmarket. The pub on the facing corner, **The Old Ship Bank**, recalls the first Glasgow bank, set up in 1750 to meet the needs of the influential and rising merchant class. Going left down the Saltmarket, the new **High Court of Justiciary** extension is tucked into Jocelyn Square behind the old Mortuary. Further along is the old High Court, with its forbidding grey-pillared portico, which has seen the black cap donned for a procession of murderers. It fronted onto Jail Square, where the guilty were hanged before cheering crowds in the shadow of Nelson's Pillar, giving rise to the maternal Glaswegian warning to recalcitrant children: 'You'll die facing the monument.'

TOWARDS AND OVER THE CLYDE

Saltmarket runs down onto the **Albert Bridge**, or Hutchesontown Bridge, a cast-iron structure built in 1871 on enormous granite piers on the site of a crossing first created in 1794. Just upstream is the weir which marks the tidal limit of the river and

Above: St Andrew's in the Square has been restored to its 18th-century glory.

Above: inside the Citizens Theatre.

controls its natural vagaries. Over the bridge, appropriately at the river's junction with the sea, is what was the **Glasgow College of Nautical Studies**, which merged with the City of Glasgow College in 2010.

Turning right onto the south bank of the river at the start of the college, a tree-lined walkway leads to the peaceful colonnaded grounds of the **Central Mosque** ❻ (tel: 0141-429 3132; www.centralmosque.co.uk; daily 9am–5pm for visitors, booking essential; 24 hours for prayers), which in 1984 became the first purpose-built mosque in Scotland and is now one of the largest in Europe. Its green, multi-faceted dome and soaring minaret combine Islamic architecture with traditional Scottish sandstone. It provides the facilities of worship for 2,000 Muslims, a community whose numbers have increased dramatically in the 1980s and 1990s and who now play an integral part in city life.

The forbidding black-and-grey-marbled building on the other side of Gorbals Street is the **Sheriff Court** where solicitors gather to ply an ancient trade. It moved here when the old, smaller, city-centre court became unable to cope with the numbers that make it the busiest court in Europe.

Further south down Gorbals Street, across the junction with Ballater Street, is the **Citizens Theatre** ❼ (tel: 0141-429 0022; www.citz.co.uk), a cornerstone of Glasgow's artistic life and a major contributor to its ambition to be considered as a European city. The Citizen's Company was established in 1943 amid a row of Gorbals tenements, in a grand Victorian

ⓖ Clyde Walkway

This 40-mile (65km) -long path has been developed to link Glasgow with the Falls of Clyde at Lanark. Cyclists and walkers will particularly enjoy the Glasgow section between Victoria Bridge and the SECC, which passes the PS *Waverley* Terminal – home of the world's last sea-going paddle steamer – and the colossal 176ft (53m) -high Finnieston Crane, which once raised railway locomotives. There are a number of other long-distance paths that link up with the Clyde Walkway, including the Kelvin Walkway, the Glasgow to Inverness National Cycle Route, and paths to Edinburgh, Greenock and Irvine.

Above: see ongoing riverside development from the Clyde Walkway.

building originally called His Majesty's Theatre, which had been opened in 1878. Scottish playwright James Bridie drove the project as part of a plan to establish a Scottish national theatre. It drifted from drama into crisis until the arrival in 1969 of director Giles Havergal and his flamboyant designer Philip Prowse. Their ground-breaking productions – sometimes shocking and disturbing – attracted headlines and interest far beyond Glasgow and continue to fill the hall. The theatre houses a main auditorium and two small studio theatres which offer cutting-edge works.

Below: the Albert Bridge.

Above: Gothic-spired St Andrew's Cathedral is now dwarfed among the modern riverside buildings.

HEADING BACK NORTH OF THE CLYDE

Returning along Gorbals Street, the road comes to **Victoria Bridge**, where the city's first river crossing, a wooden structure commissioned by Bishop Rae in 1350, stood for 450 years. The present bridge is faced

Below: the Clutha Vaults pub is renowned for its live acoustic and folk music and is a real Glasgow institution.

with Dublin granite and affords excellent views down river past the Carlton Place Suspension Bridge to the Jamaica Street and Central Station bridges. The Gothic-spired building on the north bank is **St Andrew's Cathedral** (www.cathedralg1.org; daily 8.15am–5.45pm), the main Roman Catholic church, which is reflected in the modern glass-walled diocesan headquarters next door. The cathedral reopened in 2011 after a substantial renovation and includes a new baptismal font and a new artwork of St Andrew and the city's patron saint St Mungo. The glass pyramids rising above the rooftops behind it are the canopies of the St Enoch shopping centre.

Across the bridge on the north bank, two adjoining pubs, the **Clutha Vaults** and the **Scotch Corner** (both 11am–midnight), may look a tad scruffy from the outside but are a focus for the folk circuit. Above these pubs is the three-tiered spire of the old fish market, topped with a golden sailing ship. Nearby, the Scotia Bar at 112–114 Stockwell Street stages folk acts as well as poetry and literary events.

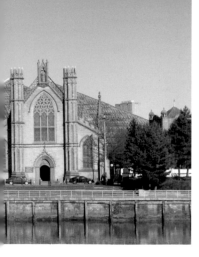

Under the railway bridge, on waste ground between St Margaret's Place and the new High Court buildings, is where **Paddy's Market** was held until May 2009. The defunct market had its origins, as the name suggests, in the floods of refugees from the Irish potato famine. Labelled a 'crime-ridden midden' by the council, the area is set to be transformed into a new cultural quarter to link up with the exciting new artsy venues and bars on the Trongate and Merchant City *(see p.40)*. Some residents have not taken too kindly to the attempt to gentrify the area, but most see the benefits of encouraging new initiatives to clean up and hopefully transform squalor into a bustling centre of arts and enterprise.

Turning left at the end of the Briggait, the **Saltmarket** – so named because the original market for salt for curing river salmon was here – curves back up to the High Street past restored tenements and busy shops.

A NEW CULTURAL QUARTER

Veering right into the Bridgegate, or Briggait, one of Glasgow's oldest streets, this tour passes second-hand shops, cheap restaurants and the expanse of the King Street car park.

ⓔ Eating Out

Café Source
1 St Andrew's Square; tel: 0141-548 6020; daily lunch and dinner.
Locally sourced ingredients go into the hearty fare served in the basement of St Andrew's in the Square. £

Maggie May's
60 Trongate; tel: 0141-548 1350; daily lunch and dinner.
Hidden in the back of the busy Maggie's Bar on the Trongate, this intimate place concentrates on traditional Scots fare with some imaginative additions. Standouts include cullen skink, a potato and smoked haddock soup, and crème brulée. £

Mono
12 King's Court, King Street; tel: 0141-553 2400; www.monocafebar.com; Sun–Thur noon–8pm, Fri–Sat noon–10pm; bar noon–midnight, noon–1am Fri–Sat.

A popular music and arts venue with a great record shop, Mono also squeezes in a café with a vegan menu. Top dishes include the falafel platter served with vegetables and hummous, and the Mono veggie burger. £

Above: Café Source offers a range of traditional and modern Scottish fare.

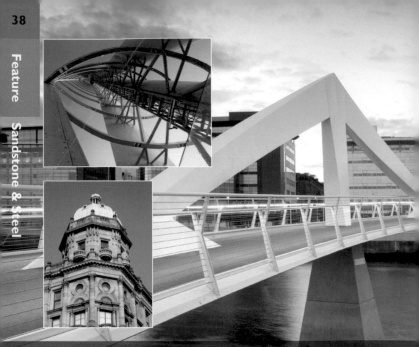

Sandstone & Steel

Roads, slum clearances, high-rise schemes and recession may have savaged the city in the past, but Glasgow's innovative spirit is reinvigorating the urban landscape

SOLID SANDSTONE SPIRIT

In Glasgow's city centre, grand drama and extravagance in sculpted stone predominates.

From the weathered 13th-century remnants found in the vicinity of Glasgow Cathedral and the 17th-century mercantile optimism around the Trongate, to the grandeur of the mansions of the Tobacco Lords in the Merchant City in the 18th century and the robust flowering of the Victorians in the British Empire's heyday, Glasgow developed into a city carved painstakingly from sandstone.

Although Charles Rennie Mackintosh *(see Tour 9)* and Alexander 'Greek' Thomson are foremost in the current view of Glasgow's architectural heritage, others such as William Young – who created the City Chambers as a monument to civic pride in 1888 – J.T. Rochead, J.J. Burnet and Charles Wilson all contributed mightily. Rochead's work in St Vincent Street sets the tone for the commercial centre, and his Grosvenor Hotel is a true Venetian marvel, Burnet's former TSB banking hall on the corner of Ingram Street and Glassford

small-scale confections like James Miller's miniature version of France's Azay-le-Rideau in the centre of St Enoch Square.

GLASS, STEEL AND THE FUTURE

Modern architecture in Glasgow is following a bold tradition. Atlantic Quay on the Clyde has waterfront grandeur, as does the Clyde Auditorium (dubbed the Armadillo for its distinctive shape) by Sir Norman Foster. The Glasgow Science Centre complex has titanium curves and a soaring viewing tower, called the Titan. The open-plan interior of the new BBC Scotland building on Pacific Quay is equally bold; so, too, is the Clyde Arc Bridge.

Other visionary projects include the striking Riverside Museum, designed by Zaha Hadid, with its wave-like 'pleated' aluminium shapes, and the new Glasgow School of Art Garnethill Estate redevelopment, opposite Mackintosh's architectural masterpiece is due for completion in 2013. In September 2009, Steven Holl Architects' (New York) light-filled design won a high-profile competition to build the GSA's new teaching and research centre.

Other recent projects have imaginatively adapted some of Glasgow's old sandstone architecture. To the innovative renovations at the Italian Centre, Tron Theatre and Princes Square can be added Trongate 103, a cutting-edge arts hub hewn out of an Edwardian warehouse. It's all part of Glasgow City Council's plan to regenerate this part of the Merchant City down to the River Clyde, and in doing so create an enlarged cultural quarter.

A great way to absorb Glasgow's architecture is on a guided tour. For information about Glasgow Architectural Walking Tours, including a visit to the GSA, check out www.glasgow architecture.co.uk.

Street outshines the bigger surroundings, while Wilson created an Italianate skyscape in the Park Circus area which is unequalled in Britain.

Huge enterprises like Robert Anderson's Central Hotel and the Edwardian mass of the Royal Technical College (now the University of Strathclyde) vie for attention amongst

Above: Tradeston Bridge in Atlantic Quay, nicknamed 'squiggly' because of its S-shaped design. **Top Left**: the Glasgow Tower, part of the Science Centre complex and the tallest tower in Scotland. **Centre Left**: classic Glaswegian sandstone architecture. **Left**: Charles Rennie Mackintosh.

Tour 3

Merchant City

From Trongate's vibrant arts centres, this half-day ¾-mile (1.2km) walk delves into the heart of the Merchant City's cool hangouts, conversions and enterprising institutions

The Merchant City fell into decline during the 1980s recession, leaving huge warehouses abandoned and businesses boarded up. Ambitious developments and stylish conversions, added to visionary arts projects such as the Tron Theatre and Trongate 103, have brought the area back to life. Expect an earthy mix of arty creativity and working-class wit.

While other cities have wrestled with inner-city problems, Glasgow perversely had an outer-city problem. Huge schemes – Drumchapel, Easterhouse, Castlemilk and Pollok, which were created after World War II to facilitate slum clearance – stand guard at each corner of the boundaries. In the late 1970s and early 1980s, Glasgow was tagged

Highlights

- Tron Theatre
- Trongate 103
- Old Fruitmarket
- Ramshorn Kirk and Cemetery
- City Halls
- Old Glasgow Sheriff Court
- Hutchesons' Hall
- Italian Centre
- Trades Hall

Doughnut City – plenty round the outside and nothing in the middle. The Merchant City was Glasgow's attempt to bring life back to the central warehouse district. The square-mile area is now home to a core of

Left: the Glasgow Jazz Festival is held at the Old Fruitmarket *(see p.42)*.
Above: the stylish Trongate 103.

pavement. This is **Tron-St Mary's**, a former church. Like the street, it's named after the weighing machine, or tron, introduced by the Bishop of Glasgow in 1491 to weigh and tax goods coming into the city. The church has been operating as the **Tron Theatre ❶** (tel: 0141-552 4267; www.tron.co.uk) since 1982, first as a club, and since 1990 as a full public venue. The Tron Theatre features a programme of both contemporary and traditional Scottish drama, and its restaurant – which offers cracking lunchtime and pre-theatre menus – is a popular meeting place.

Continuing westwards along the Trongate you come to the impressive **Trongate 103 ❷** (tel: 0141-276 8380; www.trongate103.com; Tue–Sat 10am–5pm, Sun noon–5pm), a massive Edwardian warehouse converted into an exciting arts centre, which opened in 2009. Beyond the cavernous contemporary atrium – imaginatively hewn out of the old handsome red-sandstone warehouse – are five floors of print studios, retail shops and galleries, where artists and the public can mingle and exchange ideas *(see box p.43)*.

young professionals and arty types. The blend of old and new architecture creates an exciting fusion which is echoed in the many restaurants serving up innovative cross-cultural food. Alongside exciting new arts developments including the Tron Theatre and Trongate 103 there's a wealth of pubs, clubs and independent shops. Keep your eyes peeled on partnership plans with Glasgow City Council for the Merchant City's next phase of arts-led regeneration, which is heading south of the Trongate, to create a cultural quarter down to the Clyde *(see p.39)*.

ALONG THE TRONGATE

Starting the route at the old heart of the city at **Mercat Cross** *(see p.14)*, go west along the Trongate. The tenements along each side date from the middle and end of the 19th century, and their rich facades funnel the street along to an almost Central European steeple whose base is an open arch across the busy

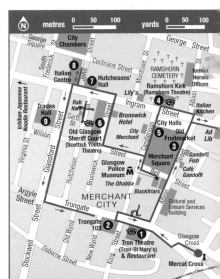

Above: exploring the Trongate, the old centre of the city.

UP ALBION STREET AND THE OLD FRUITMARKET

Crossing Trongate, head back eastwards then up Albion Street, past a magnificent red-sandstone bas-relief on the Cultural and Leisure Services building on the right, to the junction with Bell Street. This intersection has more pubs than the rest of both long streets put together. On the left, **Blackfriars** is large and lively, with a basement which hosts live music nights; **Café Gandolfi**, on the right, was one of the original Merchant City restaurants and contains the fantastical wood furniture of Tim Stead. **Gandolfi Fish**, an excellent seafood haunt, is just a few doors along. There are lots of lively pubs and restaurants which occupy various old buildings, including the **Old Fruitmarket ❸**.

The fruit market moved here from its former congested home in 1969 and now nestles, with the fish market, beside the M8 at Blochairn. The south end housed a successful general market for many years before closing to accommodate the new pubs. The north end, however, lay closed

for years, until enthusiasts from the performing arts section of the council realised that its cobbled streets and balconied offices, which used to ring to the iron wheels of carts and the shouts of traders, would make an ideal, New Orleans-style venue for the annual

Above: Café Gandolfi has been serving for 25 years and is known for its good food and stylish interior.

Above: the Old Fruitmarket packs lots of period charm under its vaulted roof.

Glasgow Jazz Festival. The extensively refurbished Old Fruitmarket is a much-loved performance space and hosts regular events and parties.

The building above the excellent **Italian Kitchen** pizzeria and café, where Albion Street crosses Ingram Street, housed the original Mitchell Library collection on two floors in 1877. Stephen Mitchell came from a tobacco family and left a huge estate to provide books 'on all subjects not immoral' for the edification of the city's working classes. His initiative was the impetus

Ⓕ Scots and International Arts at Trongate 103

Resident organisations at Trongate 103 include the Russian Cultural Centre and Café Cosachock, Glasgow Print Studio, Street Level Photoworks, Transmission Gallery, Glasgow Project Room and Project Ability. Don't miss a journey into the darkly magic world of wonders and nuances of the Sharmanka (Russian for hurdy gurdy) Kinetic Theatre. This atmospheric space chimes with the workings of Edward Bersudsky and Tatyana Jakovskaya's fantastical inventions: a mesmerising, gently unfolding whirl of mechanical finds, *objets trouvés* and sculptural inventions, accompanied by crackly old Eastern European music.

Above: artworks for perusal at the Glasgow Print Studio.

for the public library service; today, the
Mitchell Library *(see p.63)* is the largest
public reference library in Europe.

On the opposite corner, Greenwich
Village-style loft apartments are situated in a former Strathclyde University building. Further up Albion Street,
the four-storey black-glass office formerly housed *The Herald* newspaper, which prides itself on being the
world's oldest English-language daily.
The newspaper has moved to offices
in the city centre and the old offices
have been turned into flats.

INGRAM STREET AND
THE RAMSHORN

Looking right along Ingram Street,
the **Ad Lib** bar/diner (tel: 0141-
552 5736) on the right-hand side is
housed in a red-sandstone building
with a splendid coat of arms over the
entrance. This was the Central Fire
Station, built in 1899, and the home

of Wallace the Fire Dog, the mascot
who faithfully escorted the engines
on their dangerous missions. The
engine room used to contain a memorial to the 19 firemen who died in the
Cheapside Street whisky bond blaze
in 1960, an event which still scars the
memory of many families in the city.

As you turn left along Ingram Street,
the **Ramshorn Kirk** ❹ looms out
of a grove of unlikely urban elms. The
Gothic church with its square clock
tower is properly known as St David's
(Ramshorn) and was built in 1824 on
the Ramshorn estate. Thomas Rick-
man, a Birmingham architect, was
chosen to design the present building
upon the site of an 18th-century 'God
Box'-style church. Its alluring design is
based on a late 13th- and 14th-century
Gothic design. Those tall and narrow,
beautifully proportioned dimensions,
soaring stained-glass windows, and
substantial crypt show all the hallmarks

Left: lit up at night, the full impact
of the Ramshorn Kirk's Gothic
architecture can be felt.

S Retail Therapy

The Merchant City has swanky boutiques and foodie places aplenty. **Boudiche** (203 Ingram Street; tel: 0845-475 0250) stocks chic lingerie labels including Stella McCartney and Christian Lacroix. If it's jewellery you're after, head to **Brazen** (8 Albion Street; tel: 0141-552 4551) where you'll find unique pieces by independent designers and cool watches by Lip. If your tummy is rumbling, go to **Peckham's** (61–65 Glassford Street; tel: 0141-553 0666), a superb deli with a fine selection of cheeses, wines, beers and gourmet treats downstairs, plus a sleek ground-floor café and a cooking school upstairs (see p.119).

Above: Peckham's sells delicious delicatessen goodies.

of Gothic Revival Scots Style. It is built in handsome blond sandstone mined from a nearby quarry at Cowcaddens, and its tower – towards the front of the building – is 120ft (36m) high and houses a set of bells which have never been rung. The building is now used by the Strathclyde University Theatre Group, which stages an eclectic repertoire in the small performance space (see local press for details) and uses the crypt as rehearsal rooms. The intimate, atmospheric space is well worth visiting, especially for a performance.

The **Ramshorn Cemetery** is a verdant respite from street noise and a fascinating voice from the past. Many gravestones are so old as to be illegible, and some are still barred and spiked against the predations of grave robbers. Emile L'Angelier, arsenic victim of the infamous Madeleine Smith, is buried here, as is David Dale, philanthropic co-founder of New Lanark, and John 'Phosphorus' Anderson, the ebullient father of Strathclyde University. On the pavement outside,

worn by thousands of careless feet, are the initials RF and AF, marking the resting place of the Foulis brothers, a pair of enterprising and painstaking printers who perfected the craft for Glasgow University in the 18th century. Robert Foulis was also instrumental in establishing an Academy of Arts some 14 years before the Royal Academy in London.

CITY HALLS AND CANDLERIGGS

The Ramshorn stands sentinel at the head of Candleriggs, a street which takes its name from the noisome candleworks which initially operated well away from the main population. This is the heart of the Merchant City, with coffee houses and fashionable bars on the right and the substantially refurbished **City Halls** ⑤, where Dickens drew crowds for his readings and where every hue of political opinion has been heard, on the left. When the halls were built in 1841, they could accommodate an astonishing 3,500 people.

Above: the City Halls is a renowned concert venue.

The traditional shoebox-style auditorium is still renowned today throughout the world for its incredible acoustics. It's a busy hub for musicians which is well worth checking out: the Glasgow Centre for Music inside is a friendly organisation based here which has lots of information about upcoming concerts and public workshops. The BBC Scottish Symphony Orchestra is also based here; in addition, the auditorium hosts performances by the Scottish Chamber Orchestra. For all the latest about City Halls performances and affiliated venues nearby (the Old Fruitmarket, Glasgow Royal Concert Hall) pop in, call 0141-353 8080 or check out www.glasgowconcerthalls.com.

Further down on the left, the pavement outside the City Halls has some interesting marblework, created when the street cobbles were renewed and which reflects the area's age.

Below: Hutchesons' Hall has been at its present location on Ingram Street since 1806.

WILSON STREET

At the junction of Candleriggs and Bell Street, the **Glasgow Police Museum** (www.policemuseum.org. uk; summer Mon–Sat 10am–4.30pm, Sun noon–4.30pm, winter Tue and Sun, same hours; free) gives an insight into the history of Britain's first police force, as well as featuring exhibits on international policing.

Turning right from Candleriggs into Wilson Street, new flats mix with the imposing bulk of the old warehouse

The building is currently being used as the home of the Scottish Youth Theatre *(see box below)*, a retail complex and smart residential apartments.

Passing the **Brunswick Hotel** on the right, the flats at the corner of Brunswick Street and Ingram Street are a fine example of facade retention. The site was originally the warehouse premises of Campbell, Stewart & McDonald, and was one of the first in the Merchant City to tear out and replace the whole interior while keeping the architecturally important shell. The same thing is now happening with new district council buildings across the road.

district and smart design shops nestle below. Continuing right into Brunswick Street, a sandstone Victorian building with huge Ionic columns occupies the entire block. This was the **Old Glasgow Sheriff Court** ❻, which opened in 1892 and closed in 1984, having witnessed nearly a century of unmitigated villainy. It once housed a whipping table (now in Strathclyde Police's Black Museum in Pitt Street) and was said to be haunted by a lady in white.

HUTCHESONS' HALL

The white building on the opposite side of Ingram Street is **Hutchesons' Hall** ❼. Statues of George and Thomas Hutcheson, brothers from a landowning family, peer down from niches in the classical front.

On his death in 1639, Thomas Hutcheson made provision for a hospital for 12 'poore decrippet men'. George added more funds on his death two years later. The hospital was originally in the Trongate, and

ⓚ Scottish Youth Theatre

Established in 1976, the Scottish Youth Theatre (Old Sheriff Court, 105 Brunswick Street; tel: 0141-552 3988; www.scottish youththeatre.org) organises an eclectic programme of classes and performances dedicated to young people of all ages, up to 25 years old. Productions are staged in the Brian Cox Studio (named after the Dundonian star of Hollywood blockbusters *Rob Roy*, *Braveheart* and *The Bourne Supremacy*) and theatres around the country.

Above: inside the light-filled Scottish Youth Theatre.

moved to its present location in 1806 to a design by David Hamilton, with further reconstruction work by John Baird in 1876. The interior is quite simply stunning. It was acquired in 1982 by the National Trust for Scotland (www.nts.org.uk) whose renovations over the years have been scrupulous and sympathetic. The building is, once again, undergoing restoration and is currently closed to the public.

ITALIAN CENTRE AND TRADES HALL

Just past Hutchesons' Hall is the pedestrianised concourse of the **Italian Centre** ❽ in John Street. In this short stretch, on a sunny summer day, Glasgow can consider itself to be a European city. White-aproned waiters rush back and forth to tables of animated diners talking on their

Below: the Italian Centre, with its restaurants and cafés, feels like a continental European city in summer.

mobiles below the restaurants' canopies. A bronze of Mercury keeps an eye on the shoppers with their Armani and Versace bags, and the view up through the arches of the City Chambers (see p.51) is a symphony in stone. Shona Kinloch's humorous sculpture entitled Thinking of Bella and the Zen-calm slow flow of a water feature counterpoise the clamour for la moda italiana fripperies.

Leaving the Italian Centre, the squat domed building on the corner of Glassford Street houses a retail outlet. The building was designed by John Burnet and is a splendid example of late Victorian confidence. Slightly further down on the same side is the **Trades Hall** ❾ (tel: 0141-552 2418; Mon–Fri 9am–4pm, Sat 9am–noon; self-guided audio tours available), which is, apart from the Cathedral, the oldest building in the city which still fulfils its original function. It is the home of the 14 trades of Glasgow, which include hammermen, fleshers, bonnetmakers, weavers and barbers (who were the early surgeons). Their symbol – 14 arrows bound together – adorns the magnificent curving staircase which leads into the grand hall. The hall is lined with a magnificent mirrored silk frieze – the 3-D of its time – showing the trades about their business.

The Trades Hall is also the home of the Trades House, whose business these days is mainly philanthropic – it dispenses more than £1 million a year in charity. It is worth a visit, especially for the benches carved by Belgian refugees in the entranceway, the Adam plasterwork and wood ceilings, and the kists, or chests, which are opened only once a year and contain a time capsule of trinkets dating back to 1604.

Return to Glasgow Cross by following Glassford Street south and turning right into Trongate.

Above: the Trades Hall offers a fascinating look at the 14 traditional city trades.

E Eating Out

Café Gandolfi
64 Albion Street; tel: 0141-552 6813; www.cafegandolfi.com; daily all day.
A stylish, light-filled bar-restaurant with beautiful wood furniture serving simply prepared dishes like linguine with crab, cherry tomatoes, coriander and chicken. Neighbouring Gandolfi Fish is its sleeker cousin. £

City Merchant
97–99 Candleriggs; tel: 0141-553 1577; www.citymerchant.co.uk; Mon–Sat lunch and dinner.
Quality modern Scottish cuisine specialising in meat and seafood. Try the superb Loch Etive oysters and mussels. ££

The Dhabba
44 Candleriggs; tel: 0141-553 1249; www.thedhabba.com; daily lunch and dinner.
Superb North Indian cooking; their speciality is dum pukht, curry cooked in a special dish that seals in the juices. Dishes such as tiger prawns from the clay tandoori oven are also recommended. ££

Ichiban Japanese Noodle Restaurant
50 Queen Street; tel: 0141-204 4200; www.ichiban.co.uk; Mon–Thur noon–10pm, Fri–Sat noon–11pm, Sun 1–10pm.
Minimalist, with steaming bowls of noodles served at long benches. £

Lily's
103 Ingram Street; tel: 0141-552 8788; Mon–Sat lunch only.
This great little café has veggie options and caters for kids. Alongside burgers and baked potatoes there are Eastern tastes including spicy chilli and vegetable Thai wraps. £

Rab Ha's
83 Hutcheson Street, Merchant City; tel: 0141-572 0400; www.rabhas.com; Thur–Sat dinner only.
This cosy restaurant offers seafood and meat classics. £

Tron Theatre Restaurant
63 Trongate; tel: 0141-552 8587; www.tron.co.uk; Sun–Mon lunch only, Tue–Sat lunch and dinner.
Serves no-nonsense British dishes using locally sourced ingredients. Great pre-theatre meal deals. £

Tour 4

City Centre

This 1-mile (1.6km) tour takes you from the sumptuous George Square and merchants' powerhouses to the shops of Buchanan Street, stopping to visit the Gallery of Modern Art

This half-day walk starts amid the bustle around Queen Street Station and the grand expanse of George Square, which contains the lavish City Chambers and the main tourist information office. Keep your wits about you amid the workaday melee as you will find your eyes are constantly drawn upwards to scan the wealth of mighty stonework built by Glasgow's old governmental and mercantile powerhouses.

Between visits to old bank building conversions and the experience of being swamped by the Buchanan Street shopping crowds, take a breather in the popular Gallery of Modern Art and enjoy the light-filled environs of one of the many swanky Princes Square top-floor eateries.

Highlights

- George Square
- City Chambers
- Glasgow Tourist Office
- Gallery of Modern Art (GoMA)
- Stock Exchange Building
- Buchanan Street and Princes Square Shopping
- Merchants' House

QUEEN STREET STATION AND CITY CHAMBERS

Queen Street Station, the starting point of this tour, runs frequent train services to Edinburgh, Dundee and all points north, as well as a suburban service from the Clyde coast to Lanarkshire. Built on the site of a

Left: Buchanan Street is always busy with shoppers. **Above:** George Square is a popular meeting place.

witnessed momentous events in the square below, including the raising of the hammer and sickle by the Glasgow Soviet in 1919.

The interiors are a riot of marble, mosaic and alabaster. The vaulted ceiling of the entrance hall alone is covered with one and a half million Venetian mosaic tiles. Linger in the entrance hall, where tours begin and excited local schoolchildren often linger to admire the Chambers mosaic coat of arms on the floor, with arms that reflect legends about Glasgow's patron saint, St Mungo. There are four emblems: the bird, tree, bell and fish, as remembered in the following verse:

Here's the Bird that never flew
Here's the Tree that never grew
Here's the Bell that never rang
Here's the Fish that never swam

quarry in 1842 with a daring curved glass roof, it is Glasgow's oldest station. Beside it, **George Square ❶** began as a muddy hollow in 1781 and developed into a civic meeting place over two centuries. Its beautiful lawns have been replaced with red tarmac, much to the chagrin of office workers who used to sunbathe there at the first blink of sunshine.

The **Millennium Hotel** to the right of the station as you face it was, naturally, a railway hotel, and the BR initials can still be seen above the doorway.

The next office block on the left is best sped past in order to come to the **City Chambers ❷** (Ground Floor only, Mon–Fri 8.30am–5pm; guided tours of whole building, Mon–Fri 10.30am and 2.30pm; free), the towering statement of Glasgow's Victorian confidence, based on the east side of the square. It was opened in 1888 and, according to the architect, was a 'free treatment of the Italian Renaissance'. The ornate front has

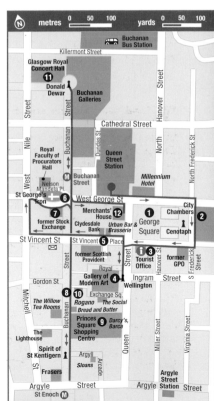

🅕 Glasgow Hotel Stories

It was at a Millennium Hotel (see p.51) dinner in 1941 that Roosevelt's World War II envoy Harry Hopkins pledged American support to Britain against Hitler with the biblical reply: 'Whither thou goest, I will go; and where thou lodgest, I will lodge; thy people shall be my people, and thy God my God.' Winston Churchill, who also had a Central Hotel suite during World War II, nearly choked on his cigar. A Glasgow myth goes that Roy Rogers also had a suite in those grand Central Station lodgings, and rode his horse Trigger up and down the main staircase.

Above: the American envoy – and eloquent speaker – Harry Hopkins.

Granite and marble staircases lead like Escher paintings to the council chambers where the Lord Provost (the Scottish equivalent of Mayor) presides over the city's affairs. There are seats for all 79 councillors, all facing the Lord Provost, his Depute, and the Chief Executive, who are seated behind the mace. If you are interested in visiting while the council is in session you can book a place in the public gallery which looks down on the proceedings, or take a pew in the small press gallery, from which much of the lively banter emanates during debate. Civic functions are regularly held in the great Banqueting Hall, under murals painted by 'Glasgow Boys' Henry, Lavery and Roche, which portray the city's colourful history.

GLASGOW TOURIST OFFICE

Below: the Cenotaph in front of the City Chambers.

Passing the white, lion-flanked monolith of the **Cenotaph**, the south side of the square begins with the former General Post Office, which has been redeveloped as offices and luxury flats. Across Hanover Street, the middle office on the block is that of the **Glasgow Tourist Office** ❸ (tel: 0141-204 4400; www.seeglasgow. com; May–June and Sept Mon–Sat 9am–7pm, Sun 10am–6pm, July–Aug Mon–Sat 9am–8pm, Sun 10am–6pm, Apr–Oct Mon–Sat 9am–6pm).

It's a grand space for learning all about the city, although queues to gain information can be very long and service can seem a tad slow. If you are

Above: the much-decorated statue of Wellington outside the GoMA.

really desperate, the tourist office can book accommodation on your behalf but it's not the best service and many leading hotels prefer to deal independently of VisitScotland, which gives you a clue as to the efficacy of the operation. It's a great place to pick up leaflets and maps though, and to find information about travelling around all of Scotland. A small shop next to the information desk also sells specialist guide books, Ordnance Survey maps for outdoor enthusiasts and an entertaining selection of kitsch souvenirs.

GALLERY OF MODERN ART

Turning left down Queen Street, past bars and fast-food restaurants, the great pillared hall on the right in Royal Exchange Square is the **Gallery of Modern Art ❹** (GoMA; tel: 0141-287 3050; www.glasgowlife.org.uk; Mon–Wed and Sat 10am–5pm, Thur 10am–8pm, Fri and Sun 11am–5pm; free). Guarded by a statue of Wellington by Baron Marocchetti (which revellers grace most Friday and Saturday nights with a traffic cone), the gallery was previously the Stirling Library. It grew out of a house owned by tobacco baron William Cunningham of Lainshaw, and the huge Corinthian columns at the front and the hall at the rear were added later.

Above: a striking view of the roof of the Gallery of Modern Art.

GoMA opened in 1996 to a welter of controversy about its collection. Many critics damned it for populism, but the citizens voted with their feet, and attendance continues to exceed expectations. It is divided into four galleries and there is a great café in the basement by the Martyr's Library. The cavernous ground-floor space retains its columns and original classical features, lending itself to bold pieces like Jim Lambie's eye-popping geometric floor of 2008, entitled *Forever Changes*. The upper galleries use natural light wonderfully, and concentrate on group shows which often tackle challenging themes.

In 2009, the exhibition *shOUT* caused a furore in the right-wing press and even stirred up condemnation from the Vatican. The show focused on gay, lesbian, transgender and intersex life – with explicit images created by the likes of Nan Goldin, David Hockney and Robert Mapplethorpe. One exhibit, *Made in God's Image*, in which visitors were invited to add comments to the pages of a Bible, attracted 600 complaints.

Above: St George's Tron on West George Street.

ST VINCENT PLACE

Returning up Queen Street and turning left, **St Vincent Place** ❺ opens up an august street of banks and offices faced with the full repertoire of Victorian masonry. The Clydesdale Bank on the north side has bas-reliefs, crouching men and encircled emblems

---

Ⓕ Handsome Pubs

Some of Glasgow's gorgeous, solid buildings are now devoted to the Glaswegian passion for having a blether over a drink. **The Counting House** (tel: 0141-225 0160) on the corner of George Square has been converted into a pub and restaurant with splendid interior statuary, cornicing and glass dome above the bar; **The Auctioneers** (tel: 0141-229 5851) in North Court is also a pub and restaurant furbished with the kind of bric-a-brac which used to pass through McTear's showrooms; and **78 St Vincent** (tel: 0141-248 7878) is beautifully lit by the vaulting windows of a former bank, and has an interior reminiscent of Le Chartier restaurant in Paris.

Above: the stunning interior of The Counting House pub.

Above: elegant buildings on St Vincent Place show off the Victorian stonemasonry that characterises much of the architecture in this district.

of the towns where the bank has had a presence. Opposite, the former Scottish Provident Building's red sandstone reaches skyward.

ST GEORGE'S TRON AND GLASGOW STOCK EXCHANGE

Passing a variety of city shops on the left, the tour turns right into West Nile Street and right again into West George Street. The church in the centre of the road is **St George's Tron** ❻, built in 1807 to accommodate the westward movement of the city. It was designed by William Stark, who was also responsible for a jail on Glasgow Green and a lunatic asylum. The Tron has a long tradition of being at the evangelical wing of the Church of Scotland: Tom Allan was a key figure in the Scottish evangelical movement of the mid-20th century, and if you pop in today you are sure to be greeted by an enthusiastic minister.

On the north side of the square, Nelson Mandela Place, is the former

Right: the red sandstone former Scottish Provident Building.

Old Athenaeum which, on opening in 1888, offered classes in science, philosophy and literature to more than 1,000 students. It now houses shops and restaurants. Tucked into the corner is the Royal Faculty of Procurators Hall, with the heads of law lords carved on the window arches. On

the other side of the square is the early French Gothic extravagance of the former **Glasgow Stock Exchange ❼** building, which brings to mind the London Law Courts and is a rather rare flight of fancy amid the solidity of its surroundings. It, too, now houses shops.

BUCHANAN STREET

The wide avenue of **Buchanan Street ❽**, the city's most prestigious shopping arena, stretches southward. It starts at Argyle Street, with Frasers on its domed corner site, and leads up a Victorian canyon fronted by designer names. In the pedestrianised centre is the winged *Spirit of St Kentigern* statue, and buskers, from lone evangelists to full string quartets, provide daily entertainment.

Shopping
Further along on the right is the **Argyll Arcade**, an enclosed walkway lined with jewellers' shops, which right-angles back to Argyle Street. Nearby is the entrance to **Princes Square ❾**, a beautiful mall packed with trendy boutiques and bars on several levels. It is best entered via the central escalator, past the *trompe l'oeil* paintings of worthies like Sir Thomas Lipton, Keir Hardie and John Logie Baird.

On the top floor, while looking down at the mosaic of the central well, you will not fail to notice the huge **Foucault's Pendulum**, a replica of the device by which Jean-Bernard-Léon Foucault proved the rotation of the Earth in the dome of the Pantheon in Paris in 1851. The centre is a

Above: the ornate Glasgow Stock Exchange building.

veritable shopaholic's dream, with the presence of top names in fashion such as Vivienne Westwood, as well as upmarket high-street chains like Ted Baker, while the top floor has a range of cafés, bars and restaurants including the stylish Darcy's, Barca Tapas and Cava Bar, November and Cranachan.

It's a wonderful building to visit and especially welcome during a rainy spell of Glasgow weather – not uncommon of course – as the twinkly lights, inviting shops and top-floor cafés provide a cheery diversion before braving the elements again.

Galleries and Royal Concert Hall

Back on Buchanan Street, the shopping choice is wide, from chic labels and brands like Hugo Boss, L'Occitane and Apple. Weary shoppers can stop at the Mackintosh **Willow Tea Rooms** (see Eating Out p.99), which is a replica based on the many remnants of the architect's original restaurant

Left and Below: out and about on Buchanan Street.

Above: the Willow Tea Rooms (*see pp.57 & 99*) re-create the designs by Charles Rennie Mackintosh for a restaurant at the turn of the century.

designs owned by the City Council, or **Rogano** ⑩, a splendid Art Deco shellfish restaurant in the passageway leading to Royal Exchange Square.

Past Graham Tiso, Hobbs and The White Company and back across St Vincent Street to the Stock Exchange, the view northwards takes in the

Buchanan Galleries, an enormous shopping complex development which encompasses several city blocks and a pedestrianised area at the **Glasgow Royal Concert Hall** ⑪ (tel: 0141-353 8000; www.glasgowconcerthalls. com), the main venue for classical concerts. The centrepiece here is a statue of the late Donald Dewar, credited as the driving force behind the new Scottish Parliament.

MERCHANTS' HOUSE

Returning along West George Street to George Square, the oriel-windowed **Merchants' House** ⑫ (tel: 0141-221 8272; Mon–Thur 9am–12.30pm, subject to functions) reflects the confidence and self-importance of the guilds which created it. Housing the Chamber of Commerce, which is the second-oldest in the world after that of New York, it hosts occasional concerts (see local press for details).

The original Merchants' Hall, constructed around 1600, acted as a

Left: Rogano is an Art Deco *tour de force* and a memorably decadent dining experience.

meeting place for merchants and as an almshouse for merchants and their families who had fallen on hard times. The Hall was rebuilt in the 1650s to a design by Sir William Bruce of Kinross, who would later be architect to King Charles II. The old layout consisted of ground-floor lodgings for old couples and facilities for pensioners. The imposing present-day building was opened in 1877 according to a design by John Burnet; his son added two storeys in 1908. The Merchants' House of Glasgow bought part of the estate of Wester Craigs in 1650, and funded the landscaping of the city's grand Necropolis in the 1830s (see p.22).

Above: the dome of the Merchants' House is topped by a sailing ship.

E Eating Out

Barca
Level 2, Princes Square; tel: 0141-248 6555; daily noon–midnight.
Wonderful traditional Spanish tapas such as prawns in chilli sauce and chorizo sausage or a full paella of meat or fish (two people sharing), as well as a cava bar just for drinks. £

Bread and Butter
74 Buchanan Street; tel: 0141-221 4383; www.breadandbutterglasgow. co.uk; daily lunch (Sat until 6pm).
Located down a side alley, this café-bar with a club downstairs serves up great-value British grub including hearty pies. £

Darcy's
The Courtyard, Princes Square; tel: 0845-166 6012; Mon–Sat lunch and dinner, Sun lunch only.
For some café-style panache in the Princes Square shopping centre, book a red-leather booth at this basement joint. As well as decent coffee, the varied menu includes Scots Angus burgers and Thai green chilli. ££

Rogano
11 Exchange Place; tel: 0141-248 4055; www.roganoglasgow.com; daily lunch and dinner.

Glasgow's homage to the days of ocean liners and cocktails exudes 1930s glamour. Top-class service and the place for oysters. Dress up. £££

Sloans
62 Argyll Arcade, 108 Argyle Street; tel: 0141-221 8886; www.sloans glasgow.com; daily lunch and dinner.
An Edwardian-style pub-restaurant with Grade A-listed interiors including a grand ballroom and a cosy, snug bar. Serves simple British cuisine. £

The Social
27 Royal Exchange Square; tel: 0845-166 6016; daily lunch and dinner.
A swanky bar full of suits by day and dressed-up Glaswegians by night with a brasserie menu that includes pasta dishes, juicy steaks and veggie-friendly wraps. There is also a decent brunch menu at weekends. £

Urban Bar & Brasserie
23–25 St Vincent Place; tel: 0141-248 5636; www.urbanbrasserie.co.uk; daily lunch and dinner.
This stylish bar-restaurant, housed in the former Bank of England HQ, has a monthly brasserie menu with excellent fish and meat creations. Perennial favourite is the fish soup. ££

Tour 5

Going West

This 1¼-mile (2km) walk follows architecturally fascinating St Vincent Street to the historic Mitchell Library, then on to the cutting-edge CCA arts centre – all in half a day

The city has been moving west since medieval times, and, since the more prosperous were the first to decamp, the buildings become noticeably more ornate. Starting the route at the junction of Hope Street and St Vincent Street, the Victorian offices spiral upwards in ever more detailed flights of the stonemason's fancy. Looking south, the clock tower of the Central Hotel looms above Central Station, the main link to the south, in an austere welcome.

UP AND DOWN ST VINCENT STREET

St Vincent Street, named after the naval battle at Cabo de São Vicente, is a thoroughfare devoted to Mammon, so it is fitting that its long incline is

Highlights

- St Vincent Street Free Church of Scotland
- The King's Theatre
- Mitchell Library
- Tenement House
- CCA: Centre for Contemporary Arts

crowned with one of Scotland's finest temples to God. On the way up the hill, there's a beguiling mix of imposing classical, Art Nouveau, Art Deco and modernist buildings including: the old **Phoenix Assurance building** (1913) in American Classical style at No. 78, the eccentric **Hatrack** (1902) with its rich red sandstone, stained glass and spiky lead roof at No. 142–144, and the elegant 1929-built Royal **Sun Alliance Building** at No. 200, with its angular Art Deco statue added in the 1930s.

St Vincent Street Free Church of Scotland ❶ is the best remaining example of the work of Alexander 'Greek' Thomson (1817–75). Thomson, paradoxically, is famous for being Glasgow's 'forgotten architect', forever in the shadow of Charles Rennie Mackintosh (see p.97). Like Mackintosh, he wanted to design every detail of a commission, down to the decorations on the walls. This is the only one of his three city churches still intact, and it has been added to the World Monument Watch for endangered buildings. Light from enormous windows bathes the sumptuous interior, and a recently repaired tower, which recalls India rather than Greece, dominates Blythswood Hill.

On the right, slightly further down the hill, the needle spire of **St Columba's Gaelic Church** soars heavenwards. It has its roots in the influx of

Left: steep St Vincent Street. **Above**: Alexander Thomson's St Vincent Street Free Church of Scotland.

Highlanders who flocked to the city in the 18th and 19th centuries after the Clearances, when landlords evicted crofters to make way for sheep.

The western end of St Vincent Street is enveloped by the roar of the

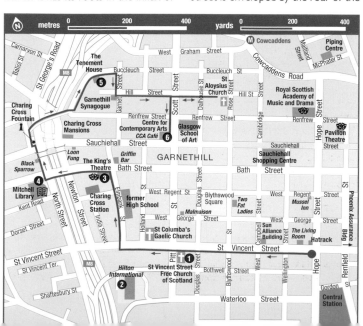

traffic on the M8, which cuts through an underpass on its way to Edinburgh. The marble and mirrored glass tower on the left is the **Hilton International** ❷, a once state-of-the-art hotel (built in 1990) which is looking a bit tired inside and out these days.

TOWARDS MITCHELL LIBRARY

Turning right into Elmbank Street, the white building on the right is the former **High School**, with statues of Galileo, Cicero, Homer and James Watt. The school dates back to the 15th century, but it has gradually moved west from its original home and is now situated in more space in Anniesland. Today, the buildings are occupied by council offices. On the corner of Elmbank Crescent, the ornate grey-stone building provides rehearsal rooms for Scottish Opera and Scottish Ballet, two of Scotland's most prestigious companies. It used to be the home of the Institute of Shipbuilders and Engineers, and a

bronze plaque just inside the entrance pays tribute to the engineers who went down at their posts on the *Titanic* in 1912.

The King's Theatre ❸ (tel: 0844-871 7648), on the corner of Elmbank Street and Bath Street, was the most fashionable Glasgow venue of the Edwardian age. Built in 1904, with a lion mascot in stone above the entrance, it provides a stage for a variety of shows, catering for most ages and tastes. Expect lots of West End-style musicals – such as *Chicago* and *Blood Brothers* – stand-up comedy shows from the likes of Frankie Boyle and Dave Gorman, and the odd ballet production or popular musical extravaganza chucked in for good measure. The **Griffin Bar** opposite the theatre dates from the same period. Known as The King's Arms up until 1969, the refurbished (2008) Griffin is a 'B' listed building with original wooden interiors, window panels and lead work. It's worth popping your head in and ordering a pint and a sneaky

Below: the Mitchell Library is the largest of its kind in Europe.

K Childhood Life in the Auld Tenements

A tour around the 1892-built Tenement House *(see p.64)* makes for
a thought-provoking and fun visit
for adults and kids alike. It's not
often you can hear the tick-tock of
the grandfather clock while poring
over old labels and utensils around
the basic kitchen range. Eyes and
minds wander through the assorted
contents – old jam jars, food tins and
household bills – and back in time to
a much simpler cramped existence.

Above: the Tenement House reveals
Glaswegian life in years gone by.

wee dram to take a closer gander at
the main bar, with its handsome tiled
floor and back-to-back rows of fixed
leather seats.

Mitchell Library

Heading left down Bath Street through
a canyon of modern offices, the splendid dome of the **Mitchell Library** ❹
(www.glasgowlife.org.uk; Mon–Thur
9am–8pm, Fri–Sat 9am–5pm, closed
Sun), adorned with its statue of Min-
erva, rises above the motorway traffic. It was the legacy of tobacco heir
Stephen Mitchell, and, after homes in
Ingram Street and Miller Street, the
collection moved to the present site
in 1911. It is now the biggest public
reference library in Europe, and its
comprehensive Glasgow Room is a
boon and a blessing to those with an
interest in the city. Take a peek inside
and the friendly janitor will direct you
along the handsome marble and dark-
wood lined corridors. There's a good
little café next to the modern IT suite
amid miles of crazy, lurid geometric
carpet and books.

The Mitchell Library has fabulous,
free resources for those looking to
research family history or anyone just
curious about the city's past. Level
3 and the Family History Section is

manned by knowledgeable staff who
help people from all over the world
delve into records such as the Glasgow newspaper archive (starting in
1715), censuses, war deaths, parish
registers and monumental inscriptions.
Leaf through the trade directories to
discover intriguing old professionals
like the phrenologist who studied the
skull's lumps and bumps to determine
personality traits.

Below: the ornate King's Theatre
stages a wide range of productions.

Above: the red sandstone grandeur of Charing Cross Mansions.

BACK EAST TO TENEMENT HOUSE

Up North Street past the excellent **Black Sparrow** pub *(see Eating Out, opposite)* and across Sauchiehall Street, the ornate fountain at Charing Cross may not have the cachet of Pisa, but the drunken angle at which it leans is every bit as dramatic. Walking north, head for the pedestrian bridge which spans the motorway. A

Below: the CCA is known for staging an eclectic programme.

pause here affords a close-up look at the graceful red-sandstone curve of Charing Cross Mansions and, on the left, the turrets, arched windows and balconies of St George's Mansions, both testament to the graciousness into which tenement living evolved.

It pays to keep this Edwardian splendour in mind on the walk from the end of the bridge on the path up through grass and trees to the **Tenement House** ❺ (www.nts.org.uk; Mar–Oct daily 1–5pm, last admissions 4.30pm; charge). It lies at the end of the walkway at 145 Buccleuch Street and is fascinating because it offers a glimpse of tenement life. It was the home for 50 years of a spinster who changed nothing in her 'wally close' (tiled common stairway). The gaslit parlour, black range and rosewood piano are, as the National Trust for Scotland which now runs it says, 'a sure sign of gentility'.

Returning along Buccleuch Street, turn right into Garnet Street and then left into Hill Street: this was for many years the heart of the ethnic Chinese community. On the other side, Italy is recalled by the domed grandeur of **St Aloysius Church**, which is attached to the Jesuit school further up the street.

Above: Charing Cross Mansions detail.

CCA – CENTRE FOR CONTEMPORARY ARTS

Turn left down Scott Street to hit Sauchiehall Street, renowned for its vibrant nightlife, music venues and bars. At No. 350 stands the superb **Centre for Contemporary Arts ❻** (CCA; tel: 0141-352 4900; www.cca-glasgow. com; gallery Mon–Sat 10am–6pm; free), which has six exhibitions a year and mounts an eclectic programme. Alongside the changing visual arts exhibitions there are interactive performance-based art workshops, cinema screenings (lots of independent films, shorts, documentaries and classics) and a superb programme of musical events, ranging from improvised soundscapes to traditional Gaelic nights and dancey DJ sets. Visiting performers and artists from all over the world mean you never know what strange delights might be on the bill. The glass-roofed courtyard café is a wonderful space and the Saramago Café Bar has a stylish terrace with some of Glasgow's best weekend music events.

Ⓔ Eating Out

Black Sparrow
241 North Street; tel: 0141-221 5530; www.theblacksparrow.co.uk; daily noon–9pm.
Stylish bar with decent food menu that includes mains such as mustard-crusted salmon and pork belly in cider batter. Also serves up a selection of burgers and pizzas. £

CCA Café
30 Sauchiehall Street; tel: 0141-352 4920; Mon–Sat 10am–10pm.
A vegetarian venue offering a variety of mezze dishes, salads and mains such as courgette and lemon linguine, served in a wonderfully airy enclosed courtyard. £

The Living Room
150 St Vincent Street; tel: 0141-229 0607; daily lunch and dinner.
Cocktail-style glitz, popular with an after-work crowd. Live music is played on the baby grand piano most evenings. ££

Loon Fung
417 Sauchiehall Street; tel: 0141-332 1240; daily lunch and dinner.
Long-established but still admirable Cantonese cuisine, much frequented by the Chinese community. £

Malmaison Brasserie
Malmaison Hotel, 273 West George Street; tel: 0141-572 1000; daily lunch and dinner.
The restaurant in this smart hotel chain serves brasserie classics with high-end presentation. The grill offers a variety of steaks as well as lobster and there's curry made with Scottish mutton. £

Mussel Inn
157 Hope Street; tel: 0843-289 2283; www.mussel-inn.com; daily lunch and dinner.
Features the best of west coast seafood – oysters, scallops, prawns and, of course, mussels. ££

Two Fat Ladies
118a Blythswood Street; tel: 0141-847 0088; www.twofatladiesrestaurant.com; daily lunch and dinner.
An elegant dining room – usually packed – serving seafood creations such as seared scallops, sea bream and ling, plus enticing desserts. ££

D.I.Y. Glasgow

Glasgow's music and arts scenes have a D.I.Y. spirit at their heart and, for many, the city's rough-hewn edge makes a refreshing change from London, Paris, New York and Venice

The flux of Glasgow's riverside post-industrial landscape – all old decrepit warehouses rubbing alongside sleek, contemporary architecture – seems to flow into the city's creative population. Likewise its indie music labels eschew the corporate and bland, creating a vibrant scene with lots of great bands and venues.

AN ART LEGACY

The swinging doors of the Charles Rennie Mackintosh-designed **Glasgow School of Art** (GSA) building continue to whir with the comings and goings of students and artists. It was the home

of the influential *fin-de-siècle* Glasgow Group of modern artists – which included Charles Rennie Mackintosh – and also boasts celebrated alumni such as Alisdair Gray, Ian Hamilton Finlay, and contemporary artists Jim Lambie, Roddy Buchanan and Simon Starling.

Glasgow's D.I.Y. spirit flourished in the late 1970s and early 1980s, when the city was deep in recession and blighted by sectarian violence. New Glasgow Boys and Girls took over warehouse spaces and set up gallery collectives, the most influential being **Transmission** in 1983 (www.trans

continues. The GSA is building a new teaching and research centre. Studio collectives are renovating warehouses and government-led partnerships continue to regenerate the Merchant City by creating a cultural quarter.

A THRIVING MUSIC SCENE

Glasgow's music scene was born out of bedroom obsession with exotic sounds. In 1979, the D.I.Y. punk ethos of Postcard Records squeezed Orange Juice and Edwyn Collins from bedroom to Top of the Pops. The city's Gaelic roots, flirtation with Country and popular Americana can be heard in the uplifting Motown beats and West Coast jangly pop of many Glasgow bands. Teenage Fan Club recast the sunshine harmonies of the Byrds and Big Star in late 1980s Glasgow. Some have an art-school sensibility, like Franz Ferdinand, while Electronica DJ duo Slam mined Teutonic beats and Detroit techno music, founding Soma Quality Recordings in 1991.

A good place to start is the independent record shop-café-venue **Monorail** (www.monocafebar.com), part owned by Pastels front man Stephen McRobbie. It stages film nights, gigs and other cultural events, including the odd appearance by artist David Shrigley.

missiongallery.org). By 1996 contemporary art was part of the mainstream and Glasgow got itself a grand building to showcase its artists: the **Gallery of Modern Art (GoMA)**. Arts hubs **CCA** (Centre for Contemporary Arts), **Tramway** and **Trongate 103** followed.

Both the **Glasgow Art Fair** and **Glasgow International Festival** – the city's answer to the Venice Biennale – attract an international crowd. The impetus

Alongside big venues like the **Scottish Exhibition and Conference Centre** (SECC; *see p.10*), there are many intimate venues and bars where Glasvegas, The Fratellis and Camera Obscura regularly appear. Top names include the legendary **Barrowland Ballroom** (www.glasgow-barrowland.com/ballroom). **O2ABC** (www.o2abcglasgow.com) and **King Tut's Wah Wah Hut** (www.kingtuts.co.uk) host established indie bands. **Nice N' Sleazy** (www.nicensleazy.com) and **Stereo** (www.stereocafebar.com) showcase up-and-coming acts. **Òran Mór** and **Captain's Rest** on the Great Western Road, West End, are also on the music map.

Above: a work by Jim Lambie at GoMA. **Top Left**: the band Glasvegas at Nice N' Sleazy. **Centre Left**: a work by David Shrigley. **Left**: the Glasgow School of Art is key to this scene.

Tour 6

From Kelvingrove to the Clyde

This half-day, 2.5-mile (4km) stroll around the green surroundings of Kelvingrove Art Gallery and Museum leads to museums and landmarks on the Clyde waterfront

This walk is a welcome escape from the noisy M8 and is a journey to the heart of Glasgow's Victorian achievements as part of the British Empire. Calm prevails along curving streets lined with handsome Victorian sandstone terraced houses, and the twisting paths around leafy Kelvingrove Park lead to the impressive Kelvingrove Art Gallery and Museum. Then it's all modern achievement with the new architectural highlights of 21st-century Glasgow.

Highlights

- Lobey Dosser
- Kelvingrove Park
- Kelvingrove Art Gallery and Museum
- Riverside Museum
- Glasgow Science Centre

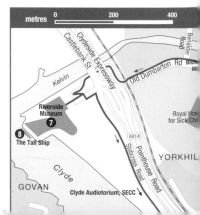

Left: an exhibit at the Kelvingrove Art Gallery and Museum. **Above:** the beloved statue of Lobey Dosser.

LOBEY DOSSER AND PARK CIRCUS

Glasgow is peppered with bronze memorials commemorating the cream of Queen Victoria's empire, but the statue that holds the fondest place in the hearts of Glaswegians is of a mustachioed sheriff astride a two-legged horse. It is to be found at the start of this walk on the corner of Woodlands Road, which runs west from Charing Cross and Park Drive.

Lobey Dosser ❶, as the statue is called, was the creation of newspaper

The West End has an interesting array of independent shops, most of which are just north and west of this route on Byres Road and Great Western Road. Among the foodie places near the start of this walk is **Grassroots Organic** (20 Woodlands Road; tel: 0141-353 3278; Mon–Wed 8am–6pm, Thur–Fri 8am–7pm, Sat 9am–6pm, Sun 11am–5pm), an organic wholefood market with lots of healthy takeaway options including pasta dishes, burritos and salads. **Damselfly Crafts** at 380 Great Western Road (tel: 0141-341 0119; Mon–Sat 9.30am–5.30pm, Sun noon–5pm) is a colourful craft shop with lots of gift ideas. Nearby **Galletly & Tubbs** (431 Great Western Road; tel: 0141-357 1001; Mon–Sat 9.30am–5.30pm, Sun noon–5pm) stocks elegant home furnishings and artworks.

Above: Grassroots Organic sells a selection of tasty wholefood treats.

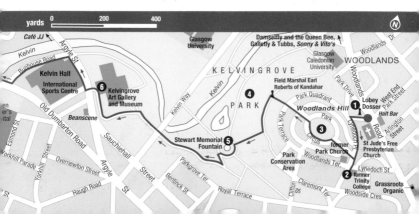

cartoonist Bud Neill who, more than anyone before or since, captured the city's sharp but skewed sense of humour. Regulars in the **Halt Bar** across the road were instrumental in raising the public subscription in 1992 to the memory of the Sheriff of Calton Creek and his masked adversary Rank Bajin. The question 'What was the name of Lobey Dosser's horse?' has sparked a thousand pub arguments, and knowing the answer (El Fideldo) will give you instant credibility with Glaswegians.

Leaving the mix of antiques shops and restaurants in Woodlands Road, the route runs from the spire of St Jude's Free Presbyterian Church up through the greenery of Woodlands Hill and left into Lynedoch Place. This wide street leads to an area of flats and offices dominated by the Italianate towers of **Trinity College ❷**, formerly the college of the Free Church and now converted into much sought-

Above: a statue of a scholar on a bridge over the River Kelvin.

after flats. Along with the lonely white tower of the Park Parish Church – the rest of it was demolished in the late 1960s – they form a dramatic focus for the city skyline.

Above: autumn colours in Kelvingrove Park.

Ⓖ Cycling and Walking along the Kelvin Walkway

There are lots of fabulous opportunities for cycling and walking in and around Kelvingrove Park and the Botanic Gardens. One less well-known route follows the Kelvin Walkway and links up with the Forth and Clyde Canal towpath at the Kelvin Aqueduct – an impressive feat of 18th-century engineering and architecture, which was once the largest functioning aqueduct in Europe. Ask at the tourist office in George Square for detailed maps and consult the Ordnance Survey Explorer map 342.

Above: a handy marker denotes the Kelvin Walkway.

Turn right into Park Circus Place and enter the splendid oval of **Park Circus ❸**, with its air of Victorian elegance. The grand curving terraces rising to a bluff above the River Kelvin were designed as private housing for the emergent middle classes by Charles Wilson (1810–63) and can justly be regarded as his masterpiece.

KELVINGROVE PARK

They lead to **Kelvingrove Park ❹**, the first custom-built park in the city and site of three great International Exhibitions, in 1888, 1901 and 1911, which proudly proclaimed Glasgow's contribution to the British Empire.

The Victorians viewed public parks as the lungs of their smoky cities, allowing their workers the physically and morally beneficial effects of clean air and uplifting scenery. **Glasgow Green** (see p.31) was the only public space in the city until 1846, when a grand plan was proposed by the city council to create three huge sculpted parklands – **Kelvingrove** in the west, **Alexandra Park** in the east and **Queen's Park** (see p.87) in the south – under the hand of designer Sir Joseph Paxton, of Crystal Palace

fame. The city now boasts more than 70 parks, and although the recreations reflect Victorian tastes – boating ponds, playgrounds, putting and bowling – the work of the inventive and industrious Parks Department has given each its own character.

Above: a Trinity College tower in the Park district.

The entrance to Kelvingrove Park is guarded by a spectacular statue of Field Marshal Earl Roberts of Kandahar (1832–1914), surrounded by the bas-relief trappings of his Indian campaigns. There is a similar statue of the field marshal in Calcutta. The park itself is a fine example of the ornamental pleasure garden, with winding paths and wide boulevards. Descending into the park, the main thoroughfare and bridge are marked by a memorial to the officers and men of the Highland Light Infantry who fell in the 'South African War' or Boer War (1899–1902). Turning left here, the road leads through dappled shade to the extravagance of the **Stewart Memorial Fountain ❺**, a tribute to the Lord Provost who, in 1855, finally managed to secure a supply of pure water to the city from Loch Katrine in the Trossachs.

Turning right past the skateboard park and the duck ponds, the tour

Above: in the Kelvingrove Art Gallery and Museum.

emerges onto the Kelvin Way, and a bridge cornered by four groups of bronzes representing peace and war, commerce and industry, shipping and navigation, and prosperity and progress. They were badly damaged by German bombers in 1941 and restored by sculptor Benno Schotz 10 years later.

KELVINGROVE ART GALLERY

The path opposite the park gate leads to the red-sandstone grandeur of **Kelvingrove Art Gallery and Museum ❻** (tel: 0141-276 9599; www.glasgowlife.org.uk; Mon–Thur and Sat 10am–5pm, Fri and Sun 11am–5pm; free), a superb repository of one of the finest civic collections in Europe. The gallery had its origins in the paintings of Trades House Deacon Convenor Archibald McLellan, which the city acquired in 1854 along with his gallery in Sauchiehall Street. The need to house these and other displays led to the 1888 Exhibition – a mammoth event attended by Queen Victoria and nearly 6 million of her subjects – and the profits were used as pump-priming money for the new building. The project was conceived on a breathtaking scale, with

Below: the Stewart Memorial Fountain in Kelvingrove Park.

Above: some say that the Gallery was built the 'wrong way round', because the main entrance is from Kelvingrove Park, while most visitors enter from Argyle Street.

its twin towers, which shelter a massive bronze of St Mungo, facing the lace-work spire of Glasgow University, and the other side leading down a grand staircase onto sunken gardens. Visited by over 1 million people each year, the Kelvingrove reopened its impressive interior in 2007 after a £27.9 million, three-year refurbishment. Its enormous galleries are arranged around two naturally lit halls on either side of the Great Hall, which has an immense Lewis pipe organ still used for recitals.

Kelvingrove's Art Collections

The collection, which includes more than 8,000 objects over three floors and many interactive displays, also

---

Ⓚ Discovery Centres and New Enlightenment

The Kelvingrove Art Gallery and Museum also has much to appeal to children. Glaswegian kids and visitors wander around excitedly and open-jawed, taking in myriad exhibitions, lifelike scale models of animals and the Spitfire LA68 (City of Glasgow Squadron), hanging from the ceiling of the west court. As well as the child-friendly exhibits there are Discovery Centres (info: 0141-276 9505) dedicated to art, environment and history, while the Centre of New Enlightenment (TCoNE; info: 0141-276 9506), in the Campbell Hunter Education Wing, offers interactive educational adventures for young people aged 10 to 14 years.

Above: the Spitfire LA68 is suspended above the west court.

Above: Kelvin Hall now houses a major sports centre.

features many 17th-century Dutch, French Impressionist and post-Impressionist paintings. Rembrandt's *Man in Armour*, Millet's *Going to Work* and Dalí's *Christ of St John of the Cross* are particular favourites. The Glasgow School, in the forefront of the departure from classical tradition, and the Scottish Colourists are well represented, and among the 3,000 oils and 12,500 drawings and prints are works by Rubens, Pissarro, Van Gogh, Degas, Matisse and Monet. Within the walls of this cultural treasure trove, visitors to the West Wing will find a World War II Spitfire hanging from the ceiling *(see box p.73)* and Sir Roger, a stuffed elephant that was once a resident of Glasgow Zoo.

Leaving from the west end of the art gallery, past the 'machine-gun Tommy' war memorial, cross the street to the **Kelvin Hall** (tel: 0141-276 1450), which for many years was Glasgow's foremost exhibition centre, fondly remembered for its annual carnival and circus, complete with elephants and their distinctive aroma. Built in 1927, it served for 60 years – including war service as a barrage balloon factory – before its functions were transferred to the Scottish Exhibition and Conference Centre next to the Clyde. It is now known as the **International Sports Centre** (Mon–Tue and Thur 7.15am–10pm, Wed 10am–10pm, Sat 9am–5pm, Sun 9am–8pm), which includes an athletics track, a climbing wall and a gym, and stages occasional events such as wrestling and basketball.

RIVERSIDE MUSEUM AND THE TALL SHIP

From Argyle Street turn left down Bunhouse Road and then right on to Old Dumbarton Road. Continue to the end of the road, under the railway bridge and take the underpass beneath the Expressway to reach the impressive sight of the **Riverside Museum** ❼ (tel: 0141-287 2720; www.glasgowlife.org.uk; Mon–Thur and Sat 10am–5pm, Fri and Sun 11am–5pm; free). This striking new multi-million-pound transport museum, designed by Zaha Hadid, opened in 2011 and has quickly become one of the UK's top ten attractions. More than 3,000 objects trace the history of transport, most of them relating to Scotland, from a velodrome of bicycles suspended from the ceiling to a wall of classic cars spanning the decades. Most popular, particularly with children, are the old trams, bus and subway carriage – climb aboard to get a real sense of travel in days gone by. Continuing the nostalgic theme, there are two areas recreating streetscapes

Above: the Riverside Museum at Pointhouse Quay was developed for the Museum of Transport. It opened in 2011.

from the 1890s to the 1960s with replicas of specialist shops and pubs.

To the rear of the museum is **The Tall Ship** ❽ (tel: 0141-357 3699; www.thetallship.com; daily Mar–Oct 10am–5pm, Nov–Feb 10am–4pm; charge). The restored *Glenlee*, a Clyde-built three-masted barque, sailed the globe from the 1890s to the 1920s – the boat made journeys as far afield as Japan, Argentina and Australia – before becoming a naval training ship. The four decks can now be explored to find out what life was like on board. Visit the crews' cabins, galley, hospital and map room.

Next to The Tall Ship, **Seaforce** (tel: 0141-221 1070) runs exciting powerboat rides along the Clyde, weather permitting.

ALONG THE CLYDE

Return to the front of the Riverside Museum and follow Stobcross Road, running parallel with the busy Pointhouse Road, around to the SECC and the Clyde Auditorium. Unless you're attending a conference or a concert at the **Scottish Exhibition and Conference Centre (SECC)** (tel:

0844-395 4000) or the neighbouring **Clyde Auditorium** ❾ (tel: 0141-248 3000) you're unlikely to go inside either of these two colossal buildings. But the architectural splendour – particularly of the latter, known affectionately as the 'Armadillo' – makes them must-sees and they have become symbolic of the whole regeneration of Glasgow from the 1980s onwards. The acclaimed architect Sir Norman Foster took inspiration from this former ship-building area, designing an exterior intended to emulate ships' hulls. On a sunny day, as the light hits the silvery curves, it's a stunning sight. Adjacent to these two buildings, yet

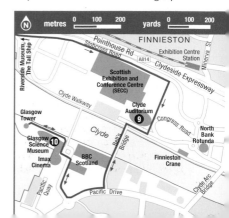

Above: the Finnieston Crane is no longer in active use, but remains as a landmark to Glasgow's industrial heritage.

another live venue, The Hydro, is currently under construction and due to be completed in 2013.

Walking down towards the river along Lancefield Quay, the hulking **Finnieston Crane** comes into view. This huge cantilever crane was in use for more than 50 years as a means of lifting heavy machinery, but it became redundant as industry died out in the city in the 1990s. Today, however, it stands as a dramatic tribute to the great industrial heritage of Glasgow.

ACROSS TO PACIFIC QUAY

At Congress Road on the riverfront take the footbridge over the Clyde, looking to your left as you do so to admire the Clyde Arc Bridge, also known as Squinty Bridge to the locals and another great symbol of modern Glasgow.

Turn right onto Pacific Drive then follow the signs to the **Glasgow Science Centre ⑩** (tel: 0141-420 5000; www.gsc.org.uk; Wed–Fri 10am–3pm, Sat–Sun 10am–5pm; charge). The main permanent attraction here is the planetarium, with various dif-

ferent staged exhibits to demonstrate and explain the solar system and the universe by exploring the night skies, but the science halls, with plenty of interactive exhibits for adults and children alike, hold great appeal too.

Above: the Glasgow Tower is the tallest tower in Scotland.

Above: the Science Mall and the IMAX theatre - two of the buildings that make up Glasgow Science Centre.

An IMAX theatre is also on site, while further along the quay and associated with the science centre is the rotating **Glasgow Tower**, a 416ft (127m) freestanding edifice. In theory, visitors can ride to the top via a lift for 360 degree views of the city. However, the tower has been plagued by engineering problems since opening, so don't be too disappointed if it's out of operation.

To return to the city centre, backtrack to the SECC and take bus No. 100 to George Square.

ⓔ Eating Out

For the best eating options, see the adjoining Tour 7's Eating Out box, p.85. There's a great café in the Kelvingrove Art Gallery. Other options include these deli-cafés and an Oriental restaurant near the SECC:

Beanscene
1365 Argyle Street; tel: 0141-357 4340; daily breakfast, lunch and dinner.
There are three of these outlets in the West End offering a relaxed setting where you can pick from the varied blackboard menu, which usually offers tempting cakes, tapas, nachos, pizza and rice dishes. £

Café JJ
180 Dumbarton Road; tel: 0141-357 1881; daily lunch and dinner.

A homespun place with a selection of vegetarian enchiladas, pasta dishes, panini, crêpes and cakes. £

Sonny & Vito's
52 Park Road; tel: 0141-357 0640; daily lunch only.
A popular and friendly deli just off this tour, which serves excellent home-made sandwiches, pies, tarts, salads and sweet treats including huge apricot and chocolate muffins. £

Yen
28 Tunnel Street; tel: 0141-847 0330; daily lunch and dinner.
In a lovely rotunda building next to the SECC, Yen specialises in cuisine from the Far East: Japanese teppan-yaki dishes on the ground floor; classic Chinese and Thai dishes on the first floor. £–££

Tour 7

West End

Explore the West End's enthralling academic collections, boho Byres Road and the luxuriant Botanic Gardens on this 1.3-mile (2km) tour, which will take a minimum of 4 hours

In the hungry 1930s, the young bucks of Govan would cross on the Kelvinhaugh Ferry on a Sunday afternoon and stage their own version of the Latin *paseo* (walking out) with the local girls along the bosky grandeur of the Kelvin Way. And to the boys from the shipyard tenements it must have seemed like a foreign country. This wonderful walk takes in the Kelvin Way – which cuts through Kelvingrove Park – to the fascinating Hunterian art and museum collections on University Avenue, before exploring the boho shops, cafés and restaurants of Byres Road and Ashton Lane. Our jaunt continues to the exotic hothouses of the Botanic Gardens and ends amid Glasgow artist Alasdair Gray's vibrant murals at the Òran Mór cultural centre.

Highlights

- Kelvin Way
- Wellington Church
- Glasgow University
- Hunterian Museum
- Hunterian Gallery
- Byres Road
- Ashton and Cresswell Lanes
- Botanic Gardens
- Òran Mór

KELVIN WAY AND GLASGOW UNIVERSITY

Starting at the Sauchiehall Street end of the **Kelvin Way**, the Art Galleries open up on the left and the imposing Gothic front of Glasgow University

Left: winter walkers cross a snowy bridge over the River Kelvin.

looms on Gilmorehill. Mature trees canopy the Way after it crosses the bridge with its four dramatic bronzes by Paul R. Montford. On the right is the Kelvingrove bandstand, now sadly derelict (although a restoration is planned), and by an azalea-studded rockery further along on the left sit statues of the figures of the great scientist Lord Kelvin (1824–1907) and surgery pioneer Joseph Lister (1827–1912), both in their university robes.

At the end is a cluster of university buildings, with the imposing gothic

Glasgow University Union straight ahead and the Gilmorehill Centre in a former church on the right. Turning left onto the hill of University Avenue is the gilded gatehouse of **Pearce Lodge ❶**, a remnant of the 17th-century Old College in the city centre, which until recently housed the very 21st-century Computing Service.

Uphill on the right is **Wellington Church ❷**, a grand classical structure influenced by the Madeleine in Paris, with 10 massive fluted pillars supporting its portico. Its predecessor stood in Wellington Street in the centre of the city and attracted a well-to-do congregation, evidenced by the fact that its

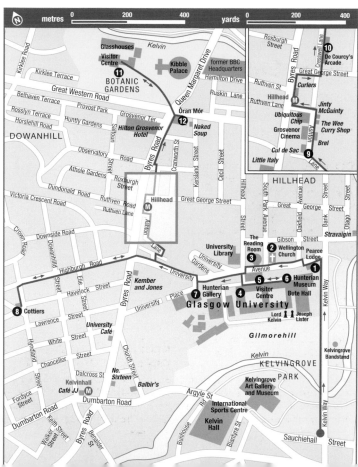

war memorial lists mainly officers, with only a scatter of enlisted men. There is a small café in the crypt. Next door is the bright, galleried circle of **The Reading Room** ❸, a quirky but practical study area built in the grounds of Hillhead House, given to the university in 1917 in memory of city merchant Walter MacLellan of Rhu.

Glasgow University ❹, directly across from the Reading Room, is one of the world's great seats of learning, with an outstanding academic history (see p.15) and worldwide influence. The University of Glasgow is the fourth oldest in Britain after St Andrew's, Oxford and Cambridge. In 1870 it moved to its current site, a leaded-windowed building designed by Sir John Gilbert Scott in what he called 'a 13th or 14th century secular style... with Scottish features'. A complex wrought-iron gate carrying the motto *Via Veritas Vita* contains the names of

Above: Glasgow University is one of the most prestigious in the country.

such luminaries as Bute, Kelvin, Lister, Watt, Stair, Adam Smith and Foulis.

HUNTERIAN MUSEUM

Just inside the gate is a monument to William and John Hunter, the medical brothers whose collection forms

Above: inside the fascinating Hunterian Museum.

the basis of the newly refurbished Hunterian Museum, and the award-winning **Visitor Centre** ❺ (Mon–Sat 9.30am–5pm) provides comprehensive information with guided tours of the university (May–Sept Wed–Fri and Sat 11am and 2pm, Oct–Apr Wed 2pm; charge).

A staircase by the Visitor Centre leads to the sunlit quadrangles and the contrastingly gloomy cloisters. Here also is the lusciously ornate Bute Hall and the **Hunterian Museum** ❻ (www.gla.ac.uk; Tue–Sat 10am–5pm, Sun 11am–4pm; free), Scotland's oldest, which displays the death mask of founder William Hunter. Its splendid galleries house material of great antiquity, from dinosaurs' eggs and rare material from Captain Cook's voyages to ancient coins and a history of the Romans in Scotland. Leaving by the Visitor Centre and turning left, you reach The Square, home to the Principal's residence and the University Chapel.

HUNTERIAN GALLERY

Directly across from the university gatehouse is the refurbished **Hunterian Gallery** ❼ (Tue–Sat 10am–5pm, Sun 11am–4pm; free) and the Mackintosh House within (see p.97), with its internationally famous Whistler collection and works by

Rembrandt, Pissarro, Sisley and Rodin. The museum has put together an impressive collection of contemporary art in recent years through the National Collecting Scheme for Scotland. All the recently acquired works have a naturalistic, scientific element that complements the overall collection. The fascinating work of Mark Dion is

Above: there is a rich collection of Old Masters at the Hunterian Gallery.

Above: Mackintosh's *Porlock Weir* at the Hunterian Gallery.

inspired by the powerful historic role of great museum collections such as the Hunterian's. Other contemporary art highlights worth seeking out are Christine Borland's delicate skulls entitled *Family Conversation Piece: Head of Father* (1998), and Matt Collishaw's strutting peacock, which accompanies the works of Whistler.

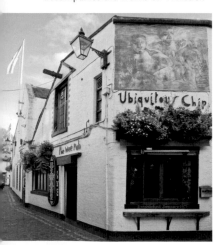

Above: the Ubiquitous Chip restaurant (*see Eating Out p.85*) is a mainstay of Ashton Lane.

The University Library, which contains more than 2.5 million books and journals, is just a few steps further up Hillhead Street.

BYRES ROAD

Abandoning academia for more hedonistic pleasures, **Byres Road**, at the junction with University Avenue, presents itself as the students' playground. Named after a small *clachan*, or village, which once stood there called Byres of Partick, it is a cosmopolitan mix of restaurants, bars and cafés, and comfortingly solid tenement architecture. Kember and Jones (No. 134), an upmarket deli and café, and The University Café (No. 87) are both excellent eateries on Byres Road. A brief detour up Highburgh Road opposite the junction leads to **Cottiers** ❽ (tel: 0141-357 5825), a superb theatre, bar and restaurant in a Victorian Gothic church by architect William Leiper, featuring the beautifully restored stained glass and interior design of Daniel Cottier. It hosts shows by Scottish Opera and Scottish Ballet, as well as experimental companies. Jazz is played on Sundays, 5–8pm.

Above: Ashton Lane is a focus for eating out and nightlife.

This leads down an alley into an explosion of constantly busy bars and restaurants. In less than 100 yds/m, this narrow, cobbled lane offers Brel (tel: 0141-342 4966), with Belgian beer and 'rustic' food, Cul de Sac (tel: 0141-334 4749), an eclectic bar and restaurant, the Grosvenor Cinema with its huge loft café-bar (tel: 0845-166 6028), Jinty McGuinty's packed Irish bar, the Ubiquitous Chip *(see Eating Out p.85)* and the Ashoka Indian restaurant (tel: 0141-337 1115). Ruthven Lane close by has antiquarian bookstores and vintage and designer clothes.

CRESSWELL LANE

Going north up Byres Road past Hillhead Underground and Curlers, an old coaching inn, turn right into Great George Street and then left into **Cresswell Lane ❿** for De Courcy's Arcade, a warren of stalls selling linen, jewels, games and records. At the end, turn left and then right again

ASHTON LANE

To return to the route, just before University Avenue reaches Byres Road, turn right into Ashton Road and right again into **Ashton Lane ❾**.

Ⓢ Shopping Frenzy

Independent boutiques and foodie outlets line Byres Road, while Ruthven Lane and De Courcy's Arcade in Cresswell Lane lure vintage fashion and 20th-century antiques fans. Vintage store **Circa Vintage** (37 Ruthven Lane; tel: 0141-334 6660) bursts with interesting threads, jewellery and curios. At No. 382 Byres Road, **Demijohn** (tel: 0141-337 3600) is a self-styled 'liquid deli' full of whiskies, liquors, oils and vinegars. The sweet-toothed will head for **I Love Candy** (261 Byres Road; tel: 0141-337 3399), filled with tempting old-school sweets, lollipops and Scots fudge. Still on Byres Road, at No. 388, **Boxwood** (tel: 0141-357 6642) features rustic home furnishings, twee treats and quirky clothes. Bookworms will enjoy

a visit to **Voltaire & Rousseau** (12–14 Otago Lane; tel: 0141-339 1811), a wonderfully dusty second-hand bookshop, crammed full of finds and collectable first editions.

Above: sweet treats galore at I Love Candy.

Above: inside one of the Kibble Palace glasshouses, at the Botanic Gardens.

into Byres Road to the junction with Great Western Road. On the right is the pyramid spire of the former Kelvinside Parish Church, which has been converted into the Òran Mór music centre, restaurant and bar. On the left is the terrace of the **Hilton Grosvenor Hotel**, a quarter-mile repetition of the facades of Venetian palaces. The eastern half was destroyed in a fire in 1978 and rebuilt with glass-reinforced concrete cast from the original pillars.

Directly opposite are the city's **Botanic Gardens ⓫** (Gardens: daily 7am–dusk, Glasshouses: 10am–6pm,

Above: Òran Mór is a cultural centre in a converted church.

winter until 4.15pm, Visitor Centre: 11am–4pm; free), a restful recreation garden relocated from Sauchiehall Street to Kelvinside in 1842, with a herb garden, vegetable garden (highlighting a number of uncommon species) and walks along the Kelvin. The dramatic glasshouses nurture tropical plants. The delicate dome of the Kibble Palace was brought here from the Clyde coast home of John Kibble in 1873. An impressive structure, covering 23,000 sq ft (2,137 sq m), it was originally designed by John Kibble for his home at Coulport on Loch Long in the 1860s, and the components were cast by Walter Macfarlane at his Saracen Foundry in Possilpark.

Prime Ministers Benjamin Disraeli and William Gladstone were both installed as rectors of the University of Glasgow under the curved wrought-iron roof in the 1870s – these were the last public events to be staged here before the palace became solely used to house temperate plants. After a £7 million restoration, which involved its complete dismantling and the repair of its rusty parts, the palace was reopened in 2006. The ruins of the Botanic Gardens railway station – opened in 1896 and closed in 1939 – can be seen at the side of the gardens through railings.

Just up Queen Margaret Drive on the right is a building that once housed the women students of Queen Margaret College, as well as the old BBC headquarters, which is due to be converted into a luxury hotel.

ÒRAN MÓR

Just across from the Botanic Gardens on the city-bound section of the Great Western Road is the fine old Kelvinside Parish Church, converted and opened in 2004 as **Òran Mór** ⑫ (meaning 'great melody of life' or 'big song'). This cultural centre offers bars, venues and an eclectic programme of musical and theatrical events (including the afternoon A Play, A Pie and A Pint series). Pop

Above: studying the plants in the Botanic Gardens.

in to view the cavernous auditorium and its wonderful murals by artist and novelist Alasdair Gray.

Return to the city centre by bus from Great Western Road or by Underground from Hillhead (Byres Road) or Kelvinbridge (down Great Western Road).

ⓔ Eating Out

Balbir's
7 Church Street, West End; tel: 0141-339 7711; www.balbirsrestaurants.co.uk; daily dinner only.
Don't let the soulless interior fool you. This is an excellent choice for a quick curry packed with flavour and fresh ingredients. £–££

Little Italy
205 Byres Road; tel: 0141-339 6287; www.littleitalyglasgow.com; daily lunch and dinner.
This popular Italian does takeaways and eat-in pizzas, pasta dishes and delicious Portuguese custard tarts. ££

Naked Soup
6 Kersland Street; tel: 0141-334 8999; daily lunch only.
This small wood-panelled eatery is the place to find hearty, delicious casseroles, curries and soups such as tomato with mascarpone and chickpeas. £

No. Sixteen
16 Byres Road; tel: 0141-339 2544; www.number16.co.uk; daily lunch and dinner.
No. Sixteen serves impressive cuts of fish and meat, including sea bream

and braised belly of pork, with imaginative accompaniments. ££

Stravaigin
28 Gibson Street, Hillhead; tel: 0141-334 2665; www.stravaigin.com; Mon–Thur dinner only, Fri–Sun lunch and dinner.
Renowned for serving up the finest local ingredients with a laid-back vibe. Standouts include chargrilled Aberdeen Angus steak, mussels with chilli and coriander, and root vegetable Wellington with mushroom velouté. ££

Ubiquitous Chip
12 Ashton Lane; tel: 0141-334 5007; www.ubiquitouschip.co.uk; daily lunch and dinner.
The Chip is an institution in a converted mews stable. Enjoy fresh Scottish ingredients and a wonderful wine list amid stylish surroundings and playful artworks by Alasdair Gray. £££

The Wee Curry Shop
29 Ashton Lane; tel: 0141-357 5280; Mon–Sat lunch and dinner, Sun dinner only.
Mother India's chain of curry shops offers a vast array of spicy offerings at reasonable prices. £

Tour 8

South Side

Heading south of the Clyde, this 8-mile, half-day tour takes in parks, grand old houses and arty attractions aplenty, from the Tramway to the Burrell Collection

This tour travels amid abandoned factories and red-bricked chimney stacks, the landmarks of Southside's post-industrial past. First stop is the old Copelawhill Tram Shed reborn as Tramway, a contemporary arts centre renowned for its fabulous visual and performance art shows, and its magical Hidden Gardens. Nearby Queen's Park offers magnificent views towards Loch Lomond and Lanark, while heading west, the wide green expanse of the Pollok Estate contains woodland walks, opportunities for mountain biking, and the late 18th-century period grandeur of Pollok House.

The famous Burrell Collection, containing priceless artworks, is displayed in stunning, light-filled galleries close by. There are more uplifting delights at

Highlights

- Tramway
- Queen's Park
- Cycling and mountain biking in Pollok Country Park
- Burrell Collection
- Rouken Glen Park
- Greenbank Garden

Rouken Glen and the walled, verdant oasis at Greenbank Garden, with its elegant Georgian mansion built by an 18th-century tobacco merchant. If you don't have the use of a bike, a car would be the best means of transport for this tour, since it is not feasible on foot and public transport is complicated.

Queen's Park Views

Queen's Park rises to an impressive summit, with panoramic views as far as Ben Lomond in the north and Lanark in the south. Near the main walkway is an oak tree planted by Belgian refugees after World War I and a beech tree planted in 1945 to commemorate the 20th anniversary of the founding of the United Nations.

Left: the sweeping view from Queen's Park over Glasgow and its glorious backdrop of hills.

HEADING SOUTH TO TRAMWAY

Start this walk from Argyle Street at Jamaica Street and, crossing Glasgow Bridge – built in 1899 following a Thomas Telford design – get in the middle lane, pass the classical tenements of **Carlton Place** to the left and head south along Eglinton Street. This area was a riverside hinterland for much of the 20th century and still bears the marks of commerce with warehouses, disused factories and railway arches.

On Albert Drive, the road leading to Pollockshields East railway station, is the fabulous **Tramway ❶** arts centre (tel: 0845-330 3501; www.tramway.org; Tue–Fri noon–5pm, Sat–Sun noon–6pm; free) below a red-brick chimney stack. It is known for its compelling programme of visual and performance art, dance and experimental music. The Scottish Ballet is now based at Tramway too, in superb new studio facilities.

The majority of the art shows explore challenging, adult-orientated themes which may not be suitable for children. This shouldn't dissuade families from visiting the centre, though, as one of Tramway's most popular attractions is its urban sanctuary, the Hidden Gardens, which sprouted from factory wasteland. Audioguides are available to help you identify the birdsong while you are walking around. Tramway's café-bar has views of the garden and is a great place to refuel and relax.

QUEEN'S PARK

Head east via Coplaw Street across to parallel Victoria Road, a wide avenue of small shops, pubs and restaurants which leads to the gates of **Queen's Park ❷**. Although built in the reign of Victoria, and laid out by Sir Joseph Paxton of Crystal Palace fame, these rolling grounds take their name from Mary, Queen of Scots, whose supporters lost the Battle of Langside nearby in 1568. The 148-acre (60-hectare) park

Above: Pollok House mounts an impressive collection of Spanish art, in addition to works by William Blake.

occupies a commanding site, which was considerably enlarged in 1894 by the enclosure of the grounds of Camphill. It is a wonderful place for a picnic and has lots of amenities, should you be feeling more active, including five floodlit tennis courts, pitch and putt,

bowling greens and a skateboard park. There is also a pond teeming with birdlife, including tufted ducks, moorhens, mallards, little grebe, coots and mute swans. The large boating pond provides serene moments during the summer months.

TOWARDS POLLOK HOUSE AND COUNTRY PARK

Turning left at the gates, Langside Road, which is not signposted, runs round the park past the **Victoria Infirmary** – a huge hospital serving the whole of the south side of Glasgow – to the monument on Battle Place, designed by Alexander Skirving in 1887, and an imposing stone-cleaned former church which has been converted to the Church on the Hill bar and restaurant.

Going straight ahead at the roundabout, follow Millbrae Road into Langside Drive, turn right at Newlands

Left: a snowy day brings out the sledges in Queen's Park.

Above: light streams into the bucolic Pollok Country Park.

These beautifully sculpted grounds were given to the city as late as 1966 by Mrs Anne Maxwell Macdonald and now form **Pollok Country Park ❸**, where morning joggers and evening strollers enjoy the Highland cattle, heavy horses, art collections and woodland walks. The driveway runs past the Police Dog and Mounted Branch and parkland grazed by 'toffee-wrapper' cattle with their glowering fringes to **Pollok House ❹** (tel: 0844-493 2202; www.nts.org.uk; daily 10am–5pm; charge), a masterful William Adam construction dating from 1752. Its exquisite interior retains many original features and houses a fine collection of Spanish School paintings, and the gardens – including a particularly fine parterre and a full and productive walled garden – are bounded by a lazy curve of White Cart Water.

It has undergone a sympathetic restoration programme, and there is a good café-bar in the kitchen. Pollok Country Park offers wonderful surroundings for cycling and is reached via Routes 7 and 75 of the National Cycle Network (www.sustrans.org.uk), or take your bicycle to Pollokshaws West station from Glasgow Central.

Road (you'll see a sign for Diarsie House School) and follow it to Riverford Road. Go through the Pollokshaws area, once a thriving working-class heartland but now much demolished to make way for modern housing and a new railway line, and turn right onto Barrhead Road for the entrance to the Pollok Estate.

Ⓖ Cycling and Mountain Biking

Pollok Country Park has three mountain-bike circuits suitable for different abilities. The **Green Circuit** offers a gentle ride; the **Blue Circuit** has steeper, more varied terrain and requires more skill; the **Red Circuit** is more akin to wild mountain topography and is not for the fainthearted. Those seeking more two-wheeled thrills should head a few miles further south to **Cathkin Braes Country Park**, which is the venue of the Commonwealth Games 2014 Mountain Biking event.

Above: Pollok Country Park is ideal for cyclists of all abilities.

Above: Sir William Burrell's incredible collection of artefacts from all over the world is on display at the famed Burrell Collection.

Above: medieval archways have been incorporated into the Burrell Collection's building.

BURRELL COLLECTION

Retracing the tour and forking left leads to the internationally famous **Burrell Collection** ❺ (tel: 0141-287 2550; Mon–Thur and Sat 10am–5pm, Fri and Sun 11am–5pm; free), the outstanding legacy of the shipping magnate Sir William Burrell, whose collector's instinct and eye for a bargain were on a par with his occasional rival, the American newspaper magnate William Randolph Hearst. He perfected the business method of selling his fleets of ships in a boom period and buying in a slump, and realised his considerable fortune in 1916 when he sold up to concentrate on his first love, art.

The collection is eclectic and idiosyncratic, with more than 9,000 objects from Egypt, Greece, the Middle East and South and East Asia, plus tapestries and stained glass from medieval Europe. Favourites with Glasgow visitors are the Degas collection, Rodin's *Thinker* (one of 14 casts made from the original) and the *Warwick Vase*, an 8-ton marble which dominates the courtyard. Volunteer guides with specialist knowledge lead tours of the Burrell Collection – for a detailed list of upcoming tours tel: 0141-287 2550 or consult the website www.glasgow life.org.uk.

In Glasgow City Council hands
Glasgow city received this fascinating collection in 1944 in a bequest of restrictive conditions, largely concerning Burrell's fears about the potential damage to his treasures from industrial air pollution. This meant that they lay in storage until 1983 when cleaner air and the acquisition of Pollok Estate allowed the construction of an award-winning building with deceptively simple lines, which has drawn as much admiration as the museum's contents.

Medieval archways from the collection are blended with new red sandstone, and some halls have glass walls to the floor, giving the impression that the exhibits are being viewed in the open air. Others are completely enclosed and provide a warmly lit backdrop for some of the world's most exquisite tapestries. The collection also includes exhibits of entire rooms from Burrell's home at Hutton Castle in Berwickshire, and there's an excellent café-restaurant.

Above: the imposing *Warwick Vase* is the centrepiece of the Burrell Collection's courtyard.

ROUKEN GLEN PARK
The road out of the park on the left – look for the carved woodpecker – leads onto Haggs Road. Turn right, get in the middle lane and follow it to Pollokshaws Road and the Round Toll roundabout, then take the B769 for Thornliebank. Stay on this road until the next roundabout and turn

Ⓚ Family Tours

The Burrell Collection organises special tours for kids and families that explore art, crafts and scientific themes. Perennial favourites include the Weaving Magic tour, which has a hands-on workshop, the Charcoal Fun drawing class with an artist, and Hidden Treasure, which challenges children to solve clues and find the booty, always a popular activity! For the latest events tel: 0141-287 2564.

Above: the collection offers several absorbing child-friendly activities.

Above: a sculptural feature in the Greenbank Garden.

left onto the A727 for East Kilbride. Soon after joining the dual carriageway, take a right turn into Rouken Glen Park.

Rouken Glen Park ❻ was donated to the city by Mr A. Cameron Corbett (later Lord Rowallan) in 1906 and passed to the adjoining Eastwood Council in 1984, after a dispute over running costs. Its loss to Glasgow was felt on an emotional level by many who remembered school trips to the large boating pond, where a motor launch would carry day-trippers round the islands, much to the indignation of nesting ducks.

Fears of the park's demise, however, were groundless, and a thriving range of commercial concerns – an attractive garden centre, art gallery and a signposted walkabout trail – have given it a new lease of life. The old attractions, however, remain unchanged: the waterfall tumbling into a mossy glen, the walled garden, a golf course and generous parkland.

Below: Rouken Glen's natural waterfall was doubled in height in the early 1800s.

GREENBANK GARDEN

Turning right at the exit, follow the A727 over Eastwood Toll roundabout, through the suburbs of Clarkston to Clarkston Toll, where Greenbank Garden is signposted on the first right after the roundabout.

Greenbank Garden ❼ (garden: daily 9.30am–sunset; shop and tearoom: Nov–Mar Sat–Sun 1–4pm, Apr–Oct daily 11am–5pm; house: Apr–Oct Sun 2–4pm; charge), which lies on Flenders Road, off Mearns Road, is a substantial walled garden which many city dwellers regard as an oasis of calm. It is one of the few substantial properties the National Trust for Scotland has near the city. The gardens surround a tobacco merchant's 18th-century mansion; there are tours of the interior with its remarkable billiard room most Sunday afternoons. A tennis court has been converted into a garden for disabled visitors, with raised plant beds; the floral profusion encourages wildlife.

To return to the city, go to Clarkston Toll and follow the signs for the M77, taking junction 3 for the city centre.

Above: the atmospheric walled Greenbank Garden is set around an 18th-century house.

ⓔ Eating Out

Boaters Café
Rouken Glen Park; tel: 0141-638 3078; daily, closed evenings.
This homely café located on the edge of Rouken Glen Park is very popular with families who queue for the ice cream. Savoury options include panini, salads, pasta dishes and fish and chips. £

The Kitchen Restaurant
Pollok House, Pollok Estate, 2060 Pollokshaws Road; tel: 0844-493 2202; daily lunch only.
Amid the grand basement interiors of this award-winning restaurant, discerning diners are served a limited but excellent choice of mains including good veggie options. The home-baked cakes are legendary. £

Moyra Jane's
20 Kildrostan Street; tel: 0141-423 5628; Tue–Sat lunch and dinner, Sun–Mon lunch only.
This former bank building has marble-topped tables and wood-panelled walls – suitably solid surroundings for traditional, quality fare including lamb dishes, Thai fishcakes, vegetarian moussaka and massive meringues. £

Tramway Café-Bar
25 Albert Drive; tel: 0845-330 3501; Jan–Oct Tue–Sat 9.30am–8pm and Sun noon–6pm, Oct–Dec Tue–Sat 10am–6pm and Sun noon–6pm.
An airy space looking onto the Hidden Gardens serving excellent, healthy vegetarian and pasta dishes, superb lamb burgers and sandwiches. £

Tour 9

Mackintosh Tour

Charles Rennie Mackintosh, pioneer of the Modern Movement, left the city of Glasgow a handsome artistic and architectural legacy which never ceases to inspire

Rarely has a whole industry been founded on the designs of one architect, but Charles Rennie Mackintosh (1868–1928) was no ordinary architect. His vision and originality were at the forefront of the Modern Movement, and his imaginative buildings and clean, simple interior design were unique. Many of Mackintosh's buildings, however, were sadly neglected until the 1980s, but then his importance was realised and much-needed restoration of his works commenced. They lie spread across the city and a comprehensive day tour moving from one gem to another is difficult, but the following guide highlights the most accessible and representative works, which are marked with an Ⓜ on the maps.

Highlights

- The Lighthouse
- Glasgow School of Art
- The Mackintosh House
- Queen's Cross Church
- The Hill House
- House for an Art Lover
- Scotland Street School
- The Willow Tea Rooms

The best source for information about Mackintosh himself, the history of the buildings and about access to Mackintosh properties as well as specialist tours is the **Charles Rennie Mackintosh Society** (tel: 0141-946 6600; www.crmsociety.com). They

Left: the House for an Art Lover (p.98) is based on Mackintosh's drawings.

have an ongoing campaign to increase awareness of the architect and a push to have Mackintosh buildings designated as Unesco World Heritage sites. The **Glasgow Tourist Information Centre** (see p.123) is another valuable port of call. It's worthwhile buying a one-day Mackintosh Trail Ticket

(£16) which allows visitors entry to all participating Mackintosh attractions and unlimited travel on the SPT subway and First bus services.

CITY-CENTRE SIGHTS

Starting in the city centre, **The Lighthouse** (tel: 0141-276 5360; www. glasgow.gov.uk; tours Mon, Wed–Fri 10.30am–5pm, Tue and Sat 11am and 3pm; charge, Sat free) features a

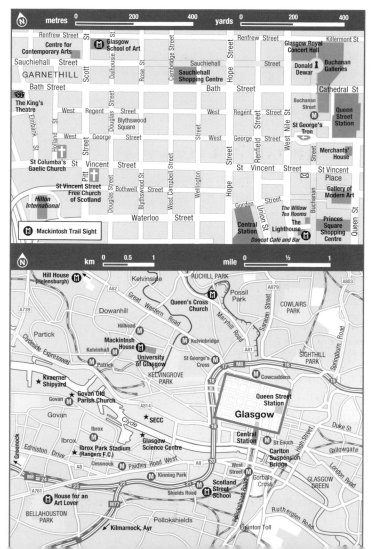

Above: an architectural exhibit at The Lighthouse.

Mackintosh Interpretation Centre to place the artist in his cultural context and help visitors find his buildings. Built to a Mariscal design beside the tower of the old *Glasgow Herald* building in Mitchell Street, its rooftop platform offers close-up views of his work. It hosts a variety of temporary exhibitions exploring design and architectural themes and has a fabulous café. In 2009, the Lighthouse Trust organisation – set up to champion Scottish architecture and design – found itself in financial trouble and went into administration. However Glasgow City Council stepped in to keep the centre open and there are now plans afoot to extend it further into a National Centre for Architecture and Design.

GLASGOW SCHOOL OF ART

Along Sauchiehall Street and up Scott Street on the right is Mackintosh's crowning achievement, the **Glasgow School of Art** (www.gsa.ac.uk; guided tours Apr–Sept daily 11am–5pm on the hour, Oct–Mar Mon–Sat 11am and 2pm; charge for tour). One of the most venerable art schools in the UK,

every stone, window and railing is redolent of the architect's unique style.

The east wing was started in 1897 under the influence of revered headmaster Fra Newbery, but the west wing was not completed until 1909. Hefty sandstone block and soaring gridded oriel windows make the first glance of 'the Mac' as you approach from a steep hill laden with drama. Inside there are dark, woody spaces with handsome detailing – the church-

Above: the Queen's Cross Church houses the Mackintosh Society HQ.

Above: the Glasgow School of Art.

MACKINTOSH IN THE WEST END

In 1906, Mackintosh completely redesigned the interior of an ordinary terraced house at 78 Southpark Avenue for himself and his wife Margaret, whom he had married in 1900 just before being made a full partner at Honeyman & Keppie. They lived in it for eight years and, before it was demolished in 1963, the fittings were removed and are now on display as the **Mackintosh House** (charge) in the **Hunterian Gallery** (see *p.81*; Tue–Sat 10am–5pm, Sun 11am–4pm), which is a brief taxi ride from the School of Art.

Another short taxi hop away from here is the **Queen's Cross Church** in Garscube Road, which is now the headquarters of the **Charles Rennie Mackintosh Society** and is open to visitors. After admiring the red-sandstone exterior with its unusual blocky turrets, dip your head inside to marvel at the interiors. The blue stained-glass window designs play on the Gothic style to startling effect, while the handsome relief carving on wood and stonework complements the feeling of sparseness, light and space. As well as being the best place for finding out

like library with its grid-layout wooden pillars and hanging lights is one of the many inspiring spaces Mackintosh created. Studios and windowsills in far-flung corners are bathed in light and provide awesome views. A visit to the building – join one of the guided tours with an expert if you can – gives a compelling insight into this working building which continues to inspire art students more than 100 years after its inception.

Ⓕ Rennie Mac's Early Years

One of 13 children of a police superintendent, he was born in Parsons Street, where he would later create the Martyrs' School. He attended night classes at Glasgow's School of Art – then in the McLellan Galleries – before joining Honeyman & Keppie, for whom he did his best work. His first major public building, the former *Glasgow Herald* office – renamed The Lighthouse in a design by Barcelona Olympics maestro Javier Mariscal – was the focal point of Glasgow's year as City of Architecture in 1999.

Above: Glasgow's architectural hero, Charles Rennie Mackintosh.

Above: the House for an Art Lover, set in attractive gardens.

Ⓚ Back to School

Kids and adults will enjoy a look around Scotland Street School's three classroom reconstructions, which show the changing face of teaching and childhood from the Victorian era through World War II to the classroom of the 1950s and 1960s. Particularly evocative are the barrel-vaulted cookery room, cloakrooms and ceramic-tiled drill hall, which have been restored to Mackintosh's original 1906 designs.

Above: a classroom reconstruction at Scotland Street School.

about Mackintosh events and tours, the Mackintosh Church at Queen's Cross has a superb library. The shop stocks an extensive range of Mackintosh books and objects based on the great man's designs.

THE HILL HOUSE AT HELENSBURGH

The Hill House (tel: 0844-493 2208; Apr–Oct 1.30–5.30pm; charge) is not in Glasgow, but it should be included in any tour of Mackintosh works. A 40-minute train ride away in Helensburgh (First Scotrail; tel: 0845-748 4950), it's by far the most attractive of his domestic commissions. Built on a commanding site for the publisher Walter Blackie, the fittings have been meticulously conserved by the National Trust for Scotland.

SOUTHSIDE MASTERPIECES

House for an Art Lover (www. houseforanartlover.co.uk; Apr–Sept Mon–Wed 10am–4pm, Thur–Sun 10am–1pm, Oct–Mar Sat–Sun 10am–1pm; tel: 0141-353 4770; charge) was created from a portfolio which Mackintosh presented for a design competition in 1901. Following his drawings, the

house was built in a beautiful parkland setting beside the Victorian walled garden in Bellahouston Park, and contains striking details and interiors, plus a café and shop. The nearest underground station is Ibrox; nearest mainline station is Dumbreck. The house is about 15 minutes by taxi from the city centre.

Scotland Street School (tel: 0141-287 0500; www.glasgowlife.org. uk; Tue–Thur and Sat 10am–5pm, Fri and Sun 11am–5pm; free) is most easily reached by underground. Get off at Shields Road station, and the school's twin towers of leaded glass and red sandstone are clearly visible across the road.

Built between 1903 and 1906, the school is clearly Glasgow-style and offers a fascinating look at developments in Scottish education. There are interactive displays which explore the school world and design tools to see if you can match the master draughtsman Mackintosh. Even more fascinating are the accounts of former pupils' recollections of their school days. The archive follows the decades, detailing the minutiae of childhood and background events in Scottish and world

Above: inside the elegant House for an Art Lover.

history. Themes covered include classroom discipline, school trips, school attire, evacuation and World War II, playground antics and the changing local environment. The excellent Back to School role-playing programme has interactive displays allowing the visitor to experience the classes of yesteryear *(see box opposite).*

E Eating Out

Art Lovers Café
House for an Art Lover, Bellahouston Park; tel: 0141-353 4770; daily lunch only.
Set within one of Mackintosh's finest houses, this popular café is open to people visiting the house and those who simply want to come and eat. The elegant surroundings embody Mackintosh's design ideals, and the dishes are presented with style and skill. The menu places huge emphasis on seasonal produce so it changes regularly, but you may find sea bass, Aberdeen beef or pork belly at any given time. In summer there is a lovely outdoor seating area. £

The Willow Tea Rooms
97 Buchanan Street; tel: 0141-204 5242; www.willowtearooms. co.uk; Mon–Sat 9am–5pm, Sun 11am–5pm.
This is a faithful re-creation of the innovative design work Mackintosh carried out for well-known restaurateur Kate Cranston at the turn of the 20th century. The originals of the White Room and the Blue Room are in the care of Glasgow City Council. More Mackintosh interiors, afternoon tea and scones can be enjoyed at the other Willow Tea Rooms located at 217 Sauchiehall Street (tel: 0141-332 0521). ££

Tour 10

Excursion to Loch Lomond

An 80-mile (130km) foray into the Highlands, Loch Lomond and the Trossachs National Park, dipping into Britain's largest lake and visiting beguiling villages

You tak' the High Road,
and I'll tak' the Low Road,
and I'll be in Scotland afore ye.

The words of the Loch Lomond song distil the romance of the glens for Scots the world over, but for the most part, the reality of the High Road these days is a wide dual carriageway. Following signs for Crianlarich, the A82 continues westwards from Great Western Road in the centre of Glasgow along the north bank of the Clyde past Bowling, Dumbarton – the ancient capital of Strathclyde, with its castle on the rock – and Balloch.

This is a long excursion, but once at the loch, the roads mellow out and the countryside ranges from the lush and rolling to true Highland drama. The route includes points at which you

Highlights

- Balloch
- Drymen
- Balmaha
- Priory of Inchmahome
- Aberfoyle
- Loch Katrine

have to double back on yourself, but not for more than a few miles.

LUSS, ON THE BANKS OF LOCH LOMOND

The first is at Loch Lomond itself. Still following the Crianlarich signs, head first for the village of **Luss** ❶. Although surrounded on the outskirts by tourist services, the rose-clad cottages and the

Left: peaceful Loch Lomond.

old pier are attractive. On the other side of the main carriageway, a farm road signposted for Glen Luss runs up to some of the best hill-walking within easy reach of the city. A series of Corbetts (Scottish hills ranging between 2,500ft/762m and 3,000ft/914m) afford spectacular views to the Clyde estuary and the western islands. The weather in the mountains can change quickly, so always carry a map and dress warmly.

BALLOCH, DRYMEN AND BALMAHA

Returning south, turn left at the roundabout signed for **Balloch ②** and left at the next roundabout. This leads into the heart of Loch Lomond's only town of any size. It hosts **Loch Lomond Shores** (tel: 01389-751 031; www. lochlomondshores.com; free), a visitor centre with shops, café and innovative aquarium (tel: 01389-721 500; charge) complete with sharks. Boats of all shapes and sizes crowd the banks and pontoons as the loch empties into the River Leven on its way to the Clyde.

The A811, signposted for Drymen, wanders through undulating farmland, passing only one village of note, **Gartocharn ③**. The small hill at the back is called **Duncryne** and is worth the gentle climb for views of the water meadows of the southern loch, the wooded islands and the higher hills in the distance, including Ben Lomond.

At the junction with the A809, turn left to **Drymen ④**, a delightful village 11 miles (18km) north of Glasgow. It retains a charming rural atmosphere. The cosy **Clachan Inn** (tel: 01360-660 824), established in 1734, is a good place to eat or enjoy a wee dram.

The B837 from the centre runs 5 miles (8km) to **Balmaha ⑤**, a village lying on the Highland Boundary

ⓖ West Highland Way

The West Highland Way, a 95-mile (152km) walk from Milngavie, on the outskirts of Glasgow, to Fort William, starts at a granite obelisk in Douglas Street. The route follows ancient communication tracks as well as drove roads, military roads and disused railway tracks. The first 5-mile (8km) stage to Carbeth involves 500ft (148m) of ascent – a tame but enjoyable preamble to later challenges like climbing the Devil's Staircase below Glencoe's jagged Aonach Eagach ridge. See also www.west-highland-way.co.uk.

Above: the beautifully scenic terrain.

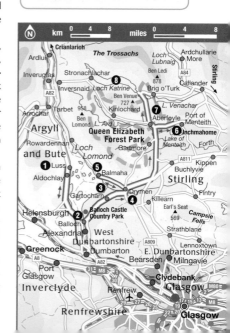

Above: Balmaha's boatyard is the place to pick up a loch cruiser.

Fault, separating the Highlands from the Lowlands. A scatter of white-washed houses surrounds the small inlet where **Balmaha's boatyard** (tel: 01360-870 214) caters for fishermen and loch cruisers, and offers places on the regular mailboat round the islands – an unusual day trip. The

Below: the historic Inchmahome priory, on the Lake of Menteith.

Oak Tree Inn (tel: 01360-870 357) is a good place to eat or stay. A path leads from the car park to Conic Hill; from the summit it is possible to see the 37 islands in the loch.

LAKE OF MENTEITH

Returning to Drymen, the A811 meanders north and east before joining the A81 north across the flatlands towards the hills of the Queen Elizabeth Forest. At the Rob Roy Motel, the route goes left to Aberfoyle, but turning right along the A81 for a short distance to the B8034 brings you to the island priory of **Inchmahome** ❻ (Apr–Sept daily 10am–4.30am, Oct daily 10am–3.30pm; charge includes ferry) on the Lake of Menteith, the only 'lake' in Scotland. These beautiful 12th-century Augustinian remains once sheltered Mary, Queen of Scots.

ABERFOYLE

Follow the A821 for the Trossachs. You'll next hit **Aberfoyle** ❼, a tourist honeypot. The road north negotiates a startling series of hairpins as it climbs

past the **David Marshall Lodge** to Duke's Pass – watch for a kilted piper here in summer – then descends to Loch Achray. One of the small peaks on the far side of the loch is **Ben A'an** which affords a superb vista of Loch Katrine, Sir Walter Scott 's inspiration for *The Lady of the Lake* (1810).

Before Ben A'an, the main road branches off to **Loch Katrine ❽**, where the steam yacht *Sir Walter Scott* sails on Glasgow's water supply (Apr–Oct; call to check times; tel: 01877-332 000/376 316). Bikes are available

Above: the banks of Loch Katrine are ideal for a peaceful bicycle ride.

to hire for a ride along the loch road. For the quickest way back to Glasgow, travel 10 miles (16km) to Callander, then on to Stirling to join the M9.

ⓔ Eating Out

Balloch
Balloch House Vintage Inn
Balloch Road; tel: 01389-752 579; daily lunch and dinner.
Serves hearty fish and chips alongside more adventurous dishes. £

Near Balloch
Cameron House Hotel
A82; tel: 01389-755 565; www.devere hotels.co.uk; Cameron Grill: daily breakfast and dinner; Martin Wishart's: Wed–Fri dinner, Sat–Sun lunch/dinner.

This luxurious lochside former stately home offers several dining options including Martin Wishart's Michelin-starred eatery, which serves delicious dishes such as turbot with sweet garlic cannelloni. £–£££
Duck Bay Marina
tel: 01389-751 234; www.duckbay. co.uk; daily lunch and dinner.
This modern hotel has large picture windows with glorious loch views. Expect classics like cullen skink, plus pasta dishes and crêpes. ££

Loch Lomond

Everyone has heard of it, but the loch bit of Loch Lomond is just one of the shimmering jewels in what is Scotland's most famous and diversified national park

OUTDOOR TREATS

Loch Lomond and the Trossachs National Park stretches a little west of the loch, north to Tyndrum, east to Callander and south to Balloch. Straddling the West Highland fault line, the heather-clad hills abound with 'darksome glens and gleaming lochs', as wrote legendary Scottish author Sir Walter Scott.

This area has a magnetism for walkers, cyclists and those who love water sports. Loch Lomond and the Trossachs National Park Gateway Centre in Balloch (www.loch lomond-trossachs.org) has every kind of information about the park, including geological history, walking routes, cycle paths and details about all the guides and companies who provide  tours, mountain-bike excursions, horse riding, fishing and boat trips on the lochs (notably the *Sir Walter Scott* steamer on Loch Katrine; see p.103).

WALKING COUNTRY

There are a multitude of easy and short walks, such as the **Creag an Tuirc** walk, which begins at Balquidder (2.5 miles/4km, about 2 hours), and the hillier **Cruach Tairbeirt** walk (4.7 miles/7.5km, about 3 hours),

Flora and Fauna

As you travel away from the sparkling shores of the loch, you're greeted by spectacular hills, glens with densely wooded forests and a real sense that you're surrounded by the wild. The national park boasts 200 species of birds, including buzzards, ospreys, golden eagles, peregrine falcons, pied flycatchers, and capercaillies – although you're more likely to hear the cricking noise of these than see them among the heathery thickets. The park is home to 25 percent of Britain's wild plant species: there are 500 flowering species and ferns, with rarities such as wood anemone, wood sorrel and, magnificent in May, thick blankets of bluebells. As for fauna, take your time and keep quiet and you have some chance of being in the presence of – if not seeing – red deer, polecats, pine martens and wildcats. Meanwhile, Loch Lomond is the largest freshwater loch in the UK; within it swim salmon, pike and powan, a whitefish only found in one other place.

taking you up to 1,485ft (450m). In exchange for your efforts you receive glorious views of Loch Lomond – weather permitting.

If you must climb a hill, try **Ben Ledi**, classified as a Corbett, a smaller set of Scottish hills (5 miles/8km, about 4 hours). It might be wee but on a clear day you can see the Firth of Forth from the summit at 2,508ft (760m). For those craving to bag a Munro, Scotland's

highest peaks, 3,465ft (1,050m) -high **Ben Lui** (13 miles/21km, about 7 hours) is a must-climb. For much of the year its Coire Gaothaich (Windy Corrie) is filled with snow, lending it an alpine character. Ben Lui is reached from Tyndrum.

For those with time, the inclination and broken-in boots, the famous **West Highland Way** (92½ miles/148km, up to 2,650ft/800m) from Milngavie to Fort William is one of the most trampled and loved walks in Scotland. It takes between 7 and 10 days.

Whatever walk you choose to do, be prepared for a dramatic change in the weather, even in the warmest months, and have proper footwear, a map and compass (the ability to use these properly is a must too!) as well as waterproof clothing. Also, leave word of your plans with your accommodation.

Above: the Loch Lomond park is perfect walking country. **Top Left**: a Loch Lomond walkway. **Centre Left**: a local pine marten. **Bottom Left**: the rare, vocally impressive capercaillie, a woodland grouse.

Tour 11

Excursion to Clyde Valley

Two country parks, riverside walks, the David Livingstone Centre, Craignethan Castle and fascinating New Lanark make this a stimulating jaunt

Highlights

- Strathclyde Country Park
- Duke of Hamilton's Mausoleum
- David Livingstone Centre
- Chatelherault Country Park
- Craignethan Castle
- Lanark
- New Lanark

The River Clyde, the wonderful Clyde, The name of it thrills me and fills me with pride.

When Glaswegians sing praise of the river that gave their city meaning, they think of the clatter of shipyards and the sway of giant cranes. But further down the valley is an altogether different river, wandering through gentle hills and watering fertile orchards and fruit farms. This 45-mile (70km) tour requires a car, or a bike for the very fit, taking in country parks, lots of intriguing history and a Unesco World Heritage Site at New Lanark.

STRATHCLYDE COUNTRY PARK

The M8 snakes through the centre of Glasgow, and it is possible to join it at many points. Once on the eastbound carriageway, follow signs for Carlisle and Edinburgh through the industrial eastern suburbs until you reach junction 8 with the M73, then follow signs for Carlisle.

Off the A723 between a cluster of Glasgow's satellite towns – including **Hamilton** and **Motherwell** – is

Left: the picturesque Falls of Clyde.
Above: there are thrills of all sorts at
Strathclyde Country Park.

Strathclyde Country Park ❶. It's
accessible via junction 5 of the M74.
This huge recreation area includes
a man-made loch that offers sailing,
windsurfing and water-skiing, along
with an amusement park, **M&D's**
(tel: 01698-333 777; www.scotlands
themepark.com) featuring some of
the biggest rides in Scotland.

The **Low Parks Museum** (tel:
01698-328 232; Mon–Sat 10am–5pm,
Sun noon–5pm; free), built on the site
of the Hamilton Palace, complete with
a mezzanine café, is located on Muir
Street. It tells the turbulent history
of the town, its regiment – the Cam-
eronians – and the Hamilton family,
whose spectacular **Mausoleum** ❷,
built by the 10th Duke in the 1840s,
has impassive stone lions guarding the
enormous bronze doors and beautiful
marblework within.

DAVID LIVINGSTONE
CENTRE

A few miles up the A724 at Blantyre is
the **David Livingstone Centre** ❸

(tel: 0844-493 2207; www.nts.org.uk;
Apr–Dec Mon–Sat 10am–5pm, Sun
12.30pm–5pm; charge), a memorial to Scotland's greatest missionary
explorer, who was born here in 1813.
Brought up as a poor factory boy, he
led an eventful life which included the
discovery of the Victoria Falls on the
border between Zambia and Zim-
babwe while on a journey across the
African continent in 1855. He died
of dysentery in 1873 while searching
for the then unknown source of the
River Nile.

CHATELHERAULT
COUNTRY PARK

Returning through Hamilton, join the
A72 for Lanark and, as the suburbs
give way to countryside, the gates
of **Chatelherault Country Park**
❹ (tel: 01698-426 213; Mon–Sat
10am–5pm, Sun noon–5.30pm)
open up on the right. A visitor centre, once the kennels for the hunting
dogs of the Duke of Hamilton, butts
onto the main building, designed by
William Adam for the Fifth Duke and
completed in 1744. The building fell
into dereliction – mining subsidence
has added a jaunty slope to some
floors – but a masterful restoration
was completed in 1987 allowing visitors to fullly appreciate the superb
plasterwork with its ornate figures
from classical mythology.

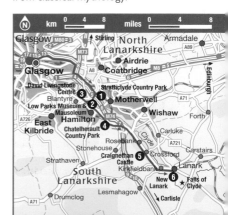

Above: the fascinating New Lanark is a Unesco World Heritage Site.

Riverside Walks

Chatelherault Country Park consists of nearly 500 acres (200 hectares) of the Avon Gorge, one of the least polluted of the Clyde's tributaries. There are miles of riverside walks and picturesque sights here including the dramatic Duke's Bridge, the medieval mystery of Cadzow Castle and rolling parkland featuring cattle whose lineage dates back to Roman times.

Above: the Chatelherault Country Park is packed with bucolic charm.

CRAIGNETHAN CASTLE

The A72 now follows the twists and turns of the Clyde as it runs through a valley of soft-fruit, tomato and vegetable growers, past Dalserf's 1655 church and the pretty half-timbered village of Rosebank with its three-star Popinjay Hotel (tel: 01555-860 441). Slightly further on, a sign points right to **Craignethan Castle** ❺ (Apr–Sept Mon–Sun 9.30am–6.30pm, 1 Nov–31 Mar Sat–Sun 9.30am–4.30pm; charge), a sombre keep situated 2 miles (3km) up a narrow and twisting road. Dating back to around 1530, this rambling ruin was one of the last great family tower fortresses, and from it the Hamilton family played a pivotal role in Scottish politics, including supporting Mary, Queen of Scots, whom they sheltered here after her abdication in 1567.

Although Sir Walter Scott denied that its ivy-clad ruins were the inspiration for Tillietudlem Castle in the Waverley novel *Old Mortality* – and indeed he is said to have considered settling here instead of Abbotsford – its remote location and air of mystery are resonant for many of Claverhouse and the Covenanting bands.

LANARK AND NEW LANARK

Back on the A72, the road continues through Kirkfieldbank to the historic town of **Lanark**, a slope trodden during the Wars of Independence (1286–1328) by the raggle-taggle hordes of William Wallace, whose statue looks down from an 18th-century church along a bustling main street divided by pretty floral displays. This busy market town was founded in 1140 by King David. He established a castle here, long since disappeared.

Following the signs at the top of the street for New Lanark, the road twists down again to the Clyde and one of the most remarkable episodes in Scotland's industrial history, as well as one of its most adventurous heritage restoration projects. At first sight, **New Lanark** ❻ (tel: 01555-661 345; www. newlanark.org; Apr–Oct 10am–5pm, Nov–Mar 10am–4pm; charge) seems little more than a group of stone-built warehouses, but it was here that David Dale and his son-in-law Robert Owen conducted a social experiment that was to have lasting repercussions for the bitterly oppressed working classes.

Dale, from Stewarton, made his fortune in weaving and French yarns. In 1785, using the abundant water power of the Clyde, he set up the New Lanark Mills which, at their height, employed over 2,000 workers, many of them children. Along with Owen,

who assumed management in 1799, he introduced a regime of decent housing, reasonable wages, education and healthcare, to prove his theory that contented workers were productive workers. His message did as much to create a social revolution as the mills had done for industry, and as a result workers' rights began to be considered seriously elsewhere.

The village, now a Unesco World Heritage Site, has been restored as a living community complete with hotel and shops, and the millworkers' tenement rows are desirable properties. There is also a youth hostel here (tel: 01555-666 710). In the Visitor Centre, various audiovisual rides show life in the mill past, present and future.

Along the river, a sylvan walk leads to the **Falls of Clyde**, where the Scottish Wildlife Trust organises badger watches and the keen-eyed may spot kingfishers, owls and pipistrelle bats as night descends.

Below: the handsome hunting lodge at Chatelherault Country Park has been sensitively restored.

ⒺEating Out

Hamilton

Di Maggio's
42 Gateside Street; tel: 01698-891 828; daily lunch and dinner. Child-friendly Italian restaurant serving decent pizzas and pastas, American diner classics, and decadent *dolci* treats such as rum and banana pancakes. £

Tour 12

Excursion to Burns Country

On the trail of poet Robert Burns, visiting auld hair and Rabbie-raising haunts – including the Bachelors' Club and Burns Cottage, his birthplace

For a' that, an' a' that,
It's coming yet for a' that,
That Man to Man, the world o'er,
Shall brothers be for a' that

Scots, with their tradition of struggle for social justice, embrace the egalitarian theme that runs through the works of their National Bard, Robert 'Rabbie' Burns (1759–96). The memory of his turbulent life is kept alive at Burns Suppers across the world at the end of January. Burns's associations with Glasgow were tenuous – minor dealings with publishers – but the literary legacy he left and the memorials to his origins in Burns Country are easily accessible from the city. A car is required for this excursion to the southwest coast taking in the various Burns-related monuments and sights.

Highlights

- Burns House, Mauchline
- Highland Mary Monument
- Bachelors' Club
- Ayr
- Burns National Heritage Park
- Burns Cottage
- Auld Alloway Kirk
- Brig O'Doon
- Souter Johnnie's Cottage

MAUCHLINE AND FAILFORD

Leave the city on the M8 westbound and join the M77, then the A77 towards Ayr. Turn off just after Kilmarnock on to the A76 (signposted

Left: Crossraguel Abbey, dusted with snow. **Above**: Burns' old hangout, the Bachelors' Club.

Dumfries). This road leads through typical Ayrshire countryside to the village of Mauchline, on the outskirts of which stands the Scots baronial folly of the **National Burns Memorial Tower**, established in 1896. The **Burns House ①** (tel: 01387-255 297; Apr–Sept Mon–Sat 10am–5pm, Sun 2–5pm, Oct–Mar Tue–Sat 10am–1pm, 2–5pm; free) in which the poet lived is in the village centre, as is **Poosie Nansie's Tavern**, said to have inspired part of *The Jolly Beggars*.

Leaving the village on the B743, the road winds towards **Failford ②**, a scatter of houses in a small dip. A path behind a sign to Failford Gorge – easy to miss – leads to a monument to **Highland Mary**, the mysterious but beautiful woman for whom Burns wrote *My Highland Lassie O*. This is one of the lesser Burns monuments, but the inscription on the pillar is touching:

> *That sacred hour can I forget,*
> *Can I forget the hallowed grove,*
> *Where by the winding Ayr we met,*
> *To live one day of parting love.*

BACHELORS' CLUB

Past Failford, a brief diversion on the right leads to Tarbolton, where the National Trust for Scotland is the custodian of the **Bachelors' Club ③** (tel: 0844-493 2146; 1 Apr–30 Sept Fri–Tue 1–5pm, last admission 4.30pm; morning visits available for pre-booked groups; charge). The 17th-century thatched house just off the main road is where the poet and his cronies formed a debating club with, it has to be said, easy access to the inn next door. It was here that Burns was introduced to the Freemasonry that shaped his philosophy of the brotherhood of Man.

Returning to the B743, it is 6 miles (10km) to **Ayr ④**, a resort town with sandy beaches and a statue of Burns in the main square. Crossing the main road over the River Ayr, the 15th-century pedestrian bridge on the left is

Above: the spooky graveyard at Auld Alloway Kirk.

the **Auld Brig** and the pillared steeple straight ahead is Ayr Town Hall. Burns was baptised in the Auld Kirk.

ROBERT BURNS BIRTHPLACE MUSEUM

Heading out of town on the A719 (signposted for Maidens), look for a sign for the Heads of Ayr then turn left at the first sign for **Alloway**, a pretty village of rose-entwined cottages that

⑥ Burns by Bike

During the summer months Cycle Ayrshire (tel: 01290-550 276; www. cycleayrshire.co.uk) organises Burns by Bike outings led by expert riders over mainly minor roads. Various excursions cater for all abilities, including beginners and families. The more taxing 38-mile (60km) ride starts at Rozelle Park in Ayr, then takes in Tarbolton Mauchline, Coylton and Dalrymple before returning to Ayr. A decent level of fitness is suggested for this ride.

is at the heart of Burns Country. A car park on the left at the junction with the B7024 to Maybole serves the **Burns National Heritage Park**, which includes **Burns Cottage**, the poet's birthplace, and the new **Robert Burns Birthplace Museum** ⑤ (tel: 0844-493 2601; www.burnsmuseum. org.uk; Apr–Sept daily 10am–5.30pm, Oct–Mar daily 10am–5pm; charge), which opened in 2011. His birthplace is a clay wall-and-thatch house, which the poet's father William built and where he instilled young Robert's love of language and learning. The new museum contains the most important collection of Burns's work, including the original copy of the *Kilmarnock Edition*, the first collection of poems he published to raise cash in order to emigrate to Jamaica. The state-of-the-art technology aims to bring the life, loves and demons of the poet to life. As well as these permanent collections there are a variety of temporary exhibitions of Burns-related art, and poetry readings and musical events. There are also tours of the site with expert guides to tell the history of Burns and the area.

Auld Alloway Kirk, also in the complex but just a little further on, is a 16th-century refuge that was a ruin even in Burns's day and was last used in 1756. Its gloomy graveyard holds the remains of Burns's father, and the mossy crypts and worn stones with their goblin carvings are a suitably chilling setting for the dance of the witches as the Devil – '*a tousie tyke, black, grim and large*' – played the pipes and '*gart them skirl*'.

When Tam, inspired by John Barleycorn, interrupted their dance with the shout: '*Weel done, Cutty Sark*', his mare Meg fled to **Brig O'Doon** nearby to escape minus '*her ain grey tail*'. This 13th-century cobbled bridge with its ancient arch now stands below the **Burns Monument**, a Grecian tower designed by Thomas Hamilton and opened in 1823.

TOWARDS SOUTH AYRSHIRE

The B7024 carries on to **Maybole**, where Burns's father and mother met in 1756. Joining the A77, signposted for Stranraer, the road leads past the 13th-century ruins of **Crossraguel Abbey** ❻ with its abbot's tower and dovecote, to the village of Kirkoswald. Here the National Trust for Scotland maintains the thatched **Souter Johnnie's Cottage** ❼ (tel: 0844-493 2147; Apr–Sept Fri–Tue 11.30am–5pm; charge), a representation of the daily life of the cobbler who was the inspiration behind Tam O'Shanter's '*ancient, trusty, drouthy crony*'.

This is a long but fascinating run. Finish with drinks at the **Westin Turnberry Resort Hotel** (tel: 01655-331 000), scene of so many memorable moments in Open golf history.

Ⓔ Eating Out

Ayr
Fouters Bistro
2a Academy Street; tel: 01292-261 391; Tue–Sat lunch and dinner.
In the vaults of an old bank, this renowned place serves excellent dishes using quality ingredients such as Gressingham duck, Ayrshire lamb and John Dory. ££

Below: Burns Cottage, the birthplace of the beloved Scottish bard.

Travel Tips

Active Pursuits

For all its municipal grandeur and urban chic, this 'dear green place' is surrounded by hills and water and full of things to do.

Walkers are less than an hour away from the splendours of Loch Lomond and the Trossachs National Park *(see feature p.104)*, which has Munros, Corbetts, heather hill rambles, forest walks and nature trails that will allow you to glimpse some of the 500 species of flowering plant and 250 species of bird that reside here. For the really serious outdoors enthusiast, there's the West Highland Way to explore, which takes about five to seven days to walk. It takes you from Milngavie, just north of Glasgow, to Fort William, a distance of 92 miles (148km), passing through some of Scotland's most stunning scenery. For information on all the walks that can be done in this area, visit www. lochlomond-trossachs.org.

BOATING

Glasgow is a city built on its maritime might, but it's only in recent years that marinas and boat clubs have really started to pop up. Sail out of the Firth of Clyde and head north along the shores and you will

Above: cycling along a canal towpath.

be gobsmacked by the beauty of the sea lochs, rocky outcrops and inlets, not to mention the isles of Islay and Mull. Experienced sailors should visit www.westcoastboating.org for information on all the routes, charts, sites, nature and companies that offer boats for hire. For those who can't sail but want to go out on the open waves, the *Waverley* (www.waverley excursions.co.uk) is the last remaining seagoing paddle steamer in the world and does summer sails along the Clyde, as well as to the northern lochs and nearby islands of Arran, Bute and Mull.

Previous Pages: natural splendours await for those keen to get active.
Left: the PS *Waverley* paddle steamer.
Above: boating is popular.

CYCLING

There are lots of cycle paths around Glasgow and along the Clyde. Within the city, the Glasgow Mountain Bike Circuit in Pollok Park has a green circuit for those wanting a gentle ride through the woods, a blue circuit for a bit of bounce and climb, and a red circuit for those who want really rugged terrain. You can rent a bike from www.cosybike.co.uk.

FISHING

One benefit of the demise of heavy industry is that the Clyde is less polluted now, and trout and salmon have returned. Angling is becoming increasingly popular on the banks of the rivers of Glasgow. The United Clyde Angling Protective Association Ltd looks after the Clyde and its tributaries, and you can buy a permit from local tackle shops to fish on a particular stretch.

Ⓕ Football's Old Firm

Football fans will associate Glasgow with its two big teams, Celtic and Rangers. The rivalry between the Old Firm (as they are collectively known) is embedded in the history of the city and passions are as fiery as ever – joint initiatives to confront its nastier side continue. Celtic Park, otherwise known as Parkhead (or Paradise), is in the East End (www.celticfc.co.uk), while Rangers, who were forced to begin their 2012 season in the lowly ranks of the Scottish third division after going into administration, make their home at Ibrox in the Southside (www.rangers.co.uk). Both clubs offer stadium tours.

Above: Old Firm clashes are notorious for their intensity.

Above: playing a few holes at the Pollok Golf Club, with the impressive Pollok House in the background.

GOLF

There are dozens of golf courses in and around Glasgow. Douglas Park (tel: 0141-942 0985; www.douglas parkgolfclub.co.uk) is an attractive 18-hole course north of the city near Milngavie. Lethamhill (tel: 0141-276 0810; junction 8 off the M8) is a municipal 18-hole course overlooking Hogganfield Loch.

HORSE RIDING

There are a few horse-riding centres around the outskirts of Glasgow. Easterton Stables in Milngavie (www. eastertonstables.co.uk) offers lessons, or, if you can already handle a horse, you can hack along the dips and dells of Mugdock Country Park in the Campsie Fells, surely one of the most delightful ways to see the scenery.

Ⓚ Children's Activities

Glasgow is a city with activities for all ages. At **Hampden Park** (tel: 0141-616 6139; www.scottishfoot-ballmuseum.org.uk; Mon–Sat 10am–5pm, Sun 11am–5pm), Scotland's national football stadium, kids and adults alike will enjoy the Scottish Football Hall of Fame, and have an opportunity to tour the stadium.

  Kelburne Country Park, which is located near Largs (tel: 01475-568 685), boasts waterfalls, falconry displays, an assault course and 'The Secret Forest'. The refurbished **Summerlee Heritage Trust** at Coatbridge (tel: 01236-638 460) offers kids the chance to ride on an old tram as part of Scotland's only electric-driven tramway. Also out this way, the **Time Capsule** (tel: 01236-449 572; www.thetime-capsule.info), with swimming and ice-skating among volcanoes and cavemen, is worth a visit.

Above: a falconry demonstration at Kelburne Country Park.

Themed Holidays

Whether you have a day, a weekend or a week, Glasgow is full of opportunities to learn a new skill or to do something useful.

Artistic breaks
Glasgow School of Art (tel: 0141-353 4500; www.gsa.ac.uk) is the alma mater of many of Britain's edgiest artists, such as Roddy Buchanan, Nathan Coley and Christine Borland. During July, the school runs a summer course allowing you to learn and work alongside resident lecturers and guest artists located in a number of the studios across the campus, including the famous painting studios in the Charles Rennie Mackintosh Building. You can also book cheap accommodation within the student halls of residence (en-suite accommodation at Margaret Macdonald House).

Bagpiping
If you've ever dreamed of mastering the bagpipes, you can learn to pipe at the **College of Piping** (tel: 0141-334-3587; www.college-of-piping.co.uk). There are day and week-long courses at hugely attractive prices at the centrally located school.

Buddhist retreats
If you feel the need for inner peace, you have a good chance of finding it at **Kagyu Samye Ling** (tel: 01387-373 232; www.samyeling.org), Europe's oldest Tibetan Buddhist monastery. A range of retreats and courses cover all aspects of the practice. The monastery is a two-hour drive from Glasgow or 90 minutes by train.

Cooking classes
The **Cookery School** (tel: 0141-552 5239; www.thecookeryschool. org) at Peckham's in Glassford Street offers even the most hopeless cooks a chance to learn how to bring food together in a tasty and attractive way. Choose from a one-day course in Italian cookery (making minestrone and pesto among other dishes), up to a full five-day course of cooking, eating and drinking.

Nature
The National Trust for Scotland's **Thistle Camps** (www.nts.org.uk/ThistleCamps) recruit volunteers to repair upland and lowland footpaths, control rhododendron growth and erect fencing. You can even learn how to restore bogs in the estates and properties of the NTS, which include the likes of Ben Lawers, Ben Lomond and Brodick Castle in Arran. A week's volunteering includes basic accommodation and food.

Above: learn to play the most Scottish instrument of all at the College of Piping.

Practical Information

GETTING THERE

By air

Glasgow has an excellent international airport to the west at Abbotsinch (tel: 0844-481 5555), which is served by flights from all main UK airports and has connections to Europe and North America. It has direct motorway links to the city centre, a journey of about 15 minutes. A taxi to the city centre costs around £20 from a rank outside the terminal building. Frequent Service 500 buses (Glasgow Flyer Airport Express), which cost £5 one way and £7 return, connect with Glasgow Central (15 mins) and Buchanan Bus Station (25 mins). The Paisley Gilmour Street Railway Station is closest to the airport; around eight trains an hour depart for the city centre.

British Airways and British Midland operate shuttle flights from London. British Airways (tel: 0870-850 9850; www.britishairways.com) operates flights from Heathrow and Gatwick. Flybe (tel: 0871-700 2000; www.flybe.com) has flights from Belfast and Manchester. Easyjet (tel: 0870-600 0000; www.easyjet.com) connects Glasgow with Stansted, Luton and Gatwick, as well as Bristol, Belfast and the European hub of Paris Charles de Gaulle. Ryanair (tel: 0870-728 0280; www.ryanair.com) operates from Stansted to Prestwick, which is about 40 minutes south of Glasgow near Ayr but has efficient road and rail links. There are also direct flights available to various other UK, European and North American destinations. For details of flights, and to book tickets online, visit www.glasgowairport.com and www.glasgowprestwick.com.

By car

From the south, the west-coast route follows the M1 to Birmingham, then the M6 to the Scottish border, then the A74 and M74, which joins the M8 into the city. The slower east-coast route follows the M1 and A1 into Edinburgh, then the cross-country M8 to Glasgow. From the north, the A9 joins the M9 near Stirling and then the M80, A80 and M8 into Glasgow.

By coach

National Express (tel: 08717-818 178; www.nationalexpress.com) runs a regular coach service from all points in England and Wales into Buchanan Bus Station.

By rail

Virgin Trains (tel: 08719-774222; www.virgintrains.co.uk) currently operates the main west-coast route from London, Birmingham and Manchester, but the running of the franchise will

Below: the Clyde Arc, also known as 'Squinty Bridge', was opened to vehicle traffic in 2007.

Above: pedestrian walkways make it straightforward to get around on foot.

be up for negotiation again in 2013. Queen Street Station has a shuttle to Edinburgh and serves the north. For general rail enquiries in Glasgow and Scotland: tel: 0845-484 950; www. firstgroup.com/scotrail. Buy tickets online at www.thetrainline.com.

GETTING AROUND
On foot
A colour-coded sign system facilitates navigation of the city centre and main visitor areas. Distinctive blue panels provide directions and information about sights, maps and pedestrian routes. The Glasgow Tourist Information Centre on George Square *(see p.123)* has decent free maps and some more detailed ones for a few pounds.

By public transport
Glasgow's subway network is one of the oldest in the world, but 15 stations on a 24-minute circular track mean that no journey will take longer than 12 minutes. Packages are available, such as the Family Day Tripper Tickets (unlimited travel on First Scotrail services, subway, some ferries and many bus operators). A single ticket costs £1.20. The subway's 'Discovery' ticket is good value: for £3.50 you can enjoy one day's unlimited travel after 9.30am Monday to Saturday and all day Sunday.

Above ground, First Scotrail (www. firstgroup.com/scotrail) runs the extensive rail network. Glasgow Central Station serves the South and England while Queen Street Station handles trains to and from Edinburgh and the north. City Sightseeing Glasgow runs open-air bus tours from George Square. National Express, Citylink and Megabus coach companies operate out of Buchanan Street Bus Station.

Car hire and parking
Glasgow city-centre traffic is heavy, but a car is useful for excursions to outlying areas. Car-hire firms in Glasgow include: **Arnold Clark** (tel: 0141-954 1963), **Avis** (tel: 0844-581 0147) and **Europcar** (tel: 0141-249 4106).

Cycling

There are great cycle paths, including the 21-mile (34km) Glasgow to Loch Lomond Cycleway, from Bell's Bridge, beside the Clyde Auditorium on the Clyde, to Balloch. Bikes are carried free on all Strathclyde Passenger Transport-supported rail services. For information on cycle routes, visit www.sustrans.org.uk, tel: 0845-113 0065, or ask for the *Clyde and Loch Lomond Cycleway* leaflet at the tourist office.

Above: Glasgow and its surrounding area has many clear cycle paths.

Car parks are plentiful but busy, with spaces around St Enoch Square filled by mid-morning. Multistorey car parks are at Mitchell Street, Cambridge Street, Montrose Street, Waterloo Street, Oswald Street and Buchanan Galleries. Unauthorised parking is not advisable, as tow-away trucks and clamping units abound. If your accommodation is in the West End, take the subway into the city centre.

Steamer and seaplane

The world's last surviving paddle steamer, the PS *Waverley* (tel: 0845-130 4647), makes its home berth at Pacific Quay by Glasgow Science Centre. A relic of the great days of steam, its massive engines are still open for inspection on summer cruises down the Firth of Clyde to Rothesay, Arran and the Kyles of Bute (www.waverley excursions.co.uk).

For a breathtaking flight over Loch Lomond, Tobermory, Oban and the west coast, charter a Loch Lomond Seaplane (tel: 01436-675 030; www. lochlomondseaplanes.com). Planes take off from a purpose-built dock by the Glasgow Science Centre.

Above: a vintage transport sign.

Taxis

Black taxis are licensed by Glasgow City Council and can be flagged down in the street, but there are also many private taxi firms which are slightly cheaper.

FACTS FOR THE VISITOR

Disabled travellers

The Glasgow Tourist Information Centre dispenses advice and leaflets for disabled travellers. The city's main sights have improved provision and access in recent years. For information on disabled access regarding hotels and other businesses, consult www.disabledgo.com.

Emergencies

Fire, Police, Ambulance: tel: 999
Fire HQ: (north of the river) Port Dundas Road, tel: 0141-302 3222; (south of the river) McFarlane Street, tel: 0141-445 2223
Strathclyde Police HQ: 173 Pitt Street, tel: 0141-532 2000
Royal Infirmary: Castle Street, tel: 0141-211 4000
Western Infirmary: Dumbarton Road, tel: 0141-211 2000

Opening hours

City centre shops are generally open 9am–5.30pm (Mon–Sat). Many stores

Left: a Loch Lomond seaplane returns to land at its floating dock in Glasgow.

stay open later – some until 8pm – on a Thursday. Sunday opening is now common in the city centre: noon–5pm is the norm.

Most major banks open 9.30am–4.30pm weekdays; some open Saturday mornings until 12.30pm.

Postal services
Most post offices are open Monday to Friday 9am to 5.30pm, and Saturday 9am to 12.30–1pm. For help and advice on all post office counter services, tel: 08457-223 344; www.postoffice.co.uk.

Tourist information
The **Glasgow Tourist Information Centre**, 11 George Square (tel: 0141-204 4400; www.seeglasgow.com; May, June and Sept Mon–Sat 9am–7pm, July–Aug 9am–8pm, Oct–Apr 9am–6pm, all year Sun 10am–6pm), provides practical guidance on getting around the city and the surrounding areas. Staff are on hand to help with information on the vast range of tours available, the city's historical and cultural attractions, as well as providing an accommodation

Above: crowds at the busy Queen Street train station.

booking service. There's also a small shop on site.

Bureaux de change can be found at **American Express** (66 Gordon Street, tel: 0141-225 2905) and **Thomas Cook** (15–17 Gordon Street, tel: 0844-335 7296).

F Gay and Lesbian Scene

Glasgow has a thriving gay scene and is home to Scotland's biggest gay festival, Glasgay! (Sept–Nov), which encompasses everything from film to club nights. Glasgay's **Q! Gallery** (27–9 Trongate; tel: 0141-552 7575; www.qgallery.org; Mon–Fri 11am–5pm) showcases art and has a bookstore. Popular gay-lesbian hangouts are centred on the Merchant City and include **Delmonica's** (68 Virginia Street; tel: 0141-552 4803) for food, cabaret and club nights; and **Underground Bar** (6a John Street; tel: 0141-553 2456), a stylish place big

on home-cooked food and friendliness. For more information and latest listings check out www.glasgay.co.uk and www.thescottishgayscene.co.uk.

Above: girls' night out.

Accommodation

Glasgow's hotels range from the swanky and expensive to cosy B&Bs housed in handsome Victorian houses. New boutique hotels – some contemporary-style new-builds and others imaginative conversions of historic buildings – have been added in recent years, which have upped the standards generally. Look out for the new luxury hotel and spa, The Hamilton, currently being incorporated into the old BBC building and due to open in 2013. The Glasgow Tourist Information Centre (see p.123) provides an accommodation booking service.

Prices of hotels listed here vary seasonally; the ranges below (quoted as a guide only) suggest prices for one night in a double room on a bed-and-breakfast basis in peak season:

££££   over £150
£££   £100–150
££   £60–100
£   under £60

CENTRAL GLASGOW AND MERCHANT CITY

ABode Glasgow

129 Bath Street; tel: 0141-221 6789; www.abodehotels.co.uk.
Located in an elegant Edwardian Bath Street building which once housed the atmospheric Arthouse Hotel. New landlords ABode have added mainstream design touches and modern comforts, plus the fabulous Michael Caines restaurant and basement BarMC. ££

Brunswick Hotel

106–8 Brunswick Street; tel: 0141-552 0001; www.brunswickhotel.co.uk.
In the heart of the Merchant City quarter, this stylish hotel is extremely good value in terms of both location and elegance. There's also an on-site Italian café-cum-restaurant. ££

Hotel du Vin at One Devonshire Gardens

1 Devonshire Gardens, Great Western Road; tel: 0141-339 2001; www.hotelduvin.com.
Luxury accommodation in an elegant tree-lined terrace comprising five sandstone houses. Quality and comfort abound, from the Egyptian cotton bedding to the Whisky Snug and its 'Glasgow Restaurant of the Year'-winning eatery. ££££

Radisson SAS Hotel

301 Argyle Street; tel: 0141-204 3333; www.radissonsas.com.
Around the corner from Glasgow Central Station, the jaw-dropping glass-fronted lobby area impresses anyone interested in contemporary design. The cavernous art-filled atrium bar is a social hub, while the Collage bar and restaurant has picked up awards. Standard modern rooms can seem a tad dull but the corner suites are gorgeous. ££

Above: a truly luxurious bathing experience at the Hotel du Vin at One Devonshire Gardens.

Above: the stylish bar at ABode Glasgow.

WEST END AND BY THE CLYDE

Alamo Guest House
46 Gray Street, Kelvingrove; tel: 0141-339 2395; www.alamoguesthouse.com.
A popular family-run hotel opposite Kelvingrove Park set in a grand terraced house. The cosy rooms are simply furnished, well maintained and offer great value. £

Crowne Plaza Glasgow
Congress Road; tel: 0871-423 4896; www.ichotelsgroup.com.
Modern high-rise by the Clyde, situated beside the SECC, offering a range of functional rooms and suites, a grand reception with bar-restaurant and shop, and a pool. £££

Hilton Garden Inn
Finnieston Quay; tel: 0141-240 1002; www.hiltongardeninn.hilton.com.
A stylish yet comfortable place to stay next to the Clyde, with a fresh contemporary design and beguiling café-bar with views of the river from the terrace. Free Wi-fi in every room. ££

Kelvin Hotel
15 Buckingham Terrace; tel: 0141-339 7143; www.kelvinhotel.com.
Family-owned hotel in the West End within an impressive Victorian building. Guest rooms have high ceilings and free Wi-fi. The Kelvin apartment sleeps up to four and is ideal for families. £

SOUTHSIDE

Glasgow Guest House
56 Dumbrek Road, near Pollok Park; tel: 0141-427 0129; www.glasgow-guest-house.co.uk.
This bed and breakfast offers homely accommodation and is handy for the parks detailed in Tour 8 *(p.86)* and the airport. £

Mar Hall
Earl of Mar Estate, Renfrew; tel: 0141-812 9999; www.marhall.com.
Stunning Gothic mansion located 10 minutes west of Glasgow airport in Renfrewshire. Comfy rooms and suites come in calming hues. The Aveda Spa offers treatments and gym facilities. ££££

Number 10
10–12 Queen's Drive; tel: 0141-424 0160; www.10hotel.co.uk.
The long-established Dunkeld Hotel has been spruced up, rejigging the layout to make many rooms more spacious. Expect warm hospitality and professional service. ££

Sherbrooke Castle Hotel

11 Sherbrooke Avenue, Pollokshields; tel: 0141-427 4227; www.sherbrooke. co.uk.

A Victorian mock-Gothic pile complete with baronial turrets near Pollok Park. Tartan carpets, period furnishings and antiques give the public areas a cosy atmospheric feel, while guest rooms have modern bathrooms, warmth and free Wi-fi. ££

NORTH OF THE CITY

Cameron House Hotel

Loch Lomond; tel: 01389-755 565; www.deverehotels.co.uk.

This five-star hotel is housed in a luxurious baronial-style mansion in a stunning Loch Lomond waterside setting. There are first-class spa and golf facilities, and you can even arrive by seaplane. ££££

Dakota Eurocentral

Eurocentral Junction of the A8/M8; tel: 01698-835 444; www.dakota hotels.co.uk

A stylish yet cosy hotel with lots of contemporary design touches and useful high-tech facilities, including free Wi-fi. The award-winning bar and grill serves Scottish fish dishes and the sweetest oysters from Borough Market in London. ££

Red Deer Vintage Inn

1 Auchenkilns Park, Cumbernauld; tel: 01236-795 861; www.vintageinn. co.uk/thereddeercumbernauld.

Great-value accommodation with functional, clean rooms and a pub-style restaurant. Popular with anglers who cast off at nearby Broadward Loch. The Vintage Inns chain also has a hotel at Balloch near Loch Lomond. ££

WEBSITES

For a comprehensive list of hotels in the city, see www.glasgowguide.co.uk/ hotels.html.

Guesthouses/Bed & Breakfasts: www.information-britain.co.uk; www.scottishaccommodationindex. com; www.laterooms.com

Green: www.organicholidays.co.uk; www.ecofriendlytourist.com

Self-catering: For those staying for more than a few days, an apartment is a sensible option:
www.citybaseapartments.com;
www.glasgowloftapartment.co.uk;
www.max-servicedapartments.co.uk;
www.dreamhouseapartments.com;
www.hot-el-apartments.com

Below: the pool at the Crowne Plaza Glasgow (see p.125).

Index

Credits

Insight Great Breaks Glasgow
Written by: Ron Clark, Colin Hutchison
and Nick Bruno
Updated by: Zoe Ross
Commissioning Editor: Rebecca Lovell
Picture Researcher: Richard Cooke
Maps: APA Publications
Publishing Manager: Rachel Fox
Series Editor: Carine Tracanelli

All pictures by Douglas Macgilvray/APA
except: Abode Hotels 125; akg-images/
annanphotographs.co.uk 38B; Alamy 33T,
98; Axiom 81T; Murray Barnes 121B; Mike
Beltzner 16T; Bruno Bord 59; Tom Brogan
11, 122T; Crawford Brown/Rex Features 40;
Cornell Univeristy Library 8T; Citizens Theatre
Ltd 34T; David Cruickshanks/APA 4BL, 5TL,
9, 25B, 28T, 29B, 41, 45, 54T&B, 57T, 58B,
62, 64B, 69L&R, 80B, 103, 104T&B, 123T;
Jean-Pierre Dalbéra 88T, 94T, 96B; Elspeth
Durkin 36B; Epic Scotland 46/47; Dreamstime
2/3, 5ML, 72BL, 75, 76, 77; Fotolia 117T;
fotoLibra 5TR&BL, 100T, 106/107, 107, 113;
Getty Images 66/67, 66T; Giant Productions
Ltd 31B; Glasgay! Festival 123B; Glasgow City
Marketing Bureau 43B, 111, 116T, 118T;
Glasgow Film Festival 10B; Stéphane Goldstein
55T&B; David Grinly 4BR; Paul Hart 105;
Hotel du Vin 124; Hunterian Museum and Art
Gallery, University of Glasgow 78B, 79T&B,
80T; iStockphoto.com 4TR, 5CR, 18B, 19T&B,
20T, 21T, 22/23(all), 24T&B, 26, 27, 30B,
33B, 35B, 36/37, 38T&C, 51, 52B, 56R, 70T,
71B, 76, 86T, 87B, 101, 108/109(all), 110,
116B, 118B, 119, 121T, 122B; Ilpo Koskinen
60; Leonardo 126; Library of Congress
52T; John Lindie 17B, 82B, 84, 87T; James
Macdonald 5CL, 32B; Graeme Maclean 117B;
Seth Mcanespie 44B; Raymond McCrae 86B;
Jim McDougall 90T, 91; Alistair McMillan 112B;
Photolibrary 12/13, 63T, 102, 112T; Pictures
Colour Library 38/39, 48, 114/115; Sheep
Purple 25T; Colin Reilly 14; Stuart Reynolds/
Rex Features 50; John Robertson 44T; Paul
Robertson 37B; Scottish Viewpoint 34B, 99;

Scottish Youth Theatre 47B; stevecadman on
Flickr 46B, 49, 61; Nigel Swales 106B; Stephen
Thomas 89B; Topfoto 42B, 90B; Ville.fi 43T;
Nesbit Wylie 63B.
Cover pictures by: (front) Superstock (T),
Fotolia (BL) & iStockphoto (BR); (back)
Douglas Macgilvray/APA (T); Dreamstime.

No part of this book may be reproduced,
stored in a retrieval system or transmitted
in any form or by any means (electronic,
mechanical, photocopying, recording or
otherwise), without prior written permission
of Apa Publications. Brief text quotations
with use of photographs are exempted for
book review purposes only.

CONTACTING THE EDITORS: As every
effort is made to provide accurate information
in this publication, we would appreciate it
if readers would call our attention to any
errors and omissions by contacting:
Apa Publications, PO Box 7910,
London SE1 1WE, England.
insight@apaguide.co.uk

Information has been obtained from sources
believed to be reliable, but its accuracy
and completeness, and the opinions based
thereon, are not guaranteed.

© 2013 APA Publications (UK) Limited.
Second Edition 2013

Printed in China by CTPS

Worldwide distribution enquiries:
APA Publications GmbH & Co. Verlag KG
(Singapore Branch), 7030 Ang Mo Kio Ave 5,
08-65 Northstar @ AMK, Singapore 569880
apasin@singnet.com.sg

Distributed in the UK and Ireland by:
Dorling Kindersley Ltd (a Penguin Company)
80 Strand, London, WC2R 0RL, UK
customerservice@uk.dk.com